SWEET ROME

A Sweet Home Novel

Tillie Cole

DEDICATION

To my fabulous readers, who demanded more Molly and Rome! Without your unbelievable amount of messages, emails and posts, this novel would never have been.

I'm forever grateful for your support.

PROLOGUE

Tuscaloosa, Alabama
Present Day…

I sprinted down the hospital hallways, panting, my heart pounding in my chest.

Five missed calls. I had *five* fucking missed calls. Something was wrong with Mol, and *God*, I felt sick at the way I'd left things between us. Everyone talks about never leaving arguments on a bad note just in case one of you never comes back. Folks never listen, but now, the thought of never seeing my girl again had me almost turning myself inside out with regret.

My feet faltered as I ripped my way through corridor after corridor, pure dread stealing my goddamn breath. What if something bad happened? What if the surgery hadn't been a success after all? What if something had gone

1

wrong after we fought? And *I* left her on her own, got pissed at her depression and left her on her fucking own, alone with only her dark thoughts for company.

Forfeiting the busy elevator, I climbed the stairs two at a time, all the way to the fourth floor, practically smashed through the entrance to the ward, and sprinted to Mol's room. I passed the nurses' station without stopping and heard my name being called, but I ignored it to get to my girl, to get to my Mol, to see with my own two eyes that she was okay.

The door to her room was closed, so I slammed down on the handle. The door swung open, the wood smashing against the wall. My blood froze in my veins as I stared at the empty room: fresh sheets on the bed, the floor reeking of Lysol, and her packed bag gone.

My hands began to tremble and my heart seemed to stop.

No! No, no, no, no... she couldn't be...

Stumbling backward on shaky feet, my back hit the doorframe and I could feel my legs giving out, my ass hitting the floor a second later with a dull thud.

"Romeo?" I could hear a voice beside me, trying to get my attention, but I couldn't focus; everything was hazy, stilted.

A hand pressed firmly on my arm, shaking me out of my stupor.

"Romeo?"

I couldn't move, couldn't speak.

"*Mr. Prince!*"

Looking up, I saw Marnie, Molly's nurse, standing above me, staring down at me with a worried expression.

"Where—" I cleared my clogged throat. "Where is she? What happened?"

Marnie's face blanched. "Oh, no, darlin'! You think…? No, no! Molly is fine. She's *fine*."

My heart lurched back to life at her words. "What?" I whispered, needing to hear her again.

"Molly is *fine*, but…" Her eyes softened and dimmed with sadness.

"But what?" I demanded, getting to my feet. Her jaw began to click with nerves. "Christ, Marnie! But what?" I snapped more forcefully.

"A couple'a hours ago, your momma paid Miss Shakespeare a visit."

My heart sank and an uncontrollable rage surged within me. "She did what?" I asked. Marnie stepped back in fear.

Shit.

I backed away, fists clenched. "What did that bitch do?"

"She… She attacked her, hit her… She was arrested, Romeo. Molly had to make a statement to the police."

"*Fuck*!" I swung around and punched the wall, the thin plaster cracking under the pressure, my breath and anger way out of control. "Where's Mol now, with the cops?"

Marnie briefly looked down at the floor before meeting my frantic gaze. "Darlin'…"

"What?" I questioned curtly. I didn't like her tone. It seemed like she was trying to be soothing or something, prepping me for a fall.

She stepped forward, hands outstretched, placating. "Darlin'… she…"

Groaning and losing patience, I took a long look around the empty room. As my gaze landed on the narrow bed, I couldn't help but remember Molly's broken face as I left tonight. It was like she was done: with me, with our entire fucked-up situation… with life.

Wait.

As I cast one last unseeing look out the small window, it all became clear…

My gaze swung to Marnie's, and she visibly sagged where she stood. The gesture alone gave me my answer.

She'd left me. She'd run. She'd fucking run away.

"I'm so sorry, Romeo. She made sure no one saw her leave. Earlier, she told me she couldn't cope, and I guess she just broke down. We checked the security cameras. She walked right outta the front doors and got into a car." Her eyes regarded me sympathetically. "She had all her belongings with her."

My heart crumpled in my chest. Unable to speak, I backed down the corridor, pulling out my cell. The other nurses on duty watched me go with varied looks of pity. I pressed on Molly's name, but it went straight to voicemail, so I left a message:

"Molly! Where are you, baby? I'm so sorry for what I said and for leaving you like that. I've just heard from the nurse about my momma. My God, Mol, they said she attacked

you… again! Please tell me where you are… You just left the hospital without telling anyone. Please, call me."

I ran toward my Dodge, mind buzzing as I tried to think of the people I should call and the places I should look.

I had to find my girl.

"Mol! *MOLLY!*" I yelled, bolting up the stairs of the house, ignoring the screams and yells from girls as I passed each floor. She had to be here. Where else would she damn well be?

I stormed into her room, and, instantly, a wave of despair hit me. She wasn't here. Everything was still as it had been: bed slightly crumpled from where we'd made love before the homecoming dinner, her class notes scattered all over her huge desk—and, *God*, that book she was reading like it was the friggin' Bible in the center, pages folded over, colored labels scribbled with her thoughts, line after line of highlighted paragraphs… and that small, treasured polaroid picture as the bookmark.

It cut me like nothing I'd ever felt before. I hadn't kept her safe like I'd promised. I'd failed her.

Fighting the urge to break down, I slumped down on her bed and stared at the silver moon through her white curtains, wondering out loud to the large, empty room, "Where the fuck have you gone, baby?"

Two pictures on her night table caught my eye. The only two pictures beside her bed—hell, in her entire room. One of the two of us kissing before one of my games, her dressed in my Tide jersey, her legs wrapped around my waist and her arms gripping my neck as she smiled in happiness against my lips. The second was of Mol as a kid, with her Grandma, back in England. I couldn't help but crack a small smile as I picked up the image of the tiny girl with too much hair, freckles, and the biggest fucking glasses I'd ever seen. But that smile soon turned into a whole world of pain. She'd gone. She'd fucking broken her promise and left me. No girl, not one person left who was mine. She'd been put through too much, and when the shit hit the fan, she'd cut and run.

As I stroked my thumb over that cute, smiling, five-year-old face, a tear trailed down my cheek and splattered onto the glass. I didn't know what to do without her; she'd become my whole friggin' life. I could barely think back to the days when she wasn't by my side, loving me and giving me what I needed. *Christ*, it'd been that way since the day she literally ran into my life, trampled on my shit, and stole my dead fucking heart.

The bedroom door cracked open and Ally, my cousin and one of Molly's best friends, crept into the dark room. "Hey, Rome," she said, her voice soft and guarded. I didn't look back at her—*couldn't*—and eventually she sat down beside me, not uttering a word.

I was still staring at the picture when Ally reached over and took it from my hands. "She's definitely one of a kind, isn't she?" she said with a sad smile.

I huffed out a strained breath and nodded, taking back the frame, feeling a lump clog up my throat.

Ally sighed and grasped my hand tightly. "She ran?"

My silence gave her the answer, and my head fell forward with dejection. "What the fuck am I gonna to do without her, Al?"

"She'll come back. I'm certain. She just had too much to deal with. Hell, I bet she never thought people like your parents even existed, never mind that she'd be on the receiving end of their shit. Most folk don't believe people are capable of such cruelty. It's just we know better, that's all."

"I can't do this without her. I can't fuckin' live without her by my side." I finally looked at Ally, whose brown eyes watched me helplessly. "I like who I am now with her, *because* of her. I hated the man I was before."

"She *will* come back," she reiterated, this time with stern conviction.

I wasn't so sure.

"I can't stop thinking about the day we met. It keeps playing on a loop in my mind."

Ally laughed and laid her head on my shoulder. "I remember it, too."

"There was always something about her, you know? Something I wanted, *needed*. Even back then. I knew she'd understand me if I just let her. I could see something special in her, and she in me."

"Then hold on to that because Molls sure felt it too, still *does*. She's just clouded by grief. Think of everything you guys have been through. She won't leave you permanently after that. You're meant to be."

Lying back on the unmade bed and staring at the ceiling, I let the anger buried inside me rip loose, growling a loud "*fuck!*"

My hands tightened, cracking the photo frame's glass, but I ignored the slicing pain in my palm, too concerned with cleaning Molly's beautiful five-year-old face, now smeared with my blood.

"*Christ*, Shakespeare," I rasped, fixated by those caramel eyes. "Where the hell have you gone?"

"Rome?" Ally said quietly.

"What?"

"You're getting all angry again." She paused for a long moment. "I don't want you going back there. You've been so much better lately."

Sucking in a pained, stuttered breath, I said, "Because of her. I've been better because of her."

"Then tell me about it. Tell me how y'all fell in love. I know a little bit, but not the whole story. Talk to me."

Slowly sitting back up, I looked my worried cousin in the eyes. "I'm not sure I can, Al. It's all so raw."

Ally rubbed a soothing hand down my back. "It'll be good for you. You need to remember why you changed, what brought you guys together. It's good to talk. I can't see you go back to Rome, pre-Molls. It was like you'd been numb your entire life, never letting anyone in, and meeting Molly woke you the heck up."

Feeling a burning in my chest, I glanced over to the balcony—*our* balcony—and my eyes blurred at the onslaught of memories racing through my mind.

"I... I guess it all began months ago. I recall it so clearly. It was just like any other normal, typical day…"

1

The University of Alabama, Tuscaloosa
Several months ago…

I felt it the minute it left my hands. It was perfect: the spiral just right, the speed and angle faultless. I watched, holding my breath, as the ball sailed through the air, gliding smoothly down the field, then landed right into the outstretched hands of Gavin Sale, the wide receiver. It was the sixth pass I'd hit with such accuracy in the last hour alone, and this time, the team all stopped and stared at me standing frozen, still in my position.

Coach Dean ran over, looking at me funny, and went to slap his hand on my shoulder until I flinched and backed away. He hadn't noticed my reaction—that I'd expected him to cause me pain. I was thankful. Daddy wouldn't want rumors to start.

"Rome! What the hell, son? I've never seen an arm like yours in my entire twenty years of coaching! The way you pop that ball is like… like… a bullet being fired from a gun!"

A burst of pride spread across my chest at his praise, and I straightened a little taller on seeing all my teammates nodding their heads in agreement.

I was good at football. I was actually good at something.

I may not be the perfect son, the best-behaved kid in the world, but this meant I wasn't a complete failure like Momma always said. I'd found something I could do well and, it seemed from Coach's reaction, better than most.

My face muscles twitched, and I could feel myself begin to smile; it was only small, but it was there. It was something I never, ever did—express joy—and when Austin Carrillo, my best friend and teammate, ran over, giving me a high five, I let myself be happy. Just for once, I let myself feel content with who I was: a quarterback, the best the coach had seen in twenty years.

I shouldn't have bothered being happy, though, because, of course, the minute I let down my guard, he arrived to take it all away.

The large silver Bentley pulled to a stop right at the side of the field, and out stepped my daddy: big, dark, and intimidating. All the parents stopped their chatter and watched as Joseph Prince glared toward my place on the field. He was dressed in his silver-gray suit, exerting raw power. The other parents kept their distance; folks around Tuscaloosa knew not to go near him unless invited.

Coach Dean didn't get that memo, though, and on seeing my daddy arrive, he ran over, excitedly pulling me with him.

Of course, Coach didn't know my daddy's view on my playing football. No one did. Coach didn't know the level of punishment I would face at being caught here at the field or that I'd sneaked out of my room in order to make today's practice, acting directly against my daddy's orders.

My head lowered as we approached—I couldn't face seeing the anger in his eyes.

"Mr. Prince, I'm so happy you came. I have to say, sir, I've never seen a talent like your son's in my whole coaching career, and he's only ten! I honestly believe he could go all the way." Coach put his arm around my shoulder and squeezed. "Your boy will play for the Tide, you mark my words. In eight years' time, we'll be seeing him lead Bama to the championship!"

I stared at the floor, never once daring to lift my eyes.

"Rome, get in the car," my daddy ordered coldly, and my heart sank as I broke loose from Coach's hold and ran into the back seat, shivering at the too-cold temperature of the black leather under my legs.

I strapped myself in, watching my daddy's back bunch as he spoke to the coach. Coach Dean swallowed hard, looking shocked at whatever my daddy was saying. He'd be telling him I couldn't come back, that I couldn't waste my time on football anymore, that I had a duty as a Prince and football wasn't it.

Leaving the coach standing frozen in shock, my daddy spun on his heel and stormed back to the car.

Slamming the driver's side door, he started the engine. I made sure to keep my head low. I knew he'd be looking at me in the mirror, his brown eyes lit with fury, so I kept my chin tucked down to my chest, avoiding looking him directly in the eyes.

"You fucked up today, Romeo," he said calmly.

I flinched.

Romeo. *I hated that name. It always caused my stomach to tighten and my breath to come out too fast. My fingernails dug into my palms as my hands clenched into fists at my sides. I'd been getting real angry of late, so mad that sometimes it was a struggle to contain it. I didn't know how to make it stop.*

"You think it was smart to sneak out and come here when you'd already been told not to?"

I didn't reply, was too scared, too angry *to reply.*

"Answer me!" he shouted, hitting the steering wheel with his large hand.

"N-no, s-sir, it wasn't smart," I whispered, trying to keep my voice from breaking. He would just laugh if I cried; it always just made things worse. He said it made me weak.

My daddy hated weakness.

"You want folk around here spreading the word on how good you are at football?"

I did, but that wasn't the answer I was expected to give.

"No, sir."

"Then from now on, do as you're told! How many times do we have to go through this? I have plans for Prince Oil, plans that you will need to see out. Football is unacceptable, boy!"

We drove the rest of the way home in silence. When the Bentley pulled to a stop in the driveway, I rushed into the house and up to my room, curling into a small ball on top of my bed, waiting for what I knew would happen next.

And it did. It was the one constant in my life.

After a few minutes, I heard the creaking of the old stairs, and a moment later, the bedroom door opened and my daddy entered my room, jacket and tie off, the sleeves of his white shirt rolled up to his elbows. He was always calm, collected. I'd never really seen him flip. The quieter he was, the more scared I became.

He was deathly quiet today.

I held in a cry as he glared at me and snapped a thin black leather belt in his hands. "Get up, Romeo. This will be over quicker if you don't put up a fight. You need to be punished for disobeying my orders."

Taking a deep breath, I got to my feet and stood in the center of the room, eyes squeezed shut, wrists held out, waiting for the lashing I knew was about to come. I would take the pain. Football was what I wanted and I wouldn't give up on that dream, not for anything...

I snapped my eyes open, body stiffening at the old memory that haunted my dreams, my heart pounding in my chest and my breathing erratic.

It was only a dream... It was only a dream, I told myself over and over again as I pushed my long, sweaty hair from my eyes, breathing in deeply through my nose, trying like hell to calm the fuck down.

My alarm cut through my panic, the bastard thing blaring out its annoying tone at a stupidly high volume.

"*Uhh*! Bullet, turn it off," a female voice moaned.

Dreading who I would find next to me this morning, I looked down, following the sound of the voice. Sprawled on my bare chest, was... was... fuck if I knew. Some random chick.

That familiar sick feeling burst in my stomach and I squeezed my eyes shut.

Hell, I needed to stop with the drinking and the fucking. This was my year—time to get serious, no more distractions, no more feeling like shit.

Lifting my head cautiously, I tested the severity of my hangover and winced at the bright morning sun shining through the window. *Jesus, what the hell did I drink last night?*

The chick groaned again at the movement, and I pushed her off me, her hung-over ass flopping to the mattress as I slid off the edge of my bed, sighing in disgust as I spotted the used rubber still on my dick. Nice.

Looking back, I tried to remember something... *anything*, a small bit of info about who the hell she was. There was nothing, just fragmented flashes of a party and being led to my room... then sweet. Fuck. All.

Same shit, different day.

I stood, stretching out my arms. Seeing a crumpled red dress on the wooden floor, I picked it up and threw it at Jane Doe's naked ass. "I'm going to shower. Feel free to let yourself out."

She muttered something unintelligible and gradually awoke at those words. Doing what I said, she put on her slip of a dress, scooped up her shoes, and smiled in satisfaction as she left the room. "Catch you later, Bullet. It was worth the wait. All the rumors about you were true."

Hell, treat 'em mean, keep 'em keen. *Or* be the starting QB for the Tide and do whatever the fuck you like. They still come running back for more. It was a novelty to fuck the great *Bullet* Prince.

After my shower, I threw on my training shorts and shirt and, grabbing my cleats, headed down the stairs of the frat house. Austin and Reece were already waiting for my lazy ass in the kitchen, so I grabbed my shades off the island and slid them on, flipping a huge fuckin' bird to Austin, who was laughing at my sorry state as he passed me a protein shake, and we headed out the door.

"Is that chick who left just now yours, Rome?" Reece asked, almost jogging to keep up with Austin and me as we made our way to the gym.

Shrugging, I answered, "She ain't *mine*, but all evidence suggests I fucked her."

"You better'd wrapped that shit up," Austin scolded.

Damn straight. Last thing I wanted was some wannabe NFL wife trapping me with a kid. "Done deal. Never ride bareback. Evidence was still on my cock this morning. I'm classy like that."

Austin slapped me on the back, laughing and Reece nudged me in the ribs. "She was hot, man. Remember anything 'bout what she was like? Was she any good?"

Reece. I loved the damn kid, but he needed to get laid more and stop trying for my castoffs. Reece looked about twelve—blond hair, blue eyes—and it felt a whole load of *wrong* when he talked about screwing chicks. The preppy fucker was one polo shirt short of being on a damn Ralph Lauren ad.

"No fucking idea." I turned back to Austin, who was smirking at me. "What the hell did we drink last night?"

"More like what *didn't* we drink."

Yeah, that felt more like it. I remember now why I slipped. My folks had called… *again*, about the bastard engagement, and I'd immediately turned to the Mexican worm. Austin, being my best friend, joined me in getting completely wasted.

"Shit. Coach will have our asses. I fuckin' stink of tequila," I groaned.

I knocked back the protein shake in one, ignoring Reece as he grinned and said, "Damn, Bullet. I'm always wishing I was you: never without a girl, the whole damn school following your every move. But when Coach sees you looking like this, he's gonna make you wish you'd never been born."

The Abercrombie-and-Fitch little fucker was right; Coach made me pay. *Hard*. You don't drink in season without some serious consequences: suicides, hang-cleans, and laps being his chosen form of punishment that day. The Tide was still on two-a-day training, which meant working like a bitch and puking at every task. I ached, I sweated, but I loved every minute of it. It gave me the opportunity to get out my rage, to hit and pummel out my anger… to get through another damn day of this sorry excuse of a life. Ten months left until I could get the heck out from underneath *their* thumbs, and I was counting down every damn minute.

2

"Momma," I greeted flatly, seeing her name flash up on my iPhone screen, en route from practice to my classes.

"You need to come to dinner tonight," she commanded.

I clenched my jaw at her usual icy tone. "Sorry, busy."

"Then change your plans! The Blairs are coming and you need to be here so we can discuss the engagement, thrash out the details, get the whole arrangement tied up once and for all. Shelly's hosting her sorority's initiation of new pledges this evening, but you should be here regardless of her absence."

"I have practice again tonight. Coach has us on two-a-days. I've told you this."

Silence.

"You will come tonight, Romeo," she finally replied, her words dripping with authority. I stopped dead, right outside the humanities block. I was already running late for this friggin' introduction class due to the overrun team meeting, and now Momma was droning on in my ear about this fucking engagement and calling me that bastard name... again. Almost twenty-two and it still made me feel like a kid. The hairs on the back of my neck stood on end and I could feel my tolerance for her shit about to snap.

Pinching the bridge of my nose, I focused on the relaxing feeling of the burning summer sun pounding on my back, attempting to calm myself.

Didn't work. Nothing ever does.

"Look, I'm going to practice. I'm not coming," I snapped with finality, slamming my finger on the END button and stuffing the cell in my jeans pocket.

Heading inside the building, I tried to let the blast of air from the air-conditioner cool me the hell down from the usual friggin' anger boiling me from the inside out. My blood felt like acid pumping through my muscles. But I embraced it—welcomed it even. It was a reminder that I needed to get away from those people, finally break free from their overbearing ways. I'd had too many years of putting up with their degrading crap. I couldn't take much more.

I sometimes asked myself why I was sticking around. I had my own money, a full scholarship, but the truth was I felt trapped. They completely controlled me and I hated that harsh piece of reality. I had no real family except my folks, and pathetically, I couldn't bear the thought of being on my own. Plus, I did have some good memories of my daddy before the money changed him. I still remember the first time he took me to his office downtown, showing me off to his colleagues and proudly stating how I would one day be the CEO of Prince Oil, his protégé. I remember feeling important… loved even, but when the years passed and football became my passion, that pride my daddy had felt toward me seemed to fade, and it continued to spiral downward until there was nothing but contempt.

My parents were powerful and ruthless, and truthfully, I was terrified of what they would do if I shamed them publically by cutting myself off. Reputation was everything to the people they mixed with, and they wouldn't tolerate any humiliation on my part. I only had ten months to get through before I could leave the state, leave *them*, only ten more months to keep up the charade.

Forcing myself back to the present, I smashed open the second set of doors, hearing the wood splinter against the wall, and stormed down the empty halls, pressure building in my chest with each step at the thought of getting hitched to Shelly.

Shittin' Shelly Blair.

Christ, I fucked her twice in high school and, stupidly, once freshman year, and she acts like we're soul mates, in love. I'm not even sure I have the capability to love anyone. Had that shit beaten out of me a long time ago. It's amazing how little emotion you can feel when you've been ripped apart on a daily basis, told you weren't loved repeatedly, until your heart ceases to feel anything. Well, anything apart from anger—constant physical and verbal abuse just seems to help that shit grow.

My phone vibrated again, but I didn't look; I knew it would be my daddy, demanding I attend tonight. Momma would have called in the big guns.

I'd answer and he'd tell me my refusal was "*Unacceptable, boy!*" Then he'd threaten me, blackmail me, tell me how much he and Momma hated me, regretted me, how he could make my life hell if I pushed him too far.

Same ol' same ol'.

I turned the corner, fists clenched at the thought of having to sit next to Shelly for the next half hour, trapped in a room, no way out of her long-clawed grip, listening to some stuck-up old Brit drone on about damn religious philosophy, of all things. I was too fucking mad. I just couldn't sit next to Shelly pawing at my arms, rubbing against my leg, hoping to make me hard enough to give in and fuck her after class.

Never. Happening. Again. My cock went limp just looking at her. She thinks she looks hot—all that big hair, expensive plastic tits, and fake red lips. But all I see is a fucking praying mantis, ready to rip me apart.

I set off, head down, toward the classroom, and then I heard it. Shelly's laugh. The laugh that sounded like a thousand cats being strangled… slowly, painfully, one by one.

I wasn't proud of what I did next.

Bullet Prince, star quarterback for the Crimson Tide, dived to the right and hid behind a staircase.

I flattened my back against the cold white wall, praying no one would see me hiding like a pussy, when a flash of movement to my right caught my eye. Some chick holding a mass of papers came flying around the corner, muttering to herself, checking her watch, brown curls piled on her head, thick black glasses, and the brightest fucking shoes I'd ever seen.

Neon orange. *Christ.*

I couldn't help but crack a smile at her whole package, and I almost felt along my lips just to check it was actually there.

When was the last time I fucking smiled? That is, when was the last time I was smiling because of something other than looking at some asshole I'd knocked clean out on the floor?

Shaking my head in disbelief, I risked a peek around the corner and saw Shelly lock her eyes onto the chick and turn to say something to her friends, a spiteful smile on her lips. I tensed, suddenly feeling protective of the flustered brunette; the poor girl was completely unaware of what was about to go down.

I couldn't help but stare at her. She looked so fucking tragic as she blew her crazy hair from her thick glasses, scurrying down the long hall, her plastic shoes squeaking against the tiled floor with each hurried step.

I was too preoccupied, hooked on the scene, and realized too late that Shelly was up to something. I could only watch as Shel shouldered into the girl as she passed, causing all her papers to fall to the floor.

Fury possessed me.

She'd always been a bitch, but seeing her do that to that innocent girl just made me pissed beyond measure. Hell, it wouldn't have taken much, the mood I was in.

Shelly said something to the girl on the floor—I couldn't hear what—but the brunette never looked up, kept her head down, ignoring what I imagined to be a shitty slight.

Why I ever dipped my stick in that was beyond me. I blamed it on too many head knocks in football. That and being too horny to function. I didn't understand why Shelly had to treat people so bad. She had everything in the world and still, on occasion, showed moments of being a good person deep down. But those moments weren't nearly enough to salvage any friendship we'd ever had. I just couldn't work the girl out.

Stepping out of my hiding spot, I headed to tell Shelly to get the fuck on, but I was too late. She'd already sauntered into class, looking like the cat that got the cream.

As I approached the brunette, she leaned forward to reach for the papers that had landed way out in front, and I almost groaned out loud, my cock springing to life.

Fuck me.

That ass.

That perfect, curvy ass.

I quickly tucked my boner into my waistband and tried to think of something to cool down. *Jimmy-Don in a two-piece. Jimmy-Don in a thong. Actually...* I smiled derisively. *Shelly sucking on my dick...* Yeah, deflated like a defective balloon.

Running my hands through my hair, I stopped behind the new chick, avoiding staring at her ass in those short

23

dungarees and those long, tanned legs that were just tempting me to reach out and wrap them around my waist.

Shit. My cock hardened again.

I opened my mouth to ask if she needed help just as she spat, "Fucking arseholes!" to herself and got to her feet. Her glasses crashed to the floor in the process, the shitty frames landing right next to my feet.

Time stopped.

What the hell was that accent? English, maybe? Whatever it was, it was the hottest thing I'd ever heard in my entire sorry life.

Before I could stop it, a loud laugh jumped out of my throat at the sweet, proper voice cussing. She paused, frozen, as she heard me behind her.

Her head bowed, her shoulders bunched, and the sigh she let out said it all—pure defeat. Hell, I knew how she felt.

I reached down and scooped up her glasses, then, holding her arm, spun her to face me.

Jesus. H. Christ.

Large brown eyes, full, juicy pink lips, smooth, clear skin, and a soft blush to her cheeks. She was so close I could smell her skin—sweet, like vanilla.

Damn, I needed to say something, *anything*, not just stand here like some creepy fucking weirdo.

"Can you see now?" I muttered, my voice sounding rough even to me.

Her eyes squinted and she looked up. Her lips parted, her eyes studying every part of my face from behind the huge frames. Brown eyes, long blond hair, tanned skin—I had the perfect outer shell, but one fucking bitter center.

I tensed, waiting for it to come, the moment she saw it was me—Rome "Bullet" Prince. The attention would piss me off and then I'd come off like an asshole.

Golden brown eyes drank me in—the usual—and then... *nothing*.

Snatching the papers from my hands, the chick tried to take off. No stuttered recognition, no flirting, just... rushing to get the hell away from me.

What the—

I wondered for a moment if she didn't know who I was. But... nah, we were in Bama. She was at UA. Every fucker knew my face, whether I liked it or not.

Without realizing it, I took hold of her wrist. "Y'okay?"

She didn't look up but politely muttered, "I'm fine."

Negative.

Still no eye contact.

Still no recognition.

"You sure?" I asked again—absolutely no idea why.

I saw it in her shoulders: she was done with the day. Her long, black lashes fluttered on her cheeks before her caramel eyes fixed on mine. The wind knocked right out of my chest, and I couldn't seem to move.

"You ever have one of those days where everything turns into a bloody nightmare?" she asked tiredly.

English. Not English like the queen, though. Her accent had a lilt to it that I couldn't place. Christ, but it was hot.

"Having one myself, actually."

Her tight eyes softened and she sighed. "Then that makes two of us." Full lips crooked into a smile.

My heart did something it never had before.

It felt.

It felt something… indescribable. Each subsequent beat seemed louder and heavier than ever before and I started freaking the hell out.

"Thank you for stopping to help me. It was very nice of you," she said politely, the sentiment snapping me right back to reality.

Nice? Don't think so.

Her eyes measured me, waiting patiently for a response.

"Nice. Not normally what people say when they're talking about me," I said, finally seeing sense. What the fuck was going on?

I watched as her lips parted slightly, sucking in a sharp, shocked breath. I had to get the hell out of here, away from her, and stop acting like some damn dumbstruck pussy. Hell, I was acting like Reece.

I walked off without looking back, realizing that was the longest damn conversation I'd had with anyone in a long time, and it didn't involve anything about being the shitting oil prince of Bama or the next big football star. There was something different about her, something… intriguing. Like she didn't give a shit what anyone thought of her, wasn't caught up in the football hype. Her outfit and her reaction to me were proof of that. It was… refreshing, if not a little strange.

Almost as if I watched from a detached body, my boots abruptly ground to a halt and I looked over my shoulder.

Brit girl was still standing on the same spot, still looking in my direction. "I'm Rome," I offered, almost involuntarily, the words spilling out of my mouth as her eyes met mine.

Her long lashes fluttered down, touching the lenses of her glasses, and when they lifted, a shy smile transformed her face. "Molly."

I nodded and licked my lips, roved my gaze down her body, then made my way to class.

"Rome Prince, I take it?" the stuffy new philosophy professor said with a raised gray eyebrow as I sauntered into the classroom, nodding a silent greeting and making my way to my seat on the back row. She'd no doubt been briefed; teachers knew the score when football was in season. Of course, those from outside the States never quite got their heads around the fact that we, the players, got special permission to miss classes when on away games, or could rock up late after practice with no repercussions.

Climbing the steps slowly, I avoided Shelly's laser-beam attention until it was no longer an option. I slipped into my usual seat beside her, her snake arm sliding over my thigh as soon as my ass hit the wooden seat. Ally, my cousin, who I normally sat next to in class, couldn't make it today, leaving me all alone with Shelly.

Perfect.

"Hey, Rome," she said, all breathy, trying her best to be seductive. Shelly, to most of the male student body, was hot, but I knew the girl underneath, the one with all the personality of a gnat.

"Shel," I answered flatly, not reacting to any of her strokes and caresses. My jaw ached from clenching it in annoyance.

A huge bang sounded, drawing my attention, and the door to the classroom suddenly burst open. Molly fell through, still doing a shit job of balancing all her papers. The whole class zeroed in on her awkwardness.

Straightening up and blowing her crazy hair from her eyes, she pushed her thick glasses back on her nose, flushed bright red, and began sidestepping toward the professor, her back almost pressed flat against the wall as she grimaced in embarrassment. She looked so goddamn cute all flustered, shuffling across the length of the whiteboard.

I snickered involuntarily, feeling my heart speed up again as she put down her papers and stood beside the professor, fidgeting on the spot.

"What's *with* this girl?" Shelly snarled under her breath, nudging her best friend Tanya beside her. I stiffened, feeling my blood rush through my ears. Shelly turned to me. "And did you just laugh?" Her mouth gaped open. I shrugged without answering.

"Didn't think anyone dressed like that once outta kindergarten," Tanya bitched.

Shelly leaned in closer to me, the smell of her strong perfume almost making me gag. She had me in her trap, but there was no point in throwing her off. She had my folks on her side, and if I wanted to get through this year without too much of their shit, I needed to stay *way* under their radar and not do anything to rock the boat... then crush the selfish fuckers when I got my draft ticket out of here and squashed all their fascist, money-grabbing plans.

The professor asked Molly to introduce herself. I watched, fascinated, as the clumsy, geeky girl transformed as she spoke: back straighter, chin higher, eyes brighter and brimming with confidence.

I sat back and listened intently to every word she said.

She was smart, *really* fucking smart, and this class' new teaching assistant. Young, English, and already on her master's, with a goal of becoming a professor in philosophy. And to top it all off, she was in Bama to help the professor write an academic paper. Shit. She put all the undecided fuckers I knew to shame.

"So, Rome, are you coming tonight—" Shelly tried to speak to me, not listening to the introduction taking place, but I shushed her. I needed to hear Molly. For some reason, I wanted to hear her speak again, wanted to know her deal.

That didn't stop Shelly, though, and her hand skimmed over my stomach, her lips closing in on my ear. "*I said* are you coming tonight?! I—"

Whipping toward her, my face pulled into a hard expression, and I spat out quietly, "And *I* said shut the fuck up! I won't tell you again." Her beady blue eyes narrowed. She glared at Molly, then back to me, repeating the friggin' routine a few more times, and I saw the moment she realized the newbie Brit had caught my attention.

Molly was still speaking. I shifted my focus back to her and ignored Shelly's fury building beside me.

"I have loved religious philosophy for as long as I can remember, and I'm happy to be here to help Professor Ross in the lectures and seminars and to try and make the wonderful world of philosophy just that little bit more interesting!"

Shelly's long nails began to dig into the arm of her chair as Molly spoke easily to the class. Her top lip curled and I just knew she was about to go into full-on bitch mode.

"I'll be happy to answer any questions about—"

"I have one," Shelly snapped, interrupting Molly's speech. The whole class glanced toward her as she smiled an ugly, smug smile. I watched as Molly's eyes searched the crowd and widened slightly when they landed on Shelly... and the placement of her hand near my crotch.

Jesus.

"*Don't,*" I warned for Shelly's ears only, removing her hand, but she ignored me.

"Why the hell would you want to be a professor in philosophy? Don't you think it's a bit of a waste of your life?"

Molly was unfazed and simply replied, "Why not philosophy? Everything in life, on Earth, can be questioned—why, how, how can that be? To me, the mystery of life and the universe is inspiring, the vastness of unanswered questions floors me, and I love immersing myself in the academic journey of scholars both ancient and new."

Tanya snorted. Shelly laughed mockingly. "How old are you, honey?"

"Erm… twenty," Molly said, a red flush quickly covering her face.

"Twenty! And you're already on your master's?"

"Well, yes. I went to university a year young. I tested out of high school early."

"Damn, girl, you need to stop being so damn serious and learn to live a little. Life's not all about studying. It's about having fun. Lighten the hell up!"

The blood in my veins cooled to ice. I was about to say something to shut Shelly the hell up, when she added, "I swear, I'll never understand girls like you."

I snapped my attention to Molly, who had moved from her lectern and placed her hands on her hips. A smile tugged at my mouth again as she stood there, fiercely getting ready to take on the megabitch of Bama.

"Girls like me?" she asked coldly.

She was one pissed-off Mary Poppins. I found myself liking her even more. She had spunk, was ready to fight for what she believed in.

"Bookworms, nerds… wannabe *professors!*" Shelly drawled. I was sure she still thought she was back in high school, only able to make herself feel better by picking on a new girl. Pathetic.

"Studying and knowledge, I believe, gives a person power, not money or status or what designer you wear," Molly answered coolly, but I could see the fire in her golden eyes even through those fuck-off thick lenses.

"Really? You actually believe that?" Shelly asked, sounding less confident now.

"Of course I do. Opening your mind to unknown possibilities and learning how other cultures function, what they believe, gives people a richer, more holistic understanding of the human condition. Philosophy offers answers to an array of questions.

"For example, why do some people coast through life with ease, devoid of all compassion for others, whilst others—good, caring, and honest humans—are dealt blow after blow but somehow find the inner strength to carry on? Don't you think if more people took the time to be conscientious to mankind's troubles, then maybe the world would be a better place?"

I'd never heard anything like it. It was like she was profiling *me*. Everyone thinks if you're from the richest family in Alabama and you can throw a ball to rival Peyton Manning, then you're golden, no fucking worries in life. But then no one knows about *them,* about what I grew up with, about what I still go through every day, and no one knows because they wouldn't understand. But for a brief second, I entertained the notion that maybe she would. She sounded like she spoke from a place of knowledge, from personal pain. I'd come to find that only others in similar situations could pick that out in someone else, like there was some kind of hidden signal that they were in a whole load of hurt too.

"*That* is why I study over getting drunk every night. The world deserves to have people who think of others before themselves, that strive to be less selfish and superficially concerned." I took in her whole package from head to toe—perfect tight-but-curvy body, smooth, lightly

32

tanned skin, face brightened by the argument—and I quickly decided she was kind of fucking hot under all that... *wrong*.

"I hope that offers you some insight to why I want to be a professor. It's who I am and I'm very proud of that fact."

I quickly looked at Shelly, who was rooted to her seat. Sure, she may have looks and money, but she sure as hell didn't have a high IQ; in fact, I'm pretty sure a sea urchin had more intelligence than she did. I knew I was an ass, but seeing her sitting there squirming, witnessing this fashion-challenged brunette bring down a Bama titan, made my entire fucking day.

Before I could stop myself, I quipped loudly, "*Fuck*! That told you, Shelly! *Schooled*!"

A pissed-off gasp sounded beside me, but I couldn't pull my gaze from the British brunette to even spare Shelly a glance. Molly stared back at me and her lips moulded into a satisfied smirk. My cock hardened. I'd actually made her happy.

Fuck.

"*Whatever!* Good luck fitting in around here acting like that!" Shelly snapped moodily. I knew I'd probably just made things worse, but seeing her belittled, when she did it so regularly to everyone else, meant I really didn't give a shit.

The professor whispered something to Molly, and I zoned out as I watched her react to the professor's words. Unintentionally, Molly'd gotten my attention, and Christ, if I didn't feel like a stalker, eyes glued to her making her way down each row, handing out those bastard papers that only minutes prior were scattered all over the hallway floor.

Shelly staked her claim, almost straddling my thighs, as Molly approached our row. I missed if Shelly said anything to her at first. I was too busy trying to get a read of the new girl, absolutely wrapped up in the things she'd just said. That was until Shelly snapped, "Nice shoes, Molly. Do all future philosophy professors have such fantastic taste in fashion?"

I heard that slight loud and clear and decided that was it. I threw Shelly's legs off mine—counting her lucky that I didn't throw her right across the room—and hissed, "Quit it, Shel. Why do you have to be such a fuckin' bitch all the time?" The other students didn't dare meet my eyes. It was the only time I was glad I was a moody, scary fucker that no one dared mess with.

Molly's feet shifted from side to side, and she looked everywhere but at me. She was mortified and clearly wanted to split.

I needed something from her first. I needed to know if she believed everything she said or if it was just some regurgitated academic shit for the sake of impressing her new class.

Her eyes fluttered to mine again and I breathed deep, asking, "You really believe what you said just now?"

She frowned as though it were a stupid question. "Which part?"

I felt Shelly and her Barbies listen in, but I needed to know, something in me *really* needed to know. "About life being unfair. About philosophy giving answers to why some people get dealt shit and others don't."

Determined eyes met mine, leaving absolutely no room for doubt, and she replied, "Vehemently." And that was it. A wash of something soothing seemed to settle in my chest and yeah, it may sound soft, but it was the first time I felt like I could breathe in years. She knew pain too. She'd been through shit too. Someone could relate.

Molly turned to run to her desk and the class was dismissed. As I grabbed my bag off the floor, Shelly grasped my arm. "Rome, don't forget about the initiation tonight. Your brothers are part of the task. Come too, okay?"

"Don't count on it," I said in response. I could feel Shelly's hard stare as I sat in my seat, completely lost in my thoughts. I couldn't move, too busy reflecting on the things Molly had said. *Why do some people coast through life… whilst others are dealt blow after blow?* As the room began to clear, I snapped out of my daze and quickly left.

The minute I exited the classroom, two arms snaked around my neck and I groaned. "Shel, fuck off!"

As I turned around, a pair of red, pouting lips protruded and large hazel eyes tightened. "Not *Shel*, Bullet!"

I sighed as I was pushed aggressively against the wall. "Caroline," I greeted tightly as she rubbed up all she had against my cock. I ignored the watching students walking past, and no doubt Shelly too, which I actually decided would be a good thing. It'd piss her off, maybe get her to back off for a while.

"Come back to my dorm," Caroline said seductively, her sharp nails slipping under my shirt and digging into the skin—she was one kinky bitch. I gritted my teeth at the pain and her eyes lit with arousal. She leaned in, right to my ear, and murmured, "I've been dreaming about your cock in my mouth all week."

Christ. I shut my eyes for a second, debating whether or not I could actually do this new change in lifestyle I'd set for myself, but I pushed her off, deciding to stick to my original plan. For the first time ever, Caroline and her wonder mouth held absolutely zero appeal. Time to put my plan into action—a cull on all *distractions*. She was getting too clingy anyhow.

Meeting Caroline's hungry eyes, I stated, "Not happening. In fact, I'm cutting you out for good. Go suck someone else's junk. I don't want it no more."

"But… but… why not? You never refuse me!" It was true, I never had before, but, hell, I was done.

"Things change." Her nails, at my words, dug in farther into my stomach, and her face flushed red with anger. Glaring, I grabbed her wrists and pushed her away.

"*Change? You?* Since when?" she shrilled.

"Since right fucking now! You're not required anymore," I shouted, and she blanched, storming off down the corridor. It was true. I did need to change. I was sick to the back teeth of the groupies, of the fame whores. *Ten months.* I reminded myself. *Just ten more fucking months.* And I turned against the wall, head against the cold cream paint… *Just ten more months to get through.*

3

"Nope, not going," I said for the fiftieth time to Austin, Reece, and Jimmy-Don as we chilled in the lounge area of the frat house—me lying on my back on the couch, throwing a football up into the air, them watching some shit reality show about fuck knows what.

"What you gonna do, then? Stay here on your own?" Austin asked from his place on the recliner. Austin was ex-gang: Italian, heavily tattooed, piercings everywhere, ear plugs, the works—and looked as scary as all shit, but he was the best guy I knew and one of the only people I could actually tolerate.

"Yeah, I guess."

A bunch of the guys—mostly Tide players—came bustling in the room, hyped up and carrying kegs. I sat up and flicked my chin at Porter. He was an asshole but still a teammate, so I put up with his loud mouth shit… *just.* "Why the fuck you all so happy?"

Porter stepped forward, rubbing his hands together. "Initiations, bitches! You know what that means: drunken pussy on tap."

"They'd have to be drunk to fuck your rancid ass," Austin remarked, and I smirked at his cutthroat tone. There was absolutely no love lost between the two wide receivers, history going back too far to get into.

"C'mon, guys, let's go. We can leave if it's a washout," Reece said, a hint of desperation in his voice. When he came to school last year, Coach asked me to show him the ropes, you know, as the leader. I hadn't been able to shake the little fucker since.

Rolling back my head, I groaned, throwing the ball at the second-string QB's head. "Fuck, Reece, you need to get laid by your own efforts. I'm sick of your randy ass needing me to hook you up. You're a football player. Fuckin' use it for the perks! What's the point of playing for the Tide if you can never get your own chick?"

He ducked, ignored my jab, and smiled. "I'll take that as we're going! Let me change."

I rubbed my hands down my face in exasperation, hearing the door close as Reece left the room. As I looked back up, I noticed Austin staring at the floor and Jimmy-Don, my only other close friend, flicking his head at me, hinting that I should speak to him.

Shit. I hadn't even noticed anything was wrong.

"You okay, brother?" I asked.

Austin darted his eyes up response. The three of us were tight. I'd known Austin my whole life, the two fucked-up kids from opposite sides of the tracks, finding each other through football. Jimmy-Don came along during our freshman year. He was a big Texan cowboy and the most genuine guy I'd ever met. Fucking hilarious too. Reece didn't know us too well yet, and Austin didn't fully trust him, didn't trust *anyone* much. It was obvious Austin was preoccupied with something, and the minute Reece left, he'd dropped his shield.

"It's my brothers, man," he said in a tight voice. "Levi got roped into the crew, and fucking Axel let him do it, saying it was necessary to pay for my momma's medical bills. Levi's fourteen. He's too young to be caught up in that crap! I ain't got no money to give. Axel's telling me to keep up football for the payout and they'll handle everything in the meantime. I need to be drafted this year so fuckin' bad." He tipped his head to the ceiling, then dropped it again, his damn tortured eyes meeting mine. "Let's go to this initiation tonight, Rome. I'll go crazy if I stay here thinking about it all. I need to get out, need to forget all this shit for a while."

I could see he was hurting. His younger brother Levi was a good kid. Axel, his older brother, not so much. Austin had fought to keep Levi out of the gang that had long ago sucked in Axel, and I could see how it pained him to know that Levi had now gone down the same road.

"You know I'll give you the money, Carillo. Just say the word," I said quietly. Austin's eyes darkened with embarrassment.

"Rome, I know you mean well, but there is no way I'm taking a hand-out from you. I'll deal with it. I always manage to work something out."

Yeah he does, but it ain't often legit.

"You need us to pay your brother a visit? Talk to him, figure out a way to get him out of all that shit?" Jimmy-Don offered.

Austin shook his head. "No getting out once you're in. Hell, look what they still expect me to do." He placed a hand on Jimmy-Don's shoulder. "I appreciate it, though, but this is family business. I'm not involving you two."

Shifting impatiently off the couch, Austin asked, "We going?"

"Done deal. Let's go," I replied.

Jimmy-Don stood and offered his hand to me. He pulled me from the couch with a huge, happy grin, and once Reece got his ass back downstairs, we headed out the door.

"Hey, guys! They're all waiting for you in the back room," Ally said as we walked through the door of the sorority house, my cousin looking bored out of her mind as she sat on a stool at the entrance, acting out her role of "welcoming committee."

She walked over to me, rolled her eyes, and kissed me on the cheek. "Didn't think I'd see you here. It's not exactly your thing."

"Yeah, kind of forced to come." I watched as the guys filtered into the room, then tipped my chin to the door. "What's Shel having them do this year?"

Ally shook her head in disgust. "Kissing a brother and guessing what they've just eaten."

I ran my hand across my head. "Shit, how old is she?"

"I know, right? Anyway, there's all ages pledging this year. We needed upperclassmen. Well, that and transfers. Even bagged ourselves some genius Brit or something. Most of the girls are happy with that acquisition, seeing as though all the other charters wanted her with them to fill their quotas. I haven't met any of the newbies yet, though. I'm just hoping they're not all mini-Shels and at least one of them has a brain and doesn't get all tied up in her games."

Running a hand through my hair, I asked, "Genius Brit?" I tried to sound casual, but, yeah, I came off sounding like a douche.

Ally's eyes narrowed and she tilted her head, regarding me shrewdly. "Yeah, she's on a master's program or something. Apparently she's a TA in our philosophy class too. I don't know. Why you being so weird all of a sudden?"

I sniffed and crossed my arms across my chest. "No reason." I pointed to the room. "Pledges in there?"

Ally stepped back and crossed her arms, mimicking my stance. "You're going in?"

"Yeah."

As I walked past my annoying cousin, she grabbed my arm tight, wrenching me back. "*You're* going in?"

"*Yeah!* What're you not getting?" I bit out, jerking out of her grip.

"Mr. *I fucking hate all the Greek shit*—direct quote!—suddenly wants to get involved in Shelly's messed-up initiations?"

"I'm just curious," I answered, trying to sound casual, but she just continued to look at me with an unnervingly suspicious glint in her brown eyes.

I pounded away from my pain-in-the ass cousin, shoulders bunched with tension at her questioning, and marched through the doors of the back room.

Looking up through the thick crowd, the first thing I noticed was a long line of pledges decked out in tight togas and opposite them, a line of football players, most sporting hard-ons as they waited their turn to kiss the blindfolded girl before them.

Shelly was such a child at times, and I couldn't believe she was having these girls do this shit.

"What the fuck? You're actually coming to enjoy the show? You feeling okay?" Austin said from his place lounging against the wall, sounding more than shocked at my presence. I decided to ignore him too as I searched along the line.

Bingo.

Molly was at the very end, standing awkwardly, fidgeting nervously, but still looking her unique kind of hot under that thick, black blindfold. And hell if my mind didn't wander to what I could do with that piece of material and all the ways to make her scream.

Shelly walked past each pledge, grinning and snickering as she went. I saw her signal to Brody MacMillan, the worst-looking guy on the team—a guy who waits at least two weeks before showering. His drunken face brightened and he stood before Molly. On instinct, her hand flew to her mouth, and I knew she'd smelled him, his body odor and his complete disregard for hygiene. Mac didn't care, though, never had.

He leaned in, but my feet were already moving, and just as their lips were about to touch, my hands landed on his chest, and I launched him out of the way, his fat ass hitting the floor, his flailing arms bringing down the table of spare blindfolds as he went. "Move, MacMillan. I think you're in my spot," I said in a way that invited no backchat.

I couldn't take my eyes off Molly as her thumb went to her mouth. I was hard, real fucking hard, and couldn't wait one damn minute longer to taste her.

"Ah n-no… B-bullet! Shelly said… said…" I glanced at him on the floor, his beer belly flopping over his too-tight pants, eyes rolling all over the friggin' place.

"I don't give a shit what she said. Go get a fucking drink, or pass out, or something. You get me?"

He sagged to the floor, and I signaled for a few of the freshman players to get him the hell out of this room and into a bed. "I-I get you. I get you, man," he slurred as they dragged him out by his arms.

"Wait! Mac has to—"

I held up my hand and glared at Shelly as she approached.

"Shut the fuck up, Shel!" I bit aggressively, and she slinked back to her friends, face outraged and seething at Molly. I still couldn't have cared less.

Turning back to Molly, I edged in. She still smelled faintly of vanilla, and I couldn't remember a time I wanted to kiss anyone more.

Moving her hand from her mouth to my waist, I almost groaned as her fingers inched up my sides, her lips parting on a small breath. At that small reaction, I knew she was feeling this weird energy too.

I cupped her cheeks so she couldn't get away and so I could control our every move, then leaned in, brushing a kiss across her lips. I was trying to be soft, gentle—Christ knows that's not how I usually operate. But then her hand dropped to my stomach, accidently skimming the tip of my cock, and I lost it. Plain, outright lost any ounce of control I was holding on to.

In an instant, I smothered her, taking all she was willing to give. My tongue launched into her mouth and I pulled her body hard against my front, the feel of that contact only forcing my tongue to work harder against hers. I fucking wanted it, wanted *her,* and I was taking it, and thank fuck she was giving me all of it right back, reacting perfectly to my every forward move. Eventually, she withdrew, but not before licking my lips with the tip of her tongue, that action alone almost making me lose my damn mind.

"It's mint. The flavor in his mouth is—" She started on about the fucking initiation task, but I needed more of her, and at that moment, what I wanted trumped everything else.

Cutting off her answer, I groaned loudly and dived back in, finishing what I started. She anticipated my aggression and gripped my hair, bringing me in to her as far as I could go, meeting every rough move with her own. My hands began to roam. I needed to feel more of her body. I was about to explore her every God-given curve— but then Shelly had to choose that moment to let her friggin' mouth fly.

"*Enough!* What the hell, Rome? Get off her, *now!*"

Tanya moved behind Molly and untied her blindfold, glowering at me behind her back. My attention went straight to Molly, though, and the startled look she gave me when her eyes flitted up to mine and she realized it was me.

"Hey, Mol," I said, still not ready to let her escape my hold.

"Hey, you," she answered, and fuck, at those simple words, I wanted her again. I started to reach for her once more, until the bane of my goddamn life grabbed my arm and pulled me back, slapping my cheek in the process.

That did it. Shelly finally broke me and I reached out and grabbed her wrists. "Don't fucking hit me. Ever. Again."

I hated being hit. Yeah, that's a stupid thing to say. No one *likes* it—well, unless you sway that way in the bedroom—but for me, it just reminded me of what I'd had to go through for most of my life: pointless beatings.

"Rome tasted of mint. That's what you wanted, right, for this ridiculous initiation task?" Molly snapped, not seeming intimidated at all by Shelly's shit and immediately stopping me from exploding in rage.

I stared, couldn't stop staring, as her determined gaze met mine. I needed to leave before my anger became too much or I completely snapped and began nailing Molly to the floor. "She's right. I'd just chewed gum."

With that, I stormed through the full room, only pausing briefly to meet Ally's sympathetic gaze at the exit. I hit her with my best "don't start" glare, then got the hell outta Dodge.

"Rome, Man! Wait!" Austin shouted from behind.

Swerving to face him, I held up my hand. "I'm good… I… *shit,* I just need to be on my own."

"What the hell just happened? Who's that chick? And why the fuck were you kissing her?"

I glared at my best friend, clenching my jaw. "Carillo, I'm telling you to leave it. I can't be around Shel right now, so I'm gonna split, okay?"

"You sure?" I could see the questions in his eyes, but simply nodding, I headed up the stairs to the top floor, Ally's private balcony calling my name.

4

Three bottles of beer, two long hours of people watching, and five texts from the folks. *No… wait…* I checked my phone. Make that six.

Daddy: Can't avoid this for long, boy. Spoke to Martin Blair tonight. Looking like a summer wedding next year after graduation. Don't fuck this up. And from now on, MAKE the arranged dinners I plan. Not a request.

I cleared the message and tipped my head back, searching the constellations above just for something to distract my mind.

Didn't work.

Summer. A summer wedding.

Perfect.

My mind wandered to what it would be like being married, or even being in love. I couldn't imagine it—what my ideal girl would look like, what the hell we would talk about, if she would be able to cope with my mood swings, my past.

I shook my head, trying to rid myself of my dark mood, hearing laughter and music down below me in the yard. Kegs were popping, folks were doing shots, but none of it appealed, and to top it all off, I still smelled Molly's vanilla scent on my shirt.

Damn.

I kinda liked her. The way she kissed, the way she clung to my hair, pulling me close with her fists, and, mostly, the way she wasn't fazed by all the football shit, didn't look at me and instantly think, *Tide QB, must try and tame.*

I was in the middle of chastising myself for thinking too much about Molly when suddenly, the door to Ally's room clicked open, and I craned my neck to try and see who was there. "Al, that you?"

There was no answer, so I got to my feet, ready to kick out whichever horny bastards had sneaked in. I just wanted to be left alone. I walked into the bedroom and stopped dead.

Speak of the devil and he shall appear, I thought idly.

Molly. Fucking English Molly, gripping the bedpost in shock. Molly in a tight, figure-baring toga, staring at me with those huge, stunning eyes, and Christ, if her hanging on to that post didn't give some pretty interesting ideas.

"This room is off-limits, Mol," I said gruffly as I zoned in on her full lips and caught the way her eyes drank in my bare arms. She was affected by me.

Good, *not* just me, then.

I quickly took a swig of my beer to stop the nerves. I felt nervous for the first time in my friggin' life, and that never happened—not in football, not even when dealing with my folks—but here we were, a geeky librarian with shit dress sense weirdly unnerving me.

She lifted a key into the air and said quietly, "Yeah, I know. Ally gave me her key to use her bathroom." I stared at her for a moment longer and turned back to the balcony, needing to put some space between us... *and* get away from Ally's damn inviting bed.

Once back outside, I pulled out my chair, propped my legs up on the table, and fought my conflicted feelings. I couldn't get the idea of inviting her here on the balcony out of my head, but I knew I should leave it and not give in to my want.

I have ten months left, I reminded myself again. I couldn't let anything fuck that up, not even pretty English girls with the innate ability to harden my cock on sight.

Resolute to just let my interest in her go, I settled back, once again watching the crowd below. I chuckled as I watched Jimmy-Don get hit on by the female equivalent of him: big, loud, and country to the core. The girl walked straight up to him, hooked her arm around his neck, and planted a wet one right on his shocked lips. Jimmy-fucking-Don, the best guy I knew: kind, funny, and loyal to a fault. I was happy he was finally getting some, even if the girl, from up here, looked as scary as shit.

My ears pricked when I caught the sound of the bathroom door clicking shut, and I had a decision to make: let Molly slip away, no harm done, or seize the day and get her out here with me, actually find out her deal.

Insanity won out and before I could stop myself, I quickly shouted, "Mol?"

But there was only silence from the bedroom. My feet slammed to the ground and my head whipped in the direction of the doors. "Mol?" Had she left already?

"Yeah?" a timid voice finally sounded from inside.

Exhaling in relief and putting all my worries aside, I asked, "You wanna hang out here for a while… with me?"

"Yeah… okay."

We'd been sitting out on the balcony, just talking. I don't think I'd ever been alone with a chick that long before without getting naked. Girls came to me for one thing: a good fuck. But this was different. I kinda wanted to get to know this girl beyond the bedroom.

After watching her almost down her bottle of Bud, she asked, "So why are you up here hiding out?"

"Don't feel it tonight."

She dropped her hand to her chest and gasped, "Mr. All-star Quarterback doesn't want to mix with his adoring fans?"

Every ounce of me froze. She'd found out I played football—*perfect.*

I ripped off the label of my beer; it was that or launch the brown glass at the wall. "Well, that didn't take long. Who told you?"

"Lexi and Cass."

"Who?" I asked in a far-from-friendly tone.

Her eyes dropped and she fiddled with her hands again. "My roommates, they told me after we... erm, after we... you know..."

"Kissed?"

"Erm... yeah."

"So what did they say about me?" I pushed.

"That you were *the* Romeo Prince, quarterback extraordinaire for the Crimson Wave and that you were the Prince William of college football, yada, yada, yada..."

"What?" she asked, taking in my blank face.

"The *Tide*," I corrected, the anger lifting and complete fucking hilarity taking its place.

"Huh?" she asked again, completely confused, her expression making that more than clear. It was probably the first time in years that her genius ass had felt at a loss.

"It's the Crimson Tide. Not wave." I couldn't help it. I laughed, stomach tightening, uncontrollably bursting out laughing. Wasn't "the crimson wave" code for a chick being on the rag or something? Christ, she'd be lynched around here talking like that about the beloved national champs.

"Whatever. Tomayto tomarto," she dismissed with a casual wave of her hand.

"Well, we'd better keep that between us. It's not tomayto tomarto around here. It's... everything. It's life and death." And wasn't that just the friggin' truth? Sometimes the pressure to be perfect was insane.

I could feel her stare, her inquisitive mind working overtime. "So, Romeo, eh?" She finally asked after minutes of silence, and I froze.

"It's Rome," I corrected immediately. I was "Rome" to everyone but my fucking parents, and I hated any reminder that I was actually named after a pussy-whipped, poison-drinking asshole.

Her face lit with amusement, and she half danced, half shuffled on the spot. "Ah-ah! It's Romeo. I've been reliably informed."

"No one calls me that, Mol." I tried to be as polite as possible because fuck, she didn't know, but that name had me wanting to snap someone's neck.

"Just like no one calls me Mol," she immediately snapped back, not taking any of my moody shit.

At that burst of confidence, I wanted nothing more than to close in and kiss that impressive scowl off her face. "Touché, Molly...?" I waited for her finish, relaxing some at the new turn in conversation. Fuck me, I was having fun. Actually having fun. Alert the friggin' media: Rome Prince had cracked a little!

"Molly Shakespeare."

Okay, call off the press. I was back to being fucked off.

"What?" I asked, edging in closer.

"Shakespeare. Molly Shakespeare," she answered with a shaky voice and a slight tremble to her hands.

Someone had to be setting me up. *Maybe Michaels?* That fucker would give anything to screw me over. "Are you trying to be funny?" I asked bitterly.

"Nope. Romeo, I'm a Shakespeare—born and bred." Hell, she was telling the truth. *Shakespeare.* Her fucking name was Shakespeare! This couldn't be happening.

I couldn't help it, but I laughed, and she said, "That's not the only weird thing about our names."

"Really? Because things have been all kinds of weird since meeting you today. I'm not sure I understand what it all means yet." They really had. It was a sobering thought. They say your life can change in a matter of minutes, but up until now, I'd never really given that much thought.

"Well, get a one-way ticket to freaky-ville, my friend, because my middle name, Romeo, is Juliet."

Man, that was a mindfuck right there. It was a setup, *had* to be. We couldn't really be that tragic, that pathetic... could we? *Romeo* Prince and Molly *Juliet* Shakespeare... Pass me the fucking bucket. Or was it an omen, a big fuck-off neon sign shouting, *Stay the fuck away! Tragedy awaits!* Damnit.

"Are you serious?" I finally asked.

"Yep, my dad thought it would be a fitting tribute to our family surname."

"Very fitting." But all that came to my drunk-ass mind when I thought of Romeo and Juliet was death, fucked-up parents, and that dude from *Gangs of New York* looking at that chick from *Homeland* through a fish tank.

"Yeah, but at the same time, kind of embarrassing." I shook my head, re-concentrating on Mol. *Molly fucking Juliet.*

"Well, Shakespeare, you going treat me differently now too? Now that you know I'm Romeo 'Bullet' Prince?" I asked, trying to see if her attitude toward me had changed from earlier today.

"Bullet?"

She didn't have clue.

"Yeah. Football nickname. Because of my arm."

Blankness. Complete blankness on her pretty face.

"My throwing arm…"

Still nothing.

I tried a new tactic, pointing to myself, talking slowly. Maybe she wasn't getting the accent. Mine *is* pretty strong. "Quarterback… Quarterbacks throw the ball… in football… to the other players… They control the game."

"If you say so," she delivered with an equally patronizing tone.

She was serious. I'm guessing you could throw a pigskin at her head and she wouldn't recognize it. "Shit, you really know nothing about football, do you?"

"Nope. And no offense, I don't want to either. It doesn't interest me. Sports and I don't mix." Shit. Would've thought knowing the Tide would have been a requirement to even step foot in the state. Obviously not. I wondered what the hell British folks did for fun.

"I like that you know nothing about football. It'll be a change, talking to someone about something other than the new blitz defense or spread formation."

54

"Eh…?"

"I love that you have no clue what I'm talking about." I shifted closer, feeling the heat off her smooth skin.

"Happy to be of service," she said with a bewildered smile.

It felt freeing, speaking to someone new. She didn't know who I was, didn't understand the level of my sport or who my parents were, and it felt insanely good. I relaxed, completely chilled the hell out for the first time in months, and reached for another couple of beers, flicking off the tops against the table, and started talking, determined to find out more.

"So, Shakespeare, what's your deal? I take it you're a brainiac if you're already on your master's and been Professor Ross's research assistant for the last couple of years. In fact, you must be fuckin' unreal for her to bring you all the way to Bama with her?"

"Err, yeah. Something along those lines."

"You don't like to talk about how great you are in school, do you?" Modest too. I'd won the fucking lottery.

"Not really. It gets embarrassing, talking about being good at something. Anyone who enjoys that kind of attention, I think, is weird."

"Then that's something we have in common." The phrase "putting the pussy up on a pedestal" came to mind, but I couldn't believe she was this good, and I was still waiting for some kind of fault in her, something to *make* me walk away.

"Well, that and our Elizabethan epic playwright names," she teased, and I watched as her gaze darted down to our touching arms, a bright-red blush covering her entire face and chest. I tried to not focus too much on that area.

"That too," I replied with a reluctant smile.

And then Shelly piped up from the lawn. "Rome? Rome? Has anyone seen Rome? Where'd he go?"

That bastard girl was going to end me. She slaps me, then comes looking for me to fuck her. Crazy. As. Shit. I suddenly remembered why I avoided nights like tonight.

Molly abruptly launched herself from her chair, the whites of her eyes shining bright in the twilight, her breathing shallow. "You going somewhere?" I asked immediately.

I watched as she moved to the balcony rail, peering over the top. She was going try and split. Fuck that. She was staying. I *wanted* her to stay with me. To feel this connection for a little while longer, even if it could just be for tonight.

"Are you not going to go to her? She's pretty wasted by the looks of things."

"Am I fuck! She can just want. She'll sleep it off with some other guy," I threw out bluntly, kicking the chair she'd been occupying her way, pointing for her to sit down. "Sit your ass back down, Shakespeare, and have another beer with your most famously tragic character. You're not leaving me yet." For a moment, I thought I'd gone too far, my abrupt insistence too much, too soon.

But she surprised me again, rolling those golden browns and joking, "If I don't stop drinking soon, I'll be the one tottering around the lawn. You want me shouting for you, too?" She'd scatter if she knew just how much. Her letting me take control of her tight body, coming at my every move.

She watched my tongue lap around my lip and I watched hers in return. And there it was, that chemistry I'd felt earlier, the pull, the draw. "It's sounding more tempting by the second," I said quietly, my hard cock becoming painful in my jeans.

Her eyes darted back toward the backyard. I'd gone too far, needed to change the direction of the conversation. "So you've joined a sorority?"

Her shoulders relaxed. "Yeah, and Ally wants me to move into the main house, with Lexi and Cass, of course. It's not exactly my thing, but I'm trying my best to embrace college life."

Ally? *What the hell was she up to?*

"You and Ally been speaking?"

"Yeah. After you left... the room... earlier... after the... erm..."

"Kiss." It was all I could think about, taking that mouth again, tasting her again... tasting her all over.

"Err, yeah. Well, Shelly screamed at me to leave and Ally fought in my corner and basically told Shelly to bugger off."

Okay. Now I was thankful my cousin stepped in. I could imagine Ally verbally knocking Shelly down. "She's not exactly Shel's biggest fan. Al's cool. She'll be a good friend for you to have around here. She's my cousin and best friend. Hence, I got the spare key for this room when it gets too crazy out there."

"She seems nice."

"She's the best." Molly smiled and nodded.

"So, Shakespeare, where you from in England? Don't you dare say Stratford-upon-Avon or I'm checking myself into an insane asylum."

"Nope, nowhere near. I'm from Durham."

I wasn't exactly great with Geography and had no idea about Durham, England. "Nope, never heard of it."

She paused and thought real hard, her face suddenly lighting up. "Have you seen Billy Elliot?"

Ashamedly, yeah. One of Ally's cheer-up sessions after my daddy had ripped me a new one over football. She was trying to show me that even though you're background's shit, you can still achieve your dreams... Subtle.

"The film about the dancing kid?"

"Yep. Well, I'm from the exact estate that he's from in the movie."

"Really?" I racked my brain, trying to remember something about the setting. The kid in it was poor, real poor. That meant... Shit. Here I was moping, but one thing I never worried about was money. I had that in abundance. My grandparents leaving me most of their fortune pretty much set me up for life, despite my parents' objections.

Her hand landed on mine and I jumped, startled. "It's okay. I know I'm poor. You don't need to feel bad for thinking it."

"I wasn't—" I was. There was no judgement there, though, and the strength behind her eyes floored me. She went to move back her hand, but I gripped it, turning to connect them palm to palm.

"Yes, you were thinking that. It's okay. I know where I'm from isn't exactly glamorous, but I'm proud anyway. It's where I grew up and I love it regardless of its reputation, although I haven't been back there in years."

"Is your family still there?" I asked curiously.

Molly instantly changed. She began to visibly shake and rubbed at her chest. Her eyes were huge and her breathing choppy. "You okay? You've gone all white," I asked, panicked, rubbing at her back to calm her down.

"Yeah, thanks," she whispered, seeming a little better.

I never removed my hand from her back. I liked touching her, in any way.

"No, I don't have any family," she announced, her voice barely audible.

I jerked back, grimacing at my stupidity, and asked, "Shit, you're an orphan?"

"No, but I have no family left. I'm not sure an adult can still be classed as an orphan."

"Your momma?"

"Died giving birth to me."

Christ. "Daddy?"

"Died when I was six."

Jesus. "No grandparents, aunts, or uncles?"

"One, a grandma."

Thank fuck. At least she had one person. "And?"

"Died when I was fourteen."

Shit. "But then, where…?"

"Foster care."

"And that's it? You've been on your own for… You're twenty, right?"

"Yes."

"On your own for six years?" My chest actually ached. She'd lost everyone. *Everyone.*

"Well, I went to university so I had some friends there, and Professor Ross took me on as a research assistant in my first year and watched out for me when she realized I had no other family. But yeah, I've been on my own for a long time. It's been… difficult."

I leaned in, trying to give comfort, but fuck if I knew what the hell to say. What was there to say? She was completely on her own.

Her fingers skirted up my arm and she said, "Not to be rude, but this conversation is kind of bringing me down, Rome. Death and Budweiser should never go together."

She was trying to joke, but I had no humor for the shit hand she'd been dealt. I'd sensed that pain within her in class, but fuck, not the level she was at.

"So you and Shelly?" She interrupted my thoughts with the worst topic possible.

"Good subject change," I answered dryly.

"Well, there had to be a reason she was so pissed at our kiss. Even if it was just for the initiation."

"We're… complicated." I never talked about this, not even with Ally. But she'd shared who she was and for the first time ever, I wanted to do the same.

"That sounds like a copout if ever I've heard one."

"Nah, not a copout. She's been hounding me since sixth grade. Our families are pushing for an engagement.

You know, to protect their investments, keep the company's money in the family. Our fathers are business partners. I don't even fucking like her. She's a big old thorn in my side." That was putting it mildly.

"But… are you going to go through with it? The engagement, I mean. I'm surprised you'd settle down with someone you don't want. Or even settle down at all, if the rumors are to be believed."

And there it was. The shit that came with being me had already reached her ears, in a matter of hours. The gossip mill doing its job to fucking perfection. Time to set her straight, share a few home truths.

"Fuckin' rumors. Look, girls just throw themselves at me. When it's offered, I take it. Why the hell not? I don't have a girlfriend, never have. Sex helps me calm down from being so riled up all the time and shows folks that I'm definitely not with Shelly. I won't apologize for it. I just like to fuck a lot and never the same girl twice." I saw her jaw drop, but she'd asked. It was the truth. "My parents have a set plan. I'm expected to graduate, marry Shelly, take over the family business, and live the American fuckin' dream."

"So you don't want to play football professionally? I thought I heard that you were destined for big things?"

That completely changed my mood. "Yeah, I do want to play. I love it. It's as natural to me as breathing—the rush, the camaraderie, the roar of the crowd on game day, popping the perfect shot for a touchdown. My parents don't support it. They just… Hell, it don't matter. I just fucking hate my life being dictated by my folks, that's all."

Saying something, telling someone about them, was helping, ridding me of my anger.

"Then do what you want. Screw everyone else," she said, as simple as that.

"Easier said than done."

Her soft hand squeezed mine. "You can't live your life for other people, Rome. You have to do things that you want, achieve your dreams, in any way you want to do it. If you're happy, then your parents surely will be too, and if not, they'll get over it in time. Don't be with someone you dislike like Shelly. Be with a girl you can't resist, who you truly want above anyone else. Someone you connect with."

What was she trying to say? "Like you, Mol...? A girl like you?"

"You don't even know me." She was pushing me away, so I said the first thing that came to mind, running my finger down her cheek, loving the effect it had on her breathing. "It only took Romeo one look at Juliet and his fate was sealed. Maybe I'm just like my namesake, and maybe you're just like yours."

Smooth, Rome, real smooth. Oh, and I was sure that comment was an instant deduction of a thousand man-points, but it had the desired effect. She wanted me, and shit, at that moment, I wanted her too.

Placing my hand on her bare knee, I continued running it up her thigh, the heat of her skin increasing the closer I got to between her legs. My cock was as hard as granite as I watched those plump lips part, and I moved in, about to take her, when the fucking door handle began to shake. "Rome? Rome? Open up! I know you're in there!"

Molly sucked in a breath and, knocking my hand from her thigh, straightened her toga.

Ruined.

"Fuck!" I screamed, turning and launching my beer into the trash, hearing the glass shatter.

"That girl!" Molly hissed and stared at me, looked me dead in the eye, waiting for me to say something. As I stared at her hopeful face, reality came crashing down. What the hell was I doing? Molly was damaged, too damaged to be just a fuck. From everything she'd told me, meaningless sex would just be cruel, and shit, I couldn't give her anything more. I needed to get the hell out of Bama—*had to*—and being with a girl that wasn't Shelly was just going cause a shit storm of problems with my folks.

Nothing was worth that.

"I'm going to go, Rome," she finally said with a disappointed sigh. "I'll leave you with her. It's probably for the best."

"Mol—" I started, but she was probably right. It *was* for the best.

But when she walked past, something in me clicked, and I grabbed her hand, smashing her into my chest. Her golden eyes were huge as she stared up at me, waiting... just fucking waiting for something. "I liked talking to you, Shakespeare. It was different..." I eventually confided with a strained voice.

Gripping her toga, I pulled her closer to me, holding the back of her neck in my hand, but her expectant gaze told me she needed more.

TILLIE COLE

Her face dropped as I stalled, and she said disappointedly, "You too, Romeo. But our little conversation seems to have come to an end. I imagine it's probably for the best anyhow."

Before I could stop her, she pulled away, walking to the bedroom, and I followed. Mol pulled on the handle and the door burst open, Shelly came running straight toward me, jumping into my arms and crushing her fat lips against mine. "I want you, Rome. Fuck me, right here, right now."

Her legs tightened around my waist and she began grinding her panty-less crotch against my jeans. Clasping the top of her arms, I pushed her back, my attention honing in on the door. It was shut, and Molly was gone.

Fuck!

Turning, I threw Shelly off me and onto the bed. "What the fuck, Shel?" I hissed.

She wobbled to her knees, smiling, her red lipstick smeared all over her teeth. "Daddy called, told me we're getting hitched next July. I wanted to celebrate with you."

Something within me broke, and Molly's advice circled my brain. *You can't live your life for other people, Rome. You have to do things that you want, achieve your dreams, in any way you want to do it.*

She was right. *Fuck,* she was right! What the hell was I doing?

Staring at Shelly on the bed, I asked, "Why do you want to marry me, Shel? You don't love me. I don't love you. What's the pull?"

"I do love you! I always have," she slurred.

Shaking my head in exasperation, I argued. "No, you love the *idea* of me. Fuck, Shel, you don't even *know* me. How can you love me? How can you want this friggin' engagement? Don't you want a man who'll love you back?"

Her eyes glossed and her shoulders slumped. "My daddy wants it to happen. My momma taught me from a young age what it would be like to marry for money, and like most women in my position, I would have to let you do your own thing, have your little *flings*. I accept that. But in society's eyes, *I* would always be your wife. *I* would be the one on your arm at social functions and *I* would be the mother to your kids. We could give each other what our folks—and Tuscaloosa's society—expect."

Her gaze had dropped during her speech, but then she looked up at me with her bloodshot eyes and said, "I'm not stupid, Rome, despite what you think. I know you don't love me, but, let's face it; it's not about love, is it? It's who we are, who we were raised to be."

"Don't you want more for yourself? Don't you have dreams? Things you want to achieve away from all the pressure to be something that we're not? Hell, Shel, I'm not made for that kind of life! I'm football player. That's what I was born to be, not some miserable suit!"

Her head began to shake back and forth. "No! I don't *have* something like football as an alternative. I don't *have* a perfect four-point GPA or some other skill to use as a backup. I'm a Blair, and you know what, Rome? I *want* the life my momma has, and I need *you* to make that happen." Her eyes narrowed and, glancing at the open balcony, she stated, "And I will do anything to get it."

65

I straightened at her thinly veiled threat, realizing there was no getting through to her in this state. "It ain't happening, Shel. I'm sorry."

Whipping back to face me, she once again adopted her usual bitch façade and shouted, "You're such a selfish prick! Think of me! If it's about sex, don't worry. You know I'd fuck you anytime you wanted. It's all here for you to take! The perfect life on a silver platter!"

"Have some damn pride, woman!"

"I have pride, but I'm starting to wonder if you even have a dick, pussying out of your duty and acting like a whining little bitch instead of just doing what you're told!"

I strode to the end of the bed, Shelly shuffling back at the severe look on my face. "You and me—never happening. You're pathetic and I hate everything you stand for. I'll never marry you. Ever. You get me?"

She faltered for a moment before answering. "You will, Rome. I've known you my whole life and you've always done what your folks told you to do. What's changed?"

It was rhetorical, but I glared at her for the longest time before smiling victoriously. *"Everything."*

I pounded out of Ally's room, not bothering to evict Shelly, and went searching for Molly to make sure she was okay. Down on the lawn, I spotted her on a bench with Ally, Jimmy-Don, the scary girl I'd seen with Jimmy-Don, and some chick with black lips and jet-black hair.

Molly looked so pissed off, so sad, and, not wanting to cause a scene, I got the hell out of there. I needed to do something while I had the courage, something that was in no way going to be easy but had to be done to finally break free.

I just hoped I didn't live to regret it.

5

"Mr. Prince will see you now, Rome."

I rose from the cold, hard leather couch in the vast, sparsely decorated white lobby and, nodding at Jean, my daddy's assistant, I entered his office, firmly closing the door behind me.

There he sat, king of the whole fucking world, dressed in his black pinstriped power suit, behind his desk, scowling as I approached. "Rome. To what do I owe this pleasure?" I caught the sarcasm in his voice but ignored it and slumped into the free chair at his desk.

"I need to speak to you," I said firmly, embracing the detached numbness I always felt in his presence.

He sat back, smirking, crossing his arms. I'd never come to him like this before, and it had obviously humored the bastard. "Go ahead. I'm all ears."

Taking a deep breath, I met his cold eyes and declared, "I'm done."

That wiped the smirk off his face, and his graying eyebrows pulled together in confusion. "Done with what, boy?"

"All of it. Your controlling shit, Momma being overbearing and ragging on me nonstop for being such a fucking mistake to you both." I leaned forward to hammer the final nail into the Prince Empire's coffin, seeing my daddy's lip curl in annoyance at the bold gesture. "And I'm not marrying Shel, not for anything. There isn't enough money in the world or any threat you can issue that would make me want to legally bind myself to her for life. Cut me out of your lives if you want, but I can't and I *won't* do it."

The silence was suffocating in the expansive, antique-decorated room as the two Prince men stared each other down. Finally, my daddy sat forward, calm as the sea, and said, "I don't know where the hell you got the idea that you had any choice in this."

Exactly the response I was expecting.

"I *do* have a choice. And I'm not going through with it. I'm going to enter the draft, and this time you can't stop me. I'm gonna leave this place once and for all, and live my own goddamn life. God, you should be proud! Why do I get the only father in the whole of Alabama who *doesn't* want his son to enter the NFL? I'm good, Daddy, real good, if only you'd realize it. Maybe if you come to one of my games, you'd see I wasn't right for a life in the business world."

Daddy stilled, his face burning red. Then he launched to his feet, swiping at his desk. It took me completely by surprise, and I jerked back in my seat. He'd always been physical, domineering, but this reaction seemed kind of extreme, even for him. He was always calm and collected, especially in public, *especially* at his work.

Slamming his hands on the solid mahogany desktop, he yelled, "You will do it, boy! It's your *duty*! Prince Oil needs the Blairs, and I will not allow some nobody from outside the family to weasel his way into my company when Shelly finally marries! The business has been passed down to the next generation for years, but, oh no, *I* get the punk of a son who decides against it. Jesus Christ!"

I quickly stood and, shocked at his outburst, shouted back, "What the hell? What's wrong with you? Why're you reacting like this? This can't be just about me not wanting to marry Shel. You're acting crazy. What's really going on?"

His eyes narrowed and a strange, almost panicked expression flashed across his face. "It *is* about the marriage! You're gonna do it, if it's the last thing you do!"

Running my hands through my hair, I sighed deeply and began backing out of the room. "I'm done. Deal with it. And don't bother trying to convince me otherwise."

I opened the door to the lobby, and Mr. Blair, Shelly's daddy, spotted me. "Rome!" He held his arms wide, smiling his expensive veneered smile. He wasn't a bad man, just had his priorities messed up: money and social standing first, and they trumped everything else. Shelly clearly had daddy issues, and the way he put most things above her, it didn't take a genius to figure out why.

"Hey, Mr. Blair," I said as he embraced me.

"You here to talk about the wedding? Just think, by this time next year, you'll be officially family." My stomach dropped and I stepped back. Mr. Blair lost his smile as he glanced over my shoulder and saw the state of my daddy's office. "Joe? What the—"

"I'm not marrying your daughter, sir. I don't want her as my wife and I don't want anything to do with the company either. I just came down here so my daddy knows I'm serious. Sorry if it causes you any problems, but I just can't do it." With that, I left the building.

I'd stood up to my daddy. I'd actually fucking done it. But the determined look in his eyes as I left made me feel nothing but dread for what lay ahead.

* * *

Texas A&M, Kyle Field, College Station, Texas.

"What's going on, son?" Coach sat before me in the locker room. We'd just finished playing the Aggies, and to say I'd just had a nightmare of a game would be an understatement. Three interception passes… Six sacks… *Six fucking sacks!*

Sitting head down, still in my dirty uniform, still in my cleats, I shrugged my shoulders. "I can't focus. Shit! I was terrible! Thank fuck we won or I'd be getting run out of

Tuscaloosa!" I threw my head back, running my hands down my face, feeling completely drained.

Coach sighed, moving his chair to sit opposite me. "Rome, I've known you nearly four years now, went to some of your high school games before persuading you to join the Tide. This is no time for you to mess up. The world knows you're certain to be a first-round draft pick." He grew silent for a moment before he asked, "Is it your folks?"

That surprised me, and I snapped my head back to face him. "What?"

"Look, son, I don't know much about your home situation. You keep your personal life pretty locked tight. But I know when someone don't have the support of their folks. I've been coaching a hell of a long time, and you're not the first player to leak his home life onto the field."

A lump bobbed in my throat, and I checked around me, only to find that the rest of the team was long gone. I stared Coach straight in the face and nodded. "They don't want me to enter the draft. They want me to take over the family business and marry a chick I don't want. I had a huge argument with my daddy a few days ago over it all. I can't stop reliving it."

"And what do *you* want, Rome?" Coach gently questioned.

There could be no hesitation. "Football. It's *all* I've ever wanted."

"It ain't *my* place to tell you what to do, Rome. But I will say this. You are one of the best... if not *the* best quarterback it has been my honor and privilege to coach.

You're at a crossroads in your young life. Only you can mess up the decisions you must make." For a few seconds, he left me to ponder what he'd said, then continued. "NFL teams have you on their radar. Everyone expects you to make it at the next level."

I stared at the dirty white-tiled floor, unseeing, when coach sighed heavily. "Look, what can I say? Try hard to get yourself into a better place. Rome… no matter what it takes… yeah?"

"Yes, sir!" I exclaimed, lifting my head and looking Coach straight in the eye… at the same time silently thanking the Lord that Coach hadn't threatened to bench me.

Slowly standing up, giving me a fatherly pat on the shoulder, he quietly said, "Get changed. We head out in twenty."

6

That was two days ago. The team… *my team*… was now back at practice. After Coach's talk with me, things felt easier, and I was thankful to be back in Tuscaloosa. Of course, the texts *ordering* me home to discuss the marriage were constant, but I decided I needed to put some space between my folks and me for a while.

I'd been thinking hard about what coach said and came up with a plan. One, get my head back into football. Two, sharpen my focus on what I do best. Three, try real hard to shut out all the shit screwing with my game—drinking and whoring around being top of the list.

My cousin and I were walking to class, and Ally was talking nonstop about some chick she lived with pissing her the hell off, but I zoned out, a feeling close to excitement in my stomach as we approached the Humanities building. Yeah, that had never happened before, especially not for philosophy, but here I was, almost sprinting to get to the classroom. I wasn't in denial about why.

"Hell, Rome! Slow down!" Ally said, running to meet my quick strides. "What the hell you in a rush for?"

"Nothing. Just don't want to be late."

Her hand gripped my elbow, pulling me to a stop, brown eyes huge. "Since when?" she asked with a disbelieving laugh.

"Since when, what?" I tried to evade her questioning. She was too fucking nosey for her own damn good.

"*You!* Why're you so concerned with class all of a sudden? You're not exactly student of the year."

"Let's go or I'll leave your ass behind." I started walking again, and she let out a huge gasp from behind.

Turning, I groaned in exasperation. "What now?"

Her lips pouted and then she broke out into a smile. "I'm on to you."

Ignoring her, I made my way to the class. As we headed through the door, Ally was still chuckling beside me—which only served to piss me off more—and I immediately checked out Molly's TA desk, feeling instantly disappointed when she wasn't there. As hard as it was to admit to myself, I'd missed seeing her all week. Was sick of her image in my damn head, preventing me from sleeping, and thought it was about damn time I viewed her in the flesh again.

"Aww, Rome, would you look at that? No Molly," Ally lilted as she climbed the stairs. I was used to her trying to rile me up, like a little, annoying sister would, but this time, she was really getting to me.

Someone entered the room, and I caught a look at them from the corner of my eye. It was Molly, head down, dressed in jean shorts, a tight white tee, and a white version of those fucking horrendous shoes. She skirted past me to her desk, not even acknowledging me.

That pissed me off.

"Shakespeare," I greeted, trying to get her attention. But still nothing. She was completely ignoring me and it wasn't sitting well, my good mood now completely gone.

I made my way up the stairs to my seat next to Ally, trying to pay no attention to Shelly, who, as always, began batting her eyelashes in my direction.

Shaking my head, I questioned why she was being so fucking stupid? I couldn't believe she would keep up the fake flirtations after the mindfuck that was our last meeting.

I sat in my seat, wondering why Molly was being so weird, when she strode up to the lectern, face tight, tapping the small microphone, the echoey dull thuds attracting everyone's attention.

"Hey, everyone. Professor Ross asked me to lead today's seminar on the introduction to utilitarianism, and in the coming sessions, I will be giving brief notes on the main arguments before exploring some examples for discussion."

There was that confidence again, almost arrogance when it came to her subject, and she moved from the lectern, dropping her notes, her tight ass flexing under those shorts. I shifted as my cock grew hard. She licked her lips, adjusting her glasses, and I struggled not to groan out loud at the sight.

"In simple terms, the idea of utilitarianism is the theory that actions of an individual are based on the fact that we, as humans, actively seek pleasure when making decisions. Therefore, this argument is seen as the hedonistic approach to ethics—we do things to feel good, are driven by the quest for pleasure. Jeremy Bentham proposed that humans operate on a pleasure-pain principle, i.e. that we seek pleasure and avoid pain at all costs."

She never once looked my way as she spoke. The class was small and she met every pair of eyes in the room except mine. It got to me… *really* fucking got to me.

"Bentham believed that this principle could be adapted to society as a whole and that it would function better if it operated on a system that considered *the greatest good for the greatest amount of people.* This is evident in many sectors of society, but a good example is the way we vote in a democracy. The majority vote benefits most people. Therefore, the majority of people in that society are happy, i.e. feel pleasure at the outcome, creating a more utilized society."

After minutes of still getting nothing, not even a glimpse, I decided it was time to cut the shit and *make* her acknowledge me. What Shakespeare didn't know was that I had a firm grasp of this topic. And I'd use it to show her I didn't like to be ignored.

I waited until she paused in her lecture and let out a dramatic cough, edging forward in my seat and pretending to listen intently, purposely being obnoxious. Her eyes darted to mine and they narrowed. *Perfect*. I'd started to piss her off too.

"Where was I?" she said out loud, subtly glaring in my direction in admonishment. "Oh, yes. Today we will be discussing the concept of the pleasure-pain principle and whether humans really do function this way. I, for one, tend to agree in the most part with this theory—"

"Really?" I blurted, stopping her mid-flow. My classmates gaped at me from their seats. Yeah, I never participated in class. Hell, most of these people probably hadn't heard me say anything in nearly four years of sitting in this room. I knew I had the reputation of a dumb jock, and what did I care? Let the fuckers believe what they wanted. I was going to speak today, though, and it was all because I wanted a certain girl's attention.

Molly had stopped still, the pulse in her neck beating furiously under her exposed skin. "*Pardon?*"

There it was, that fire, that spark she kept so well hidden. Taking my pencil, I rolled it in my fingers as if I didn't give a shit and, by the look on face, succeeding in riling her up.

"I was expressing my surprise that you agree with Bentham, *for the most part,*" I said, exaggerating the last four words.

"Then the answer is yes, you heard correctly," she snapped.

Christ, she looked even cuter when she was mad as all hell, and her attitude was turning me on. "Huh!" I muttered, biting on my pencil. The room was absolutely silent, and even the professor was watching us both with rapt attention.

Ally struck me with her elbow in my rib and hissed out, "Quit it, Rome. She ain't finding you funny. Leave her the hell alone." For a moment, I did feel a bit guilty, but I was having too much damn fun sparring to really give a shit.

"Huh, what? *Romeo?*" she queried with a bitchy smile. That stilled me, and any humor I had soon morphed into rage. She used that fucking name, *knowing* exactly how I felt about it… and in public too? It was so far below a low blow it was arctic and I couldn't believe she'd done that to me, didn't believe her capable of being so damn mean.

Her eyebrow rose, a clear challenge, and I snarled. She wanted to play dirty? Game on.

Taking a deep breath, I said, "I just think it's foolishly idealistic to think in such a way, *Shakespeare,* and for someone of your supposed intellect, I'm surprised it came out of your mouth at all."

"*Rome!*" Ally warned quietly beside me, but I couldn't stop myself. I had a burning desire to fuck her off after calling me that bastard name so maliciously.

"I mean, look at the voting analogy you gave: *greatest good for the greatest number of people.* You mentioned how it was considered good for society, as most people would be happy with the result, but all I see are flaws. What if the 'majority' of the people voting are bad or have ill intent and the minority are innocent, and good people are put in danger due to the fact that they're outnumbered? What if the person you voted in has ulterior motives and goes back on what they said they would do?"

She opened her mouth to butt in, but I kept going, raising my voice even louder so she couldn't stop me in my tirade.

"Look at Hitler. He was elected by a democratic vote, and for a time, he was what was right for the majority of the people who were living in poverty with no real hope. But look how that ended… I'm just saying that although it seems good in theory, the practical side don't really pan out, now does it?"

I tipped my chin arrogantly, challenging her to step up her game. Leaving the protection of the lectern, she marched forward, purposefully walking up the first two steps toward me, her hair bouncing, long brown strands falling into her eyes.

"For a start, do me the honor of letting me finish before rudely interrupting." Her teeth were gritted together and her eyes alight with ire. "*What* I agree with is the idea that individuals *do,* in many situations, live for pleasure over pain, at least *for the most part*. Surely you'd agree with that, Mr. Oh-so-fantastic QB. Don't you make the majority of your decisions based on your illustrious football career, something that brings you pleasure?"

So she was going to go for the jugular, try and bring me down. I wondered what the fuck I'd done to deserve her wrath. "You're right, I do, but I also do it for the spectators, for my teammates. They find joy in football, unlike some," I said pointedly.

Her hands landed on her hips. "Meaning what?"

"Meaning that in Alabama, *Shakespeare*, football is the greatest pleasure there is—playing it, watching it, coaching it. My training and therefore my success benefits both me and others. You seem to be the only one who don't like it."

Her lips twitched and a victorious smile settled on her face. "Then you've proved me right. In Alabama, the greatest good for the greatest number of people is football, as it brings pleasure to the majority of the population."

"In this respect, you may be right, but it's not always that simple."

"Go on," she said, her arms folded under her chest, her foot tapping loudly against the wooden stairs.

"You talk about individuals doing things for pleasure and to avoid pain, things they dislike?"

"Yes."

"But many individuals do things that cause themselves pain or displeasure to suit other peoples' wants and desires." She should've gotten that reference. Christ, she'd been the only person I'd ever confided in. Only she knew about the pressure from my folks to marry Shelly and do their bidding. I'd be damned if I was going to let her start spouting it back at me in front of total strangers.

"Oh, I'm not sure they're always that painful—doing certain things or certain *acts* that others want, I mean." Yeah. She *was* going to go there, and I almost snapped the desk in rage.

"Be *completely* clear, Shakespeare. What you getting at?" I gripped onto the pencil like it was a stress ball.

"Well, let's use sex, for example. One of the two people partaking in the act might want it more, and the second person may be altogether quite indifferent in their affections, but the second person ultimately gives in and

81

does it anyway to make the first person happy. However—and herein lies the irony—the one that is unhappy still finds sexual release. Therefore, that party doesn't really experience displeasure at all. Do they?"

Shit. Realization hit. This was about Shelly. She thought I'd fucked Shelly the night we talked on the balcony, and she clearly didn't like it.

The pencil in my fingers snapped, along with my patience and tolerance for Molly's public form of revenge... And for something I didn't fucking do! She wanted to air all the dirty laundry? Then I'd air it the fuck out.

"Or how about a person decides it would be a good idea to kiss another, due to some weird, unexplainable pull, but then, in hindsight, decides it was a fuckin' mistake? That they spoke about personal things for the first time ever with someone different, someone new, thinking, *Maybe I can trust this person with knowing the real me?* Only to realize that what you did was stupid and should never have happened at all. Cementing that people are just one big ol' disappointment!" I ran my hands through my hair, letting the now-shredded pencil fall to the floor.

"Jeez, Rome," Ally whispered from beside me, her sympathetic gaze falling on Molly. I lifted my eyes to see what had her so upset. Molly was still standing on the second stair, eyes watering, complete embarrassment in her stance. *Shit!* How the fuck had all that just happened? It was meant to be a stupid debate, not a full-on verbal massacre. Fuck, but the girl could rile me—in more ways than one.

Golden eyes quickly left mine, and she glanced at the clock, announcing quietly, "Next seminar will look at Bentham's personal notes. The essential reading is on the course outline. Class dismissed."

Slinging my bag over my shoulder, I raced down the stairs, not even looking at Molly at her desk, the need to get the hell out of the stifling room taking precedence over everything else. Shelly stormed past me, almost taking off my shoulder in the process, and the other classmates scurried past with hurried whispers. Walking to the corner of the hallway, I leaned against the wall, breathing deeply.

A light cough broke through my daze. "*What?*" I said, knowing it was Ally.

"You okay?" she asked softly.

Opening my eyes, I laughed sarcastically. "Fuckin' peachy! I love my personal life being the subject of the UA rumor mill."

She stared at me for a while before shaking her head. "I need to get to my next class. Don't do anything stupid."

"Shut up, Al."

"I mean it. I know you're waiting for her." I was. Shakespeare and I needed to have a private little talk about how to keep a fucking secret.

"Look, Rome, I've become real close to that girl lately. Heck, she's become one of my closest friends. I don't want you giving her a hard time, you hear? She's not used to the likes of you. Hurt her and you'll have me to deal with!"

Crossing my arms without giving a response, I dropped my gaze, watching Ally's feet as she marched away with a frustrated sigh.

Two minutes later, Shakespeare walked out of the classroom and, instantly, I was in her face. "What the fuck was that all about?"

Her shock at my presence was obvious in her huge eyes and the rhythm of her stuttered breath.

"You were rude," she said sternly, checking all around us.

We were alone, I'd made certain of it. This was between her and me.

"I was debating. That's what you do in philosophy. *You* made it personal." I could hear the rough edge to my voice, but Molly wasn't intimidated, just stood tall, meeting me glare for glare.

"So did *you*!" She hit back, her face flushing with anger.

Could she not see what she'd done? How she'd brought me to the brink of losing it in front a class with her words…? With that fucking *name*?

"Why did you bring up the other night? What I talked about was in confidence. I told you things I've never told another living person and you threw it back at me in a public class?" I closed in, smelling that damn vanilla scent of her… What? Her hair, her skin? *God*, it was driving me insane. Up this close, I noticed more about her, like how her skin was perfect, not one mark or blemish, and her eyes had a strange shade of caramel around the iris. Jesus, I was furious but wanted nothing more than to take her against the wall. Fuck her into submission. Fuck her until she learned to not cross me again.

I refocused my mind and said, "I put my trust in you and you dredge it up in your lecture for your own fuckin' smartass gain?"

My jaw clenched as she rolled her eyes and laughed. "Confidence, my arse! The whole college knows you use girls for sex, which, quite honestly, makes me feel sick."

She'd just earned strike one.

"From what I saw the other night with *her*, you did then too, after you confided to me that you didn't like her, after you connected so deeply with me. "

Strike two.

"Where's the morality in that? Couldn't resist her open legs I take it?"

Fucking strike three!

Completely losing my mind, I backed Molly against the wall and into a dark corner. We were completely hidden from view. Inching closer, I asked, "Why do you care who I fuck? What's it to you?" Anger was quickly being replaced by lust, the two blurring in my mind. Her heavy breathing and the goose bumps on her skin were only goading me further.

She may not have realized it, but Molly couldn't take her gaze off my lips. "It isn't *anything* to me," she said between gritted teeth, but those hooded eyes gave me all the indication I needed. She fucking wanted me too but couldn't just come out and say it, could she? No, Mol was content to push every damn button I had.

I slapped my hand against the wall, edging in closer, to the point that we were almost touching. "You're lying."

Her firm tits pressed against my chest as she hissed, "I'm not lying. It has nothing to do with me who you *fuck*, as you so eloquently put it!"

"Bullshit! I don't fuckin' believe you!" I spat out as she hit my chest, and I tried once again. "I *said* I don't believe you! Tell me why the fuck you care and don't fuckin' lie!" I felt her hands brush my stomach, almost causing me to moan out loud.

"*Fine*!" she screamed. "I care because you kissed me! You kissed me like you had no other choice, dammit! I don't like being just another plaything when I trusted you with *me*. I never do that and now I remember *exactly* why!"

Now we were getting somewhere.

"For your information, I didn't *screw* her. In fact, I told her in no uncertain terms that I was done for good. What you'd said to me made sense… about living my own life. You got through to me. You… *affected* me. And get this straight… you are no one's plaything, Shakespeare. I may fuck around, but I wouldn't fuck around on you."

Those damn lips opened again, but I'd had enough of her shit so I laid my finger over her mouth, trapping her in my hold. "You're brave, Shakespeare, speaking to me like this. I don't… *tolerate* it from anyone. People around here know not to approach me. They have the sense to leave things alone."

Her eyes narrowed and she asked, "Are you threatening me?"

My cock was iron-stiff, my tether about to snap, but this small English chick was taking me on like a gladiator.

"Not threatening, Shakespeare, *commending*. I'm finding you and that mouth of yours a real turn-on. But I'm more interested in teaching you how to keep it shut."

Her body was betraying her; I caught the swallow of her throat and the squirming of her thighs. She liked the way I was being with her, and the thought that this Miss Goody Two-Shoes might actually like me like this was only driving me more insane.

"Save that kind of talk for when you screw Shelly again," she snapped.

"I told you I didn't fuckin' touch her!" I tried to say calmly, but it came out as more of a low growl.

"That's not what *she's* been saying." Her voice was getting breathy; she was losing the hard-ass front she'd adopted.

Both calmer now, I tried to make her understand how I was feeling. "I couldn't care less what she says. I thought you were different, Mol. Why make a dig about Shelly or football after what I'd told you I was going through?"

Sucking in a sharp breath, she began rubbing at her temples. "Look, I'm just in a crappy mood. I shouldn't have come at you like that and I apologize for betraying your confidence. It was bad manners on my part. I was pissed off at you, have been pissed off at you for days. I don't know how to be around you. You... *confuse* me."

Talk about conflicted. I was so pissed at her for that earlier performance, but I craved her. I had no idea why, but I'd never wanted a chick like her before, every fiber of my being screaming at me to take her, possess her. As my mind swirled with these thoughts, my grip on her momentarily loosened, and she attempted to slip past me.

"Where the hell do you think you're going?" I snapped.

"I'm leaving. I'm done with this… done with us and whatever the hell just happened."

Done? She wasn't done. We were just getting started.

When she tried to wiggle past me again, I gave up my restraint and growled, "You're fucking driving me insane, Shakespeare!" And grabbing her tightly around the back of her neck, I smashed those fucking pouting lips against mine.

Shit it felt good.

I ate at her mouth, devoured everything she had like a starving man at a feast. My tongue relentlessly explored, and she welcomed everything I gave. She was perfect, *this* was perfect, and I was becoming more than a little obsessed.

I heard the thud of her books as she threw them to the floor and felt her hands grip the loose material of my shirt. I was taking her and she was taking me right back. She wanted this as much as me.

I was a man possessed. Gripping her tightly around her arms, I thrust her against the wall, my cock pressing against her pussy, grinding, and groaning against her mouth. She expelled a loud moan, and suddenly, reality came crashing back. I was mauling Mol in a friggin' hallway.

Dread built in my stomach. I was supposed to avoid doing shit like this, get through this year with ease. Molly was proving to be a huge fucking distraction. On the one hand, I wanted to taste more of her, but on the other, I wanted her to stay really fucking far away.

I expelled an angry groan. "Fuck, Mol, why can't I get you outta my head? You're all I fuckin' think about and I don't know how to deal."

She looked stunning: face flushed, lips swollen, eyes bright with need. "You do?" she whispered, and I could see she liked those words that were stupidly spilling out of my mouth.

"Every minute. Of. Every. Day."

Thrusting my hands behind my head, I watched as she began to gather her things, preparing to leave. We needed to clear up this shit between us, whatever the heck it was.

"I don't know what to do about you. It's rattling me and I don't like it. I've never gotten like this over some girl." I cursed myself for saying that. This was Molly I was talking about, not some groupie slut. "But I don't think you're just some girl. I've thought that from the minute I saw you all flustered in the hall on the first day of classes. *Christ,* I haven't been able to taste anything *but* you since we kissed at the damn initiation."

I waited for her response, but instead, she took off, running, shouting back, "I-I n-need to get to the library."

I almost punched the wall as her tight ass ran away from me as fast as possible. I started to follow but decided to just let her go and made myself stand still. I watched her bluster away, but when she shyly glanced back, I assured her, "This is far from over, Shakespeare… far from fuckin' over!" And then she was gone, leaving me pent up with anger, confused to all hell, and stuck with the biggest hard-on I'd ever had in my life.

Molly Shakespeare was going to kill me.

7

Fayetteville, Arkansas

"Shit, Bullet, that chick can't take her eyes off you!" Reece said excitedly.

Lifting my head from my beer, I checked out the attractive blonde, catching her inviting smile but shaking my head in dismissal.

Jimmy-Don put his hand to my head, pretending to check my temperature. "You feeling all right?"

With a smile, I said, "Yeah, just not interested."

"You *sure* you're all right?" This time he was serious. His mouth gaped open and he stared at me in shock. I just nodded my head slowly in response and tapped my beer to his, laughing.

"How can you not be interested in that? She's a freakin' goddess!" Reece complained, getting up off the couch, walking across the room and trying his luck with the blonde.

"Fifty bucks says she knocks him back," Austin said with a smile as he nudged my arm.

"Hell, she ain't going to touch him. She's a nine. He's… *not*. I'd just be giving my money away taking that bet."

Jimmy-Don shuffled forward on the couch, hand held out. "Hey now, give him a chance. He'll be first-string QB next year. Heck, Rome, he'll be you! I'll take the bet… from you *both*."

The three of us sat back and watched Reece as he strutted up to the blonde, cocky as all shit. She glanced over his shoulder at me, but whatever Reece said had her slumping where she stood and her "fuck me" smile falling off her face.

He worked the talk good, whispering in her ear, touching her cheek and her bare arm with his fingers.

Austin gaped at me, clearly thinking the same thought: the little fucker was in.

The blonde ran her hand down his chest, then, taking his hand, began leading him out of the room. Reece glanced back at us, the biggest damn grin on his face, and then disappeared upstairs.

"*Whew!* I knew it!" Jimmy-Don howled and, facing Austin and me, said, "Pay up, bitches!" with a shit-eating grin.

Shaking my head, I reached into my pocket, pulling out a fifty, Austin doing the same, and we each slapped it into Jimmy-Don's outstretched hand. "I never thought I'd see the day when he scored on his own."

"He's been watching you—on the field, off the field—like a damn hawk. He's gonna be friggin' dangerous next year," Jimmy-don said jokingly and moved off the couch to join some of our teammates heading to the backyard for food.

We were at a house party courtesy of one of the players' cousins from the Hogs. It was the usual—pussy on demand, liquor flowing—but what was *unusual* was that I didn't have an ounce of fucking interest in any of it, too busy wondering what Molly was up to back home, too busy wondering if she'd seen my shit show of a game.

I'd just about given up trying to rid her from my mind.

Austin got up to get more beer, and a few minutes later, the couch cushion dipped next to me, signaling his return. Tossing me another bottle, he asked, "You okay?"

I nodded, biting off the cap with my teeth before taking a long swig.

"You'll get your form back, you know. You're just having an off start to the season."

"Off start? Fuck. I can't *play* no more. Nothing I try goes right. I overshot my pass to you today by about five yards," I muttered sullenly.

"Shut up, Rome. You're the best damn player in the state, hell, the *country*. You're just going through too much and can't leave that baggage outta the game."

"How do you know what I'm going through?"

Austin shrugged. "Seen you like this before, when you took the football scholarship at UA. Your daddy almost beat you into hospital, and you, the sadistic fucker you are, just let him."

That memory was hard to forget. I'd gone home straight from my game to tell my daddy I'd accepted a scholarship with the Tide. Coach had been coming to some of my senior games in high school and when we took state, he offered me a place at UA on the spot. It was one of the happiest days of my life. That was until I told my daddy. I think he'd always assumed I'd eventually come around to his way of thinking, would eventually give up all the football crap and follow in his footsteps and go into the family business. But he didn't understand the passion I had for the game, never did, and that's where our present issues began.

The minute I told him I'd gotten a full scholarship, he'd snapped. I remember realizing at that moment that he was never going to let me lead my own life. And fuck knows why, but I stood before my irate father, the stocky man throwing punch after punch... and I took every one. Smiled at him through each blow. Then, bloodied and beaten, packed my shit and slept on Austin's floor for several weeks before having to go back home to wait out the rest of the year. I avoided my folks for months, stayed well out of their way, living mostly in the old cabin on their land, then left for summer training camp with the Tide and never looked back.

Snapping back to the present, metal music booming through the speakers, I said, "There was no point in fighting back. I'd learned that just made it worse."

"So what's up now? He still trying to stop you from entering the draft?"

"Yeah, nothing new there." I huffed out a tired laugh. "But now he wants me to marry Shelly. I refused, of course, haven't spoken to him since, but I know he won't give up." I glanced at the bottle in my hands and said, "Nothing ever changes for us, eh, brother?"

Shaking his head, Austin said, "Sometimes, Rome, I wonder how we both got such shit lives. You with all the money in the world but with the worst parents on Earth." I actually laughed at that. "Or me, a piece of trailer trash nothing, with two dickhead brothers and a saint of a mother who can barely walk anymore."

I tilted my bottle of beer in his direction and he clinked his against mine, no more words needing to be said.

The party carried on, most of the players scoring chicks for the night, and Jimmy-Don came back into the room finding Austin and me still on the same spot. "Guys! A group of us are heading out to a bar, you coming?"

"Your girl not going to be pissed at you if you do?" I asked with a teasing smile.

Jimmy-Don was crazy about his new girl, never shut up about the damn Texan blonde all the way to Arkansas. Apparently the chick was adventurous as all hell in bed, which I discovered after the seventh detailed explanation of their top ten sexual positions. What the fuck's *Othello's Back Grove* anyway?

"Hell no! Cass'd probably kick my ass if I *didn't* go out and drink, and she knows I wouldn't stray."

I believed him. He was a good guy.

"Gonna pass," I said. "I think I'll just head back to the hotel."

Bending down, Jimmy-Don pressed his hand against my head once again. "Seriously, Bullet, are you sick? For real? First, no women in weeks and now, refusing to go to a bar? You're *Invasion of the Body Snatchers* deal is scaring the shit outta me!"

Laughing, I stood, patting him on the back. "I'm just sick of it all, man. Need to get my head down and focus. Catch you later."

Austin came back with me, something clearly bugging him too, but we knew not to pry into each other's problems and instead talked football all the way back to our rooms.

Once in bed, I closed my eyes, and it was Molly's face I saw, her kiss I tasted, and sighing, I began counting down the hours until I could see her again.

I was so fucking screwed.

* * *

As soon as the plane hit the tarmac, the texts started. My daddy writing that he wanted to see me, *needed* to see me, warning me that I'd *better fucking see him!*

Then at six thirty in the damn morning, he called. Deciding to just answer and get his lecture over with, I greeted with a reluctant, "Daddy."

"I'm almost at the grounds of your school. I suggest you meet me immediately. Don't make me come looking."

My fists clenched and I almost crunched the bastard cell in my hands.

"I'll meet you at the quad."

Picking up my keys, I quickly left my room, almost sprinting to the quad, still wearing the same clothes I'd just traveled in. The place was deserted, too early for students to be up, but the sun was already burning hot, the campus eerily still.

Rounding the corner, it didn't take long to spot my father's treasured Bentley—silver, ostentatious—and I stopped on the sidewalk, right at the hood of the car.

My daddy opened his door, his suit slightly disheveled and his brown eyes tired. For a moment I faltered, thinking he was here to deliver some bad news, until I saw him grinding his teeth and knew he was here about me.

"Rome," he greeted, folding his arms across his chest.

I hated that he was this calm and collected, his voice quiet and low. I could never predict his mood when he was like this, never knew whether to brace for a hit or if I was about to be blackmailed into doing some shit I didn't want to.

"Daddy," I said cautiously.

"You've been ignoring my calls, texts, emails."

"I needed a break. Football has been intense, and school is only getting crazier the closer I get to graduation. And I know you still want me to marry Shelly and didn't want to argue about it anymore." His eyes ignited some at that.

"Damn right I want this marriage." He took a step closer, but at six foot three, I towered above him. "Look, I need you to marry her. I need to keep the business between the two families."

My father was acting strange. I could sense the desperation in his voice, see it in his stance, the way he was constantly running his hand through his hair. My suspicions were through the roof. Something other than the marriage was clearly bothering him, but hell if I could guess what. My daddy would never tell me if I asked. No way would he ever show weakness in front of me, but I had to try.

"Tell me why are you pushing this so much," I demanded, seeing the anger in his tight features at my line of questioning. That was one of many things that were forbidden—questioning my father's instructions. Curling his lip with annoyance, he prodded a finger to my chest.

"Do what you're told. Carry out the duty we kept you for!" And there it was. The not-so-subtle reminder that I wasn't ever wanted.

I held my ground. "You know what, old man, screw your arranged marriage. Nothing has changed. Nothing *will* change. Give it up already."

His rage took hold and the man I'd grown up with showed his ugly head, fake politeness forgotten as he gripped my shirt in his fists. "You insolent shit! Why must you defy me at every turn!" His eyes were skittish and that only confirmed my suspicions. Something bigger had to be behind this. He hadn't been this physical in years.

I didn't fight him, but bit back, "Because I don't want this life for myself. I don't want to be you!"

Leaning up to my ear, he said in a low voice, "You were never good enough for this family!" and on instinct, he drew back a hand but stopped, clearly trying to restrain himself from his old form of punishment. I could fight back now that I was bigger, stronger, and the old bastard knew it. I was seventeen the last time I'd let him hit me, but he never touched me in public. There was no way he would risk his perfect reputation. But here he was, lashing out in broad daylight, his composed persona unraveling.

"Do it!" I growled, tipping my chin in offering.

"Don't tempt me, boy!" He threatened, and I only smiled in response. I'd learned that if we got a good hit out of the way, it would buy me a few weeks of quiet. I needed a few weeks of quiet.

Desperately needed it.

I pushed at his chest and shouted, "*Do it!* Hit me! I know that's what you want!" His lips tightened as he decided what to do, so I smiled again, really goading him, and that was the moment he snapped. He pulled back his fist and in seconds it collided with my face.

He immediately dropped his hand and, walking backward, assured, "I won't stop until you are walking down that fucking aisle. It is imperative that you marry Shelly Blair! *Imperative!*" And with that he jumped back in his Bentley and drove off.

8

The blood from my lip dripped down my chin, but I let it. My cheek throbbed and my jaw ached, but it reminded me why I couldn't marry Shelly, couldn't live this life forever, eventually turning to liquor to cope like my momma and being trapped in the suffocating world of society dinners and duties.

I headed straight for the nearest tree and hit the bark until my hands grew numb, my muscles ached, and blood spilled from my knuckles. The heaviness of my breaths exhausted my body and I slumped to the floor, staring unseeingly at the grass before me.

Fuck! I couldn't keep living in this constant hell, this darkness.

How the hell had everything all gone to shit so quickly? I could feel the weight of it all pressing down on me—my folks, football, school—and I could barely breathe or

100

think. I wanted to curl into a ball right here on the ground, not really caring who would find the great *Bullet Prince* reduced to a bleeding, hurting mess.

I heard the sound of a dry twig snapping next to me, and when I lifted my head, Molly stood before me, hands shaking, tears in her eyes, whispering, "Romeo, God…"

She looked like a friggin' angel.

Dropping to her knees beside me, her golden-brown eyes softened in sympathy. She set to cleaning up my cuts, but none of it really registered; my mind was lost in a thick fog.

"Does this hurt?" she stopped to ask, but I could only manage to shake my head.

She edged closer still, her small body snug between my legs, and she pressed a pink scrap of material to my lip. Still, I could only stare.

"Swill your mouth out, Rome. That blood can't taste too good." She handed me the bottle, and I did as she said, spitting the water onto the ground, the dried soil laced with red.

Then she surprised me, gently taking my hand and sitting beside me. As I stared at her small fingers wrapped around mine, I realized this girl was turning into everything I needed but never dreamed of being able to get. On the surface, she was my exact opposite, but deep down, she was getting me like no one ever had before.

Feeling her hands squeeze mine in support, I snapped out of my daze and croaked, "Hey, Mol."

"Hey, you."

"How much did you see?" I asked, dreading the answer.

Moving in closer, her arm brushing mine, and tucking her head into my neck, she replied, "Enough."

Someone had finally witnessed my daddy in action, and, feeling like I was eight again, I dropped my head against the tree, feeling humiliated that she'd seen me like that, still stupidly a victim to my father.

"Who was the man in the Bentley?"

"My daddy," I admitted after a few seconds of silence.

"Your *father*?" That shocked her, and those eyes tensed with anger, her body curving toward me protectively. That was definitely a first. I couldn't speak at the gesture, a moment of happiness seizing my voice. I'd never had anyone comfort me before, never had anyone *care* enough to comfort me before. Being around Molly made me happy... *Fuck*... She actually made me *happy*.

I kept her hand tight in mine, not wanting to let this feeling go.

"You okay?" she asked again.

"No," I confided, the tears threatening to fall.

"You want to talk about it?" I absolutely did not, so shook my head.

"Does he hit you a lot?"

I decided to just go with it. She'd seen more than anyone else ever had; no use in pretending otherwise. "Don't get a chance much anymore. He was pissed with something I'd done. He called me to meet him and... Well, you saw the rest."

Shifting in front of me, she asked, "What was so bad that he'd strike you like that?"

I wanted to reply with the truth—because I was a blight on their perfect lives, a reminder of something they'd rather forget—but I was never going go there, never ever going to reveal that, so I simply said, "Money, disappointment, not being the dutiful son. The usual. He's never gone that far in public before, though. I've never seen him so pissed."

"But you're his son! How dare he treat you like that? What the hell have you done to deserve to be punched?"

I *wasn't* going to go there.

Sitting back in frustration, but accepting that she wasn't getting an answer, Molly changed the subject, asking about the Arkansas game. I confessed that I hadn't been playing well.

"I've never had such a bad start to a season in my entire life. My senior year, the one in which I'll enter the draft, and it's all going to hell in a hand basket."

"Why is it going so bad?" Her eyebrows were pulled down, her thick frames slipping a fraction down her nose.

Pushing them back up into position, I revealed, "Because I can't complete even one of my passes. I'm letting the team and fans down. My parents won't back the fuck off over Shelly—you just witnessed my daddy's insistence on that issue. She's being a bigger leech than normal and I'm constantly fighting her off. My head is all over the place, I can't sleep or get focused, and thinking about a certain English girl keeps me up every night. Every fucking night. She's plaguing my dreams."

Needing to feel her touch, I laid her hand against my cheek, the contact calming me right down.

"Yeah, I know what that's like." Her answer was breathy, *telling*.

It was time I told her some home truths. "I thought about our last meeting nonstop while I was away."

"Yeah. Me too. It's been... different to have my head filled with a certain Bama hottie and not Dante, Descartes, or Kant." I wanted to laugh at her cute as hell accent and thank the Lord that she'd been thinking about me too.

"You think I'm a hottie?" I asked jokingly, nudging her arm.

"You're all right." Her nose crinkled as she smiled and that blush crept up her cheeks. I'd gone from hating the world to feeling on top of it.

"Where were you going at this time of morning when you saw this hottie getting a beatdown?" I needed to move from this tree, and I sure as fuck wasn't going to class. I wanted to be wherever she was, and I pretty much always did what I wanted.

"Rome—" She went to say something, but I cut her off.

"Answer the damn question, Shakespeare."

"The library. I have notes I need to write up for Professor Ross. She has an office there where I can work undisturbed. I saw... what happened with you and your daddy and thought you needed me more than the exciting world of academia does right now."

Standing, dragging her with me, I announced, "Let's go."

"Where to?" She frowned in confusion.

"The library. I'm going to help you. We can't let the world of academia down now, can we?" I lifted her bag off the floor and placed it on her shoulder.

"Romeo… are you sure you don't want to go home or do something else? We could talk more if you'd like. Whatever you need."

Jesus, talking about my home life was so *not* what I wanted. Hell, what I really wanted was to take Molly back to my room and not bother surfacing until I'd had my fill, but I wasn't sure that suggestion would go down well.

Pulling on her hand, I said, "No. We're going to go to the library and I'm going to help you with your paper."

"You're going to help *me* with philosophy?" I should have been insulted by her disbelief, but that air of arrogance she always had when it came to her studies just made me want to prove her wrong.

Turning her around and wrapping my arms around her shoulders, I whispered, "Hey, just because I'm a jock don't mean I'm stupid. For your information, I'm acing that class. I may be able to show you a thing or two."

I let her go and quoted, "For example, *Immanuel Kant was a real piss-ant who was very rarely stable.*"

Letting out an excited giggle, she sang, "*Heidegger, Heidegger was a boozy beggar who could think you under the table.*"

"*Aristotle, Aristotle was a bugger for the bottle, and Hobbes was fond of his dram.*" I gestured for her to finish.

"*And Rene Descartes was a drunken fart. I drink, therefore I am.*"

She was British after all. Wasn't watching Monty Python like a rite of passage or some shit? Her huge grin told me I'd just racked me up some points in her book.

"So you're a *Monty Python* fan?" she asked excitedly.

"Well, you can't study philosophy and not be familiar with 'Bruces' Philosophers Song.'" Truth was, one of my first philosophy professors in sophomore year used to play it all the damn time. After that, I watched every film they'd made.

"I agree, but I never pegged *you* for a British comedy nut."

"It's Python," I said simply. I held out my hand. "So let's go. I surprised you once with my philosophy knowledge. I'm pretty sure I can do it again."

"Whatever, you're twenty-one. I'm still only twenty and I'm already on my master's. I doubt there's anything you can show me, superstar. It's my area of expertise."

There she went with that mouth again. Grabbing her hand, I pulled her to my chest, gripping her tight, and leaned in to whisper, "Maybe not in philosophy, but I can sure as hell show you other things, Mol—in *my* area of expertise."

"And what's that?" she asked, and I smiled, feeling her heart beating like crazy in her chest.

I ran my lips down the skin of her neck, kissing her pulse and teasing, "Much more... *pleasurable* things than work."

I caught her pause in breath, and, satisfied that I'd rattled her nerves, dragged her with me. "Come on, megabrain, let's go research and get your dirty mind outta the gutter."

That'd teach her to try me.

We worked in the library for hours. Not once did she push me to talk about my father, or about anything else; her mind was completely focused on her task. She kind of reminded me of *Rain Man* when she worked, totally immersed in her own little world.

"Come on, Shakespeare, I'll walk you home," I finally said when Molly yawned for the fifth time in the space of ten minutes and my ass had begun to ache from sitting in one spot too long.

"Yeah, okay." She agreed tiredly, and we set off out of the library, only a few students still pulling all-nighters on the near-empty floors.

The campus was pretty quiet as we walked down the main path, and happy that no one was around, I reached down, taking Molly's hand in mine. At first her fingers stiffened at the action and she flashed a questioning look at me, but seeing my refusal to let go, she just let it be. It felt right having her close, and I liked that if anyone spotted us, it looked like she was mine. That sentiment sat better with me than it should have. I was Rome Prince. I didn't do commitment with chicks, but Molly being on my arm just felt really fucking perfect.

Halfway home, Molly asked, "Rome?"

"Yeah?"

"Did you have fun when you were away in Arkansas?"

That question caught me off guard, and I glanced down at her head hanging low, wondering where the hell this conversation was heading.

"Not really. Truth be told, I couldn't wait to get back." I pulled her to face me, trying to get a read on her mood. "What you getting at?"

Kicking her toes into the grass beside us, she glanced up at me and said shyly, "Cass brought up some pictures of the after-game party you attended, on Facebook."

Frowning, I asked, "Yeah, so?"

"Well, I saw what some of the guys were doing. You know, shots… Beer… *Women*… I didn't see any of you, but…" She trailed off.

Placing a finger beneath her chin, I forced her to meet my eyes again. "You want to know if I fucked anyone?"

Her eyes narrowed. "Well, I wouldn't have put it quite so crassly, but… yeah, I suppose I do. I know it's none of my business, so feel free to tell me to bugger off if I've gone too far." Her eyes fell to the ground again.

"Look at me," I instructed, and she did so guardedly. "Plenty of groupies made a pass at me. They always do. I don't really have to try too hard, Mol."

"Oh." Her head bowed, and her shoulders slumped in disappointment. It made me beyond fucking happy that the thought of my being with someone else would bother her so much. "But I told them all to fuck off and went home alone," I finished, and her head shot up.

"You did?" she said with a happily surprised tone.

"Yeah." I leaned down and smirked. "None of them could argue about utilitarianism for shit!"

She burst out laughing and retook my hand. I finished walking her back home, her hand this time slightly less tense in mine.

It was the first night in a long time I slept right through with no nightmares... nothing on my mind but a certain damn cute brunette.

9

The next day, after early morning training, I showered and threw on my jeans and shirt in record time. Austin and Jimmy-Don glanced at each other from the other side of the locker room, shaking their heads in confusion at my haste.

"Going somewhere?" asked Austin.

Raking my fingers through my wet hair, I replied evasively, "Yeah, catch you later." With that, I ran to the library and straight up to Professor Ross's office, trying the handle.

Locked.

Shit.

I checked the time; Molly would be here soon. There was only one thing for it. I'd have to see Ms. Rose. A shudder ran down my spine, knowing that the minute she spotted me, she'd be too excited and all over me like white on rice.

Heading to the desk, I spotted long gray hair, and, leaning in on the counter, lilted, "Hey, Ms. Rose, how's it going? Looking good. Purple's your color."

She turned slowly on hearing my voice and beamed. "Rome Prince! How nice to see you, darlin'!" She approached the desk, her yellowing teeth showing as she pulled back her thin lips in a wide smile, moving to stand right before me. Shit, how she still worked at her age was a mystery to me. She had to be nearing a hundred.

"What brings you here this early?"

Giving her my best seductive smile, I said, "I need a favor."

She tilted her head, amused. "Now, you know I can't be giving you any special treatment. Gotta treat all the students here the same."

"Oh, I know that Ms. Rose, but I thought, well, because we're such good friends, you'd make an exception. Just this once?"

Patting my hand with her bony fingers, she gushed, "Rome Prince, such a bad boy! And Lord knows I've never been able to resist a bad boy, especially one as handsome as you! What do you need, honey?"

It always worked. "Can you open Professor Ross's private office for me? I'm working in there today and forgot the key."

Winking, she lifted the counter and shuffled painfully to the elevator. "Let's go before I get into trouble for breaking the rules."

Ms. Rose opened the office, switching on the light, and left me to it, but not before firmly patting me on my ass as she passed.

I gaped at her retreating form in shock. *Seriously?*

Throwing my bag to the table, chuckling at her audacity, I sat down and got comfortable, waiting for a certain Miss Shakespeare to arrive.

Thirty minutes later and the door creaked opened, Molly jumping in surprise at my lazy stance, lying back in my seat.

"It's about time, Shakespeare. I've already written a goddamned thesis waiting on you."

"What are you doing here?" she asked, the biggest most fucking blinding smile on her face.

Lifting off the seat, I moved to stand before her, saying, "I'm here to assist the assistant. Put me to work. I'm eager to please." I waggled my eyebrows for extra effect.

Setting down her book, she looked at me speculatively. "You want to tell me how you got in here, in a locked room?"

"I have a secret admirer in the librarian. She opened it for me after a little sweet talk." And a feel of my ass, but I didn't feel entirely comfortable sharing that piece of information.

"Ms. Rose? She's like ninety!" Mol said, choking on a laugh.

"Cougar on the prowl, more like," I relayed with a grimace and wide eyes.

Molly lost her humor and studied me. "Mm-hmm. And why, Romeo, do you want to help me write notes again?"

My stomach dropped. I'd never even contemplated that she might not have wanted me interrupting her studies again. Shit! My arms crossed and I grumbled, "You don't want me here? I'll go if I'm getting in your way. I don't want to be where I'm not wanted."

Her features softened and she placed her warm hands on my rough cheeks, her thumb dusting over my bruised cheek and lip. "Hey, I didn't say that. I'm just taken aback by the fact that *you* want to be here with *me*. It's… nice to be with you, in any capacity."

Relief coursed through my tense muscles and I moved my head to press a kiss to her palm. "I like being around you too, Mol. I feel good when I am. Plus, I owe you for what you did for me yesterday."

"You don't owe me anything," she whispered shaking her head profusely.

Feeling completely calm and even happy, I stroked down from her cheek to her shoulder. "I'm staying with you."

"What about your classes?"

Fuck my classes. They had no pull if she wasn't there. "I'm staying with you. I'm kind of becoming addicted."

"Addicted?" she asked dubiously.

Inching closer, ghosting my hand along her hip, I confided, "That's right. To you and how you make me feel."

"Right, well... err... let's get you to work, then," she said, stumbling both in footing and words.

She was so fucking cute.

Hours passed and we hadn't taken a break—I was starving. I stood, glancing down at Molly furiously scribbling away on her notepad, her hair coming loose from her bun, mumbling to herself about Paley and his watch. She wasn't stopping anytime soon.

Slipping out of the office, I headed to the student coffee shop, stocking up on cream cheese bagels and cappuccinos. After paying for the snacks, I caught that basketball fucker Michaels glaring at me from his table across the room. He was clearly back together with the chick who banged me behind his back. Classy gal. What a fucking pussy he was for taking her skanky ass back.

I walked past, trying to ignore him, but he had other plans. "You lost?"

I stopped and turned to face him. "What?" I asked tiredly.

"I said are you lost?" he said slowly, like I was dumb, laughing to his girlfriend, who kept her head firmly down. Slapping the table, he bit out, "Shit, no wonder you're spending time in the library. You're still trying to figure out the end of the alphabet, aren't you?"

Yeah, I fucked his girl. I get it, but I didn't even know who she was until he started on me after practice two days later. I may not be big on morals, but I wouldn't have knowingly touched someone else's girl. Give me some fucking credit. It was a party, I was drunk off my ass, and *she'd* led me to bed. It'd been that brief, but Michaels still couldn't let it go.

People in the cafe stopped their chatting, listening in.

"Michaels, I'll warn you once. Shut the fuck up. I'm in no mood for your shit today," I warned. I just wanted to get back to Molly. Fighting with this asswipe was the last thing on my mind.

I watched as a slow smile spread across his face. Apparently he wasn't feeling the same. "You're right. I'll let you get back to the retard section on the first floor."

If the food in my hands hadn't been for Molly upstairs, working herself toward the first stages of malnutrition, I'd have thrown the whole lot at his fucking head and kicked out his front teeth. But I simply smiled and retorted, "Will do, Michaels, and I'll let you get back to your copy of *The Kama Sutra*." I crossed the fingers on my right hand and held them up, smiling sarcastically. "Not long now before you can make your girl come without a dildo and she has to stop shopping around campus for substitutes." With that, I left Michaels raging on his seat and ordering his girl to follow him home, the listening students snickering at our show.

Five minutes later and back upstairs, I sighed as I saw Molly was still writing furiously and looking beyond exhausted, a huge stack of notes piled up on her right. My entrance finally broke her from her philosophy zone and she looked up at me in shock.

"We need a break," I told her sternly.

"How long have we been in here?" she asked with a yawn, stretching her cramped muscles and rubbing at her eyes under her black frames.

"About six hours," I answered in a reprimanding tone as I handed her a bagel.

"Oh. Crap."

"Yep, *crap,*" I answered with a laugh, her exaggerated accent amusing me to no end. I'd never known a Brit before Molly, and sometimes the things she came out with and the way she pronounced shit was fucking hilarious.

I couldn't take my eyes off her as she sat on her seat, and more importantly, I couldn't take my eyes off Molly's tongue as it ran along both lips as she stared at her food. I tightened my hand on my coffee death grip, imagining that mouth licking around the tip of my cock. And when she took a sip of her cappuccino, moaning out loud in satisfaction, the bastard lid popped off, the hot liquid scalding on my chest.

"Shit!" I shouted, launching to my feet, pulling the boiling, wet material off my gray shirt.

"You okay?" Molly asked, one eyebrow raised.

"Just… don't make those kind of noises around me, Mol," I instructed tightly, moving to adjust my now rock-hard cock in my jeans. Molly's breathing grew labored at my words and her breasts pushed against her dress. I wanted her so damn much, but she wasn't like the other girls. She wasn't just a fuck, didn't give her pussy to anyone wearing a Tide jersey. And more shockingly, I was quickly realizing that *I* wanted her for more than just one night.

Yeah. Imagine that. My feelings for her were spiraling out of control, confusing the absolute crap out of me.

Taking a seat, we both stared at each other in silence, the tension pulsing once more, until I cracked my knuckles and stretched out my arms, saying, "You must be nearly done now. I've never seen anyone work so hard at anything. I have no doubts you'll make one hell of a professor."

Losing the flush to her heated cheeks, she shrugged. "I love studying. It keeps me occupied."

"From what?"

"From thinking about other things."

"Like?" The desolation that appeared on her face at that question cut me to the core.

"Bad things… upsetting things… things from my past."

I felt that pain, *knew* that pain, so I reached out and took her hand that was resting on the table in support, throwing all caution to the wind and confessing, "So studying does for you what you do for me?"

Her hand shook slightly in mine, and she looked anywhere but at me. I pulled on her hand, jerking her closer. "It's true. You're doing something to me, Mol."

"I… What? You…?" she mumbled, moodily pulling back her hand when I laughed and then launched a piece of her bagel, I assumed, at my head, but instead it hit my chest. She may be a genius, but she had shit aim.

My heart nearly exploded with happiness as I shoved it in my mouth and she couldn't contain her laughter. It seemed we were good at doing that for each other, lightening our moods after getting lost in the memory of our dark times.

"So how are you feeling today?" she asked, genuine concern in her tone. Someone was *genuinely* concerned for me. It felt… nice.

"Better," I replied, smiling. "This pretty gal helped me get through some personal shit."

Her head bowed and she looked up playfully through her long black lashes, pretending to search under the table and around the room. "What gal? What does she look like?"

Scrunching up my face in mock concentration, I answered, "Brunette, hot accent, fucking sexy as hell librarian-with-glasses thing going on."

Molly shook her head in dismissal. "*Right.* But seriously, are you *okay?*"

Time to cut the shit. She deserved to know, and more importantly, I finally wanted to open up to someone, even if it was just a small glimpse at who I was. "Getting there. One day at a time," I confided quietly.

Nodding proudly, Molly went back to her notes, understanding I couldn't be pushed too far. I loved that about her. I couldn't take my eyes off her as she sipped on her coffee. She was pretty—there was no question about that—but she didn't try hard to make herself more beautiful, didn't coat herself in a ton of makeup or tight clothing. But sitting before me right now, she looked like a supermodel, the most stunning girl I ever saw. Her easy acceptance of my damn moody ways made her the most beautiful girl in the world to me.

At that moment, my decision was made. I wanted her, was consumed by need for her, and decided to screw the consequences.

I was making my move.

She placed the cup back on the desk; a small drop of foam rested on her lip. Rising from my seat, I stalked around the table, seeing her eyes widen with nerves as I approached. I leaned down, trapping her on the chair, my attention firmly fixed on my target.

"Romeo, what—" she whispered, but I dived in, flicking out my tongue and licking the foam off her soft lip.

"You had foam on your lip," I said as casually as I could manage, pulling back from her.

"Oh, I—" Raw disappointment shadowed her golden eyes. It was all the convincing I needed. Gripping her cheeks in both of my hands, I moved in, crashing our lips together and grasping her thick hair in my fists, on the verge of losing control as she groaned with pure need against my busy mouth.

I had to stop before things went too far. As much as I wanted to sink deep into Molly, I wasn't going to do it in the library for fuck's sake. I wanted more when it came to her, so I reluctantly pulled back.

"And then?" she asked breathlessly as she nuzzled against my hand.

Touching my forehead against hers, I confessed, "Well, then, I just wanted to kiss you." Her lips twitched and a shy smile lit up her face.

Spurred on by her affections, I dropped to my knees, running my hands up her bare thighs, and asked, "Come to my game this weekend."

"I have to study."

My heart plummeted to my stomach. "It's just for a few hours, Mol."

She began playing with her hands and shaking her head. "I know, but I get paid to assist the professor and I pride myself on getting everything done on time. I need my paycheck to survive, Rome. Living in the sorority house is expensive. I'll be here on Saturday when the game is on."

Her dismissive response took me aback, and I panicked that I'd got it all wrong. Why wouldn't she come to my game? She could study before or after. It suddenly occurred to me that maybe she wasn't feeling what I was feeling, and that thought just about broke me.

Sighing deep, I said, "Okay, I don't fucking like it, but I understand."

Gentle hands held my face, golden eyes imploring me to understand. "Please don't be disappointed. Sports are just not my thing. I have absolutely no clue about American football, or quarterbacks, remember?" She finished with placating smile.

Briefly closing my eyes, I replied, "I hear you, Mol. No one's ever there supporting me anyhow. Nothing new." It wasn't. Ally and on occasion her folks were the only ones who'd ever bothered their asses to show support.

"Romeo—" she whispered, her voice sounding conflicted.

I needed out, disappointment leaving me no other choice but to bail, so I stood, staring at the door, blurting, "I have a practice I gotta get to."

I didn't; I had absolutely nowhere I had to be, but I kind of felt humiliated at her shoot down.

Molly reached out and laced her fingers through mine, making me pause. I stared down at our hands, then to the panic on her face.

Jesus. I couldn't get a damn read on what she the hell wanted!

"I'll be here a few more hours yet. I'll catch you later though, yeah?" she offered politely, only serving to confuse me more.

Trying to find some kind of answer, I bent down, meeting her eyes, catching the blatant interest in their depths.

There it was, that look, the one that told me she wanted me all right; she just needed a gentle push in my general direction.

I left the room, and once out in the corridor, I dug in my bag for pen and paper and scribbled a quick note:

Please come to the game.
I want you there.
Your Romeo X

I read the note back to myself and almost crumpled it up. Damn, that was cheesy. *Your Romeo?* What the hell was I thinking?

Mol'd seemed quite pleased about our Shakespearean connection the other night, but was this a step too far? Would it persuade her to come to the game, or just make her think I was a fucking tool?

Pinching the bridge of my nose, I laughed at the ridiculous state of myself. *Christ*, I'd hit an all-time low— Rome Prince pining after a chick who didn't immediately fall at my feet. But hell, for reasons I couldn't fully explain, I wanted her in the packed stands, watching me play. I wanted to show her my worth, that I was *good* at something. I wanted—no, *needed*—her to *believe* in me.

Checking no one was around, I slipped the note under the door, quickly walking away and just hoping more than ever that she would be the one person in my life to not let me down.

10

My breathing echoed in my ears, whooshing loudly, the roar of the hundred-thousand-strong cheering crowd drowned out by the hard slam of my heart as I waited for the whistle to blow.

The referee moved into position for the third down, the whistle's sound only increasing my anticipation and breathing. "Red eighty-three, red eighty-*three,*" in hard count. The defense didn't buy it; no one encroached. I called the play again, this time adding, *"Down, set, hut hut."* In near silence, the snap fired out of the shotgun.

Catching the ball, I stepped back, one, two, searching for Carillo among the sea of defenders. There he was, with separation from single-man coverage. I raised my arm, drew back my hand, then released, watching the pigskin's lazy spiral in the air... miss Austin by two yards... again.

FUCK!!!

I didn't miss the growing groundswell of disappointment as it washed around the stadium. I loped off the gridiron, unable to take my clenched fist off my helmet as I screamed a string of expletives into the air, slamming my free hand on the cursed field.

Catching my QB coach glaring at me from the sidelines, I braced for his tirade. "Bullet, get your head in the game! Focus on Carillo, check down to Porter, but complete the damn pass!" He finished off his inspirational speech by throwing the game photos into my hand. "Study them! Now!"

Gripping the images, I reviewed my check down receiver options, rolling my shoulders, trying to get my head into the game, but all I could feel was crushing pressure.

With each flip of a photo, my father's words echoed in my head. *Football will never happen, boy! Do your duty!* My mother's taunts followed. *You'll mess up football anyway, just like you mess up everything else! You were born to be a failure!*

I was. I was fucking everything up and my team didn't deserve to have me screw the season up for them anymore.

Reece moved beside me, throwing his arm around my shoulders. "You got this, Bullet. Focus!" I knew the kid was trying to be supportive, but if one more person told me to focus, I was going to ram my fist through their head.

Repeatedly.

Ignoring him, my legs shaking with adrenaline, I tried to visualize the next down—just as Coach had taught me. I imagined it going perfectly, imagined the Tide scoring a touchdown, the crowd roaring in happiness.

Before I knew it, I was back on the field. *You got this, Rome. You got this,* I told myself, trying like hell to psyche myself up. If ever sports psychology was to work for me, for my team and for my school, well, its time had come.

And then it was on. Snap. Catch. Pop.

The ball sailed toward Carillo, not even coming close to his outstretched hands, and instead spiraled straight into the crowd. Whatever amount of heart I had left in this game immediately sank into my stomach as the fans began to fall to their seats in exasperation at my shit execution of pass plays.

I could throw better in pee-wee football.

Turning away from my equally frustrated teammates, I caught a glance of the Jumbotron, expecting to see my fucking horrendous replay, but instead saw a fight break out in the lower student section of the stands, right near where Ally was sitting, and I witnessed some chick get pummeled to the floor by the douchebags. A brunette chick, who, when the crowd cleared, sat up, stunned, holding her nose.

Recognition hit me like a damn truck.

Shit. *Shakespeare!*

Acting on pure instinct, I unsnapped my chinstrap, tore off my helmet, and charged off, completely ignoring the entire on-field coaching staff screaming at my back and my teammates staring at each other in absolute disbelief.

Jumping the barrier into the stands, I pushed my way through the student body, shrugging off grabs at my jersey and ignoring the chicks trying to rub up against me.

A path appeared before me and at its end, Molly peered around, looking so fucking hot in a short white dress and brown cowboy boots that showcased her tanned legs to perfection. But that didn't distract me from the panic seeping into my veins at the thought of her being hurt... because of my shit pass.

"Shit, Shakespeare! I'm so sorry. Are you okay?" Dropping my helmet to the floor with a crash, I powered through the crowd to Molly's flushed-with-embarrassment face and without thinking, grabbed her flaming cheeks in my hands—my sanity, once again, gone without a trace.

Large golden eyes darted everywhere, clearly expressing her lack of comfort at being put on display, but fuck that; I needed to know she was okay. And more than that, it quickly hit home that she'd shown up. *Shit.* She'd come here for me... because of that note... She'd actually done as I'd asked...She'd actually come for *me.*

"Rome, I'm okay. I was saved by my glasses. They laid their lives on the line to save my nose." She held the broken frames in her hands, keeping them steady against her eyes, and I couldn't help but laugh. The stadium fell away as she went on to complain about the drunken guys who hit her square in the face, but all I could think about as she rambled on was that she was *here.*

Rubbing my thumb on her grazed cheek, I shook my head and laughed. "It had to be you. Out of everyone in this entire fucking stadium, it had to be you who was involved." Tilting my head, I continued. "I'm no longer surprised; you're always there. I think someone's trying to tell me something."

A blush flooded her cheeks, the heat of the action warming my hands. "I was going for a Coke," she answered and I couldn't help but laugh at her gripping the two bits of broken plastic to her eyes, just so she could keep looking at my face.

"During my play?" I teased with mock annoyance.

Biting her tongue and scrunching that damn nose, she confessed, "Err, well, quite honestly, I didn't know what the hell was going on, and I was thirsty."

The noise in the stadium grew to a deafening volume, but I could still hear Coach screaming my name from the sideline, anger boiling up at the sight of his QB running from the field mid-drive, forcing him to call a precious timeout. I knew I was going to get my ass kicked for running off the field, but all I could think about was Molly.

Pulling her to me, commanding her instant attention, I said simply, "You came."

Her whole body seemed to melt in my arms and she sighed, "I came," with the most stunning smile, stealing my friggin' breath.

Desperation surged through my brain and I blurted, "Why did you change your mind?" I needed to know. She'd been so damn reluctant.

Shrugging playfully, she said softly, "You got through to me." And with that, something within me snapped. Any worries blocking my mind cleared, and all thoughts of my parents' taunts that'd been affecting my game disappeared into vapor.

A short, fat little shit of a medic tried to pull Molly out of my arms. Throwing him a threatening scowl, I asked Molly one more time if she was okay. After assuring me that she was, she went to walk away, but that wasn't going to happen. I needed to taste her. Without thinking anything through, I crushed her lips against mine, pulling her so close that she wouldn't be able to break away. It was short, it was sweet, and it made me feel like I was a fucking king.

Backing away, I watched Molly's mouth gape at this blatant show of public affection, and smiling, sprinted back to the field, not giving a shit that Coach was verbally ripping me a new one, *or* that Austin and Jimmy-Don were shaking their heads at my fucking stupidity. Molly had shown up, and I instantly knew I wasn't going to fuck up this game. I knew I wasn't going lose. She would see that I was worthy.

Summoning the offense into the huddle, I called, "Eighty-three on red."

Austin shook his head. "Try another, Bullet."

Yeah, I knew he didn't trust that pass play after four screw-ups, but something within me had changed.

Snapping my eyes to his, I bit back, "Eighty-three on red! And don't fucking question me!"

Glaring back and wanting to argue, but knowing you never questioned the QB, Austin just sighed and put his hand in the center as I screamed, "One, two, three, *break*!"

And we all moved into position, every fiber of my being bursting to life.

I had found my flow state. I was in the zone.

Time seemed to slow as Jeremiah Simms, the center, snapped the ball to me, and in a state of complete mental calmness, I spotted Austin, the white number 83 on his crimson jersey. It shone like a beacon.

I stepped into the throw as he sprinted downfield. Intense gratification swept through as the ball spiraled perfectly into his hands on his post route into the end zone.

The stadium erupted in thunderous celebration. A forty-yard touchdown pass, and it was the best tight spiral I'd thrown all season, hell, maybe all of college.

My teammates came barreling over, jumping on my back, and I basked in their celebration. Jimmy-Don lifted me in his arms, only to set me down and shout, "From now on, you better lay one on Molly before every damn game!"

Eyebrows drawn, I asked, "What the fuck are you talking about?"

Slapping my cheek lightly, he answered with an excited laugh, "You kissing Molly, man! Not to put it bluntly, but, hell, Bullet, you've been playing like shit for weeks, but one kiss from her and you throw like a damn demon!"

Staring at the screaming fans around the stadium, a disbelieving huff came out of my throat. "Shit, you're right."

Gripping my collar, Jimmy-Don pulled me close and declared, "Every game, ya hear?"

A slow smile tugged on my lips. Fuck yeah. Like I even needed an excuse to taste those lips again or press those damn curves up close against me. Bama fans could be beyond superstitious, and I'd gladly give in to their whims.

Gladly.

Fifteen minutes later and we'd won. I'd played as though I was possessed. I questioned if I was—hell, I was absolutely *obsessed* with Molly and couldn't get enough of how it felt being around her. Like my problems didn't exist… Like she got me… *Me, Rome*, not Bullet, not the famed QB… but *me*.

At the end of the game, Coach, the cheerleaders, and the band flooded the pitch, as reporters in their masses headed straight to my direction, asking the same damn questions as always, and I gave the same answers, avoiding any mention of Molly or any explanation of that kiss.

After fighting off Shelly and squashing her mission to get us looking like a couple on camera, I made my way straight to Ally's seats, needing to see Molly again.

Ally was standing next to Jimmy-Don and his new woman, who were all over each other. She looked relieved to see me and threw her arms around me in a hug.

"Well done, darlin'!" she squealed in excitement. I wasn't exactly being attentive to anything she was saying, too busy searching the surrounding seats for Molly, but there was no sign.

"Hey, speaking here! Devoted cousin singing your praises, getting totally ignored!" Ally shouted in my face. Turning to face her, I gave her another quick hug and asked, "Where is she?"

Crossing her arms across her chest, she smiled, lilting, "Who, darlin'?"

"Cut the shit, Al," I said tersely. "Where's she gone?"

Dropping her smug-assed smile, she shrugged. "Said she had to study."

My heart faltered at that. "She couldn't stick around a bit longer?"

Jimmy-Don and his new woman came up for air, and the large blonde held out her hand in my direction. "Cassie, darlin', but my friends all call me Cass."

"Rome."

Her eyebrows danced. "I know." She stepped forward, placing her hand on my shoulder. "One thing you need to know about my girl Molly is that studying comes first, everything else second. If she don't get at least ten hours of study in a day, she don't see it as productive and freaks the hell out. I don't know what more to say. All that time spent in her books keeps her sane." That sounded about right from everything I'd witnessed.

Looking back at my cousin, I said, "Party at mine tonight. Bring her. Don't let me down."

Ally shook her head. "I'll try, but I wouldn't hold your breath, Rome. She isn't exactly a keg and cock kind of girl."

"Do it, Al. I'm counting on you."

With that, I headed to the showers, telling the other players to spread the word about the party and to stock up on beer.

No more waiting, no more overthinking the ramifications of being with the girl I wanted... Tonight I'd make her mine. And I'd kick the shit out of anyone who got in my way.

11

"So... you want to show me your room?"

"Negative."

Sharp red fingernails ran up my arm. "Aww, c'mon, Bullet. I can show you things you've never seen before... I've been wanting you for years."

Rubbing my hand over my face, I leaned back and groaned out a frustrated, "*Please*, just fuck off!"

The scrape of a chair told me I'd successfully deterred another fucking groupie. I bet their mommas and daddies would be proud knowing they were paying for their daughters to come to college, not to learn, but instead to offer themselves on a gilded platter to the Tide QB.

A slow clap got my attention. When I opened my eyes, Austin was standing before me, laughing. "Rome Prince! Showing some friggin' restraint with the opposite sex!" His smile faltered when he glanced at the door, and looking to see what had got his attention, I spotted Ally, Cass, and that Goth chick—Lexi?—entering the party.

I questioned why the hell he was acting so weird when he slipped out of the back door without another word, casting one more frustrated look at Lexi. Her face fell as she watched him cut and run, and she spun on her heel and walked over to a group of cheerleaders chilling in the kitchen.

I wondered what the hell that was about, but more pressing matters were on my mind.

I got to my feet, walking in their direction. Ally saw me first, followed by Cass, who stumbled toward me, arms spread wide as she fell against my chest, almost tackling me to the floor. Fuck, she was wasted.

Pushing her back, helping her balance, I titled my chin at my cousin. "Where is she?"

Ally's face dropped. "She wouldn't come."

Anger and disappointment merged in my chest, and I growled out loud, "Why the fuck not?"

"Said she was tired."

"For Christ's sake!" I shouted, causing Cass to jolt upright and hold up her cell.

Fiddling with the screen, she put it to her ear, winked at me, then slurred, "Molls, get your juicy English ass out! We're getting trashed and need the fourth musketeer!" Cass smiled up at me, nodding her head smugly as though certain her drunken little call would work. I couldn't hear what Molly was saying, but by the drop in Cass's expression, I could tell she wasn't getting the answer she wanted.

Ally made a mock strangling gesture behind Cass's back and snatched the device from her hand. Cass tried to wrestle it back but was distracted by the sight of Jimmy-Don heading down the stairs and, screaming in excitement, ran over into his open arms, pretty much tackling him to the floor.

Ally was now speaking into Cass's cell phone. "You sure you won't come, darlin'? I don't like that you're alone in your room and everyone's here having a good time."

I held my breath, never taking my eyes from Ally's, but when they dulled with disappointment, I chugged the rest of my beer, hearing Ally signing off, abruptly ending the call with a shake of her head.

"She says she's just tired." Reaching out, Ally laid her hand on my bare arm. "Molly's extremely guarded, Rome. She don't really let anyone in. She's the most private person I know."

Not true, she'd fucking let me in—on Ally's balcony, that night at the initiation. I *was* friggin' different to her. I knew I was, but her never turning up or sticking around for me to see her was really starting to piss me off.

In a second, I made up my mind… Time to pay Miss Shakespeare a visit. No more hiding.

"I know that face," Ally said warily, a flood of questions in her eyes.

Backing out of the doorway and smiling at her reproachful face, I waved. "Catch you later. I got somewhere to be."

Slamming her hands onto her waist, Ally yelled, "Rome, I'm not so sure it's such a good idea to go over there uninvited! She's not one of your sluts!" Pretending not to hear the worry and censure in her tone, I kept going through the crowd but smiled when I heard her shout begrudgingly, "It's the balcony to the left of mine, top floor! *But don't say I didn't warn you!*"

Stepping out of the backdoor of my frat house and running across the street, I found myself below Molly's balcony, looking up at the stone columns, a dim light coming from her room, and I shook my head in complete disbelief.

Romeo below fucking Juliet's balcony.... Fuck. Me. Sideways.

Reaching down to my junk, I checked my balls were still there... You know, just in case they'd been revoked at such a pathetic and desperate act, but yeah—still intact and aching for the chick in that room just a stone's throw away.

I reached down to the fancy landscaped lawn borders, scooped up some of the red gravel surrounding the plants and rolled the stones in my hands. I was about ready to throw them at her window when my cell vibrated in my pocket, my fingers parted and the gravel slipped through the gaps.

Moving to a shadowed, secluded spot, I slumped down to the warm grass and read the message.

Daddy: Look, son, I went too far with you the other day. Let's talk about this calmly. I really need you to make this marriage with Shelly happen. The business

needs it, the family needs it, and if you want to keep things good between us, you need it to happen too.

My head fell forward. Even when he was trying to be nice, he couldn't help but issue a threat. I didn't know who he got it from. My grandparents were the nicest folk on Earth. His brother, Ally's daddy, a saint, but my daddy was ruined by money and greed, and meeting my momma—who was equally as money-hungry—turned him into a nightmare.

My stomach sank some as I thought of my paternal grandparents. I'd been real young when they moved to Florida, and they both passed away shortly after they left.

I remember my granddaddy taking me to pee-wee football for the very first time. He'd been so damn proud of me that day, proud that his grandson showed good promise. But he never got to see me play properly, and I wished he could've stuck around longer to see what I became. I remember it feeling so different being around my grandparents; even as a tiny kid I could tell that much. They always cared for me, and on my eighteenth birthday, I found out just how much. They'd left me a trust fund, a fucking *huge* trust fund, one that my folks couldn't touch. My daddy flipped when I told him a lawyer had turned up at my frat house with the details, and it was from that day that he knew he could no longer use money to control me, so he switched to blackmail and humiliation instead.

Fighting the urge to scream and pummel my fists into the wall, I stared up at the sky, deep in thought.

What was I doing? My folks were never going to let me out of this marriage shit, and part of me felt like just giving in for an easier life, but more of me wanted to resist it with every ounce of my being.

Rolling my neck, I stared back up at Molly's balcony. If I kept going down this road with her, I knew there was the very real danger that I'd never be able to let her go. I wasn't stupid. *Christ*, she'd already gotten into my head and I'd barely even touched her, barely even scratched the surface of who she really was. But I was addicted nonetheless, and I had to decide right now if she was worth it... worth disobeying my folks... worth facing months of hell... worth lowering my barriers.

Thoughts of today's game bolted into my mind. I'd asked her to be there for me, to support me, and although it wasn't what she wanted, she came anyway, sacrificing her precious study time... for *me*. Having her there completely changed my game, that kiss relaxing me for the first time in such a long time. I couldn't ever say that about my folks, or any other chick I'd fucked. Too many people wound me up to the point of snapping, but not Molly. She listened, comforted, and calmed me right down. Who wouldn't become desperate to have that level of connection all the damn time?

Molly made me feel good about myself. *Christ*, she made me friggin' smile, and the way she'd coped with so much shit in her own life gave me hope, hope that maybe I could get through my obstacles too... one day... maybe with her help.

Fuck it! She *was* worth every shitty text, every aggressive slur, and every strike I'd have coming my way.

After I'd been sitting debating my predicament for nearly an hour, I rose to my feet with a new sense of determination, scooping up more gravel as I went, and set to launching them at Molly's closed balcony doors. I figured if that weedy fucker Montague could get his prize this way, I had a pretty good chance of doing so as well.

Shadows danced behind the white curtains and the balcony doors opened slowly. "Shakespeare?" I called softly, checking the grounds of the sorority house to make sure no one was around.

There were a few moments filled with shuffling sounds before a mass of long brown hair fell over the balcony rail and a pair of taped-up glasses looked down at me.

"Hey, Mol," I said, my chest already feeling lighter in her presence.

"Hey, you. What are you doing here?" she asked, her eyebrows pulled together to form a deep frown.

"I came to see you."

She straightened some and asked, "You did? Why?"

Because I can't stop thinking about you. Because I want to kiss those damn lips again so bad I can't bear it... Then I want to continue south until I taste you on my tongue as you come and writhe against my mouth... Only to then strip you bare and fuck you until you can't stand. I didn't think the truth would go over too well with a girl like Molly, so I simply replied, "Because I noticed you weren't out. And I wanted to make sure you were okay after today. I've been thinking about you all night."

Pushing her broken frames back on her nose, she asked, "Shouldn't you be with Shelly?"

Those words caused my back to stiffen, and I snapped, "Why the fuck would I be with her?" The very fact that Molly thought I'd be with Shelly of all people, had me steaming with rage. *Shelly!* Why did everything always come back to her?

Clearing her throat, Molly answered, "She was with you after the game. The two of you looked cozy. I thought you might have wanted to celebrate with her tonight." Although she'd fought to hide it, I caught the disappointment in her voice. I got it. She'd heard all the rumors about me, about me fucking any piece of ass that moved, so why should she trust me? Why think she was different to me?

I needed her to be convinced.

Standing directly below her and pinning her with my gaze, I pronounced, "Let's get this straight right now. She's not fuckin' anything to me. Never will be." Molly's entire body visibly relaxed and a small smile broke on her lips.

Wait—

"Is that why you bailed on the party? Because you thought I'd be with that conniving bitch?" Even in the dark, I could see the guilty blush smother her cheeks.

Shit. That *was* why she snubbed my party and why she wasn't there for me at the end of the game.

"Rome, I just didn't fancy the party tonight, that's all. You go and enjoy yourself. You don't need to check on me." She was trying to push me away. I knew I was a scary concept to her—hell, to most—but this was one fight I

140

wasn't going to lose. She was one chick I wouldn't just throw away.

"I'm not going anywhere," I assured her, my voice stern and laced with authority. I grimaced internally, unsure if my tone would scare her off. But hell, this was me: stubborn, strict, one hell of a moody fucker, and harboring a desperate need to be in control.

As always, the girl surprised me, and instead of being deterred and telling me to fuck off, she burst into hysterical laughter.

I wasn't sure whether to be pissed off or join in on the amusement. "What're you finding so funny, Shakespeare?" I asked, a hoarse roughness to my voice.

Leaning farther forward, she sang, "That Romeo has come to my balcony to strive for my attention." I barely even noticed she said that damn name; I was too mesmerized by the lift in her spirit.

Clasping her hands, she recited, "*The orchard walls are high and hard to climb, And the place death, considering who thou art, If any of my kinsmen find thee here... they will murder thee.*"

"How the hell do you know that from memory?" I asked, fighting not to return the wide smile that was plastered on her damn cute face.

"I've read it about a hundred times. It's beautifully tragic." Pointing at me, then herself, she said, "Kind of like us, don't you think?"

She'd hit the friggin' nail on the head. We were tragic, both pretty fucked up. But we could be fucked-up together, balance it out.

Running to the side of the balcony, I spotted a trellis and, groaning at the damn irony, began climbing up the wall like a man possessed.

"Romeo, be careful! What the hell are you doing?" Molly hissed, watching me in horror.

"Coming to see my Juliet," I said in jest, watching her face pale as she stumbled back in surprise, then climbing the rest of the way and jumping onto the terrace. I hit the floor with a thud, but then I looked up... and almost had a stroke.

Brown hair to her waist, thick enough to grip, and the shortest, thinnest scrap of pink material barely covering her impressive curves, the beads of her nipples visible, tempting me to just step forward and take them in my mouth. My cock instantly hardened in my jeans, and moving toward her, noting the quickened rise and fall of her braless tits, I reached out, stroking her soft dark hair— even the thin wrap of sports tape in the center of her frames unable to distract me from how fucking stunning she was right here before me.

In an instinctive move, her hand met mine, and, taking advantage of the lust widening in her eyes, I moved in, running my finger down her neck, my restraint hanging by a thread.

"Romeo? W-what are you doing?" Molly asked, her question more of a strangled moan than anything else.

"I ain't sure. But I don't wanna stop," I whispered against her neck. Vanilla. Her. Fucking perfection.

"Rome, I don't think—" She stopped mid-sentence as she whipped around to look down at the backyard, fear on her face. Students flooded the yard, the party spilling to this side of the street. I didn't give a shit, though. In fact, let all of the student body see us like this. So with more aggression, I slammed her body against mine and nipped along the bare skin of her neck, continuing where we left off.

"We... we need to stop," Molly whispered into my ear, but there was no conviction in her tone, just breathy pleas spurring me on.

"No, Mol. I've held off for long enough. I've tried to take things slow, but no more. I won't be a nothing to you anymore. I want you. I want you so fucking bad..." I said quietly, my voice hoarse with need, my desperation increasing by the second. Reality and fantasy blurred into one, and I couldn't get the image of us intertwined on her bed out of my mind. I almost groaned out loud at the thought that in about ten minutes, I'd have her stripped bare, could be plunging deep in her pussy.

Soft hands skimmed up my bare arms, feeling so damn right against my skin. "Rome. This isn't a good idea. I can't do this." But she didn't pull away; her hips and tits were still pressing into my body

"Sure you can," I murmured, my hands slowly drifting down, hearing the hitch in her breathing as I caressed her waist.

Those damn soft hands suddenly pushed me back, snapping me to the harshness of reality. "Please... just... hold on a moment," she said in a fluster, arms locked and braced to stop me getting any closer.

Well, that was a first, a chick stopping me from fucking her. I hadn't had to work at sex since I was in high school; matter of fact, I never did then either. Chicks were just always drawn to me. Not Molly, though; she was proving one tough fucking nut to crack.

"What?" she suddenly asked, and I realized I was imitating a friggin' statue, standing gaping at her in shock. She was still panting, trying to catch her breath.

Shuffling awkwardly, I admitted, "No one's ever told me no before."

Her mouth dropped like a damn cartoon character, and she emitted a single disbelieving laugh. "Are you serious?"

"Deadly," I answered through clenched teeth. Fuck, I felt like I was in pain, my fists clenching as my cock throbbed in my boxers.

A giggle escaped her mouth, and she blurted, "That's… *pathetic.*"

Yeah… I guess it kind of was.

Dragging my teeth along my bottom lip, I moved in toward her tense body and held her by the hips. The damn sweet sound of her giggle broke through the thick wall of my aggression, and with a ghost of a smirk, I confessed, "But true."

She shook her head, actually looking pretty damn disgusted, and tipped her chin to the sky. It dawned on me that maybe my past with chicks was putting her off.

With dread pitted in my chest, I plucked up the courage to ask, "You don't want this? You don't want… *me?*" I was so damn scared to hear her response. Actually scared for the first time in years.

"Romeo... I—"

"What?" I interrupted. I didn't want to be pitied. I wouldn't be made a fool of. Not by her. Not by anyone.

I watched the conflict in her eyes, but with a sag of her shoulders, she ultimately gave in, her want for me, for *us*, overpowering her logic. "You're a lot to take on, you know," she said with a defeated sigh, but her fingers wrapped in my red Tide T-shirt, subtly bringing me closer.

"I know," I answered semi-humorously, feeling like I'd just won the friggin' lottery.

Those hypnotizing golden-brown eyes searched mine, confusion glaring through, and she confessed, "I don't know what you want from me. You tie me up in knots and I'm not used to it."

You, I want only you, I thought. But out loud, I said, "Then let me show you what I want. Stop fuckin' fighting this." I couldn't deal with any more running, any more hiding, couldn't tolerate one more day without knowing I had her as mine.

Arms fidgeted and she tried to break loose, but I held on tight, causing her to murmur, "No, Rome, this is just... just..."

I'd well and truly had enough of this back-and-forth shit.

"I want to be with you," I snapped, losing my patience, arms like a vise around her waist. "Come on, Mol. I need you. Tell me you get me. Tell me you're as fuckin' into me as I am you."

Caramel eyes closed, and any remaining shreds of resistance left her rigid body. Then two words from her mouth changed everything. "Come inside."

Exhaling a long, pent-up breath, I could only respond in the best way I knew how—with a sincere and a heartfelt, "Fuck. Yeah."

12

The minute we'd stepped into her room, I was on Mol—hands roaming on her tight body, fisting her nightgown—and I slowly backed her toward her bed. Our mouths meshed furiously, tongues thrashed together as we hit the mattress, and I set to doing what do best.

Molly gripped my shirt hard, moaning and groaning into my mouth, and when her hands met the bare skin of my back, it was the green light I'd been waiting for.

Breaking from her mouth, I slipped my hand up her thigh, working toward her core, when she slammed on the breaks with a tight hold on my wrist.

"I-I can't. It's going too fast."

Tipping my head back, I almost screamed out in frustration. I was so damn turned on I was almost blind with need. Molly released an embarrassed whimper, and seeing her flushed face, I instantly felt like an ass.

"Don't do that," I said, holding her face in my hands.

"Do what?"

"Feel bad for stopping. Never feel bad for that. When I have you, it'll be when I have you writhing in need, begging me to fuck you. Never feel bad for stopping. When you give yourself to me, you'll be so wet you can't fucking stand it."

Her pupils dilated and her lips parted. "When I give myself to you?"

She was so friggin' cute.

"*When* you give yourself to me."

Shifting slightly away, she said, affronted, "You're confident. I might refuse you."

She wouldn't. Yeah, I may sound like an arrogant dick, but the way her eyes devoured me, my body, there was *no* fucking way she'd hold out long.

She was still staring at me, waiting for me to speak, so I said, "We're going to happen. We both know it's true, and I'm counting the days until I get inside you and make you come… over and over again. Fuckin' counting the *minutes*…"

Lust took her over and she almost pounced on me there and then, but I pushed her back to the mattress. She was the one girl I didn't want to just fuck and leave as soon as it was done.

"I shouldn't have pushed you. You're not ready."

"You didn't. It's just… It's just that… I'm… not very experienced… and I…"

I sat up, reality hitting home. "Shit, are you a virgin?"

Shifting before me, she blushed and confessed, "No, not a virgin, but I'm not exactly skilled in all things... seductive. I've only ever slept with one person and only one time, this past year."

And just like that, I really fucking wished she *was* a virgin, jealously over some unknown douchebag taking hold.

Some unworthy fucker'd had *my* Mol.

"When did this happen?" I asked through slightly gritted teeth.

"When I was at Oxford. Oliver and I—"

"Oliver?" I interrupted.

Her eyebrows drew together and she said, "Yeah, Oliver Bartholomew."

I couldn't help it, but I laughed, my anger put aside for a minute. The way she said that fucking pompous-ass English name was comical. *Bartholomew?* Fuck, and I thought Romeo Prince was bad enough.

"What?" she questioned, seeming pretty pissed at me.

Clearing my throat and trying my damndest to hide my smile with my hand, I said, "Oliver Bartholomew? Very... British."

Her eyes narrowed behind those thick lenses and she stressed, "He is British! As am I! Quit making fun!"

With a frustrated groan, Molly turned her back to me, causing me to swallow my friggin' laughter and pull her back into my chest. "Okay, okay, I'm sorry."

She shook her head in admonishment, but when she threw a small smile, I knew we were good.

"So Oliver, was he your boyfriend?" I asked, suddenly in that weird state of mind where you don't want to know the answer but desperately need it at the same time.

"Yeah, I suppose. I tried to have him as a boyfriend anyway."

"Tried?" I questioned at the strange response.

Her lashes fluttered as her eyes quickly met mine, and she said, "Yeah. I... I don't really get close to people. I tried with him, but in the end, I just couldn't do it. We'd been sort of dating for a few months—coffee dates, study partners, that type of thing—and I decided to just take the next step, just get it over with. He wanted it badly. I was indifferent. So I thought why not? Olly was sweet to me and I liked him well enough. The sex—not so much."

"What? You didn't like sex?" I almost shouted. How could anyone *not* like sex?

Her face went as red as my damn Tide jersey, and she admitted, "It was awkward, fumbled, and not everything it was hyped up to be."

"Olly just didn't do it right."

Meeting her eyes, I said, "I imagine with you, Shakespeare, it'd be like nothing else. I've never wanted anything so much in my damned life—to taste you, feel you... hear you scream my name." The pulse in her neck set off thumping like a drum and that pull we both felt began drawing us back in.

"Romeo—" She edged away, but I pulled on her arm to keep her close.

"I'll stop, but I won't hide the fact that I want it real bad, Shakespeare. *Real* fuckin' bad."

I watched as her thighs clenched together and my cock slammed against my fly. Things were too tense, but Molly managed to diffuse the moment by thrusting a pillow over her head, warning, "We need to find something to do, Rome. I really need distracting right now!"

Pulling back the pillow, holding in my laughter, I said, "You've stolen my line, Shakespeare. Ain't I the one that's meant to say that to you?"

"Probably, but I'm about ready to jump your bones and would prefer not to tonight if it could be helped. I'd like it if I didn't go from near-virgin to slut after one night in your friggin' company!"

Unable to stop laughing this time, I creased up, falling on my back and pulled her to drape over my chest. "What should we do, then, near-virgin, just so you don't give in and jump my bones? Although, it's mighty tempting for me to just let you do your thing."

"I have just the thing, if you're game?"

She put on friggin' *Monty Python*.

We watched the movie. I actually *watched* a movie with a girl *and* made no move to seduce her... much. I still caught a kiss and the occasional feel, but most surprising, I *liked* just chilling with Mol. It kind of felt like I was twelve again, on some first date that I'd never had, but it was good... It made me feel kinda normal.

That was until I fucked up by taking offense at her joke.

I was just tipping the last of the popcorn in my mouth when Molly ripped the bowl from my hands. "You're meant to be an athlete! Isn't that an overload of starchy-carby crappiness for you or something? You've polished it all off, you greedy bugger!"

Snorting out a laugh, I flexed my bicep, catching Mol's small, impressed gasp, and said, "I'm a fucking machine, Shakespeare. Popcorn's no match for me!"

"Sorry, I forgot I was talking to the *Bullet!*" she quipped, but her words felt like a cold bucket of water being dumped on my head.

"Don't," I hissed, losing all humor.

"Allaaabbbaaammmmaaa!!! Get to your feet for your hometown quarterback, Romeo... 'Bullet'... Prince! 'There's a bullet in the gun. There's a fire in your heart. You will move all mountains that stand in your path...'" Molly was laughing as she sang that damn song the IT guys always played in Bryant-Denny whenever I was on the big screen, but all I felt was annoyed. She wasn't getting the hint that I was serious.

Taking hold of her wrists, I pulled her forward until her eyes met mine and growled, "Quit it, Shakespeare. *Fuck!*"

Almost choking on her words, she sat back. "I'm only kidding. You don't have to be so bloody grumpy with me."

Shit. I hadn't meant to be, but I hated that bastard name. *Bullet,* it was almost as bad as Romeo. I hated the football hype so damn much; it'd always just made shit at home that much worse.

Taking another look at Molly's hurt face, I sighed. "I know, sorry, but I fucking hate all that shit. You don't know how much. I don't want to be the Bullet to you.

You're the first person to ever not be affected by all the football fame. To you... I just want to be Rome."

Molly got me. She got I didn't want to go into why the football fame bothered me so much, and moving us away from that uncomfortable topic, she asked, "So... MVP?"

"Yeah. Crazy considering I couldn't hit a truck for the first half."

How did I tell her that seeing her in the stands changed everything, without revealing too much about my feelings? How could I tell her she was the first person to ever pull through for me without having to explain my past and my folks?

I just couldn't find the words. So instead, I just filled her in on the locker room talk. "The fans and team are pumped, saying it's because of you. That you're my good luck charm, all from that one sweet kiss."

And then she flipped the fuck out, shooting to sitting position, fighting for breath and rubbing at her chest. It looked like she was having a damn heart attack.

"What? What's wrong? What did I say?" I asked frantically.

Her eyes were as big as the fucking moon and she tried to speak but nothing came out. My heart took off beating too fast, so I held her hand, and watched as she calmed the heck down, color coming back to her pale face. I stared down at our joined hands in confusion, wondering what the fuck had just happened?

"What is it, Mol? Tell me." I pushed, needing some explanation of why she just nearly collapsed.

Taking a deep breath, she said, "I'm sorry, it's just something my Grandma used to say to me. It took me back to those days. I panicked. I-I just... I was just surprised when you said it. Of all the ways to say what you did, you quoted her word for word."

"What did she say to you? What did *I* say?"

Smiling a broken smile, she said softly, "That I had sweet kisses. Grandma would say one sweet kiss from me would make any problem just that little bit easier."

"I believe she might be right. She must have been a wise woman because that's exactly what you did for me tonight at the game."

"She was. She was everything to me." Tears fell from her eyes as her fingers tightened against mine. "We used to say we were a matching set. When she died, she took half my soul with her. I don't like to think of my past too much... It kills me to remember all that I've lost."

I stayed silent. There are no words to comfort someone who'd lost those closest. So I just let her get it all out as I pressed her into my side, lying back against the bed, using my touch to keep her calm. Fuck. My touch had kept her calm.

"So you walked out of your own party?" Molly eventually asked as I stared at the ceiling, realizing she actually may be as fucked up as me.

"You weren't there."

Molly shuffled her legs to face me and nervously asked, "Do I matter that much to you?"

I wanted to laugh in her face, convinced that if she only knew the severity of my obsession with her, she'd run for the fucking hills.

"Do you really not know?"

She shook her head no, so pushing her back into the mattress, I confessed, "I like the way you are with me. I like me when I'm with you. I feel like I could tell you anything, that I could bear my fuckin' black soul. You make me feel... well... you know... You get me?" I was such a douche and evidently no good at all the romantic shit.

But a finger stroked down my cheek, and smiling so damn big, Molly said, "I get you, Romeo."

We stayed that way for a while, just talking. She apologized for our showdown at the lecture, admitting that she was pissed at me after believing I'd slept with Shelly. I told her the truth, that I was done with everyone but her, and she seemed more than happy with that fact.

After a time, music began blaring from the backyard and it was clear that the party was only getting bigger. I didn't complain, though, because Molly asked me to stay—*only to sleep!* she'd stated—and I couldn't have felt happier.

Molly moved into bed, nervously biting her thumb and watching every move I made. When I got in bed beside her and that tight ass of hers began grinding into my cock, it took all my might to edge forward and whisper, "We need to try and sleep or things will get out of control. I only have so much restraint."

"O-okay," she whispered back, and I wrapped my arm around her waist as she tucked herself farther against me.

It felt so damn right.

"Night, Shakespeare," I said quietly.

"Night, Romeo," she replied, and I couldn't help but laugh in disbelief.

She stiffened at my amusement, so I quickly explained. "I actually like the sound of my name on your lips. Something I never thought would happen. I think it's the English accent. It sounds all proper, like the way Shakespeare intended. No one calls me Romeo, has ever called me Romeo. I don't allow it. But weirdly, I like it when you do."

I heard her exhale and felt her trying to turn and face me. For some reason I couldn't let her, too overcome with emotion to have her meet my eyes, to see the demons I fought in my gaze. But when she whispered, *"What's in a name? That which we call a rose by any other name would smell as sweet; so Romeo would, were he not Romeo call'd."* I felt like I couldn't breathe. The memories, the *pain* that name stirred in me was too much.

"Don't… please…" I begged, unable to tell her why that name was such a burden.

"Why don't you allow it?"

"Long story," I evaded, my panic now rising to the surface.

"We have time."

"Not now," I said harsher than I meant to, but I just couldn't go there yet. Maybe not ever. It was just too much.

Molly sighed in disappointment, but I was thankful when she changed the subject and asked, "What does the tattoo on your ribs say?"

"*The greatest accomplishment is not in never falling, but in rising again when you fall.* It's Vince Lombardi."

"It's beautiful. This Vince Lombardi philosopher must be good. Why have I never heard of him?" And just like that, she pulled me out of a bad place. Only Molly had ever been able to do that for me... It was addicting.

"What now?" she groaned, clearly over me laughing at every little thing she said wrong.

"He was a football coach. A very famous football coach."

"Oh. I really need to get up to speed on all things football."

"I'd like it if you didn't. You're not impressed by the hoopla that comes with me playing and I never want you to be either. It's better if you don't know in depth what it all means to folks round here."

"You mean you really don't want me to call you Bullet?"

"Fuck no."

"Whatever makes you happy."

I swear she was going to kill me. "Sleep, Mol, or we'll end up doing what makes me incredibly fuckin' happy."

"One more question, then I'll sleep."

Squeezing her tightly, I said, "One more. You're pushing your luck."

"Why *One Day*?"

Memories of getting that tattoo on my hip played through my mind, and finally taking a risk, I told her what I'd never told anyone else. "That I'd leave this place, one day. Be my own person, one day. Do what I want... one day."

Molly's hand tightened in mine. "Has it always been so bad for you?"

I couldn't, I just couldn't speak about that topic, some weird force within me stealing my voice, so I replied, "That was two questions, Shakespeare. I agreed to one. Now sleep."

"Romeo? I don't want everyone to know about us yet. I want to keep our relationship to ourselves," Molly suddenly blurted when I was halfway to sleep.

Anger zapped through me at an alarming rate, snapping me awake, and I had to move, sitting on the side of the bed. "I get it. You're embarrassed to be with me. Bullet, the aggressive, whoring QB—not boyfriend material, right? But good for a few fucks in secret..." I hated the way I was speaking—harsh, malicious—but her saying that made me feel ashamed. She didn't think I was worthy of being with her in public.

Molly's warm breath spread on my back and her arms wrapped around my waist. "What? No! I... I'm just nervous!" she said, panicked.

Feeling like a weight had been lifted, I turned, taking her hands, and asked, "Nervous of what?"

She took her hand back and smoothed down her thick hair and the hem of her nightgown. "Look, I'm not what you go for. I don't look like the others—polished, perfect, twenty-twenty vision. Please can we just wait a bit longer before the whole campus finds out? For my sake? It's going to take some adjustment on my part to be with you. I just need some time."

Awesome, I thought. The only girl I *want* to have on my arm for all the world to see, and she wants to hide away in secret.

Karma's a bitch.

Pressing my head to hers, I said, "I want to show everyone I'm with you now. I'm not fucking hiding us, and I don't give a shit what people think. As for my past, that's not what I want with you. I want more. Don't you get that by now? *Christ!*"

"Please. Just for a while. You're Romeo Prince. Your… reputation scares me a little. Let's just be us in private for a while, see how it goes without anyone else interfering."

"Fuck, Mol!" I shouted a bit too loud. I was pissed. Yeah, my reputation was as a bit of a scary fucker, but I was *different* with her, and I'd happily knock out anyone who tried to say otherwise. I would protect her.

"Please," she begged again, and hell, I couldn't resist those pleading eyes. No way was I giving her up. If we had to stay secret for now, I'd just have to friggin' adjust.

Meeting Molly's apprehensive gaze, I snapped out, "Fine! We'll keep it quiet… I don't fuckin' like it, but I'll do it for you, even if the thought of us being a secret makes me want to punch someone square in the face."

A fucking secret.

Perfect.

Hell, this was *not* going to be fun…

13

My cell vibrated in my pocket, and fishing it out, my mood instantly soured. "Daddy, nice of you to call again," I said sarcastically as I made my way through the college to the cafeteria for lunch, my muscles still aching from my weight session.

"It's a good day, Rome! Martin Blair has approved the prenup. When you marry Shelly, Martin will finally retire and gift you thirty percent of his fifty percent share as a wedding present. He's been wanting to leave for a while now, and you taking over the day-to-day running of the business beside me is exactly what we've wanted! Full Prince control."

I'd never heard my daddy sound so friggin' happy— me, though, I was just seething.

"What *you've* wanted," I immediately stressed.

"What?" he snapped, his moment of elation soon forgotten.

Bracing for the aftermath, I said, "What you've wanted. I've told you once and I won't keep repeating it: I'm. Not. Marrying. Shel!"

Silence reigned strong. Then, surprising me, he asked calmly, "What can I do to change your mind? What do you want? Whatever will make this happen, I'll do for you, *get* for you."

That shocked me to the point that I couldn't move. Was the great Joseph Prince actually trying to negotiate?

Nipping the bridge of my nose, I replied, "Nothing. Nothing will change my mind. I'm sorry, Daddy, I know you think I'm failing in my duty as your son. But it's my life and I won't marry someone for the sake of your already stupidly rich business… I won't marry just so you can get more money… I'm not cut out for that life. Football is what I'll be doing in the future."

A deep cough sounded on the other side of the line and he said, "You're not going to change your mind about this? Am I getting this right?"

Blowing out a fortifying breath, I answered, "No. I'm not going to change my mind."

"Then have it your way."

I froze, looking, unseeing, through the cafeteria windows. "What the hell does that mean?"

"You've made your choice. Now you'll have to live with it. I won't pander to you."

"What does that fuckin' mean?" I barked out again, trying to keep my voice low, as students around me began to stare in my direction.

I realized the phone had gone dead and, seeing the trash can before me, yelled out in frustration and sent the damn tin cylinder flying across the sidewalk with a huge kick. Shocked squeals from surrounding girls only infuriated me more, and, ripping into the cafeteria, ignoring the questioning looks from other people, I slumped down on my chair, staring, lost in thought, at the plastic tabletop.

What the hell did he mean? Jesus! He was forever fucking with my head. I'd rather take a beating than this damn mental torture. At least with a punch I knew where I stood.

Lifting my head, I searched the room, desperately needing to see Molly, and when I did, I found those golden eyes already staring right back at me. Her eyebrows were drawn together with worry. Feeling slightly calmer knowing she was close, I gave her a reassuring tilt of my chin.

Not being able to hold her in my arms was killing me. Not being able to pull her onto my lap, kiss her damn neck, and show the world she was mine was friggin' killing me.

The next hour was going to be torture.

I was right. Lunch seemed to drag on. And when Caroline strutted over and made a pass at me, spouting some shit about dethroning queen bitch Shelly—I didn't care, wasn't remotely interested in her slutty offer, and I sent her away with a dismissive wave, and a polite, "Fuck off."

Chris Porter watched me curiously from a few seats down, a smirk on his smarmy face.

"What the fuck you laughing at, Porter?" I snarled, my voice sounding lethal even to my ears.

"You batting for the other side now?" he tried to joke, so I flipped him the bird, hearing my teammates snicker in response.

At a loud bang, I looked toward the entrance of the cafeteria. And Shelly entered the room, immediately getting all up in Molly's face. I watched, fury building within me as she ripped off Molly's glasses, throwing them to the floor. It happened so fast, I didn't even have a chance to do anything to prevent it.

"What's wrong? Momma and Daddy got no money, sweetie? You poor, Molly?" Shelly bitched, loud enough for the entire room to catch every word. I didn't hear the rest of what else that witch was spitting; my blood was rushing through my ears, drowning out the sound. Molly rose from her seat, a furious look in her eyes, but Shelly shoved her back into the chair.

My patience for dealing with assholes had worn completely and totally thin, and slamming my fist on the table, I stood and ordered, "Enough!" so loud you could feel the vibrations in the plastic chairs. I glared right into Shelly's eyes and spat, "Back the hell off her. What are you, twenty-one or twelve?"

The cafeteria came to a standstill at my words and, not giving a shit about Shelly's reaction, I marched over to

Molly, lifted her glasses off the floor, and pushed them back onto her flushed face before pressing my hands to her shoulders in comfort.

"Get your hands off her!" Shelly hissed from beside me, like she had some fucking ownership, some claim on me. I took a quick glance about the room, noting a sea of eyes all staring at me in shock.

This day was going to absolute shit! First my daddy starting on me and issuing threats, now his golden child opening her damn mouth to one of the only two girls I gave a crap about. Fuck knows what my folks were up to. I'd find that out in time, but I was going to stop Shelly's delusion now, publicly, and cut her down off her high horse.

Feeling an ounce of control settle back over my body, I rounded on Shelly, raising my voice so the entire room could hear. "Get it through your head. We're not together, never will be. Time to cut the shit." Pointing at Shelly, I faced the gawping crowd. "Despite what shit she may be spewing, know that I am not with her, never have been, and anything she says is utter bullshit!"

I made sure Molly was okay, then practically hoisted her off her seat and instructed, "Get your purse, Shakespeare. We're leaving."

Doing as I asked, Molly followed me out of the cafeteria and into the quad. With every step, I grew more annoyed. No one would even pay Molly an ounce of attention if it weren't for me, if Shelly didn't suspect I was into her. A smart chick like Mol wouldn't even register on anyone's radar—and their sorry lives would be worse off for it. My girl was getting ripped on because of me, and if she wasn't so fucking intent on keeping us a secret, I could tell them all that she was mine and they needed to back the hell off her.

Fine. I got it, and I didn't want to rock that boat too much, scare her off before we'd really had a chance to get going, but she wouldn't be targeted anymore because of those fucking stupid glasses. I'd make sure of it.

"Romeo, slow down. Where are we going?" Molly panted from behind me. I didn't stop or give an answer, unable to slow down for fear of marching back into the cafeteria and telling everyone the truth about us.

"Get in," I ordered through clenched teeth once we reached my truck.

As we left school behind, every second in Molly's presence calmed me down further, allowing me to ask, "Sure you're okay?" She hadn't said a thing since we'd been on the road, understanding that I couldn't talk right now, that I needed some time to wind down.

Fidgeting nervously, Molly replied, "Yes. A little embarrassed, but I'm fine."

Embarrassed? Fucking understatement! She hated attention, and today, Shelly had thrust her right into the spotlight.

"How dare she speak to you like that? She's such a bitch! Why the hell did I waste so much of my fuckin' time on her?" I snapped, more to myself. I was so pissed I could barely function.

"You took the words right out of my mouth." Glancing over at Molly and seeing her tiny proud smile at her comment thawed my rage, and I couldn't help but smile a little in return.

This girl amazed me. Shelly had mocked her parents in front of a good portion of the student body—her dead parents that she never really talked about. But she took Shelly's vicious dig like a champ, taking the high road, putting me and my typically aggressive reaction to shame.

"Mol, I'm so sorry for what she said to you about your parents. I can't imagine how that must've felt."

A soft hand stroked across my knee. "You have nothing to apologize for."

Gripping her fingers, I replied, "Not true. She's ripping on you because she sees my interest in you. Saw it from our very first kiss. You're the enemy now, Mol, and I can't say sorry enough for that. I put you in this position and she's going to try and make your life hell."

With a stunning smile, she scooted closer, laying her head on my shoulder, her breath warming the bare skin of my bicep. She was fearless, never giving a shit what others thought. My body relaxed and, wrapping my arm around her shoulder, I ran my fingers through her loose strands of hair. It was the first bit of peace I'd felt in weeks. Right here, right now, just the two of us... it was perfect.

At least it was until she asked, "Rome, who was on the phone earlier, outside the cafeteria?"

Fuck. Didn't expect the conversation to go there.

Clearing my throat, I asked, "You saw?"

"Yeah," she replied sadly.

"I don't really want to talk about it." I really didn't. What the fuck was I meant to say? *Oh, yeah, it was my daddy. He's been negotiating my prenup to Shel. You know... the girl who just tore you apart for being poor? Well, her.* I never wanted Molly messed up in the shit between my parents and me, never wanted her to be on the receiving end of their crap; hell, I never even wanted them to know of Molly's existence—she was too important to me to put in that kind of situation.

"Okay. Just answer one thing. Was it your parents?" she asked carefully, snapping me back to the here and now.

"Yes," I finally admitted.

She squeezed me tighter around the waist for a few seconds, then moved back and peered out the window, no more questions about my folks.

"Why are we here?" Her eyebrows drew together as she took in the sprawling mall.

Getting out of the truck and helping Molly down, I said, "We're getting you some new glasses. Come on."

I tried to set off toward the ophthalmologist, but she dug in her heels and jerked me to a halt. Staring me down with steely resolve, she blurted, "Romeo, I can't afford them yet."

This wasn't happening! Meeting her determined gaze, I repeated, "I'm getting them. Now come on!" She stood rooted to the spot, and I began to lose it again. I wanted to help her, dammit, but her stubborn ass was being all proud and shit. I just wanted to look after her—what was a few hundred bucks to make her life infinitely easier at school?

"Romeo, I'm not a charity. I'll get my own bloody glasses when I've saved up enough money. You won't buy them for me. I won't let you. Being poor doesn't embarrass me—taking pity money does!"

I groaned and pulled her to me, loving the way lust blossomed in her eyes every time her body met mine. "Molly, don't fuckin' push me on this. I indirectly broke the damn glasses with my bad pass. I riled up Shelly by showing everyone that I liked you, and I let her ego get too inflated by putting up with her queen-of-all-Bama shit for the last three years. I'm getting you new glasses and you're going to let me. You don't have a fuckin' choice. It's not about embarrassment; it's about protecting what's mine." Her pupils dilated as she stared up at me. Yeah, she may be pissed at my pushy tone, but I wouldn't back down. She was mine and I wouldn't let her be called out for anything... by anyone.

Molly went all quiet but never flinched from my gaze. We were glaring, both refusing to submit. Groaning in exasperation, I grabbed her hair in my hands, leaned in, and asked harshly, "You get me?"

Golden eyes widened slightly at my aggressive move and, with a gentle shake of her head, followed by an amused smile, she whispered, "I get you."

Damn right she did.

Fucking Molly Shakespeare, giving in and relinquishing the control, giving me what I needed, what I craved. Fuck. Me. I wanted her so damn much it was painful.

Feeling a weird burst of something in my chest, I kissed her head and led her into the mall.

14

"My God, Rome, it's amazing," Molly whispered as she surveyed my hidden spot with the biggest fucking smile on her face. Thanks to her new contact lenses, I could see how brightly her eyes were sparkling, and her happy, beautiful face was taking my damn breath away.

Taking her hand, I led her down to the creek. This place was my haven, the only spot where no one bothered me. My folks owned acres of land but never set foot on most of it. I'd never shared this place with anyone before, never had the urge. I did now though. Molly needed to see this place; something within me just knew she'd love it.

"Okay, now you seriously have to tell me where we are. It's possibly the prettiest place on Earth," she said as we sat under the large oak beside the water.

Here goes nothing. With a deep sigh, I said, "It's the creek at the back of my parents' place."

Her brows furrowed. "Your parents' place?" I watched her throat take a huge swallow and apprehension shaded her features.

Craning her neck, she checked out every direction, every seemingly never-ending field. "They own all of this?" Her voice had weakened, and I could see that the realization of my family's wealth was hitting home.

Praying she didn't let this revelation change anything, I lay back, reluctantly admitting, "It's a plantation, Mol."

Her huge eyes were almost comical. "Plantation? Your parents own an entire plantation?"

My folks didn't even friggin' use it right—as a farm— they just wanted the biggest damn lot in Tuscaloosa. Total showboating.

Glancing back up at Mol, I could see her gaze was nervous as she checked out the surroundings.

Laughing slightly, I assured her. "Relax, they won't know we're even here. I come here all the time. It's where I get away from it all."

She tilted her head, staring at me with a disbelieving look.

"What?"

"This. You. A plantation. We're from completely different worlds." Catching the flicker of doubt in those brown eyes, I grabbed her hand, kissing it, and said, "This isn't me, believe me. If only you knew… All this belongs to my parents, not me. I'm just the same me and you're just you—Romeo and Molly Juliet."

The smile tugging on those damn full lips almost had me tackling her to the floor. "Come here," I demanded, pulling her to lie on the grass beside me. A giggle escaped her mouth as I did so. I couldn't take my eyes off her face.

Fuck, she was amazing.

Without thinking it through, I blurted, "I can't believe how beautiful you look with those lenses in. Your eyes are the strangest golden color… I'm having to try real hard to stop myself from touching you the way I want to."

That damn thumb of hers went to her mouth and I growled low in my throat, my cock springing to life. We were alone; I wanted her, the need to take her how I wanted—under my terms—beginning to take hold. She'd fucked one guy in her life and, by her own admission, didn't like it. And my style—when it came to sex—well, it wasn't exactly all romantic gestures and loving caresses. I was scared shitless that showing her that side of me could ruin it all.

And then eight words from her mouth made me snap. "You can touch me if you want to."

Sucking in a breath, like I'd just took a slam in my solar plexus, I warned, "Don't play with fire, Shakespeare. It's too much for a pretty little English girl to cope with."

A shy grin spread across her lips. Christ! I was holding on by a damn thin thread, and by the look of things, she knew it. "What can I say…?" she replied playfully. "I'm a risk taker."

"Mol…" I warned again through painfully clenched teeth. Eyes hooded with lust, my girl lifted onto all fours and began crawling toward me—the geek long gone and a fucking sex kitten taking her place.

She had one last chance to back away before I really let her have it. "Mol…" I cautioned one last time, but she didn't stop, and when she kneeled before me, the smell of vanilla made me lose all sanity. I gripped her bare thigh, never breaking eye contact, and smoothed my hand farther up the skin, right up until my fingers ran along the line of her panties.

Molly's warm breath panted quickly through pursed lips and, leaning down, she brushed them against my mouth. It was too soft, too little contact, but I let her set the pace. She was still pretty inexperienced and I didn't want to come on too strong. But when her hand moved down my stomach, tucked into my jeans, and almost brushed the tip of my cock, I fucking lost it—the time for chivalry and patience was long gone. I was going to make her come, watch her guard fall down, and enjoy every damn second.

Gripping the flesh of her thighs, I spread her across my crotch, her tits pressed right against my chest, my hand wrapped tightly around the back of her neck. My mouth smashed furiously against hers and, taking advantage of her position, I ground my hard dick right between her legs, letting my desire override anything else.

Massaging the soft flesh of her breast in my hand, I pressed farther against her mouth, then moved my hand to her pussy, and hearing her moan out load in desperation for my touch drove me crazy. She was more than liking what I was giving her, how I was giving it to her… doing it the way I needed it to be.

"Romeo…" She moaned in aroused frustration, those newly exposed eyes rolling as I ghosted my finger against her cotton-covered clit.

"Mol… I… I…" I wanted to tell her how I was feeling, but I was fighting against a lifelong-scarred blockage in my throat.

"Please…" she moaned again, pressing herself hard against my hand.

"Mol… God… you're making me fuckin' crazy…" I hissed out, biting into her exposed shoulder, trying to calm down.

"Rome… now!" she demanded, which just plain ol' pissed me off.

Taking her by surprise, I ripped her panties aside and brought her mouth to mine, shutting her the hell up, and impaled her tight hole with my finger. I worked her back and forth, feeling the heat build and the tightness of her inner walls clench.

I broke away from her, and she stared at me, couldn't take those eyes off me. "Don't ever tell me what to do," I said firmly.

Crooking my fingers just right, I skimmed the pad of my middle finger across that soft spot I knew would make her scream, teasing her, making her want more. "Do you hear me?" I barked again, the need to control my girl taking over every cell in my body. At this point, I'd gone too far to hide the real me.

"Yes. Yes," she moaned, pushing down harder on my finger,

Fuck. She was perfect, a natural fit—openly receptive to my roughness. I'd never allowed myself to be like this with any of my random fucks, was never sober enough to care enough to try. But right here, right now, it was everything—full and utter disclosure of who I was.

My attention was fixed on Molly's every sigh, every contraction of her hot center, and the flush covering every inch of her bare, tanned skin. Then those eyes opened and, licking and biting her bottom lip, her hand crept down to my jeans. My cock twitched at the thought of her hand wrapped around the base, stroking the tip, but I froze and croaked painfully, "Mol, no, you don't—" My words lodged in my throat as her soft hand folded around my dick and gently began to stroke it up and down.

Shit. It felt too good to make her stop.

"Let me take care of you. Let me give you what you need. Please…" she begged, still rolling her damn hips against my hand.

Meeting her eyes, I was lost, blinded by her. There were no sounds apart from our ragged breaths and moans amongst the miles of rural cropland, and nothing else registered but the fucking insane pleasure we were giving each other. Actually, that was a lie. I was feeling a ton, probably too much to be revealed to my girl right now. I'd never felt anything this real before, and I needed time to digest it myself.

"Ah, Romeo… I…" Molly rode me faster, her pussy clamping down as I focused on her G-spot with my fingers and her clit simultaneously.

She was burning hot. By her rock-hard nipples, flushed face, and heavy eyes, I knew she was about to come, hard. "Let go, Mol... fuckin' let go," I instructed, and with one more thrust, she cried out loudly. I wanted to devour her screams so I smashed her lips to mine, her hand unrelenting on my cock as she hit her peak.

At the sight of her letting go, my balls tightened and, quickly lifting Mol, I rolled my hips to the side, groaning as streams of cum spread onto the grass beside me. She slowly moved her hand, but I didn't withdraw my finger from within her, wasn't ready to. I didn't want this addicting feeling to end.

The reality of what just happened between us sank in. Mol leaned forward and I kissed and nipped at her damp skin. My finger gently stroked against her clit, her breath hitching when it all became too much, too sensitive.

Leaning back from the safety of my embrace, she smiled shyly. Damn, she was beautiful.

"Hey, Mol," I whispered, my hand raking through a loose piece of hair in front of her face.

"Hey, you," she murmured back, but she was giving nothing away. In fact, she was being *too* shy. I instantly began to panic that I'd been too rough, too aggressive for her.

Fuck, was she hurt?

"You okay?" I asked tersely, every muscle fiber tensed for her response.

Her caramel eyes focused on the ground and shame surged through me—I knew the way I was—no holds barred—was pretty fucked up, probably too much for someone like Molly to understand.

But then she spoke, almost knocking me to the floor in shock. "More than okay."

"Look at me," I snapped out immediately. And fuck, she did… Right away.

Searching her eyes, I asked, "You liked that? You liked how I spoke to you, how I ordered you?"

She met my intense stare but didn't say a damn word. Shifting in nerves, I demanded again, "Mol, you did like it… didn't you?"

Fuck. The thought of losing her crushed me, my voice catching with emotion.

Stroking a finger down my face, her expression filled with affection, she whispered, "I did, Romeo. I-I didn't know that I'd like it… like that… but… I think we both know I did."

Muscles stretched, lips spread, and I knew I was fucking smiling—hell, not smiling, beaming. Needing another chance to touch her, I gripped her hands, waggling my brows, and ran them down my ribs. A questioning smile tugged at her lips.

"Are they all there?" I asked, loving feeling this free—light enough to joke, watching her lips purse in confusion, not following my meaning.

"What?"

"My ribs. Is there one missing?"

Careening forward and holding my waist, she muttered in amusement, "Okay, I think you've lost it. You think you're missing a rib?"

"Just thought God took one of mine when he made you." I knew that sounded lame, but fuck, I sucked at romance, and a girl like my Mol, well, she should have the best said to her, the most romantic words written about her. I didn't have that in me, couldn't give her what she deserved... but I was fortunate enough that she wanted me regardless, and *finally*, all them damn years at Sunday School were coming in useful. Hell, the way I was feeling right now, I'd stand dead center in Bryant-Denny and spout fucking poetry if it made her smile.

"Romeo, at times you're really sweet, you know that?"

Sweet? Fine, I'd take that. "Only for you."

Molly took my hand in hers and, pressing lazy kisses on my palm, got lost in her thoughts. Her eyes glazed with worry and she licked along her bottom lip.

Something was definitely up.

"What you thinking?"

"When you say you like to order, just how far does that need to dominate go?" she blurted, her face flushing red with either nerves or embarrassment. I wasn't sure.

I couldn't help it, but I burst out laughing. Fuck! She thought I wanted to tie her to a damn bed and whip the shit out of her? Mmm... I could see how it would be enticing, but it wasn't exactly my thing.

Facing Molly once again, her bastard teasing thumbnail back in her mouth, I assured her, "I'm not a sadist, so you can take that look off your pretty face. I just like to be in control... I don't know... It's how I am. There are some pretty shitty things in my life that I can't have power over so I need it with the things I'm good at. I just need the

177

assurance that I'm in charge. I'm a good QB because I like to lead, run the show. It's the same with sex."

Tipping my chin, I urged her to respond.

Swallowing hard, she whispered, "I liked how you took control. I'm so used to having to be independent and self-sufficient, always making the decisions, and I hate it. That felt... freeing to give myself over to you, to hand over the reins."

Wrapping her in my arms, I jolted her right into my chest, my possessive desperation for her stronger than ever before. "You're mine now, Mol. You know that, right? I've never had anyone respond to me like you do—every move, kiss, and stroke—full and complete surrender of yourself." I worked a finger again, still inside her. I needed to see her come again. But this time she'd be coming as mine, full disclosure... I owned her now and she, in turn, me.

"Yes, I'm yours," she panted, slamming her hips down, then rolling back and forth. I worked her good, and I almost came myself as she exploded with a loud scream, thighs tightening almost painfully against my hand with her orgasm, then slumping against my chest, completely spent.

After a few minutes of silence, her breathing evened out and I smiled, realizing she'd fallen asleep in my arms. Staring at the blue creek, something happened. With Molly wrapped in my protective embrace, accepting me on every level, my issues, my need for control, my priorities shifted. Everything changed for me in that second, and my girl was now right at the top.

15

We watched the sunset together.

That's right, me, Rome fucking Prince, woke a girl up who was dozing in my arms to watch a damn sunset... and it was friggin' incredible. I'd never known such peace before. I'd never known such happiness. I'd always known a rough life with my folks, but until Shakespeare came into my life, I'd never really stopped to think about just how fucked up it all was.

How fucked up *I* was.

My girl was tight in my arms, and I wanted to know more about her, about her family, wanted to know her more than anyone before. Shit. As far as I could tell, she'd had it bad in her twenty years. Where I had folks I wished would disappear, Molly would give anything to have hers back. She'd never told me how her daddy died, so not really thinking it through, I asked, and fuck, but I didn't expect the answer she gave.

"… I remember it like it was yesterday. I came home from school and my grandma was upset and sat in the front room. She told me that my daddy had been taken to heaven." She laughed, but it wasn't in amusement. I could feel her tense and knew it came from a place of real pain. "At the time I thought I was being punished for being a bad child. It soon became clear that he hadn't died of an illness or because God was punishing me, but he got up as usual, saw me, his little girl, out of the door for school, got into the bath, and slit his wrists with a razorblade."

Fuck. Me. I never expected that. What the hell do you say to a person whose father had killed himself in such a way?

"Shit, baby. I didn't think… I'm so sorry."

She went on to tell me how she struggled daily with his choice, why he did it. She told me about how she coped when her grandma died, and damn if I didn't have to fight a lump in my throat at the thought of my girl alone, nursing her grandma on her own, then the only person she loved dying in her arms. I couldn't help but picture the minutes that followed her grandma's death—how she would've been feeling, the quiet, the slam of realization that she was on her own in the world.

Molly had been fourteen when she lost her last remaining relative—four-fucking-teen. I knew I was gripping onto her too tightly, but looking up at me with those golden browns, she just smiled and laid a kiss on my mouth. She was so damn strong.

As she talked of her stint in foster care, I momentarily felt pissed at her father. Yeah, it's wrong to think ill of the dead, but for three years she'd been forced to endure loneliness in a stranger's home and had to throw herself into the only thing she loved—studying—to survive. But, hell, I didn't know him, didn't know his deal, so I felt I shouldn't judge. It was scary, though, how much her life in those years was like a reflection on mine—always alone, throwing ourselves into our passions as a distraction, and using it like a lifeline to get the hell out of the mess, even if it was temporarily.

"When I was seventeen, I passed my exams early, got into university a year young, and was offered an advanced place at Oxford." I snapped out of my own thoughts and listened intently once again. "I got my degree and came here. I'll move somewhere else for my doctorate."

That stilled me… friggin' scared the shit out of me too. She never stayed in one place too long.

"So you run?"

Breaking the calm we'd been sitting in, Molly grasped my arms, trying to pry my grip from around her waist. There wasn't a fucking chance I was letting go.

"Don't struggle. Answer the question," I bit out more forcefully.

"You have no idea what my life has been like! You don't get to judge!" she screamed.

"I'm not judging you. But you run from your problems, don't you?"

"So what? I don't have a real home, no family. Why not?"

181

"That may have been true before, but now you have people who care for you, truly care for you. I won't let you run away from me."

I needed her to believe in those words, believe in *me*. Now I had her, there was no way in hell I was letting go, and her running from me when times get rough was unacceptable.

I wasn't naïve. I knew being with Molly was going to cause a bucket load of problems with my folks. Well, that's if they ever found out, which I would avoid at all costs.

Still attempting to pull away, I put my mouth to her ear. "I won't let you leave me." All the fight drained from her small body. It was the first time I'd ever seen her heavy emotional guard crack.

Molly broke. The floodgates opened and she cried and cried, unable to stop for several minutes. I rocked her until her sobs died. It could've been minutes, hours, days, and when the only sounds were a few stuttered sighs or an odd sniffle, I asked, "Why did you run from Oxford to here?"

Her head pressed back into my chest, and I laid kiss after kiss on her forehead.

"Oliver wanted more from me. He stayed on to do his PhD and wanted to take things further. I didn't—he knew nothing about me. I never told him.

"After we slept together, I knew I couldn't do it anymore. I thought being intimate with him would help me get closer, that it would bring my walls crashing down. But all I felt was strangling disappointment. I thought I was unable to ever be close to another person again. In the end, I freaked. I ran. Simple. He woke up and I was gone. I haven't spoken to him since."

Knowing that some British punk bastard had my girl naked, pinned beneath him, him coming within her, made anger pulse in my veins. I couldn't speak. It was like I was possessed, and for a moment, the severity of that possession scared me. The girl was friggin' bewitching me.

By the fidgeting of Molly's body, I knew she wanted me to say something, but I couldn't, couldn't cope with the thought of her with someone else. Eventually she settled down, accepting my inability to speak, and with a reassuring sigh, she confessed, "That was until you. I'm close to you. I let you in. Maybe I'm not as damaged as I thought."

Jesus. Those words did something to me deep inside, like a bolt of electricity billowed through my body. She was close to me; she let me in. I was an undeserving motherfucker, completely worthless—I'd been told so all my life—but that only made what she said that much more special. To her, I was worthy.

Feeling on top of the world, I said gently, "You're not the only one who feels like splitting when times get rough, baby, but from now on, I won't let you run anywhere if I'm not right there running beside you."

But then she asked about me, my family, and a jolt of panic ripped through me. How could I tell her my deal? It was beyond fucked up, and I just couldn't do it.

"We should go," I ordered abruptly when I felt her grow cold and shiver with the evening breeze.

Stiffening, she protested. "I don't want to leave yet. I want to know about you."

But I didn't want her to know, didn't want her tarnished by that shit. Molly was now the one part of my life, besides football, my folks had no control over, and I'd be damned if I infected her with that poison.

I was done with any talk of my past, my folks. So pulling her up off the grass, I dodged her questions and led her in silence to the truck.

As I drove, my mind worked in overtime. I tried to find a reason why Molly would want to be with me, memories of my parents telling me how no one would ever love me circling my brain. She didn't give a shit about my money, had no fucking clue about football, and even when she'd seen me play, still didn't seem to care for all the hype. She didn't give two shits about her social standing, didn't care for popularity; she had her own mind, her own goals, none of which would be furthered by me. It only led me to one conclusion, but I just couldn't bring myself to believe it.

"You okay? You seem miles away," Molly asked, taking my hand, looking up at me with that beautiful, open face.

"Yeah."

"You sure? You don't look it." Turning my head to meet her worried gaze, I couldn't speak the words. *Why do you want me? I'm not good enough for you. You should get out now before it's too late.*

"Rome, what is it?" she asked, this time with more insistence.

I cleared my throat and murmured, ashamedly, "I never knew before tonight what it felt like to be wanted... just me for me." I saw the sadness creep onto her face, but I needed to know something for my sanity, so I asked, "What do you want me for, Mol? I'm trying to work it out."

"I just want you," she said, inching closer and pressing into my side, kissing my bare shoulder.

"That's what I don't get. Why would you want me for just me? No one ever has before. I'm pissed twenty-four-seven. I'm possessive and not good with attachments—where's the attraction?"

"Then I'm the first, because I want you without anything in return. Why does any human want anyone? My body recognizes you as something that's good for me. My mind recognizes you as someone who's right for me, and my soul recognizes you as someone who is meant for me."

Sincerity filled every word she said.

I relaxed, embracing the fact that, for the first time in my entire life, I was wanted... just for me. Relishing the satisfaction that was settling in my blood, I whispered, "We're in fucking deep, aren't we, Shakespeare?"

"I think that's an understatement," Molly said with that huge, stunning smile of hers. When I glanced down at her happy face, I didn't think about pulling over and fucking her into next week. I didn't think of what she would taste like writhing on my tongue. I just wanted her beside me, like this, wanting me. So, tilting my head, I ordered, "Come here," and she did, no questions asked, getting me like no one before.

After dropping Mol off at her door, I drove to my frat house, parked, and headed through the front entrance. I passed the TV room, and several of the guys, including Austin, Reece and Jimmy-Don, looked up as I walked in. It already felt weird, not being with Mol and being back with guys… It felt kind of wrong, every cell in my body urging me to go to her again.

Moving to the kitchen, needing a distraction, I opened the fridge and grabbed myself a beer. When I shut the door, Austin was leaning against the island, watching me.

"Eighty-three," I greeted, using his nickname, his jersey number.

"Where the hell have you been? You skipped out of weights tonight. Had to have Reece spot me and that kid is weak!" He seemed kind of pissed.

Leaning against the counter, I shrugged. "Just out."

His eyebrows drew in. "You've been with that British chick, Molly, haven't you?"

I tensed. Austin caught it and smirked. "Heard you caused quite the scene in the cafeteria, tearing into Shelly, then dragging out the girl and driving off with her in your truck. The guys didn't know what the hell to make of it all. You, acting all crazy over that chick."

I busied myself with tearing the label off the beer bottle, not saying a damn thing in response.

"Rome!" Austin said and I looked up to see him, arms spread, waiting for a response. Dammit. Molly didn't want me saying shit to anyone about us as a couple, hell, but I wasn't going to break that promise, so taking my bottle, I backed out of the room without a word.

I climbed the stairs to my room, locked my door, and sat on the end of my unmade bed, sipping on my beer and thinking of my girl. My cock hardened as I remembered her grinding down on my hand, her mouth dropped open as I marked her as mine.

Reaching down, I slipped my hand into my jeans and began to stroke my dick up and down, running my thumb along the tip just like she did. But it just didn't feel the same, so I pumped it harder, doing it rough, just how I usually liked.

Nothing. Nothing felt like what Mol made me feel tonight, and I was desperate to have it again.

Removing my hand from my jeans and groaning in frustration, I lay back on my bed and closed my eyes. I wondered what she was doing right now? Was she thinking of me too? Of tonight? Was she horny as fuck, trying to feel that pleasure again?

The thought had me jumping to my feet.

Fuck it. I wasn't sitting here all night, obsessing about touching her, when she was just across the street. Intense or not, I was sleeping beside her from now on.

Swiping my keys and wallet off the table, I ran down the stairs, almost taking out Austin in the hallway as I passed.

He eyed me in surprise, then folded his arms, smirking. "Let me guess. You're going *out*?"

Huffing a laugh, I punched his shoulder. "You know it." He threw his head back, laughing too, and carried on up the stairs.

Within minutes I'd reached Mol's sorority house and, picking up a handful of stones from the lawn in the backyard, began pelting them against her balcony doors. Seconds later, her doors flew open and she looked down, smiling, and I couldn't help but grin in return. I quickly climbed the trellis, and seeing her standing before me on her balcony in only a tiny purple nightdress, her tits and tiny panties pretty much on show through the semi-sheer fabric, I knew I'd made the right choice in showing up.

Gripping her waist, I brought her straight into my arms. "I got back to the frat house and I immediately wondered what you were doing. I decided to stop wondering and just come find out."

Tucking her arms around my back, tilting up her chin so I could see her, she teased, "You just want to stay again, don't you? You planning on making this a regular thing?"

"Oh, you can count on that, baby. After today, I'm now entitled to certain privileges."

Fuck. This felt good—so fucking good.

"Really? And what are they?" she asked with an arch of her brow.

"You'll find out in due course, Shakespeare. Now move that fine ass, get into bed and into my arms."

And hell, she did as I instructed but looked back as she crawled on her mattress on her hands and knees, showing me a glimpse of her tight, curvy ass. "I don't remember Romeo being this pushy with Juliet!"

My cock showed its appreciation of her position, and I had to restrain myself from slamming into her from behind. "And look at how that worked out for them. My way is better—less death, more orgasms."

She burst into laughter and I pointed her way and instructed, "You. Bed. Now."

I quickly stripped down to my boxers and strode to the bed, getting in beside her, watching her golden eyes drinking in my every muscle.

Immediately kissing and licking the side of her neck, I reached around and plunged my fingers straight into her panties. God, she was so hot, wet and ready for me.

A shocked loud moan came straight from her mouth, causing me to slide my fingers into her warmth, murmuring, "Now about those privileges…"

Mol's back arched and she reached her arm up and wrapped it around my neck, rocking against my hand.

I was never leaving this damn bed again…

16

Training the next morning was the best I'd had this season. I never missed a pass, made new PBs in my weight routines, and every snap I popped was perfect.

Coach came over, smiling widely, exclaiming, "Whatever the hell got you out of your slump, Bullet— hell, keep doing it! We'll be getting another national championship for sure if you keep training like this!"

Showering quickly, feeling pretty damn good, I dressed and arranged to meet with Austin and Reece for lunch in a few hours. As I left through the gym doors to head to my Business class, I spotted Shelly leaning against the fence outside the stadium, waiting, I assumed, for me.

Stopping dead in my tracks, I tipped my head back, groaning. I prepared myself to breeze straight past her, but then I saw her face. It looked so friggin' miserable that I couldn't help but soften a fraction. I knew I treated her like shit most of the time, but there was a time when we'd been friends. We'd grown up together, been forced to go to every damn prom and cotillion together, and I'd even liked her—as a friend—for a while. But then the pressure from our folks to be together became insane and we'd drifted apart. Or at least I'd drifted; she just became crazed with the need to stick in her claws. She wanted the life that was waiting for her, that was being dangled on a string before her eyes.

I knew seeing me with different chicks over the years had killed her. God, even the thought of another guy besides me touching Mol would have me spitting mad, so, for the first time in a long time, I actually felt sorry for her. She was failing in her duty just as much as I was, and although Martin Blair wasn't as fucked up as my daddy, he wasn't exactly easy-going either.

I reluctantly walked over to where she stood—head down, arms folded—and greeted her, "Shel."

As she lifted her head, I could see she'd been crying.

"Hey, Rome," she croaked.

"What's wrong?"

Staring into the distance, she shrugged. "I just wanted to apologize for yesterday. I hated how you spoke to me in the cafeteria. I know I probably deserved it, I was in a bad mood, but… it's just… just…" She cupped her hands over her face and her shoulders began to shudder with sobs.

Clenching my jaw, I looked around us before awkwardly laying a hand on her shoulder. "Shel, calm down."

She moved forward, pressing her face into my chest, and I stiffened before patting her back a few times in comfort. I spotted some of the team walking past, throwing me suggestive gestures or knowing smiles. Most of the team would have her in a heartbeat. But I'd never felt it. Damn, it would've made my life a hell of a lot easier if I had.

Taking a step back, Shelly looked up at me, smiling in embarrassment. "Sorry about all this."

Shaking my head in dismissal of her apology, I replied, "What's up?"

"My daddy and I had a fight… over you."

Raking my hands through my hair, I cursed to myself. "What happened?"

"Daddy said it was my fault you were refusing the marriage, that I hadn't tried hard enough to be your girl. He said he only wants you to take his place at Prince Oil to keep it in the family, and if you don't, he wouldn't be able retire as planned, and he already has a heart condition and said that he'd end up working himself to death."

Shit. I couldn't imagine Mr. Blair being that harsh—he adored Shelly—but fuck, look at my folks. People are completely different when the world doesn't see.

"Shel, I'm sorry. If it helps, I know how you feel, okay?"

Sniffing, she looked up at me and smiled. "Yeah, I know."

A few moments of uncomfortable silence passed, then, suddenly, she moved in, throwing her arms around my neck and pressing her lips against mine. It only took me a second to realize what was going on, and, gripping her arms, I ripped her off me, shouting, "What the fuck, Shel?!"

"I just… just… Why don't you want me? Everyone else at this damn college does, but not you! Not the great *Romeo Prince*!" I stiffened as she said that name. Only Mol could get away with calling me that.

"Calm the fuck down, now," I said flatly.

Taking a deep breath, she seemed to mellow out. "I just don't get you. You have this perfect life mapped out for you, richer than you could dream, but you choose to fight it all the way, and for what? For football—a career that will last, what? Maybe ten, fifteen years if you're lucky. If you don't get on board with the plan, I don't get that life either, and it's all I've ever wanted… I don't know what else to do to make you change your mind!"

"Well, sorry, Shel, but I'm not marrying you. And that's the end of it." I folded my arms across my chest to keep my control.

A cold expression drifted across her face. "Face it, Rome. This marriage has to happen. The quicker you accept it, the better everything will be."

"All this, this little performance, was all fake, wasn't it?" I hissed through gritted teeth. "You haven't fallen out with your daddy?"

"No, believe me, it happened, *keeps* happening, and I'm sick of it! I thought if maybe you saw what your stubbornness was doing to me you'd reconsider. It'd be a piece of paper. It wouldn't even have to be a real marriage. Just, please, I'm begging you, change your mind!"

"I can't, Shel. Things are different for me now."

Her eyes narrowed. "It's because of her, isn't it?"

"Who?" I answered, feigning confusion.

"Molly!" I could see the disbelief on her face and she snapped, "Whatever, Rome. The sooner you get over your little obsession with that nerdy horror show, the better it'll all be. We all see how you watch her. It's friggin' weird if you ask me. People have been talking, and just so you know, I'm going to tell your folks, and we both know they won't be happy."

Fuck! I never wanted Mol to have to deal with my parents, but Shelly was playing hardball, and by threatening to tell my folks, she'd just started a fucking dangerous game. One thing made me feel better, though, and that was the knowledge that apparently everyone already saw my interest in Mol, knew I was gone over the girl. Perfect. No need to keep it a secret anymore, then.

Leaning down to Shelly, I warned quietly, "You stay the fuck away from me, you hear? Molly too, for that matter."

"You're choosing wrong, Rome."

"The hell I am! You know, Shel, you weren't always such a bitch. What happened to the happy-go-lucky girl I knew when we were kids?"

She seemed to choke on a bitter laugh. "The same thing that happened to the kind little boy you once were… *life!* We're both pawns, Rome, and we both have our parts to play."

Hell, that hit home. I suppose, in a way, we were the same, both jaded. But it didn't change anything.

I abruptly turned as fast as possible before things got out of hand, hearing the click of Shelly's heels as she stalked angrily away. The sooner she saw Mol on my arm, where she belonged, the better. My girl would hate me for it, making us so public, but by end of classes today, the whole damn campus would know she was mine. No more hiding, no more pretending we didn't belong to each other.

Just as I was about to enter my business class, a text came through on my cell. I braced, expecting it to be from my daddy over Shelly, maybe over Molly, but it was Ally.

Al: Make a habit of climbing down balconies???

Closing my eyes, I sighed. My cousin knew.
Oh well. One person less to tell…

"You want to go out for food? I have a hankering for Mexican," Reece asked, as I met him and Austin outside the Business building at lunch.

"Nah, let's head to the cafeteria," I answered and set off walking, slipping on my shades.

"Why we eating there again?" he whined. Austin rolled his eyes at Reece and his pissy attitude before slapping him upside the head.

"Something I need to do," I replied.

"In the cafeteria?" Reece asked once more, a confused scowl on his face as he rubbed his head.

"Yeah! Or the quad. Quit bitchin' and come on!"

Austin stepped beside me, leaving Reece trailing behind us, sulking like a toddler, and hushed, "What the fuck you up to? I know that look on your face, Rome. You're planning something."

"Yeah. Something I should've done a while ago." Austin eyed me curiously but stayed quiet as he kept pace beside me.

We strode through the quad; the place was teeming with people. The weather was still pretty damn hot, and everyone was taking advantage of it before winter set in.

Halfway down the path, I spotted Jimmy-Don, Cass, Ally, and Lexi on the grass. Cass momentarily leaned away from Jimmy-Don and that's when I saw Molly, sitting opposite them, smiling at something they were saying. She was stunning, and a bolt of happiness hit me as I watched her all relaxed, hanging with her friends.

I was vaguely aware that people were watching the three of us walk by. They always gawked at the football team, but I didn't pay any attention to them, too busy looking at my girl.

The moment she lifted her eyes from her friends, our gazes met. A tiny smile set on her face. I knew what I was about to do would embarrass the fuck out of her. For a moment I questioned if it was the right thing to do, but I decided to stick to the plan… It needed to be done.

"What you doing over here with us?" Jimmy-Don asked as we approached.

No one expected the answer I was going to give, but, honing in on Molly's gaze, I could see that she'd realized what I was about to do. "Just seeing my girl."

Molly's mouth dropped in shock. I sat down, pulled her onto my lap, and moved in for a kiss. I fucking owned her with that kiss, showing the world that we were together.

Pulling back, both of us breathless, I asked, "How are you today, baby?"

I braced myself for her to be pissed, but when she beamed and answered, "I'm good. Great, actually," I knew I'd done the right thing. She was happy for everyone to know about us, and it was the best damn feeling in the world.

"Well, I guess that answers my question of whether he likes you!" Cass let her loud mouth go, but I couldn't be pissed as my girl relaxed back into my arms.

I met Ally's gaze for a spilt second, and she winked. I knew she'd be pissed that I didn't tell her about us, but I could see she was happy for me regardless. She loved Mol to pieces; they'd quickly become best friends. She was the one girl Ally wouldn't give me shit over being with.

"Yesterday at the cafeteria, I thought something wasn't quite adding up. We all know Bullet don't do relationships, so I thought he was just being weirdly nice. But the contact lenses, Molls going missing for hours... totally makes sense now!" Cass went on, her voice getting more animated with every word she spilled. I knew my reputation, knew Molly's friends would probably worry I wasn't going to do right by her. I needed to show how much she meant to me.

"This is different. We're together, a couple, right, Shakespeare?" I said to Molly, laying kisses all over her face.

Blushing and lowering her long lashes, she agreed, "Yeah. We're together."

I pressed a kiss on the side of her neck, and she lay back against my chest. I could see the students around staring, completely shocked, but I loved it, loved people knowing I was actually in a relationship.

Reece was like a statue watching my girl and me, the horny fucker probably grieving over the fact he could no longer have my weekly castoffs. Beside him, Austin tilted his chin knowingly. Yeah, I guess I'd kind of given it away the other night, but he seemed good with it, even happy for me. Lexi, however, snapped at Molly for not telling her sooner, but she got over it and then couldn't take that damn giddy smile off her too-white face.

As we chatted, I caught several of my old conquests scowling and making fun of Molly from a distance, and my anger was gradually building. But when that basketball cunt, Michaels, the guy who hated me most, saw us, a cruel grin spread across his face. Fuck. He'd been waiting to stir shit with me for months, and he'd just been given the perfect opportunity.

I promised myself if he even came within a few feet of us, I would tear out his fucking heart.

Him and me were going to throw down at some point; that was a fact. It was just a matter of when, and the way he was looking at me, at my girl, it seemed like it was going to be today.

Michaels got to his feet, and I tensed, Molly's gaze shooting to mine as she sensed my unease. I watched every move he made, and my blood boiled when I saw him turn purposely to the path that led right by our group.

When Michaels reached us, he laughed, right in Mol's face, and said, "Fuck, Bullet, I don't believe my fuckin' eyes! You gave up all the pussy on campus for that? Tell me, does she at least suck your cock good?"

That? *That?* Was he for real? Mol was becoming everything to me and he had the audacity to stand there and shred her to pieces… in front of me! Letting my anger take hold, I picked up Mol and, moving her aside, got to my feet and tackled the fucker to the floor, ramming my fist straight into his face. A deep sense of satisfaction spread across my chest as I watched blood burst from his nose, but the asshole just didn't know when to stop.

"Time for payback, Bullet. I'm going to fuck your girl, see how you like it."

Edging forward, my arm pressed against his neck, and I hissed, "Like you'd even get a chance. She'd never fuck you, never even give a creep like you the time of day."

Smiling, his mouth full of blood, he whispered back, "Never say never. You'll mess up—you always do—and when that time comes, it'll be me that fucks her so hard that she'll forget you even existed."

I saw red and pounded his face, kneeing at his ribs repeatedly. Pausing momentarily, I threatened, "Don't you fuckin' dare talk about Mol like that again. You get me, asshole?"

But he just grinned and coughed out, "The geek ain't shit to look at, but she clearly fucks good if she's tamed your ass. Does she? Does she fuck like a seasoned whore?"

I lifted my arm to finally knock him out, when someone grabbed onto my wrist. When I looked back, Molly was behind me, fear in her eyes.

My stomach sank.

"Romeo, don't," she begged.

A war broke out within me. Michaels needed to pay for talking about my girl like that, but the way she was looking at me, like I was letting her down, was killing me.

Michaels laughed, and my decision was made. "Get the fuck back, Mol," I ordered and pushed her away. She let go of my arm, and my attention refocused on the smug face below me.

I lifted my arm again, but Mol suddenly shouted, "Romeo, stop. Now. You're better than this!"

Wincing at her words, I stalled, Michaels taking advantage to sneer, "Yeah, *Romeo*, stop. Listen to your girl."

With one last glance at Molly and her devastated face, I sagged. What the fuck was I doing? Here I was trying to be better for her, be what she deserved, so I would listen and back away this time.

But only for her.

Looking down at Michaels, I spat, "You're lucky I don't cave your fuckin' skull in, but I won't do it in front of my girl."

I stood abruptly and, seeing Molly behind me, racked with nerves, I held her to my chest, breathing in the vanilla on her skin, using it to simmer the hell down.

Glancing up, I saw Michaels being lifted off the floor by his teammates, and he brought two fingers to his mouth and spread them open, flicking his tongue toward Molly's back. It took all the strength I had not to go after him, the pervert.

"Fuck off, Michaels, and get outta my sight before I change my fuckin' mind and end you!" I shouted, commending his friends for dragging his dumb ass away.

I held on to Molly, the motion of her hands on my back gradually calming me down. After a few minutes, I confessed, "I should've beaten him good after what he said." I didn't go any further into the specifics, couldn't bring myself to repeat them.

Pulling back and meeting my eyes, Mol said, "No, you shouldn't have. What would've been the point? We both knew that you being in an 'official' relationship was going to cause some talk."

"Yeah, but he's had it coming for a long time, babe. He fuckin' deserves a good beat down."

I could see her thinking, always fucking thinking. Staring me straight in the eye, she asked, "Why was he so hostile towards you in the first place?"

Shit! I never wanted my past to affect her. I was so ashamed of the way I'd been living before she came into my life.

"What?" she asked, swallowing in apprehension at my refusal to speak.

"I... I—" Dammit! I couldn't tell her... She'd hate me, be ashamed.

Golden eyes clouded and she pressed, "You what?"

I panicked. I didn't want what we'd just found with each other to be put in jeopardy. I needed her to still want me the same as this morning, as last night.

"Just spit it out, Rome," she said, but this time with much more force.

Focusing on the ground, I admitted, "I fucked his girl a few months back."

Looking back up, I could see the disappointment in her expression and she stepped back, hands out in dismissal, rejecting me.

Fucking Michaels!

"Now you're pissed at me. I'm totally kicking his ass now!"

I couldn't take that look of censure in her eyes, but when I turned to go, a soft hand gripped mine. "Leave him," she whispered quietly.

"You're pissed, aren't you?"

"Well, I'm not exactly doing backflips on hearing that you shagged his girlfriend, am I?"

A whole load of hurt was evident in her voice, but her speaking to me so shittily, on top of everything so far today, really pissed me off.

"I'll let that go since you're clearly annoyed, and I suppose justifiably," I said moodily. And then she surprised me again by fucking smirking at me.

She was now finding it all funny? Christ almighty, I had no idea what the hell to think! One minute she was pissed, the next laughing… complete mindfuck.

"Did you hear what he said about you?" I pushed.

Shrugging, she answered, "Yes, but I don't care, never have cared what others thought of me." She was telling the truth; the bland expression on her face told me so.

"Come on, sit down with me a while longer." My girl held out her hand, but I couldn't take it. This kind of treatment was only going to continue. I'd done a lot of shit in the last few years, stuff that I'd give anything to take back at this moment. I needed to put a stop to it.

"Mol, let me just sort the fucker once and for all. It'll send a message to everyone else to leave us be. There are a lot of assholes who I've pissed off that'll enjoy ragging on us being together."

But she wouldn't have it and held out her hand again, nodding sternly for me to take it. She looked so damn cute, being all insistent. I friggin' loved this girl. "Fuck, Mol, I'll be getting a new rep—Rome Prince, newest member of Pussy Whipped-R-Us!"

We sat down under a tree and I held on to Molly tightly. She played with my fingers, softly kissing each one, and I caught our friends watching us, a mix of disbelief and happiness on their faces.

Being with Molly just made me better. She made *everything* in my life better.

"What the hell is this?" My eyes closed in exasperation as I recognized the voice.

"Ahh, fuck off, Shel. I've had enough of dealing with assholes for one day!" Looking up into her eyes, I could see she knew I was referring to our earlier showdown outside the gym.

"Are you seriously with her?" The surprise on her face was comical. She knew I liked Molly; she'd made that clear, maybe even expected me to fuck her, but she obviously never thought that anything had come of it, that she'd become my girl.

Smiling at her shell-shocked face, I leaned down and took Molly's mouth with my own—friggin' went for it, roughly, possessively—showing Shelly and anyone else who was still rubbernecking that she was mine.

Breaking away, I answered, "Yep, I seriously am."

"You know he won't stay with you, don't you, darlin'?" Shelly directed at Mol.

"And why's that?"

"Because Momma and Daddy Prince won't accept a money-grabbin' whore with their son, and they can be real persuasive. They want me and they'll get me, you can count on that." My heart fell at the mention of my folks, it was the one gray area I had with Mol. The one part of my life I'd kept private from her.

"Funny, a money-grabbing whore—that's exactly what Rome said about you." I almost pissed myself in laughter, but when Shelly lunged forward, fury on her face, screaming, "You're nothing! A pure piece of—"

I had to interrupt.

"Shut your evil mouth, and get the fuck on before I do something I regret."

Shelly wisely stepped back from Mol, but when she looked at me, the blood in my veins turned to ice. "I'll give it a month and then we'll see what your folks do. You'll be back in my arms in no time. Your momma's gonna flip!"

In that moment, I knew my time was up. Shelly would tell my folks about me officially being with Mol, and I, quite honestly, didn't know what the hell they would do. Shelly seemed convinced of her plan, though, and that smartass gleam in her eyes caused me to bite out, "I'd never touch you again and wouldn't be with you if you were the last person on Earth. You're a bitter, vindictive bitch. As for my folks, I'm quickly learning to not give a shit what they say anymore. I want Mol and she wants me. End of discussion. Nothing you or my folks do will make a damn bit of difference to change that. Now leave us the fuck alone."

I registered the gossiping around us, so I shouted, "That applies to everyone—leave us the fuck alone or deal with me! The next person who interferes or even breathes wrong in our direction, I won't be so fuckin' lenient with!"

Shelly quickly bailed, and the onlookers turned away. But Mol, Mol was freaking out. She'd gone all quiet, closed in on herself. "Don't listen to her, okay? What she said, they're just words. Don't mistake them for truth."

Without answering me, Mol got up and walked away to sit on her own. She'd gone from complete anonymity to being the subject of the campus rumor mill in a matter of minutes and was obviously not handling it well. The reality of being with me was smacking her right in the face, full force.

I left her on her own for as long as I could manage, then crouched before her, stating, "You've gone all quiet on me, Shakespeare. I don't like it."

"I'm good, baby. Don't worry." She tried to assure me, but I could see through her bullshit. I decided to keep going with the exposure—like a Band-Aid, ripping it off quick, showing as many people as possible that we were together. Then hopefully things would settle down.

We made plans to go out with our friends after this weekend's game, and Molly seemed slightly less tense as I led her to class, her hand in mine. I just prayed that from this point on, our lives would be less… dramatic.

17

"Molly..." *Kiss*. "Baby..." *Kiss*. "Shakespeare..." *Kiss*.

I moved down the bed, pressing soft kisses along Molly's neck, her collarbone, and back up to her pouting mouth.

Groaning, she lifted her hand and pushed me away, bringing the covers back over her body—she wasn't good with early mornings. Cracking open an eye, Mol spotted me, still hovering above her, and buried her head in the pillow.

I couldn't help but laugh, and I ripped down the quilt. "Baby, I'm going. I got practice until this afternoon."

Rolling her head and sighing in defeat, she looked at me, asking, "You'll be gone all day?" as she wiped the sleep from her eyes.

"Yeah, I'll call you later, okay?"

Grinning, she hooked her arm around my neck, bringing me to her mouth. A hand landed on a loop on the waistband of my jeans, and she pulled me on top of her, wrapping her legs around my waist. Using my arms to brace myself above her, I met her mouth hungrily before laughing again against her lips.

"Mmm... I want you," she murmured, gripping onto me like a damn spider monkey.

"I need to go, baby. I gotta get to practice."

"No, you need to stay with me." I reached up to my neck, breaking her grip. She finally opened both eyes and pouted. "Pretty please?" she said in her damn cute accent.

Pinning her arms above her head, I leaned in and nipped at her bottom lip. "If you keep begging me, I will fuck you, Mol, okay? I'll tie you to the damn bed and fuck you... hard. I'm trying to be a gentleman and wait until you're ready, but you're making it damn difficult." Her breath caught, and she arched up to lick the bottom of my throat, causing me to growl in response.

"I'm thinking that sounds pretty good, Rome. I'm starting to wonder what the hell we're waiting for anyway? I'm ready."

That stilled me, and when a teasing friggin' smile spread on her lips, telling me she was joking, I backed off the bed, saying, "Careful, little girl..."

Tucking herself back under the covers, she closed her eyes. "Have fun at practice. I'm going back to sleep to dream naughty dreams about you... and me... and what would've happened if you'd stayed right here instead of going to football to grunt and play with other men." And damn but she did; within seconds she was out, the little temptress, leaving me with a hard-on from hell.

By midday, I was pretty much done. Coach had pushed us all to breaking point, getting us prepped for the game this weekend. Going back to my locker, I grabbed my cell and headphones, needing music for my weights, when a caller flashed on the screen: Momma. I tried to think what the hell she could want. She never talked to me; hell, months could go by and we wouldn't even have said two words to one another.

The call went off, but when she started to call again, I groaned and answered, "Momma?"

"Rome, I need a favor." Straight to the point. But at least there was no pretense when it came to her and me. She had no problem with how she treated me, didn't hide her complete disregard for me as her son.

"Yeah?"

"I need a signed jersey for a charity luncheon I'm hosting tomorrow. I assume you can arrange that?"

"Yeah, I can get it for you. When do you need it by?"

There was a pause, and then she said, "I'm actually going to be at lunch this afternoon. Could you arrange it within the next couple of hours and drop it by?"

"I'm doing weights in the gym now, so that should be okay. Where will you be?"

"*Lorenzo's* downtown. Let's say one thirty?"

"Fine."

And with that, she cut the line, no good-bye or thanks.

I poured out all the tension in my body through my weights. It was always this way when I spoke to my momma. It was like I had some fucked-up Stockholm syndrome or something. I had a drive within me that always did what she asked without argument, always striving for her praise. I literally had no memories of her being attentive, of being loving, no memory I could recall where I'd made her proud. All I had were memories of pain, not physical—no, my daddy was the one who used his fists—but the pain of her hostility toward me, her utter disdain that she had me as her son.

Moving to the free weights to do my set of squats, I couldn't help but remember all the times I'd tried and failed to gain her approval. The earliest memory was Mother's Day when I was about six. My teacher'd had the class creating cards to give to our mommas after school.

I remember going home, excited, hopeful that what I'd done would make her happy. I searched the house from top to bottom and eventually found her in the parlor at the back of our huge house, drinking again. At the time I didn't realize my momma was a drunk.

I ran in, proudly showing the red card, a picture of a heart on the front, the message inside reading "I love you so much, Momma."

I remember her rolling her eyes as I entered the room, asking, "What the hell do you want? I'm busy."

Walking over, smiling wide, convinced that this would be the day she told me she loved me, I presented her the card—I wanted her to know that I loved her too.

Putting her scotch on the tabletop, she took the card and read the message in silence. I held my breath, my heart beating fast with nerves. But then she lifted her head and began laughing and laughing, and I began to cry as she tore the red card in two, throwing the destroyed message to the floor at my feet. At my tears, she just laughed even harder.

Picking up her drink, she stared out of the window, refusing to meet my eyes, and said, "Don't ever make me something like that ever again. It's insulting."

And I never have. I never cried in front of her again after that day either.

Christ. I was six.

Coach suddenly stood before me and pulled my *Beats* headphones from my ears. "Enough, Rome. You're pushing too hard. You don't want to pick up an injury."

Throwing the heavy weighted barbell on the floor, I picked up my towel and hit the showers. The team signed the crimson home jersey and I made my way across town.

I couldn't believe my eyes. As I approached *Lorenzo's* restaurant, planning to make this short and sweet, I immediately spotted my momma outside on the terrace. Sitting next to her was Mrs. Blair and friggin' Shelly on the opposite side, all three of them smiling and laughing—the perfect high society image.

It quickly became apparent that I'd been set up. So, turning slowly, I moved to walk away when I heard, "Rome, where are you going? We're right here!" Taking a deep breath, I turned around to see my momma on her feet, Shelly and Mrs. Blair smiling brightly my way.

211

Keep calm. Play it cool. Get through it, I told myself as I took a second deep, relaxing breath. I didn't want to make a scene, didn't want to make my momma suspicious.

Waving my hand in acknowledgement, I entered the restaurant, freezing when my momma kissed my cheek for show, Shelly and Mrs. Blair following suit. My momma lived the perfect double life: the quintessential society lady on the outside, fucking nightmare on the inside.

"Here's the jersey you asked for," I said, handing it over.

"Perfect! Have a seat," she instructed, gesturing toward the spare chair next to Shel.

Biting my tongue, I reluctantly sat down, playing along, saying, "Didn't realize everyone would be here. Thought I was just dropping that off." I pointed to the jersey, my voice perfectly monotone, not betraying my anger.

My momma leaned forward, eyes tight. "Well, we had an interesting call from Shelly here yesterday. She told us that you made quite the announcement at school. Something about some British transfer you've become... a little *enamored* with?"

I detected the anger, the threat in her voice, and her blue eyes never moved from mine. My heart thumped in my chest, so hard I felt like it was slamming against my ribcage. She knew about Molly, but I'd be damned if I showed that I was bothered. I had to protect her. I needed to throw my momma off the scent.

"Well?" Mrs. Blair pushed, Shelly leaning on the table to hear my response.

Shrugging, I said dismissively, "Yeah, I've been seeing her, casually, but it's not anything serious. You know me. I'm not the monogamous type. She just proved a good distraction for a while. We're done now."

Shelly put her hand on my thigh in excitement. "You mean all this time you've been messing with her? Oh my God, Rome, that's hilarious. The way that girl looks at you, she's obviously in love! She'll be devastated when you end it."

Shelly couldn't help but laugh, and I wanted to kick her off her chair. Her words, however, circled in my mind—*the way that girl looks at you, she's obviously in love.* Was she? Was Mol in love with me?

"That had better be the case, Rome. And all these girls, it needs to stop. Shelly should be your only focus now. You've fooled around long enough, but it's time to grow up, time to act responsibly."

I stayed silent. I wasn't going to get into a conversation with these three vultures about this friggin' ridiculous marriage. My momma would know where I stood on the whole damn farce. I'm sure my daddy would have said something, and I wasn't going to air all that shit out here on this friggin' terrace, in public.

Shelly moved in closer, and I could tell by the look on her face that she'd believed everything I'd just said. It was the only time I was thankful that I'd whored around in my past; my dismissal of Molly was believable 'Bullet' behaviour.

As Shelly placed her hand around my waist, that suffocating feeling crept up my throat, but I had to pretend not to be bothered, even though I felt like overturning the table before me.

Mrs. Blair went on to ask me about football and I gave her some routine answer about wins, practice, and championships. Shelly giggled beside me at fuck knows what and then laid her hand across my chest, planting a damn kiss on my cheek. My jaw clenched at the action, my hands curled into fists. When I looked up, my momma was watching me like a hawk, scowling.

She was on to me. Nothing much got past her and I could practically see the cogs whirring in her head.

"Well, hey, guys! Fancy seeing you here!"

My attention snapped to the side of the restaurant. Ally was standing on the sidewalk, beyond the white fence, arms crossed and glaring at Shelly practically dry-humping my leg.

"Aliyana, always a pleasure," my momma greeted coldly.

"Aunt Kathryn, lovely to see you too," she repeated with equal disdain.

"What you doing here, Al?" I asked, hoping she'd get the message to go away, to not involve herself in this shit.

"Well, I was just out shopping with some *friends*." My heart dropped when I saw the admonishment on her face. "Yeah, Rome, they're *all* just over the street." She turned, pointing to a row of stores, and I saw Cass and Lexi standing in front of Molly. They'd clearly been trying to stop her from seeing. Molly, was staring at me with the most haunted fucking look on her face, her eyes completely focused on Shelly's hand spread on my chest, before moving them to lock onto mine, devastation in her expression.

Shit.

Harshly pulling out of Shelly's clutch, I got to my feet, barking at Ally, "Is she upset?"

"What the hell do you think? Her whole damn day has just been ruined by you, you stupid idiot!"

"Fuck! What's she saying? Is she done with me?"

She didn't answer right away, so I asked again, "Al! Is she done with me? What's she saying?"

"I think so. I don't know? She wants to leave; she's in shock. I've tried to tell her that nothing is happening here, but, well..." She pointed to Shelly. "It kind of looks bad from where she's standing."

A searing pain shot into my chest and, groaning in fury, I threw my head into my hands.

"Rome, I thought you said she was nothing to you?" Shelly asked from beside me as Ally shot daggers from her eyes.

"Shut the fuck up, Shel!" I snarled, causing Mrs. Blair to gasp and my momma to jump to her feet in outrage.

Casting a glance back at Molly, I saw the crushing grief on her face, and I lost it the moment I saw her run. She took off down the street, hailing for a cab.

Pushing Shelly out of the way, I screamed, "Molly!" as loud as I could. She stopped and stood still on the spot, and I felt myself breathe again. Her shoulders sagged, and she slowly turned around. Our eyes met, and I tried to show her how sorry I was in my gaze, but when I smelled my mother's strong perfume right beside me and heard her mocking laugh in my ear, I froze.

"I'll ruin her, Romeo. This is the moment you decide if you want to destroy someone's life. Believe it, boy. You choose her, I'll ruin you both."

Indecision plagued me. My momma always meant what she said. She never stopped until she got what she wanted. I'd seen her in action. When she wanted to be head of some damn committee, she tarnished the reputation of others in the running until she won. When she wanted my grades to be higher than they were in middle school, she blackmailed the teacher until my GPA miraculously increased. If she wanted Molly out of the picture now, all my instincts were telling me she would work out a way to get it done. I couldn't put Molly through it. Christ, she'd been through enough—her daddy, her grandma, to name just a couple—but I couldn't lose my girl.

"Rome! Don't listen to her. She can't control you anymore!"

I stared at my cousin but couldn't speak, causing her to groan in exasperation and throw her hands up in the air.

I could practically feel my mother's sense of victory, the fucking smug smile plastered on her botoxed face, but when Molly's golden eyes fell to the floor and she caught the attention of a slowing cab, my flight-or-fight instinct kicked in.

Turning to my momma, I said, "It's over. You won't come near me or Mol again. If you do, you'll regret it; that's a promise *I'll* make sure I keep." It was the first time in my whole life I'd stood up to her and the first time I'd ever seen her taken aback, completely speechless.

Jumping over the small white fence, I took off running across the road, dodging oncoming cars, ignoring my momma's frantic, "Rome, don't you dare!" from behind me.

Molly jumped into the cab. I raced toward it, unable to bear the thought of her slipping away from me. The cab began to move. Pumping my legs as hard as I could, I ran beside it, pulling at the door handle, frantically begging her to stop, to listen. She looked so fucking broken sitting so small in the back seat. It made my heart ache when she turned her face from me and the cab screeched away, leaving me standing, alone in the middle of the street.

Backing onto the sidewalk, I sprinted for my truck, ignoring the shoppers gawking at me. Ally, Cass, and Lexi were still standing on the sidewalk in front of me. When Cass saw me approach, she stood straight in my path, blocking my route.

"Move, Cass," I warned, but she ignored me, and, damn, that crazy woman swung her fist straight into my fucking stomach.

"You stupid shithead! How dare you treat Molly like this?"

Winded and bending over slightly, I argued, "It wasn't what it looked like. I was fuckin' protecting her. I would never cheat on Mol. For Christ's sake! She's all I want!"

"Well, it sure looked like something was going on, and with that skinny bitch, too!" Cass was breathing heavily, and I could see the fury in her red face as she stared me down.

"Cass, honey, leave him be." Lexi pulled on Cass's arm, calming her down, before looking at me, shyly. "Molly won't take this well, Rome. She doesn't trust people easily and I think you just about broke her heart today when she saw you with Shelly."

"I know that, Lexi, but hear this: she's mine and I'll do anything to protect her. You have my word."

Even to me, my voice sounded strangled. But Lexi must have heard my sincerity because she smiled and squeezed my arm in support.

Ally pulled me in for a quick hug, whispering, "Go get her."

That was exactly what I intended to do.

I pulled the truck into park and ran to the backyard of the sorority house, climbing up to Molly's balcony, only to be met by closed doors.

Shit! She never locked her balcony doors; it was obvious what she was trying to say.

Panicking, I rattled the handle repeatedly and yelled, "Mol! Open the fuck up. I know you're in there!" I pounded on the doors, almost ripping them off their hinges, but they wouldn't budge.

I could see a shadowed outline of Mol curled up on her bed, and I needed her to hear me out, but it was clear she wasn't about to open the doors and let me in.

Climbing back down the balcony, I ran around the house and burst through the front doors. Some jock-looking chick ran into the hallway and began trying to push me back out of the door as I began to climb the stairs.

"*What the hell?* You can't just come in here… wait!" she shouted, jumping right into my path.

"MOVE!" I yelled. She didn't, so, picking her up by the waist, I moved her to the side, setting off running once more, the muscled brunette immediately following behind.

Catching sight of Molly's door, I quickened my pace, the chick behind me screaming, "Molly! Molly! Watch out—"

Shouldering through the door, I found Molly sitting up on her bed, eyes red and gaping at me in shock.

"I tried to stop him, but he wouldn't leave. Do you want me to call security?"

I could see Molly was considering it. But no fucker was making me go anywhere. She was going to hear me out whether she liked it or not.

"Don't. Even. Think it," I said in a stern voice, watching Mol sigh in defeat and then shake her head at her friend.

"You sure?" the chick asked again. Man, I was about to shove the damn girl out the door myself.

"Yes. Thanks, Cait," Mol answered with a small, appreciative smile.

Almost snarling at me in disgust, *Cait* insisted, "Holler if you need me." She left, and the silence that filled the room was excruciating.

"Just leave, Romeo. I have nothing to say to you," Molly said coldly, looking so damn small in the center of her bed.

She'd given up on me; that much was obvious. My desperate fury took hold, and my hands were literally shaking with fear. I marched over to the bed and shouted, "Well, I have something to say to you!"

Her brown eyebrows drew in and she lashed out, "What? That you've been lying and cheating all this time, and that when you say you're training in the gym, what you really mean is that you're meeting up with Mommy Dearest and that tart?"

"That's not what fuckin' happened at all!" I tried to explain, but she put her hand up and hissed, "Whatever. I don't care. Leave."

I couldn't let her do this, couldn't let her push me away without hearing me out, so I reached out, holding her in my arms, forcing her to listen. "My momma asked me to meet her today. Some kids charity she's on asked for a signed Tide jersey for an auction. I went to drop it off and when I got there, Shelly and Mrs. Blair were waiting with her at the restaurant."

Her lips pursed, like they did when she was studying, and I knew I had her attention. Placing her back on the bed, I explained, "They fucking bombarded me. Shelly'd told them about you and they started going off about how irresponsible I was and all that shit. My momma laid into me and told me if I didn't break it off, she'd make damn sure she did. I can't let that happen to you."

How could she understand the real meaning of what I was saying? I'd never told her about how bad my parents were. She'd seen my daddy hit me, and now my momma manipulate me, but that was just a taster of how they could be. How could I possibly tell her the extent of their cruelty?

Seeing nothing but understanding in my girl's eyes, I confessed, "My folks… they… Look, baby. They treat me real bad. Not going into it, but they do, and I'm their fuckin' son! I couldn't let her upset you in the same way, so I made up some bullshit about you being just a fling, a friend. Shelly's too stupid to even realize I was lying. I stayed for the lunch to appease my momma. No way will anything happen to you. They'd have to get through me first."

Titling her head, she asked, "Why did you lie and say you were going to the gym? Why not just be honest with me?"

"I was honest, I swear. She called when I was finishing up. The plan was to just drop off the jersey and leave."

"But Shelly was touching you. She kissed you and you let her! How could you do that?"

God, how could I make her understand? "Because I don't want my parents to come after you! I *had* to play along… to protect you. You don't understand what they're like! Powerhouses, Mol. Around here they're fuckin' powerhouses."

Leaning down, I captured Molly's flushed face in my hands. "God, baby. I would never do anything to lose you. Believe me when I say that I sat there and endured their scheming hell to protect you. Fuck Shelly, I can't stand the bitch!" It was true. Any shred of respect I had for that girl had been completely eradicated over the last few days.

Running a hand down my face, I said, "Don't matter now of course."

"Why's that?"

I hadn't even had time to think over what I'd done today and couldn't help but let out a nervous laugh as I did. "Because I told Momma to shove her Blair/Prince marriage merger bullshit when I came gunning after you."

"You did?" she said, hopeful, and I knew I'd gotten through to her, my rigid body relaxing for the first time since she'd bolted into the cab.

Molly watched me as I approached the bed, climbing up, forcing her onto her back with the weight of my body. "Mm-hmm. Told her I ain't ever marrying Shelly because I'm with you. That I'm done with their shit because I'm with you. Plus, I ran down the street after your cab, screaming and banging on the paintwork. I'm sure that hammered home my point."

Her pupils dilated, and she clawed at my hair, bringing me to her lips, only to say, "You need to tell me if you're going through stuff with your parents. Tell me so I can't doubt you. It's hard for me to trust, but I'm learning to trust you. Please… confide in me."

I wanted to, but I wasn't ready yet. I'd never told a damn soul the truth about my parents, about the years of abuse I'd suffered… Never truly acknowledged it until Molly came into my life, showing me things could be different, that I could choose a different path. "Baby…

you're safe with me, and I would've told you everything that happened when I got home. I didn't expect to see you. God, it almost destroyed me when I saw your reaction from across the road… and then you ran, after you promised you'd never run from me."

She shuffled beneath me, and, at the movement, my cock hardened and I pushed against her crotch.

Sucking in a sharp breath, she murmured, "I do trust you. I-it just looked bad. She kissed you. I… I didn't like it. I needed to get away."

Grinding harder, I said, "I'll never cheat on you, Shakespeare. You're too damn important to me for that. I told you I'd never fuck around on you, and I don't like to be doubted."

"Okay," she blurted, her breath now ragged and uneven.

I wasn't going to dry-fuck her like some damn horny teen. If she wanted me to give her what she needed, I was going to do it right.

Pushing her thighs apart and securing them in position with my hands, I leaned in and swiped my tongue from her pussy to the tip of her clit. Her hips almost lifted off the mattress as she cried out, testing the roots of my hair as her clenched fists wrapped around the long strands.

She tried to move her legs, but I held her tight as I worked her with my tongue, plundering in and out and sucking on her clit. Her moans were building and she was growing hotter—I knew she was close. My cock throbbed and I knew needed her too come before I came like a damn teenager in my boxers.

With a breathy moan, Mol fell apart, thighs tightening, her fingers pulling on my hair.

She was beautiful.

Moving back to the pillow beside her, I held her tightly in my arms, gripping onto her as if she might change her mind, as if she were going wise up and kick me the hell out of her life at any second. Today had been too close of a call.

After lying still for several minutes, Molly lifted her head, a conflicted smirk on her lips. "God, Rome. You've got me so confused. I never know whether I'm coming or going with you."

I couldn't help but make the obvious joke. "Always coming I hope."

Giggling, she jabbed me in the ribs, but the weight of today began to play on my mind, her now-worried expression pressing me to confess, "I'm not sure if you get the significance of what I did today in coming after you, in leaving my momma like that."

I was never going to tell Molly this, but I was scared shitless, petrified at what she may try to do. As I stared into Molly's golden eyes, I knew I wouldn't survive it if I lost her.

"Don't ever leave me," I whispered, the truthful words almost involuntarily spilling from my mouth in a moment of weakness.

"Hey, what's all this?" she asked soothingly as she pressed loving kisses to the top of my head.

"I just can't believe I've got you in my life. You make everything better and I don't want to lose you."

"I won't leave you."

"You almost did today. You told me to leave you." It came out sounding accusatory, but that shit hurt; it hurt to know I didn't yet have her full trust.

"It was a misunderstanding," she said firmly, but I heard her heartbeat increase slightly as I laid my head on her chest, causing me to look up at her in concern.

Swallowing, she asked, "Truthfully, Rome, how much trouble are your parents going to cause us?"

I didn't know that answer. I wish I did. There was a chance they would let everything go and cut all ties with me once and for all, but knowing my folks, I was preparing for the exact opposite. They could really try and hurt us. And I would protect my girl if it was the last thing I did.

18

"Tide star QB's lucky kiss with girlfriend to save the season!"

I smirked at Reece as he read tonight's headline from the game report, thinking back in amusement to Molly cringing in the stands as the crowd chanted for her to come to the field and kiss me, wearing the Tide jersey I'd left on her pillow for her this morning—my number on the back, of course, with another sappy note attached.

My jersey for MY girl to wear at the game.
Sit with Ally and I'll come to collect my good luck sweet kiss.
Your Romeo X

Yeah, yeah, I was whipped, and I honestly couldn't give two shits about it. In fact, I fucking loved it.

Her legs had shook the entire way to the field, but pride burst in my chest as I showed the hundred thousand fans in the stadium and millions around the world that Molly Shakespeare belonged to me.

As she approached my place at the sideline, I could see her eyes focused on the floor, her lips moving as she muttered words of reassurance to herself. I bet she never thought in a million years that my begging her to come to my game, in the library all those weeks ago, would result in her being put in the spotlight to kiss her quarterback boyfriend due to superstition.

As she stood before me, I inched forward, gripping the nape of her neck, making her focus only on me and, pressing my forehead to hers, I whispered, "Hey, Mol." With that she relaxed, a tiny smile on those pink lips.

"Hey, you."

"You going to give up that lucky sweet kiss?"

"If that's what you want."

She had no idea how much.

"It most definitely is." With that I leaned in and kissed her, my tongue searching for hers—duelling, lapping, owning—and then I broke away before I got too hard in my tight football trousers—family game and all.

The Tide won.

Molly was praised for the power of her lucky kiss, and then my bastard cousin chased me from my girl and ordered me to come back tonight at nine; she'd planned something for Mol. But only Christ knew what she was up to.

It hit eight forty-five and I couldn't wait any longer, so me and the guys headed out to Mol's sorority house. It was like withdrawal whenever we were apart, and I knew it probably wasn't healthy, but quite frankly, I didn't give a shit about that either.

Knocking on the sorority house door, Reece, Austin, Jimmy-Don, and I were greeted by the jock from the other night—Cait, was it? Perfect, we'd hit it off the first time so well.

After rolling her eyes and groaning in disappointment right in my face, Cait left the door open and made her way up the stairs, looking back only to snap, "Stay there. *Don't* come upstairs! I'll tell the girls y'all are here."

Jimmy-Don looked at me and took off his Stetson, shaking his head. "Cait, Turner, soccer jock and all-state champion. Heard she kicked the crap out of Cody Brown for grabbing her ass a few weeks back." Raising his eyebrow, he asked, "What you done for her to gun for your blood?"

Shrugging, I replied, "Barged in to speak to Mol the other day and kind of wrestled her off the stairs when she tried to outmuscle me."

Austin just shook his head, laughing. "I swear Rome, you sure know how to treat women. If they're not spreading wide for your moody ass, they're trying to kick it!"

"Carillo, fuck off."

As we waited for the girls, Jimmy-Don launched into a story about one of his brothers back in Texas who was into racing monster trucks. He was talking animatedly about a flip when Reece began tapping me on my arm. Shrugging him off, I turned my attention back to Jimmy-Don, trying to figure how the hell he moved the story on to cow tipping back in high school, but Reece didn't quit, and after a few seconds, I was ready to knock the little fucker out.

Swinging around, I asked, "What? Fuck, man, back off!" But Reece just pointed up the staircase, ignoring my attitude, mouth gaping open.

Looking up, I quickly registered what had him, and Austin—and now Jimmy-Don—gawking. Molly. My Mol looking like a friggin' supermodel walking down the stairs.

Pushing away from the wall, I shouldered Reece out of my way, ignoring the way his tongue was practically hanging out of his mouth at the sight of my girl.

Ally winked at me as she passed, but I only had eyes for Shakespeare: tight black dress showing her unreal curves, her long brown hair falling in soft curls over her shoulders, and her nervously flushed face looking so damn beautiful that it nearly made me drop to my knees.

Reaching out, I wrapped my arms around her waist, fighting the worst case of blue balls I'd ever had. Pressing a kiss to her full lips, I whispered, for her ears only, "Fuck, Mol, you're trying my restraint looking this beautiful. How the hell am I meant to get through the night? I'll be fighting off the guys with a stick. They're going to get in trouble if they even look at you for a second."

It was true; up until now I hadn't really had to worry about other guys watching Mol. She'd always slipped under their radar. But hell, she was beyond a friggin' ten as she stood before me now—she always had been to me, but now the world would see it. I wasn't sure I could stand other guys looking at her and imagining they were between her legs. It was going to drive me insane, no matter how much she assured me that she was mine and mine alone.

Tonight would be a test, that's for sure.

We sat down in one of Club Flux's private booths and ordered drinks from a blond waitress who looked vaguely familiar. I'd been right about tonight being a test—I'd already gained Molly's disapproval for nearly punching out an overeager Tide fan who'd grabbed her to congratulate her on her kiss. She'd forgiven me, but who knew how long that would last.

The blonde came back with our drinks, smiling suggestively at me, and the memory started to resurface.

It was last season, maybe after the Iron Bowl against Auburn? I'd been drunk out of my mind when she'd made her move, sitting on my lap as I almost lost consciousness on my chair, then leading me to the back of the club. I'd fucked her from behind, her face pressed against the wall, so I didn't have to see who I was screwing. It'd never mattered; a hole was a hole. But with Mol, she'd be looking straight in my eyes and I'd savor every damn second.

As I shook the memory from my mind, I focused back on the waitress. Ah, hell. By the look on the blonde's face, this wasn't going to go down well.

Molly had stiffened in my arms, and I tried to ignore the chick as she did everything but strip before me. Then she gave up trying to get my attention and finally said, "Hey, Bullet, how've you been?"

How've I been? I didn't even know the damn girl.

"We're done here," I said.

The rush of a challenge lit in the waitress' eyes, and Molly began to fidget. Ally subtly booted me under the table, and Austin rubbed at his eyes in frustration at where this was clearly heading. The two of them were just pissing me off more; I didn't need to be reminded that this was going to be real a clusterfuck of a situation.

"You never called me after our night together," the blonde said, and I knew that was it. Molly's first night in a club and *boom*, some cheap fuck tries to mark me as her territory. If roles were reversed, I'd have killed the fucker by now—as it was, I wasn't exactly sure how jealous Molly could get. I couldn't work out how she would take all this crap.

"I was never going to. I'll say it again... We're done here. Or if you need a simpler answer... fuck off," I growled.

Her mouth tightened and she spat, "I'd heard on the grapevine that you were pussy whipped—fucking waste of a good cock." She looked at Mol, taking in her natural curves and stunning face, and curled her lip. "And for that too. She must screw better than she wears that shitty dress." I caught Molly's sharp intake of breath. I knew she thought she didn't measure up to others, and that comment had hurt her.

Mol jumped out of my arms and snapped at me, which was a first. Her reaction set me to reeling mad, but before I could call her on it, she bolted to the restroom… She'd fucking run.

"Hell, Rome! You'd better go fix this!" Ally shouted, shooting daggers at me across the table.

"You fucked that waitress? Shit, can you set me up?" I glared at Reece, fighting the urge to launch him across the room. Tact, man, the kid had no tact or sense of damn timing.

"Go, Bullet, before I hit you again!" Cass pushed on my arm, and I shot up from my seat, nearly turning the bastard thing over, pounding through the crowd of dancers to get Molly the hell back.

I spotted her ahead of me. The blond waitress was standing at the bar, watching me run with a bitter smile on her face. Stupid bitch, she'd done all that on purpose, and it'd worked.

Reaching out, I grabbed Molly's arm, only to have her wrench it back, her golden eyes furious and filled with hurt. Fuck, it was the first time I'd earned that look from her, and I completely panicked. She looked… resolved… like her mind was made up on something.

No! She couldn't…

Beyond frustrated, I took her arm, dragged her with me like some fucking caveman, and locked us both in a dusty old closet.

Molly was panting, her fists clenched in anger. She didn't look like she was in the mood to be placated, so I just spat it out, "I fucked her once. Last year. There was nothing more to it. You don't need to be upset by it, and you certainly don't need to fuckin' run away."

By the way she froze, nose turning up in disgust, I realized I'd fucked up… again. "Well, excuse me if I don't enjoy your exploits flaunting their slutty selves in front of my face!"

I could feel myself getting madder. How the fuck was that my fault? I'd tried to brush her off; Molly had seen that. How could I help it if she wouldn't take no for an answer?

Closing in, watching Molly freeze in anticipation, I shouted, "You want to know all about my sexual past, all the sordid details? Fine! I've fucked a lot of girls, in many different ways, in many different places. They'd throw themselves my way and I'd give them what they wanted, and they'd fuckin' love it." I was pumped with too much adrenalin and knew I was being an ass, but when Mol's eyes blazed and she smacked me across the face, I felt like I couldn't breathe.

She'd fucking hit me! Molly, my timid little Mol, had cracked me right across the fucking face. Guess I'd found her breaking point.

"Did that feel good? Have you got it out of your system now?" I said coldly.

Molly instantly cried out, covering her mouth with shaky hands as tears fell down her cheeks. She was disgusted with herself. I could see that much.

Seeing her so sad had me backing away to the other wall, croaking, "They fucked Bullet. They only ever fucked Bullet…"

Sniffing and wiping frantically at her eyes, she whispered, "Nice, Rome. Real nice. Is that what you'll do to me? Let me fuck the great Bullet Prince, give me what I want, and move on?"

God! What else did I have to do to prove she was different? We'd done plenty in bed but hadn't gone all the way. I respected her and didn't want her to feel used. I could see the conflict on her face, that look urging me to power forward and say, "Not at all, Shakespeare, but hear this. I'm going to fuck you, but I'm also going to make love to you. I'm going to own every goddamn piece of your soul, and I'm never going to let you go. You're going to scream my name over and over until it's permanently lodged in your friggin' throat. You're not going to be just a fuck to me, Mol—you're going to be my fuckin' salvation!"

She already was. She was making my life better day by day. How could she not know that?

Molly couldn't meet my eyes, and the way she'd closed herself off was making me nervous as all hell. "Baby," I said almost inaudibly as she closed her eyes in anguish. "You'll make love to me—Romeo—not some pathetic fucking football alter ego. You'll get the real me, all of me, forever and ever. Is that clear enough for you?" She still didn't say anything, and a foreboding lump blocked my throat.

Pressing her forehead to mine, I tried to keep my voice low and calm. "Christ, Mol! I've never done this before. If I'd known you were out there waiting for me, I wouldn't have fucked all those chicks. But I can't take it back."

She sagged against my chest and looked up, completely defeated, running a finger down my cheek. "It's all too much, isn't it? Your family obviously hates me, Shelly won't back off, you turn on anyone who even looks at me, and these… girls you've had in the past seem not to be able to let go. I have my own issues, Rome—you know this—and piled with yours… it's just too much. How can we possibly work under all this stress?"

No, no, no, no…

"Don't. Don't do that!" I begged her in panic.

"Do what?" she said, unfeeling, numb even, as she focused on the floor, dejected, unable to even meet my eyes.

"Write us off. Don't run away when it gets tough." I needed her to look at me, dammit, so I forced her head up, gripping her chin. "You fight your past problems. I'll learn to control my anger. We fight back against my family. We ignore all the others. We get through this! Don't you dare quit on me now, Shakespeare. Don't you fuckin' dare!"

"Rome—" she whispered, sounding completely heartbroken.

For the first time in years, I actually thought I was going to break down. The fierceness of how much I needed my girl was surprising even me. "No! I won't let you go. I know I'm all kinds of wrong for you, but you've changed me. You've fucking changed me! Can't you see that? You're going to face this with me. Say it! Please, baby, say it to me!"

She wasn't running. I wouldn't let her. She'd promised me. Looking her dead in the eye, I insisted frantically, "Say you get me, Mol?"

"Rome, I—" Her choked cry cut her words.

I was so confused by her rejection. I knew she wanted me, maybe even close to loving me, but she wasn't fighting for us and it pissed me off so fucking bad, causing me to slam my fist against the metal rack behind her, the tall contraption swinging as I shouted, "You're not running. YOU GET ME?"

"YES! YES, I FUCKING GET YOU!" she yelled back, her palms hitting my chest before gripping onto my plaid shirt and pulling me back in close, the heavy sound of our breath like friggin' thunder.

My hands drifted to hold her neck as I asked carefully, "You're still in?"

Golden eyes dilated and, wrapping a leg around my hip, she began to grind against my cock. "I'm still in."

Feeling the building heat between her legs, lust assaulted my body, instantly forgetting all the angry tension, and I croaked, "Fuck, I want you so bad. You doing everything I say makes me hard as fuck."

Dipping my hand lower, I pushed her panties aside and felt along her soaking center. "Mol… Christ. You're killing me." She was so wet and ready.

Her teeth and tongue licked and bit along my neck, ear, and jaw, only stopping to admit, "I like it when you lead, when you assert your authority. It turns me on."

She was really fucking killing me. My cock felt like it would explode any minute if I didn't get inside her once and for all.

"Fuck… I can tell, and I like that you submit. It… calms me. You're what I need. Damn, you're perfect for me. Beautiful, sexy as all hell, with a body that makes painters weep."

Her head rolled back as I pushed two fingers inside her. "There'll be no one else. For the first time ever, you're giving me what I want, what I need. You give me full control, and I love it. You do too, don't you? You fucking love it…?" Her pussy began to clench, over and over, and her breathy moans increased in pace against my neck.

Snapping her eyes back on mine, she lowered her hands and began to tear at the fly of my jeans. Fuck that, I wanted my full attention on her face as she came. If she touched me, I'd explode. "Off! Let go. Now. This is not about me. You won't touch me unless I say so."

I worked her until she stiffened and ground against my hand, screaming in release. I held her as her body jerked and her breathing returned to normal. Then I asked her if we were okay and confessed how much I wanted her… *needed* her.

"I want you, Romeo. You give me something I didn't even know I needed too." And just like that, I had my girl back.

After a few silent seconds, she bit her lip, then asked if I thought we were wrong. I knew the way I controlled during sex could be seen as fucked up, but it was just some drive I had and, Christ, my girl told me she loved it. I couldn't believe that someone so right had been made for me, that we'd found each other in such an unlikely way. She was my equal in every sense.

Fixing her dress, Molly held out her hand, wanting to go and dance. Personally, I just wanted to go home and fuck her into the mattress, but we needed to stay. My girl needed to get back to her first real night out.

I was about to follow her to the dance floor, when she said, "I want to dance, show all your past conquests that you're mine." With that, I lost all the control I'd been fighting so hard to keep.

Slamming her back against my chest, I gripped her ass and wrapped those long legs around my waist, demanding she say it again.

With her shocked face now breaking into a sweet smile, she said, "You are mine now, just you for you."

I thrust her against the wall. The time for waiting was done. Lowering my hand, I pulled out my cock and began guiding it between her legs, inches away from finally possessing my girl completely. And that's when a jumped-up little shit of a manager began pounding on the door, demanding that we leave.

I was murdering mad and so damn desperate to finally take Mol that I was almost blind with need.

Groaning in frustration, I dropped my head onto her shoulder, the scent of her calming me down, as it always did. Molly giggled lightly, reaching down to tuck my hard dick back into my jeans, stroking it teasingly, and whispered, "Let's go, baby. Let's actually have our date."

Finding some inner friggin' chi I didn't know I had, I instructed, "You go out there and fuckin' show everyone we're together. You own this… us. Time to be bold, baby. Bring the fuckin' rain."

And she did, she never let go of my hand, dismissing the stupid blond bitch from earlier, and led me to the dance floor, completely proud to be on my arm.

I'd never been so damn happy as I was watching her relax and let loose.

A few hours later, Molly stopped dancing, her hands creeping up my torso, and stared up at me with a strange expression on her face.

"You okay?" I asked, cupping her cheeks.

She shook her head. Panic swelled once more, and I asked, "Why? What's wrong?"

"I want to go home."

"Are you sick? Is something wrong?" Her eyes had glazed and she was red hot to the touch. I worried it was a fever; she was acting so weird.

"What is it? Tell me," I demanded, my patience quickly fading.

She took a shaky breath and replied, "I want you to take me home and put me to bed."

"Okay, are you tired? It's still pretty early."

A small smile curved her lips and, rubbing up against my crotch, she leaned into my ear. "I want you to put me to bed… get in beside me… and make love to me."

Spinning her around and pressing her against the wall, I asked, "Are you serious?"

Golden eyes fixed on mine with determination. "Deadly."

Was she drunk? She'd had a hell of a lot of tequila. Sanity broke through for a second, urging me to declare, "I don't want you to do anything you ain't ready for. You've been drinking. I don't want you to regret us in the morning."

"I'm not so drunk that my feelings are untrue. I want you, Romeo, no regrets."

Thank. Fuck.

"Then beg me," I ordered, all my inhibitions gone. She knew me; she got me. I didn't have to be afraid to be myself.

I could see that I had thrown her. "I told you I'd take you only when you begged me, when you wanted me like no other. If you're at that point, Mol, you have to prove it to me. You have to beg." Her eyes widened with lust. This was us, how we should be—me in control, her giving in to my instructions.

"Romeo Prince, I want you to take me to bed, I want you to undress me slowly, and I want you to make me completely yours. Please, Romeo, make love to me... tonight."

Exactly fifteen minutes later, Molly stood before me in her room, breathless with anticipation, and I knew that after tonight, taking this last step, we would never be the same.

19

"Walk toward the bed and take off the boots." Turning, Mol did exactly as I ordered, rewarding me with a view of her full ass in her tight black dress as she bent down, shucking off her boots.

"Turn around and face me."

Christ, she was beautiful, meeting my eyes with hungry excitement, a small smile spreading over her lips.

"Take off your dress... slowly."

Inch by inch, the black strapless dress revealed a toned, soft, tanned body, her lacy black underwear almost causing me to have a damn seizure. Then my gaze zeroed in on some tiny black script at the very top of her left hip. A tattoo?

I had to touch her; my fingers were itching to feel that silky skin again. Moving to where she stood, I waited for her to meet my eyes, and she looked up shyly through those long black lashes, her long brown hair hanging low over her breasts. She was fucking... just... beyond.

Dropping to my knees, I rubbed along the fine inking and remarked, "A tattoo, Shakespeare? You surprise me. You've never let me see this before." I watched her swallow and her breath began to stutter, her anxiety taking hold. Grasping her hand tightly to stop the panic, I read, "*So are you to my thoughts as food to life, or as sweet seasoned showers are to the ground,*" and kissed along her soft skin.

"What's this, baby? Why do these words take pride of place on this beautiful body?"

Wrapping her fingers in my long hair, tears filling her eyes, she whispered, "It's William Shakespeare, from one of his love sonnets, number seventy-five."

She wouldn't tell me any more, no matter how hard I pushed, but I knew there was a deeper meaning to that story.

After I had stripped her bare, Mol couldn't open her eyes. I had no idea if it was nerves or fear. She was perfect to me, and there was absolutely no need for embarrassment, and it wasn't something I would tolerate, not from her. She was too perfect to be insecure.

Gripping her hair, I ordered, "Open." I had to see those big golden eyes.

But she couldn't. Tugging on her hair even tighter, I said sternly, "Open. I won't ask again."

She did, and all I saw was desperate need shining back at me.

Crushing my lips to hers, I took her full breast in my hand, pinching at the nipple, fucking dying at the noises slipping from my girl's throat. Picking her up, unable to wait anymore, I threw her on the bed and practically ripped off my clothes down to my boxers, my throbbing cock now completely controlling my mind.

I pressed my skin to hers, rubbing, grinding, and loving every damn minute. This feeling was so different than ever before; it meant everything to me. My hands were frantic as I gorged on her tits, sucked on her nipples, and fingered her wet pussy until she arched off the bed, screaming.

It was too much. I needed to be inside her, deep inside her—I'd never wanted anything more in my entire life.

Staring at Molly, in a moment of pure friggin' love, I pressed my head to hers. "I'm going to take you now. I'm going to show you what you mean to me, how much I want you, and show you that you're mine. You get me, baby?"

"I get you, Romeo," she replied with that sweet damn smile that she reserved just for me.

My smile, my girl… my fucking life.

Standing, I stripped naked, watching as Molly's eyes took me in, running her hands over her breasts, her thighs contracting in need. Moving over her once again, I locked her head within my arms, kissing her slowly, my cock twitching against her warmth. I stood to get a rubber when a small hand landed on my arm. "Romeo, what—"

"Condom." I pointed to my jeans on the floor.

"I'm on the pill," she said nervously.

Fuck. She wanted me raw, skin on skin. She wanted me to come inside her and make her completely mine.

"Baby…" I could barely speak, feeling halfway to insane, needing to have her moaning beneath me, clawing at the skin of my back, out of her mind with pleasure. I'd never ridden bareback before, but damn if it didn't crazy turn me on at the thought of taking my girl that way.

"Please…" she croaked, meeting my eyes. "Romeo," she whispered, "I just want you, nothing in the way."

I was so done.

In a second, I smothered Molly with my body, my dick seeking out her entrance.

Almost shaking with nerves, I leaned down and pressed a soft kiss to her full lips. Taking advantage of the distraction of our kiss, I pushed forward, slamming into her pussy to the hilt, throwing my head back, neck bulging with the strain of being wrapped inside her tight center.

Expelling a long moan, Mol wrapped her legs around my waist, shifting as I pounded into her furiously, biting, scratching, and hissing, "Romeo… God… I can't take it… It's too much…"

"Yes, you can, baby. You'll love it. This is us; this is how we should always be." Her eyes rolled back as I switched the angle of my thrusts and hit the spot that had her groaning, gripping my ass, and raking the fuck out of my back.

She wasn't coming yet. I wanted more.

Taking back control, I pulled out, catching the shocked disappointment on her face. Smiling at her despairing frustration, I said, "Now I'm going to make you scream my name."

Pounding forward as hard as possible, we both screamed at the sensation and, closing my eyes, I murmured, "Fuck, you feel amazing."

My breathing was labored and I reached up with my free hand, gripping the headboard.

"Grip my arms," I growled into her neck.

Molly did exactly what I said, and I lifted my chest, using all my strength to hold tight onto the post of the headboard and push harder, Mol's satisfied cries and hard grasp on my biceps driving me even further.

"Do you like it, baby? Do you like it this hard?"

"Yes. Yes…" she cried as I tilted my hips, my pelvis now working against her clit, her golden eyes rolling back, and her tight pussy clenching so hard it felt like it would snap my cock.

I was getting close, but so was Mol, and there was no way I wasn't going to make her come first. I pushed harder, seeing her eyes widen and her cheeks flush—she was at the brink.

"Let go, Mol. Let go now," I ordered through gritted teeth, the fragile wood of the headboard almost splitting under my clenched fists.

With a final shift of her hips, she threw back her head, screaming out as she came long and hard. Slamming into her rougher, unable to contain my own sounds, I felt the rush of pleasure, then closed my eyes and growled out a loud groan, my cum jetting inside her. My arms shook with the strain, and I let go of the headboard, wrapping my arms around my girl, tucking my head into her hair, rocking within her slowly, winding us both back down.

Completely sated, I stared down at my girl beneath me, whispering, "Hey, Mol."

Blinding me with a smile, she replied, "Hey, you."

As that stark realization took hold of me, I confessed, "You're everything I thought I could never have. Making love to you, it was... you know... beyond..."

I couldn't look at her and, like a damn coward, buried my face in her neck. I could be a possessive ass, but sharing my feelings wasn't something I found easy. I wanted Molly to know, though; she deserved to know how much I adored her.

Kissing my head and stroking my hair, she sighed. "Romeo... it was... beautiful."

We stayed that way for a while until it was necessary for me to move, and as I pulled out of her, she winced.

"You sore?" I asked.

"A little."

It made me damn proud that she was feeling where I'd just been, what we'd just done, and I told her so.

To that she simply replied, "I'm glad you're pleased with yourself."

After cleaning up, I returned to bed, smiling at Mol as she laid waiting for me back in bed. Sliding in beside her, I tucked her into my chest, combing out the knots in her hair with my fingers, her humming in response. I'd never had this, this happy after state of making love. It'd always been quick, rough and I'd roll over, ignoring whoever I'd just fucked, or even better, send them on home. But lying here, happily spent, with my girl beside me... Shit, it was incredible.

"Tell me something you've never told anyone," I said quietly, becoming addicted to our new closeness and wanting to explore it more.

I felt the instant panic seize her breath so I quickly took a hand, feeling her relax.

"Like what?" she asked nervously.

"Anything. Just something no one else knows. Some deep secret or fear that you have."

Lifting her head, she met my eyes and hers filled with water. I squeezed her hand in support as she whispered, "I get so lonely that at times I literally think it might kill me."

I was sure my heart stopped beating. I could handle my own shit, but hearing her sound so broken, so down, almost killed me.

She never took her eyes from mine, smiling a watery smile. In an instant, I had her in my arms, kissing everywhere possible, every inch of skin. She was lonely. All the studying, the solitude, was a defense... just like me with my football.

"Molly, baby, you're breaking my fucking heart," I said tightly, wondering how the hell an insensitive guy like me could take away her pain.

"It's true and I've never told anyone that until just now... until you. For me, it's been the hardest thing. It's amazing how loud the sound of silence can be screaming at you relentlessly, reminding you that you're completely on your own in the world."

"Can I tell you something?" I said almost inaudibly, as if my mouth opened of its own accord and a part of my soul fought to get free.

Bracing in anticipation, her breath held as I confessed, "I'm desperately lonely, too."

Relief and understanding flashed across her face and my girl crumpled in my arms, the floodgates bursting free and years of pent-up heartache making her almost inconsolable. I didn't know if it was the sound of her breaking or seeing her so raw, but she forced me to face my own demons, and I let my own sadness leak through for the first time in years.

Holding Molly tight, I said, "We don't have to feel lonely anymore, baby. I have you and you me."

Shifting back, she wiped at her eyes, laughing, "This is crazy, Romeo. We've known each other for such a short space of time, yet I feel as if I've known you my whole life."

It may have been the wrong time to joke, but smirking, I said, "We're star-crossed, Shakespeare. Fateful, star-crossed lovers. We have a lifetime to get to know each other, unlike our namesakes." Dropping the humor, driven intention taking its place, I assured, "I'll make sure we get our happily ever after…"

She settled on my chest, her breathing evening out, when I asked, "That quote on your hip, tell me about it."

My request caused her pain—that much was clear—so holding her hand, I said, "I've got you, baby."

Taking a breath, she said, "My… my father quoted it in his suicide note. He used to say it to me at bedtime every night and I wanted something to remember him by, just so I can never forget him."

God. The hurt, the confusion was still thick in her voice. She wasn't over it. Not at all, not even a little bit.

"Is it from memory?"

And then she explained the note, her father's suicide note, his last words to his only daughter, and that he used to quote that sonnet to her every night. I was so out of my depth. I was a jock with anger issues—I had no idea how to handle the topic of suicide.

"Would you like to read it?" she offered hopefully.

"Why?" Shock and nerves stilled me.

"Because no one but me and my grandma ever has. I'd like to share it with you. I find myself wanting to let you in more and more every day. It may help you understand some things… about me."

I reluctantly agreed. If it meant knowing more about my girl, I would be crazy not to do so.

She got up from the bed, completely naked, and I watched as her round ass swayed to the closet, her reaching up to grab a box, and I almost groaned in pain.

Christ, my woman was hot.

Peeking over her shoulder, she laughed, "You're incorrigible."

I was, and I couldn't wait to be deep inside her once more. "Just so you know. I'm going to take you again tonight. Addicted, Shakespeare. I'm fuckin' addicted."

Blushing, she reached the bed, leaning down, and pressed a kiss to my lips before handing over an old letter wrapped in a plastic. I began to read, completely engrossed in Molly's daddy's parting words.

My little Molly-pops, this is the hardest letter I have ever had to write.

Firstly, I want you to know that I have loved you more than any daddy has ever loved his little girl since the very beginning of time. You're the apple of my eye and the best thing I have ever done in my whole life.

I know that this is all too much for you to understand right now, but you will, in time. I want to explain why I have left you and I want you to know that it's not because you did anything wrong.

I have loved many people in my life, but the way I loved your mother was beyond anything I can explain. The day you were born was both the saddest and happiest day of my life. The happiest as I got you, but the saddest as I lost the other half of my soul.

I was broken, Molly, and nobody but God could fix me.

One day, my sweet girl, some lucky young man will come and help you understand the very meaning of love. He will sweep you off your feet and show you what it is to place your heart in someone else's care and to willingly offer them the gift of your soul—and he will own it completely. Make sure he is worth the treasure of your heart and do everything in your power to protect what you have together.

In the future, when you're older and wiser, you may look back on my departure and have questions, insecurities, and blame me for abandoning you at such a young age—and for that I cannot offer anything that will give you peace. People may tell you I was selfish for leaving you behind, but I believe that it was more selfish to let you live with half a father.

Since your mammy passed, I have lived a sad and lonely life, you and Grandma being the only light in my darkness. I want you to know that I am at peace now and in the happiest place I can imagine—in the arms of your mammy for eternity.

Live life to the fullest, my darling girl, and one day, when God so wishes, I will be waiting to see you again at the gates of paradise, to once again have you jump into my open arms so I can twirl you around, tell you how pretty you are, and introduce you to your mother... who looks just like you.

"So are you to my thoughts as food to life, or as sweet seasoned showers are to the ground." ~ William Shakespeare

I love you.
Daddy X

I didn't move for the longest time, reading his words of love and sorrow over and over, abruptly realizing Mol was no longer at my side. Placing the letter down on the bedside table, I looked out to the balcony. She was wrapped in her black robe, just staring out into the night.

She was so damn strong. She came across as this timid little brainiac, but fuck me, the shit she'd survived. She deserved a damn medal.

She was incredible and I loved her beyond words.

Holy Shit! I loved her... I was madly in love with Molly...

Walking to the balcony, I brushed Molly's long hair over her shoulder and pressed a kiss to the nape of her neck. Wrapping my arms around her waist, I turned her to face me. Her eyes immediately searched mine—guarded and scared—but all I wanted to do was kiss her, make love to her, show her she was mine and I wasn't ever leaving her side. I would be different from everyone else she'd ever had in her life.

As though she weighed no more than a feather, I picked her up, walking to her balcony table, watching her swallow nervously as I laid her down and untied her robe. I hadn't bothered getting dressed since we'd made love, and smoothing a hand up her soft thigh, I held it around my waist and pushed into her without a word.

I never broke from her gaze as I braced myself above her, thrusting into her slowly. I laid kisses all over her face and her neck, smoothing her damp hair from her face, along with the light tears she shed the closer we got to release. Her eyes widened and I could feel she was close, so, pressing my forehead to hers with a final thrust, she broke apart, holding my face in her hands, taking me with her.

I kissed her slowly as I came and, breathless, met her gaze, running my finger down her cheek. "Thank you for showing me the letter, baby. Thank you for trusting me with knowing your past."

She released a breath, almost as if she'd been holding it all this time, and smiled in relief. "Take me to bed, Romeo."

I did as she asked, where she immediately fell asleep, leaving me reliving our night over and over in disbelief until I too drifted off.

20

I knocked on my daddy's office door, body tense and bracing for yet another fight. I hadn't responded to any of his texts, emails, or voicemails over the last few weeks, hadn't dared to. I wanted to keep Molly safe.

As predicted, my momma hadn't been in touch since our showdown at her guerrilla-style lunch at *Lorenzo's*. Hell, the only damn reason I was here today at this fucking house of horrors was because my daddy had practically begged me… Well, that and morbid curiosity had won out. He'd never spoken to me in such a way before—so kind, so sincere—and I needed to know why he'd had a change in attitude. I prayed it was due to finally seeing reason over this marriage crap. Hell, I'd walk to the end of the earth to see that shit buried.

"Come in!" Joseph Prince shouted from within his seat of power.

Taking a deep breath, I opened the door to see my daddy sitting behind his large mahogany desk, looking all kinds of strange as he tried to crack a smile my way. I actually checked around me to see if someone stood behind me, but the coast was clear—that painful-looking smile was directed at me.

"Rome, please, sit." My daddy gestured to the seat at his desk. For a while—it was seconds but felt like minutes—I just stared at him, unsure of his intentions. He was calm, collected; this was the face the rest of the world saw, not the extreme disciplinarian I'd always known him to be.

"Rome, sit. I think we need to talk." Moving slowly, in almost in a dreamlike state, I walked forward and sat down.

Fidgeting in my seat, I looked around the room, just trying to find some sense of reason for why the hell I was here. My father shifted and I focused all my attention back on him, seeing him regard me warily and grasp his hands together.

Rubbing my head, I asked quietly, "Daddy, what's all this about?"

"I…" He took a breath and went on. "I…" Sighing in frustration, he laid his palms flat on the tabletop. "Your momma told me what happened a couple of weeks ago, and it really made me think about things."

My heart began to pound in my chest. His tone, his entire demeanor, was off and making me nervous.

"I'm getting older, and your silence toward me of late has given me time to put things in perspective, about how

I've been toward you and how it's understandable you'd feel railroaded into continuing the family business."

Gripping the arms of the chair, the heat of anger beginning to spread into my muscles, I said, "This is a joke, right? Another fucked-up ploy to get me to do your bidding?"

My daddy sat back, seeming affronted. I couldn't tell if his reaction was genuine or fake. "No, Rome, it was meant to be an olive branch."

Olive branch? I felt like overturning the desk and screaming, *Olive branch? You've belittled me all of my life, beaten me. Momma ignored me, never truly accepted me. Why now? Why change now when all you've done for the last few months is hound me to marry Shelly?* But I didn't. I just stared at him, completely shocked, unable to move.

That was until he said, "Your momma told me about your girlfriend, the British girl you've been seeing." And the overwhelming need to protect Molly took root, my muscles remembering how to function.

Abruptly leaning forward, I warned, "You leave her the hell out of anything going on between us. She doesn't need to be involved in our shit."

Graying brown eyebrows rose, and he put his hands up in surrender. "Relax, it's not want you think."

"What's not?" I hissed, suspicion creeping its way into my brain.

"Me and your momma have been talking, and we want to meet her, see what all the fuss is about. Try to be more… accommodating to you."

I was certain I'd entered the fucking *Twilight Zone*. My folks wanted to meet Mol... For me?

"Bullshit," I answered in response, convinced this was just a really elaborate scam.

"It's not—"

"Why would momma want to meet her? She told me she'd ruin us, destroy Mol. Why now, why show an interest now?" I interrupted.

Clearing his throat, my daddy agreed. "I admit, your momma took some convincing, but *I* want to meet her. Bring her to the house tomorrow for dinner."

Stony resolve set in my stomach. "Hell no."

Daddy's facial muscles began to twitch. I knew he was about blow. I sat there waiting... but his anger never came. He was massively fucking with my mind.

"Look, Rome, I understand why you don't want to dine here with us. I'm beginning to see we've not done right by you. And I get why bringing your lady friend may be causing you some turmoil, but I'm reaching out... You're my only son, my only child."

"I... I..." I stuttered, not knowing what to say.

Daddy caught my confusion and continued. "I've been too caught up in business, in making Prince Oil the best it can be, but in doing that I've neglected you. I haven't taken the time to get to know you, to really understand who you are. I want that to change, starting with a chance to meet your girlfriend. Your first official girlfriend, if I'm not mistaken?" He waited for my answer, so I gave a curt nod.

An unfamiliar warmth smothered my chest and I didn't know how to deal. Conflicted emotions duelled in my mind. I'd wanted for so long for my daddy to want me. He called me his son... with affection. Half of me could only think about how amazing that felt, but the other half screamed at me not to believe him. Granted he'd never tried this tactic before—being normal, *fatherly*—but it wouldn't be the first time I'd been lured into the fire by their promises, only to be burned when I took a chance and leapt into the furnace.

Sighing loudly, my daddy said, "Go home, ask your girl, and let me know as soon as possible, but don't make me wait too long. If you want to build bridges, you need to agree to this as a first step. You need to meet me halfway, but I won't wait forever."

"Momma will treat her badly. I won't have that," I remarked, my voice slightly calmer now, my mind actually considering what he'd offered.

"I'll have words. She won't say a thing," he assured. I stayed silent, unable to look anywhere but, unseeing, at my hands on my lap.

"Rome. I know you don't have a close relationship with your momma. She's never been able to get over what I did. But you're mine, blood of my blood, and I got a lot of penance to serve for the way I've done you wrong." Sitting back in his chair, he concluded. "I'm a physical and intolerant man, and all this marriage talk of late has pushed me to the brink. Let's start afresh... That is if you want to be part of our lives."

Abruptly standing from my seat, unaware of how the fuck to digest all this crap coming my way, I said, "I'll speak to Mol and let you know."

I didn't wait for his reply, but halfway to the door, I looked back and asked, "What about Shel and Mr. Blair? What you going to say to them?"

A smile spread on his lips, one that I couldn't read. Doubt flooded my mind once more. "I'll handle them. Don't worry," he dismissed, before saying, "Again, don't keep me waiting too long."

Without another word, I walked to the front entrance, catching sight of my momma in the parlor, her usual drink in hand, staring out the large windows... and all before two in the afternoon. I didn't even bother to stop and say hello. My daddy may have been trying to save what scraps were left of our relationship, but there was no love lost on Momma's part.

I drove furiously down the freeway, trying to decipher whether or not this was a trick. I never wanted Molly tied up in the constant war between my folks and me, but what if this was genuine? All I'd wanted was for my folks to want me, and if this was my only chance, should I take it? It was probably all a load of crap, wasn't it? A convincing—and disturbing—ruse for some other plan... Argh, FUCK! I just didn't know! Didn't know if I should risk it.

My daddy was playing with my emotions. He'd always known I strived for his approval; I just wasn't sure if he really wanted to start again or if he was being truly fucked up and using those emotions against me. My mind was in turmoil and there was only one person to calm me down, to settle me. I needed to see my girl.

21

I took one last look at myself in the mirror: black slacks and a white shirt. I looked like a total dick. I reached for my wallet and keys and headed out my bedroom door.

Austin was in the TV room, and I caught his eye as I passed. "You outta here?" he shouted out to me.

Standing in the doorway, my arms holding too tight to the wooden frame, I sighed, "Yeah." Looking back at my best friend, I asked, "Hell, man, am I doing the right thing?"

Carillo sat forward and shrugged. "I told you last night, my instinct would be to tell you not to go, but folks can change, Rome. I don't know what to tell you. Maybe your daddy has had some divine epiphany or some shit, you know, seen the light?" The fucker just laughed at that. I couldn't help but smile along with him, despite my nervous mood. "One thing's for certain. You'll find out soon enough," he said, his face suddenly serious.

Nodding, I slapped the doorframe twice. "I'm out."

"Good luck, man."

Getting into my truck, I tried to stay calm. Something in my gut told me this was all wrong, but hell, Mol had been so damn insistent. I knew she wanted me to fix the problems with my folks. She didn't have family and didn't want that same situation for me. But I hadn't told her much about my past, the relationship I had with my parents. She knew they sometimes hit me—mostly in my past—belittled me, forced me to put my duty above my dreams, but she didn't know the extent of abuse I'd suffered at their hands, didn't know why I'd been treated with such cruelty. I couldn't bring myself to tell her. I hadn't ever told anyone... I was ashamed.

Pulling in front of her sorority house, I almost just called the whole thing off. I'd nearly done that several times, but Mol's words from yesterday still played on my mind.

* * *

As soon as I left my folks' place, I drove straight to Mol's sorority house and climbed up to the balcony where she sat surrounded by her laptop and all her books.

"Still working hard I see," I said as I finished kissing my girl hello.

"Yeah. Professor Ross was told this morning that we have a timeslot of when we need to present the paper in

Oxford—we go in a few months." Her excited smile was huge.

Frowning, I sat forward on the chair I'd occupied. "You're going to England in a few months? Since when?"

"Since always…" Mol went to explain that she needed to go do the presentation at Oxford University to help her secure a PhD program, but I really didn't want her to go. She promised to be back for the championship games though, so I'd just have to suck it up when the time came. It was just one more bastard thing to mess up my day.

My girl moved toward me, seeing my drop in mood, and sat on my lap.

"What's wrong?"

Sighing, I answered, "One guess."

"Parents?"

"Bingo."

"What now?" I caught the worry in her voice.

"They want to meet you. They've invited us to dinner tomorrow night. They're notching up their tactics."

She actually reared back in shock. "Really? I never thought they'd want to meet me… ever."

"Me either." Her shock waned at that comment and hurt took its place.

Pulling her closer, I said, "Hey, I didn't mean to hurt your feelings, but they're not happy about us, Mol. They've made no secret about that."

"I know. It just sucks."

"I'm telling them no," I said, finally making up my mind. Mol was far too important to me to put in jeopardy.

Sitting up, determination on her face, she said, "No. Screw it, let's go. Show them how good we are together. By seeing us, it might help them understand."

"They won't understand and I won't have them attack you. I've coped with it for years; I'm not watching you take the same treatment. You've seen my daddy in action. He doesn't tolerate disobedience. My momma's vindictive and cruel. Why do you want to officially meet people like that?"

Smiling at me, her inner strength shining through, she pressed, "I want to bridge the gap for your sake."

* * *

And after much more persuasion and a couple of hours buried deep in her soft depths, we'd accepted the invitation and right now, in this truck, all I could think was that I'd completely fucked up.

I hadn't realized how long I'd been sat in my truck, just staring out of the window, when the sorority house's main door opened and out walked Molly, immediately stealing my damn breath.

Opening the truck door, I got out and when she was a few steps away, reached out and pulled her into my arms. "Baby..." I croaked, my anxiety showing in my voice.

Wrapping her arms around my waist, she gripped onto me tight. "Hey, Rome. You okay?"

Pulling back, I pressed my lips to hers and nodded, "Yeah, no, maybe. I don't know..."

Scrunching up her nose playfully, she tilted her head, asking, "Mm? You look kind of uncomfortable. Then again, I've never seen you in anything other than a T-shirt, jeans, and those damn cowboy boots you never take off, unless it's to put on your cleats. Is it the fact you're all suited and booted in your Sunday best that has you scowling and sitting outside my sorority like a creepy stalker?"

Unable to hold in a laugh, I put my arm around her shoulders and led her to the truck. "Get in, sexy, before I shut that mouth of yours for you." Lifting her into the high cabin, I couldn't resist skirting my hand up her bare leg and running my fingers along her panty-covered folds. Yelping at the touch, she scowled at me as she belted up.

God, I loved this girl so damn much. As I stared at her, I felt the familiar sense of dread that had been plaguing me since I'd accepted this bastard invitation. I couldn't lose her. I was non-negotiable on that, and no matter what my folks were up to, they would have to learn that too.

Jumping into the driver's seat and pulling out onto the road, I looked over at Mol, who was fiddling with radio, head nodding along to Blake Shelton telling the world they could *kiss his country ass*, singing every line, her out-of-place English accent sounding completely wrong against his southern Oklahoma drawl. Snorting through my nose, I shook my head, earning a scowl from the wannabe Dolly Parton beside me.

"What?" she asked, eyes narrowed.

"Nothing. You just look all beautiful tonight and I'm having a real hard time focusing on the road." It was true, maybe not what I was thinking right then, but she wouldn't appreciate me ripping on her for her terrible singing.

She ran her hands down her dress, no longer singing, and began worrying her lip. "It's so not me. Ally dressed me up like a bloody Barbie doll in all this designer stuff to make me look appropriate for your fancy parents—I look like I'm trying too hard. They'll see right through me." She let out a sigh and shook her head. "I guess I'm just worried they'll hate me." Flicking her eyes up at me nervously, she added, "Well, hate me more than they already do."

That sentence alone just sliced through my heart. It was so friggin' clear she didn't want to go tonight, and it became more than apparent she was doing all this for me, sacrificing her pride for me.

I'd never felt more like a selfish ass.

For the next fifteen minutes, we didn't speak.

I couldn't.

Sensing my strange turn in mood, Mol scooted over to me, pressing in close, her leg hitching over mine. A wave of protectiveness took hold and I instructed, "I want you to listen to me, okay?" We needed to be prepared, make a plan in case this so-called "olive branch" was a huge load of crap.

Sitting up, those golden-brown eyes looked at me intently.

"They will probably pick on anything they can tonight, viciously. Whatever they say, don't let it get to you. I'll protect you. If you need to leave at any time, for whatever reason, we go—no ifs or buts. But promise me you won't let them hurt you."

Swallowing hard, she whispered, "I promise."

Gripping her thigh, using the skin-on-skin contact to gain strength, I said, "Then why do I have a feeling I'm about to lose you?"

Without missing a beat, my girl made me pull over, and no sooner than I had parked on the graveled hard shoulder, she straddled my lap, saying sternly, "You will not lose me."

I wanted to believe her so bad. But if this was all a setup, if my parents somehow got to her, she'd bail on me the first chance she got. Why would she stick around? Panic swelled at that thought.

Looking her dead in the eyes, I tried to tell her how much I loved her, but the anxiety was making me lose all sense. "I can't, Mol. You mean so much to me. Do you know that? Do you realize how I feel about you? How much I need you? Because I do. I know I don't say much about my feelings, but... but... I... I..." *I love you. I fucking love you...* But the words wouldn't come, stuck in my throat, along with intense fear.

"Shh... you don't need to do this. Romeo, you've given me a reason to be happy. I haven't been okay for such a long time. You've brought me back to life. Do you know that?"

Calming slightly, I confided, "They're not good people, baby. I know you don't believe me, but there is no way tonight is about anything other than asserting their power over me. It's always about that." I pressed my head into her neck. "They're never going to let me go, never going to just let me be happy with you. They'll do something; they always do something to ruin my life."

That was true. Hindsight taught me that they had never, and I mean *never,* done anything but make my life hell. Tonight had to be bullshit; it had to be a setup. I quickly asked myself what was more important: repairing a fucked-up relationship with my folks or being good with my girl?

There was no contest.

"We're going home. We're not doing this shit," I stated, moving to unseat Molly from my lap.

"Yes, we are," she insisted, refusal etched in her every muscle. I knew that was my girl putting her foot down and I knew she wouldn't change her mind.

Fuck.

We were actually going to do this.

22

Two hours later...

Red-hot rage. That's all I felt, all that was driving me, keeping me going, not oxygen or blood, just boiling hot rage.

My foot pressed on the gas and driving like a NASCAR pro, I headed for the cabin. I wouldn't make it all the way home.

Focusing on the road, I had to drown out the sound of Molly whimpering beside me, or I was going to go back. For the first time in my life, I knew I wouldn't be able to stop myself... I'd kill them, fucking kill them both for what they'd done. Everyone had a breaking point—I'd just found mine.

The gravel crunched under the weight of the truck, the tires jerking from left to right as I wrestled the steering wheel for control down the old, bumpy driveway.

"Romeo…" Molly whispered from beside me and I couldn't look at her, I couldn't see the expression that would accompany that desperate and grief-stricken voice.

"Not now. *God!* Just… be quiet…" I snapped, wincing at what she must be thinking of me. A pained cry ripped from her throat and she curled her body away from me, the crystal clip from her hair falling to the floor.

I was right to have been suspicious of the invite and my parents' intentions in meeting my girl. The fucking vultures had circled us, lured us in, and then pounced. Hell, not pounced—ripped us apart until there was nothing left, shredding our dignity and stomping all over my girl's already broken heart.

Spotting the cabin, I practically jumped out of the truck while it was still moving. The cramped space of the seats, too small, claustrophobia fucking choking me.

Barging through the cabin, my childhood place of salvation, I began kicking and lashing out at anything in sight, thinking back over every detail of tonight…

"Mother. Always a pleasure," I said as she opened the door and immediately started on the fact that we were late.

"Shame the same can't be said for you," she'd bit back.

Gripping an old lamp, I lifted it off the floor and launched it against the wall, enjoying the sound of it smashing to smithereens.

"You kept us waiting on our invitation for dinner tonight, boy. Not acceptable!" my daddy had snarled the minute he saw us. I couldn't fucking believe it. Where was the man who was telling me he wanted to build bridges? Where was the bastard olive branch? His smirk at my obvious shock said everything. He'd planned the whole thing to make me look like a fool; he'd lied to me yesterday in his study. They were going to tear Molly to pieces right in front of me. They were going to make her leave me.

The side table was next, and gripping one of the thin, fragile legs, I picked it up and slammed it to the floor.

"So, Molly, I suppose you're aware of Romeo's plans after college?" my momma asked Molly as we sat on the couch, my daddy glaring at me, smiling in victory when my eyes met his.

"With football?" Molly had asked, pulling my focus back on my momma. My parents' laughter echoed around the huge room.

"Absolutely not! We're talking about his duty to take over the family business," my daddy said, moving closer from his place against the fire.

"Daddy," I threatened, my voice low and harsh. Molly's frightened eyes darted around the three of us, her hand gripping mine so tight it almost cut off the circulation in my fingers.

"She needs to know, Rome," my daddy went on. "She needs to know that you won't have time to continue your player lifestyle." Molly stilled.

270

"Leave it!" I shouted. "I won't do this with you tonight."

As I stood in the quiet cabin, I tried to put myself in my folks' shoes. Had I been that much of a letdown over the years? Enough to deserve such blatant cruelty? And Mol, Molly's only crime was in being with me—the first person I'd truly let in and they were trying to rip her from me. Hell, for all I knew, she could've already decided she'd had enough. She hadn't bothered coming in here after me. Then again, she was probably scared out of her mind. I was acting insane.

Expelling a loud scream that had been building in my throat, I pounded to the wall and began punching it again and again and again at what had happened next…

Then, all of a sudden, there was Shelly, striding in like she owned the place, kissing my momma and being treated like the daughter they'd never had—hell, the child *they'd never had.*

The grand plan was finally revealed. They'd wanted to get it through to Mol that Shelly was what they wanted, and like my daddy and momma always said, they always get what they want!

I flew toward my parents and snapped, "How dare you do this to us!"

"Shelly is family and Molly needed to be informed of a few things that may affect your little… relationship," my daddy said in his usual condescending tone.

"Don't start this shit again, and while you're at it, treat Molly with some fuckin' respect!"

And then the fucker bowed, ridiculing my girl. "Your Majesty, how is the queen?"

My hands began to shake with fury. Molly was friggin' mute beside me, her golden eyes huge with fear. "You invited us here for dinner, to meet her, why? Was it all bullshit? Was your plan to rip on her the minute she walked through the damn door?"

My daddy looked at Molly like she was a piece of shit on the bottom of his shoe. "Why the hell would we want to meet a gold-digging whore, let alone entertain her at dinner? She probably struggles to even use cutlery she's so poor. Shel's told us a lot about your girlfriend."

And then he put the final nail in the coffin. "Tonight was an intervention. We had to get you to bring your new titbit before us somehow. A dinner invite seemed best. So now you're here and we have your attention. You'll do as instructed and end this charade. Immediately. Send your little British slut on her way... preferably back across the Atlantic."

I couldn't believe the level of viciousness coming from his mouth. He had always been a cruel bastard, but his treatment of my girl was like nothing I'd ever seen before.

"You invited us here to break us up? Christ, this is extreme, even for you!" I remarked, rubbing my hand across my head, feeling the constant control I had on my anger beginning to slip.

I wrenched the old shitty curtains from the windows, and tore them in two in my hands, dropping the faded red shreds of material to the floor. Back across the Atlantic...

the fucking Atlantic! Agh! I hated him... HATED him! I swear the man's evil.

Still too pissed to calm down, I snapped the frail curtain rail in half, throwing the fractured pieces across the room.

My drunk-ass momma stumbled forward, pointing in Molly's face. "Molly here needs to know that her scheming won't work." Taking a large drink from her glass, she slurred, "Leave him alone. You have no idea who you're taking on, do you? Shelly is engaged to Rome and some trailer trash nothing will not get in the way of that. It's been arranged for years. I always get what I want, darlin'. You just remember that."

My control snapped and I embraced the searing hot rage pumping around my body. I looked dead into the nervous eyes of Shelly and spat, "I'm not engaged to her and never will be! Screw your fuckin' fortune; I want nothing to do with it!"

Lifting my head, I stared at the old chipped wall, now spattered with hole after hole, my fists covered in splinters and plaster, the room a complete mess, scattered with broken furniture. I stepped back, the pain in my chest affecting my breathing, and not knowing what to do next, I walked forward, pressing my forehead to the wall.

Taking tight hold of Mol, I began dragging her out the door, when my momma ran after me, lashing out and slapping me hard across the face. The smell of liquor was so strong on her breath that I was surprised she could even stand. "You insolent child! You dare speak to us like that after

273

everything we've given you? You're the worst thing that ever happened to this damn family, you ungrateful piece of shit! You never get anything right, do you? Always screwing things up, and bringing that into our lives is the worst to date," she shrilled, pointing her finger in my face.

"Take that back," I threatened in return. My mind was racing. She'd never shown such hatred toward me in front of anyone else. Was she losing it? Was she so drunk that she was about to let the truth slip?

"Enough!" my daddy shouted, obviously worrying about the same thing. "I won't discuss this any further. Quit fucking the girl and get on board with what's happening. Your one fucking purpose in this life is to do as we say and do your duty as a Prince! So do it! And stop being such a pig-headed asshole!"

Laughing without humor, I gripped Molly's hand and announced, "I'm through with y'all. I choose Molly. I choose to not be in this fucked-up life anymore. Jesus Christ! What more can you do to me?! You're the worst fuckin' people I've ever known. I'm your only son and you can't stand me." I had one more question, and even then, I couldn't help but hope the answer would change. "Have you ever even loved me? Ever just once felt anything for me?"

My daddy curled his lip in disgust. "How can anyone love you? How can anyone love a stone in their shoe? You're just one giant disappointment. But you will do your duty to this family, regardless. We'll find a way to make you see reason, you mark my words." The answer was always the same. I'd been a damn fool to ever think otherwise—they would never accept me.

My breath stuttered. Even just reliving tonight's shitshow felt like a thousand daggers being plunged into my back one at a time.

I was in a bad place, one of the worst I'd ever been… And then the door opened, and I knew my girl was here to leave me for good, to deliver the final killer blow.

23

As soon as I heard the door shut, I decided to use offense as the best defense and whirled to face Mol.

"You should never have made us come here!" I screamed, seeing her red-with-crying eyes enlarge at the lack of control I had over my anger. "I warned you! I told you they weren't happy about us, but you didn't listen to me. You told me it'd be okay, that they would see us together and realize what we meant to each other. But no! Instead, you agreed to your own fucking execution. Christ, Mol! The way they treated you..." I waited for a sign, for some indication of what she was thinking. But there was nothing. She was numb, unmoving, and my heart fucking broke.

"Rome—" She eventually began to speak, but the way she said my name was wrong... off. Panic set in my veins and I interrupted her before she could continue—I

SWEET ROME

couldn't hear that she was leaving me. It would be the final straw.

Pacing before her, I yelled, "I could've stopped it—*should* have! I knew what they were capable of and still I trusted that you could handle it. But I saw your face in there, Mol—you fuckin' checked out on me!" She had. They'd attacked and she had cowered.

Red burst across her cheeks, and she stepped forward, eyes blazing, meeting my shit head on. "I don't care about what they said to me, but I care about what they are doing to you! Why do they hate you so much, Romeo? There has to be a reason. That was beyond brutal. What kind of parent hates their child for no reason?" Tears welled in her eyes and she croaked, "Your mother, the way she hit you, how could she treat her only son that way?" She was struggling to keep her composure.

Why did she hit me? Why does she hate me? Fuck! There was a reason all right! I'd kept the damn secret for so long that I felt I was buried under its massive weight.

Staring at Molly and pulling desperately on my hair, the words not coming easily, I decided to just spit it out quickly, get it done. I'd lost her anyway; may as well tell her why my life was so fucked up.

Blood roared in my ears, and reaching forward, I let go and heard myself shout, "*Because I'm not hers!*" I sucked in a sharp breath when the sentence had finally been said.

I'd told someone. For the first time in twenty-one years, I'd told someone what my folks had fought so hard to protect, and my hands began to shake with the enormity of what I'd just done.

"W-what?" Molly whispered, her eyes huge with surprise, pulling me back to the here and now.

Skirting a finger down her cheek, needing the support, I repeated, "Because. I'm. Not. Hers. You wanted to know so badly why they hate me. Well, that's why."

"No…" I could see the disbelief. No one knew. No one had ever fucking known. It was a secret I was meant to take to the grave.

Molly's eyes darted around the room and her hands cupped her mouth, tears dripping down onto her cheeks. The slow burn of antagonism built as I thought of my folks, but my girl needed to understand.

Stepping back out of her embrace, I confessed. "Momma was barren. The fuckin' bitch was barren. The one thing she needed to be able to do as the perfect wife was breed, and she couldn't deliver, couldn't give the great Prince Oil tycoon of Alabama an heir."

"Ohmigod, Rome—" she cried, her head shaking back and forth. But I was on a roll, my untold story unstoppable, now set free.

"They couldn't adopt because that would be an embarrassment, right? They couldn't get a surrogate and risk all of Tuscaloosa knowing she was unable to have kids. But, hey, fate decided to intervene just in time."

I laughed, but there was no amusement in my mind, no humor to find in this damned messed-up story. "One of my daddy's many paid whores turned up on their doorstep, pregnant with a child she sure didn't want but was willing to hand over at its birth to his biological father… for a good price."

Molly stumbled, her eyes fixed on mine as she put two and two together.

"Yeah, Mol. It was me. My father got a private paternity test and I was his, the fuckin' heir to his fortune. The whore had one stipulation, though. They had to keep the name she'd given me. She wanted control, to play some sick, twisted game with her most frequent customer, probably pissed she would never be more than a fuck to him. My name was a lifelong reminder of where I came from, and my mother despised it, despised *me* on sight."

"Romeo," she whispered, sympathy saddening her face.

"Romeo." I still hated that fucking name—no Bama in that name.

My legs felt weak. All the fight I'd had for so long drained out like a flood. I couldn't deal with my parents controlling shit anymore, and I was pretty convinced this would be where Mol checked out too. Hell, who wouldn't?

Dropping my head, completely done, I hushed out, "So there you have it. I'm the illegitimate child of my father's slut on the side, but they had to have me, didn't they? The fact of the matter was my father wanted to keep his assets in the family. He was expected to have children, an heir. My arrival ensured that could still happen. They paid for the whore to have me in secret. Then my folks disappeared for a year, you know, off on some bullshit cruise, and they returned with a new baby—and of course, the great billionaire's lies were believed."

Moving to the couch, I used it to support my weight— I hadn't dared look Mol in the eyes during all of this shit, didn't want to see my future slipping away. "My momma fuckin' hates me. I'm a living, breathing reminder that my father was a cheat. But that's not the only reason they're like this. They expected a docile, obedient child, who, when they said jump, would ask how high. But not their letdown of a son, right? I ended up being freakishly good at sports and I had my own mind and own dreams—unacceptable for a Prince!"

The more I talked, the more the agony built back up.

"How dare I? How dare I want something for myself after they'd so selflessly taken me in? Taken me in and reminded me every minute of every fuckin' day that I was the product of a paid fuck. Beat me until I couldn't even hold a football, let alone throw one—if you're injured, you can't play, right? So my daddy made it a frequent thing, a father-son weekly tradition."

"N-no one helped you? Figured it out?" Molly stuttered out.

The thought made me laugh. "Who's going to take on a powerful billionaire and question why his kid flinches whenever someone touches him?

"Then to make it worse, their failure of a child is expected to enter the draft for NFL, twice, and was forced to say no, to sacrifice his dreams just in case people found out he's not really Kathryn Prince's biological pride and joy. The mass of skeletons must be locked up real tight!"

My voice sounded raw, all of the screaming and the emotion tearing me in two. Finally lifting my head, I stared at Molly, still rooted to the same damn spot, and walking to her, spread my arms wide—I had nothing left to give.

"So there you go, Mol. That's why my parents hate me and why my being with you has just added to their already mountain-high disappointment of their beloved fuckin' son." I worked hard to keep in the tears, didn't want to expose myself so open, but when my girl edged forward, straightening my clothes with unashamed affection, and pressed closer into my chest, I almost broke. She just made everything better.

"That's why everyone calls you Rome, not Romeo... why you hate it so much. It reminds you of your past," she stated, smoothing back my messy hair.

"Yeah," I rasped out. "My birth momma said if they didn't keep Romeo, she'd go to the media, expose the story, and they couldn't have that, so they agreed... reluctantly. Had her sign some contract to keep quiet."

Loving the feeling of her warm breath against my skin, I huffed. "What the hell kind of name is Romeo for the prized son of the wealthiest family in Alabama? My folks always called me Rome in public, but in private, I was Romeo. They used it as a taunt and curse. Romeo the whore's son, Romeo the non-returnable bad gift—and they never, ever let me forget it."

"Where did she go, your birth mother?"

My stomach churned as I thought of the woman who practically sold me off like some damn piece of meat. I used to wonder if my life would've been better if she'd kept me, but hell, she was just some whore, some bitter slut. Ironic really considering that's what I'd turned into too, a whore who treats girls like crap.

I caught Mol's expectant gaze, awaiting my response, so I shook my head and said, "Probably back to whatever hole she crawled out of."

Sighing deep, she dropped her gaze and said quietly, "Romeo, I—"

I knew this was it, the part when she let me down gently. I wouldn't recover from the loss.

I couldn't deal, so thrust her out of my arms and said bitterly, "You're going to leave me, aren't you? I knew I'd lose you. I just knew it. Who's going to put up with my parents' shit? I'm not worth everything they'll put you through if we stay together, am I?"

Flashback after flashback of my life over recent months slammed into my mind. I'd never known such happiness, and although I'd coped with a lot during my life, I knew I wouldn't be able to do it without her by my side anymore. Sometimes you just know when a person is meant for you, and I always had with her. She got me… She fucking saved me.

I could no longer control my breathing and a hollow pain burst in my stomach, causing me to slump on the sofa and, fuck, but I couldn't stop the tears this time. The thought of her leaving reduced me to a crying friggin' mess.

Gentle arms folded tightly around my back and chest and I flinched and tried to get away. Molly shushed me soothingly and pulled me down until my head was lying on her lap, her fingers moving to comb through my hair.

I didn't know if it was the comfort of her touch or the enormity of all that happened tonight, but a flood of memories raced to the front of my mind: punches, hits, harsh insults, punishments… *everything.*

Molly was sniffing and shaking above me, and I knew she was crying too. I'd never loved her more than I did in that moment, sharing my grief, and when she lifted my face with her hands, whispering, "Romeo—" I sucked up a breath, and for the first time in my life uttered the words, "I love you… I love you," as I stared into her golden eyes, praying she would just give me one more chance to make her happy.

"W-what?"

I lay back on the couch, suddenly exhausted, and brought my girl to lie above me, confessing, "I love you. I love you beyond anything I could've ever imagine was possible."

A gamut of emotions danced across her face before it melted into what looked like relief, and she whispered, "I love you, too, babe. I love you so, so much."

I'd never heard those words directed at me before. *I love you*—three little words that, up until I'd met Molly, I thought were reserved for sappy fucking films and unrealistic dreamers. But hell, hearing them from her lips made me feel alive, and I couldn't believe she meant it. She'd been verbally torn apart because of me, thrust from her quiet life into a shitstorm.

Rubbing at her cheeks, I asked, "Baby, you do? Even after—"

Pressing her finger to my lips, she said, "I'm not going anywhere. I came in here to tell you that. I was in the truck, listening to you hurting, and I knew I had to be

283

with you no matter what, tell you that I'm never going to leave you."

"But my parents…"

"Yes, your parents tonight were something else, but they won't ever chase me from you, from loving me. We're star-crossed, Romeo. Interfering parents come as part of the package."

And there it was, her unshakable strength, her ability to pull me back from the darkness, and I couldn't help but smile. She was always searching for the fairy tale, the happily ever after. But she was mine, and she fucking loved me.

"I feel stripped bare right now… like someone has ripped open my chest and all you're seeing is a mangled heart held together by jagged scars," I whispered, seeing her eyes glisten once more.

Fingers crawled up to my chest and she began shedding me of my shirt, button by button, pressing those damn soft lips against my heart.

It felt incredible.

Watching her slowly move down my body, I said, "No one has ever known what they're really like behind closed doors. I've never told a soul. You were a big old brick through their glass fortress tonight. I could see the panic in my daddy's eyes. You could destroy everything they've worked so hard for."

Pausing, she replied, "As bad as that was, I'm glad I was there, that I now know what you cope with. We can't erase the secrets and marred memories of our pasts, but we can build the next chapter of our lives together."

She wasn't leaving me.

"Mol…" I croaked, unable to finish the sentence.

"Shh…" she said, a teasing smile on her lips, and she began to push my shirt aside and shimmy down my legs.

Groaning at her touch, my hips lifted automatically as she began to undo the waistband of my slacks.

Fuck me. I knew that look in her eyes.

She pulled down my pants and boxers in one, and hard as fuck before her, she bent down and licked my cock from balls to tip, a long groan ripping from my throat. I needed this. I needed this from her so fucking bad.

Her hot mouth engulfed my dick in one swallow and any thought of tonight and all our problems left my mind. There was only my girl and me right now.

Gripping the back of her head, I pumped in and out of her mouth, and the whole time Molly just took it, giving me what I needed most—her acceptance.

But when she raked down my length with her teeth. I jerked and I groaned a desperate growl.

Fisting Molly's brown hair, I forced her off my junk. "Stand up."

With a hungry bite of her lip, she did as instructed, and within seconds I'd rid her of her clothes and she stood before me, naked, flushed, and ready.

Pushing her to the sofa, her thighs draping open, my cock twitched and I drank her in, needing a taste. "I didn't tell you to suck me, Shakespeare. You know you need to ask permission first." Her lips parted and she arched in untamed lust below me.

Leaning down and crooking her leg over my shoulder, opening her wide, I announced, "Now it's my turn," and dived between her legs. Molly expelled a long moan, only serving to egg me on further.

"Grip my hair," I ordered, momentarily lifting my head. Her fingers ran through it softly, but I wanted hard and rough. I wanted to fuck—raw and primal.

"Pull it! Mean it!" I ordered again, my voice curt and forceful.

With a rise of her hips and a guttural groan, she clawed at my hair, obeying me, and I plunged my tongue into her. My girl's breath was coming in hard pants, and I substituted my tongue for my fingers and latched onto her clit, sucking hard until she came, hot and sweet in my mouth.

Not stopping for even a moment, I turned a shifted Molly onto her stomach and bent her over the couch, kissing her lips, opening her soft thighs, and pounding straight into her warmth.

"Tell me you love me," I ordered into her long, brown hair, my nose buried in the crook of her neck.

Moaning, she murmured, "I love you. I love you so, so much."

Fuck me, those words. "Tell me you'll never leave me."

This time all I got was silence.

Her channel clenched and she tried to rock against me, but I pushed in to the hilt, making it impossible for her to move, holding tightly onto her hips, leaning down to whisper, "Do as I say or I won't give you what you want, what I know you need from me."

"Romeo! Stop it!" she cried, her voice thick with lust.

"Do it. You get me?" I growled, wrapping my fist in her long hair and taking her mouth only briefly.

"Argh!" she screamed, and glaring back at me, she said, "Yes, I friggin' get you!"

I drove into her once more. Christ, she felt amazing. "You do get me, baby. You're the only one to ever understand. You're the only one to ever know.

"Tell me you'll never leave me." I needed to hear it again. I needed the reassurance.

"I'll never leave you!" she answered immediately.

My hands were everywhere: her ass, her tits, her clit. "You'll never run," I barked out.

"I'll never run!"

"Promise me."

"I promise!"

"Romeo... I... ah!" Stiffening, she tipped over the edge, her tight center milking at my dick almost to the point of pain, taking me right over with her.

I slowly worked us down, my mouth sucking at the damp skin of her shoulder, a large red mark forming, evidence of my roughness left on her body. I didn't worry about what she would think; she liked it like this as much as I did.

Kissing and licking at the skin of her back, I whispered, "I love you, baby."

Relaxing into her exhausted body, I thought back over the day, and despite the shit we'd been through, right here, right now, holding Molly in my arms, I couldn't help but be thankful. The events of today had forced us to share our feelings with one another; it had brought us both to a better place.

After lighting a fire and lying back down on the couch, my girl draped over my chest, she asked, "Are you okay, baby?"

"I will be. I have you," I whispered. It was true. If I had Molly by my side, I could get through anything: psycho parents, delusional exes… anything.

Smiling at me shyly, she looked straight into my eyes and stated, "You chose me."

How the hell could she think I'd do anything else?

"And I'd do it again in a heartbeat," I assured, running my hand down her cheek.

"Have your parents ever been nice to you?" she asked, her fingers tracing lazy circles on my chest.

I ran my younger years through my mind, then miserably shook my head.

"Were you ever happy?"

"No."

"Are you now?"

This one was easy. "Completely. I finally know what it is to love and to be loved. But I'm scared as all hell that it'll end. My folks won't give up that easy."

"I'm staying with you," Molly said with authority, showing the determination of a little pit bull.

"Do you swear that to me?"

"I swear. I love you. I'm yours." Fuck, I couldn't speak at those words, at her unwavering certainty, so I just kissed her fingers, the palms of her hands, anywhere I could.

"So what now? Football? Greatness? World domination?"

"I guess so."

"What do you want, Romeo? What do you desire most from life?" She pushed, nodding her head encouragingly.

There was only one thing keeping me sane, so without thinking, I responded, "You."

Eyebrows drawn, she shook her head and said, "No, really, baby, what do you want? It's there for you to take."

I was unmoved. "Just you, baby. You feel like home to me."

Moving above me once again, she assured, "You have me. All of me, for as long as you want."

"Really? I've got you forever? Because I pretty much just cut myself off from the only family I have."

"Romeo, you're my family. You're it. You and my crazy friends are my entire reason for being. How can you not know that?"

I let out a pent-up breath. "Because I can't believe it's true."

"It's you and me, Romeo."

And it was. Some folks may think the way we were with each other was unhealthy, but what they didn't know was that it was Mol that had stopped me from going over the edge so many times. She diffused my anger, helped me focus on the good. She *was* my good, and I shouldn't have to explain that shit to anyone.

Molly leaned in for a kiss after all the talking was done, and that kiss turned from innocent to a whole load of not.

I pressed myself between her legs and just like that, I wanted her again.

"Romeo," Molly moaned immediately—and that was us, for the rest of the night, giving each other what we needed and then sleeping in each other's arms. Or at least she slept. I just worried about what the future held as I gripped on tight.

Turned out the next few months would be some of the happiest of my life. I heard nothing from my parents, Shelly stayed well away from both of us, and the Tide sailed through the football season undefeated.

The closer my girl and I got, the more I worried about the future. She wanted to be a professor and could move away to complete her PhD. By entering the NFL draft, I could be sent anywhere in the US, and it played on my mind all the damn time. Molly told me to relax, have fun, and it would all work out. So I let myself do that for the first time in my life.

But nothing ever stays good forever. Molly and I both had pasts that'd taught us that the hard way.

24

Three months later…

"Bring it, baby! Ain't nothing gonna stop the Tide!"

Walking into the locker room after practice, I was faced with the most fucking disturbing sight I'd ever seen—Jimmy-Don in his funky white briefs on a table, grinding a towel between his legs, his Stetson still firmly on his head… and nothing else.

"We got 'em boys. Gonna get another BCS National Championship, no doubt about it!" He didn't stop there, whooping and hollering for several minutes, and Austin moved to stand beside me, saying, "How he gets laid is beyond me, crazy fucker."

Laughing as Jimmy-Don worked our teammates into a frenzy, I couldn't help but get caught up in all the excitement too. The last three months I'd played like never before—we all had—and my girl, my girl attended every home game, even some away, and she kissed me, publicly, before each and ever one, the fans unwilling to have it any other way. They were beginning to love her just as much as me.

Coach chose that moment to enter the room, trying his damnedest to hold in his amusement of our offensive tackle working it like a pro.

"Jimmy-Don Smith! Get the hell down from there!" Grimacing, Jimmy-Don jumped off the table and followed the coach, apologizing until he was dragged away by a teammate and shoved into the showers.

Coach tried to hide his mirth, then finding me at the back, tilted his chin and signaled for me to meet him in his office.

Sitting before him, I asked, "What's up, Coach?"

"I wanted to let you in on a very interesting call I had yesterday."

Frowning, I said, "Okay…"

"It was from the head coach of the Seattle Seahawks." Excitement built in my chest, and I smiled; Coach did too.

"They're having a real tough time this season, and if things keep going south for them and we get it right, you'll be a first-round draft pick. You could find yourself heading north for Seattle, son. You'd be getting a fresh start away from Bama." I got what he was really saying—I'd be getting a fresh start away from my folks.

"I told the Hawks what I think of you."

I looked at him and frowned. *What the hell was that?*

Coach smiled and said, "Relax, I told them you're the best quarterback I've ever worked with, your work ethic is bordering on obsessive—which is a good thing—and you're one of the strongest kids I know, especially in the face of adversity. I told them you're the damn lottery, son."

Coach stood, always a man of few words, and clapped me on the shoulder, seeing I was choked up at his words, and left me alone to process all that was said.

Seattle.

Moving to my locker in a daze, I grabbed a shower and quickly dressed into my jeans and T-shirt. My thoughts were going crazy. I was excited by what Coach had just said, the fact I could get away to somewhere like Seattle. But I was also worried with when I should tell Mol. Right now the Hawks were a possibility, but I didn't want her to plan her future around it, in case things changed. Plus, we'd never even agreed that she *would* come with me. That was a conversation we needed to have.

Grabbing my things, I checked my phone. One message:

Al: Rome, when you get this, come straight to Molly's room. We're all with her until you get here. Al. XX

Frowning in concern, I turned to Austin. "Got to go. Something's up with Mol. Catch you later?"

"Sure. Hope she's okay." Slapping him on the back, I headed out of the stadium and raced to Molly's sorority house.

As soon as I arrived below her balcony, I heard a loud cry from inside her room.

Molly.

Fear saw me climbing up the trellis faster than ever, and when I landed on the balcony terrace, it was to find Molly on the floor, surrounded by her friends, all shedding tears too.

"Mol?" My girl didn't stop crying as I called out her name, but Ally lifted her head and paled at me frozen in shock. That only caused me to panic more.

"Mol! What's wrong with her?" I bit out more forcefully as I burst into the room. Molly still didn't stop in her tears, Lexi and Cass shielding her from my view.

Ally stood and came before me, chewing on her fingernail. She was nervous. I knew my cousin enough to know that. "Rome, calm down, okay?"

"No! What's wrong with her?" I looked over Ally's shoulder, but my girl still hadn't moved. Was she in pain? Was she really sick? Did she need the hospital? Shit! Did she have to leave to Bama? Too many messed-up scenarios raced through my head.

"Mol?" I tried to call out again. Still nothing, and this time I was losing patience… fast. Turning back to Al, I asked, "Is she sick? Why isn't she answering me? I got your message and came straight over."

"No. She's… erm…" Al couldn't say a damn thing either, and my stomach flipped.

"Was it Shelly? Has that bitch—"

"It's not Shelly either," Ally cut in.

"Then what's wrong…? Al, for fuck's sake, move outta my way!" I physically lifted my cousin out of my way and beelined for Mol, her friends moving so I could pick her up off the floor.

Once in my arms, I took in her too-white face, her damp skin, and the fact that her chest was convulsing from too many tears. Moving to her unmade bed, I placed her down, lying beside her, ignoring our friends, and pressed a kiss on each of her cheeks, her huge, nervous eyes scaring the absolute shit out of me.

"Baby, what's wrong?" I tried to ask gently, but my impatience was sneaking through.

Her eyes squeezed shut and she shook her head, still too emotional to speak.

I stared at our friends fidgeting nervously at the end of the bed and yelled, "Will somebody tell me what the fuck is going on?!"

Casting each other questioning glances, Cass pushed Ally forward and she said, "Rome, Molly needs to tell you. We'll go, give you some time to yourselves."

And that just caused me to worry more. What the hell could be so bad that my girl would be this hysterical and my cousin could barely make eye contact?

Within minutes, the girls had cleared, leaving me alone with Molly, my heart booming in anticipation of what she would say. Grasping her around the waist, I rolled us so she was above me. Her flushed face showed her surprise, but searching my eyes, she simply dipped forward, whispering, "I love you, Romeo."

If that was meant to soothe me, it failed, but I told her, "I love you, too." I couldn't get enough of those words, and then I just waited for her to speak.

But she didn't, causing me to groan loudly and say, "Mol—"

"I've been feeling off for a few days," she interrupted and my heart immediately sank.

She was ill? Fuck, was it serious, like really serious? I felt nauseous.

"Why the hell didn't you tell me?" I snapped out, now scared out of mind and pissed that she would keep something as important as her health a secret from me.

"I found out today why," she said almost inaudibly.

"And... what's wrong?"

"I'm... I'm..."

Fuck me, I was going to explode!

Gripping her harder around the waist, I shouted, "Christ! You're what, Mol?"

"I'm pregnant," she blurted out.

Golden eyes lowered, and my pulse took off like a hummingbird.

Pregnant. Shit, a baby. I was going to be a daddy?

"You're pregnant?" I stared at her in disbelief, feeling like every drop of blood had just drained from my body.

My girl seemed to have turned into a friggin' mute, so I flipped our positions, putting me on top. "You're pregnant?" I asked again and watched Mol's eyes well up.

"Yes, I'm pregnant, Romeo. I'm pregnant with your baby." Each word was like a punch.

Sitting up, I stared at the white wall before closing my eyes, lost in my thoughts. How would this work? Would Molly be able to finish her master's? Would it be the end of her education? Where would we live? I was going to be a daddy... And slowly, I realized that the thought of that didn't have me running for the hills like I'd always thought, but rather feeling so damn content I could barely breathe. I was having a baby with my girl.

So many questions circled through my mind, too many to keep up with, and then my girl fucking froze me to the spot with one simple sentence. "I'll make an appointment to see a doctor. I'll just get rid of it immediately."

Glaring at Molly below me, I barked, "You'd kill our baby?"

Bucking her body, trying to get up, Molly shouted, "Don't get all high and mighty on me now! I don't need to hear any moral shit! I'm trying to do the best thing for both of us. I'll cope with whatever I have to do. If that means having an abortion, then that's just what will have to happen. It doesn't mean I want to go through with it!"

"Then don't, baby, please. Getting rid of it can't be what you fuckin' want." No way was she killing our child. It was *our* child.

"I don't know what the hell I want!" she cried, the tears flowing once more. Shit. She was petrified, and I was being an ass.

Leaning down, I ran my hands through her hair. "Well, I do."

Taking hold of my wrists, she searched my face before saying, "But... you..."

"Jesus, I was shocked!" I cut in, shaking my head, then moving my hand to her stomach. "I'm still shocked, but that's our baby in there. We made it together."

Desperate for her to understand, I pulled up her T-shirt and kissed along her stomach, stating, "And it's not going anywhere. Promise me. I have real strong feelings about this, Mol. Don't destroy our God-given angel." Her silence almost killed me, but I had to make her understand how much this meant to me.

"Promise me I have a say in this. Don't have an abortion, please." She couldn't. God, I couldn't see her go through that.

I waited, barely breathing, pressing my forehead to her flat stomach until she whispered, "I promise."

Relief like nothing I'd felt before settled in my bones, and I moved back to take the lips of my girl... the mother of my child.

As soon as our mouths meshed together, the same need that I always felt around my girl shot through my veins like a drug. Ridding Molly of her jeans, I freed myself and in seconds, plunged into her wet warmth.

Wrapping her legs around my waist, Molly moaned into my ear, clawing at my back and murmuring my name.

"I love you, Mol," I said against her lips.

Tears slipped from her eyes as I pushed into her slowly; she studied my face as I took her, unhurried and slow.

We came together, holding hands, and I swear something within me changed right then. I realized I didn't need the controlling fucking all the time with Mol;

it could be different... I trusted her enough to relinquish my controlling tendencies.

"That's the softest you've ever made love to me. It felt so different," Molly whispered into my hair falling over her face. Pulling back, our foreheads touched and she smiled. "I loved it."

"You're carrying precious cargo now, baby. I need to be more careful with you... with you both."

A wave of happiness seemed to settle over us both and I sloped to the side, pulling my girl to face me, her eyes bigger than normal behind thick brown frames. I'd been so worried before I hadn't even noticed that her contacts were gone.

"You look like my old Mol with these glasses and your hair like that. The girl I looked at months ago, on her hands and knees, cussing in that fuckin' hot accent in humanities block, wearing neon-orange shoes, and I knew, without a shadow of doubt, that she would one day be mine."

"One day," Mol teased with a smile, referring to my tattoo.

Swallowing, I confided, "I always wondered if one day I'd have a family, if I'd ever be happy enough with someone... with myself, to have a child." It was true, but with Molly by my side, the thought didn't scare me quite so much.

Reaching out and gripping my hand, panic set in Molly's eyes and she admitted, "Romeo, I don't think I can be a mother. We haven't had normal families. We have no idea how to be in a normal family! How the hell can we bring up a child? We're far too young. What do we have to offer a baby?"

"Something we never had." Her eyes were as wide as saucers. "Listen to me. Together we can do it. Together we can do anything. We can be good parents."

"But your football…"

"So what? I'll get drafted in April and you'll come with me, with our son or daughter. You can still do your PhD and achieve your dreams. We can have it all. Just please… don't destroy our child, our first child." I knew we could make it work if she would only let me try.

"Rome—" She sighed, defeated.

Shaking my head, I covered her mouth with my finger. "I could've been destroyed, but my birth mother didn't. She had me." I took her hand and laid it against my chest, right above my pounding heart. "I'm here because she chose me, even if she didn't actually want me. Yeah, my family did a real number, but I got through it and it led me to you, my smart English girl—the girl that saved me. The girl who showed me how to love."

Her frown line softened and she said, sadly, "Your parents will think I've done it on purpose to trap you."

My parents.

Shit. Just the mention of them had my protective instincts roaring into the stratosphere. "I don't give a fuck what they'll think. In fact, I've no intention of ever telling them. I was serious when we left their house that night. I'm done with them. You're my life now; you're my everything. You and our baby."

She simply nodded, but I couldn't get the worry of my parents out of my head. I hadn't heard from them for months. We'd broken all ties, but if they found out about Molly being pregnant, I didn't know what they would do. *If* they would do anything. Maybe they wouldn't; maybe they really were through with me…

We couldn't hide it. Hell, Shelly lived in this sorority house. It was rare that they were ever around one another, but they did bump into each other now and again, and when Mol was heavily pregnant, it was going to be kind of hard to ignore a huge belly. And that bitch would go straight and tell my folks. I had no doubt about that.

I knew one thing, and that was that those sadistic fuckers wouldn't get within a mile of my child; they would never get a chance to sink in their claws. A fleeting thought suddenly made me stiffen.

Mol looked up and narrowed her eyes. "What? What is it?"

Breathing deep, I asked, "What if I turn out like my folks? What if I'm ingrained to be a horrible father? You can't fight genes, Mol. What if I'm like my daddy? What if I let our child down?"

Pressing a kiss to my lips, Molly pulled back, reassuring me. "You'll be perfect."

"But you don't know that, do you?" I argued, my stomach churning, a sickening fear taking root.

Taking my hand and laying it flat to her stomach, she said softly, *"I have also seen children successfully surmounting the effects of an evil inheritance. That is due to purity being an inherent attribute of the soul."*

"Who said that?" I asked, the sincere sentiment from Molly's lips meaning everything to me. She had complete and utter faith in me and anything I did.

"Gandhi," she announced and breaking a grin, play punched my shoulder. "And you call yourself a philosopher!"

"Em, no, smartass. I take philosophy as a minor. I'm a business major... and a damn good one too."

"Whatever, not everyone can be as spectacular as me!" she quipped and then burst into fits of giggles.

"Maybe not, and you'll be a hell of a spectacular momma too."

"You really believe that?" she asked nervously.

"With all my heart."

25

"Is it done?" I asked Diana, the manager of the Tide club shop, as I entered.

Face lighting up, she beamed. "Sure is, honey. It's so damn cute I almost died!"

Leaning on the counter, I waited as she disappeared out back, then came back holding it up proudly for me to see.

"Jesus Christ," I whispered, and pride burst into my chest.

"Hey, no blaspheming!" Diana joked. "But yeah, I get why you said it. Adorable, ain't it?"

"It's perfect," I replied, pretty damn speechless.

Wrapping it in tissue paper and putting it into a white gift box, she looked at me and asked, "So who's this for, darlin'?"

"A relative," I answered, not even missing a beat. No one could know yet.

Smiling wide, she giggled. "Well, you'll be their favorite person in the whole damn world giving them a gift as good as this!"

"Yeah, hope so."

Taking the gift box and hiding it in the back of my truck, I pulled out onto the road to pick up my girl. It'd taken a few weeks to get the appointment, but I'd secured the best ob-gyn in all of Tuscaloosa, and we were heading there now for our first appointment.

We'd been advised to come in early due to Molly's momma's condition. Hearing that conversation on our initial meeting with the GP nearly had me going insane. As if the worry of my parents finding out about our little angel wasn't enough, finding out that Molly's momma died of something called severe preeclampsia almost had me collapsing to the floor. We'd been advised to choose an ob-gyn as soon as possible due to this, and Dr. Adams had requested an appointment immediately.

Fucking preeclampsia—just one more worry to add to the already sky-high pile.

I knocked on Mol's front door and she answered with a nervous smile and immediately moved in for a hug.

"You okay, baby?" I asked, rubbing her back.

Looking up, she answered, "Just nervous, I guess."

Holding out my hand, I tipped my head toward the truck. "Let's go."

"You must be Molly. I'm Dr. Adams." He introduced himself, standing to greet us.

"Nice to meet you, Dr. Adams." Molly shook his hand and turned to me, laying a hand on my arm. "This is my boyfriend, Romeo."

The doctor sent me a huge smile and shook my hand, saying, "Nice to meet you, Bullet. I'm a big fan—season ticket holder."

"And I recognize your face, Miss Shakespeare. The good luck charm that's going to help Bullet here lead us to the championship again."

I watched Mol blush, still hating the attention, and I pulled her into my chest. "She sure is. Thank you, sir."

And then he asked the one question I really didn't want him to. "Any news on the draft? Seattle Seahawks are dying this season. Their quarterback was forced to retire early through injury, and you're a sure win for first draft."

I flashed a panicked glance to Mol. The day I'd learned Seattle was looking like an option, Molly found out we were pregnant, and I hadn't dared bring it up with her since. I wasn't sure what my future held for us now. We hadn't even talked about our next step beyond making sure she and our baby were healthy.

Shifting uncomfortably, I answered, "I know as much as you, sir, but from what I've been hearing from my coaches, Seattle is a big possibility for me."

We sat down, and I got the meaning of Molly's long hand squeeze. We would be talking about Seattle later—great.

"Okay, you two, let's meet your baby," Dr. Adams said excitedly.

When the time came for the sonogram, I swear I'd never been more nervous for anything in my life. The doc inserted a long camera-looking thing inside my girl and she gripped onto my hand, squeezing it like a vise as I pressed kisses along her fingers.

When a tiny picture appeared on the screen beside Molly's head, all the breath left my body. I felt Molly stiffen and once again tighten her grip on my hand, but I couldn't speak. I don't know what the hell happened in that moment, but the stark realization that what I was looking at was a baby my girl and I created was life changing.

I loved Molly more than anything and often wondered if anything else in my life would ever come close to how I felt for her, but seeing our baby, hearing its tiny heartbeat, I realized I could love another in an entirely different way. The man who never thought he would ever love anyone, was incapable of such an emotion, right here in this room held the hand of the woman who'd not only opened his eyes and heart, but was also gifting him with the perfect unison of us both: a child.

Feeling wetness on my cheek, I realized I was crying, and for the first time ever, it was in happiness.

"Everything looks great and it measures as though you are... about... ah... about eight weeks along," Dr. Adams said, interrupting my fixation on the screen.

Seven months. In seven months we would have a little one of our own.

Dr. Adams passed Molly a picture of the sonogram, and standing up, I kissed her head, watching her staring, disbelieving, at our little angel. Turning to me, she smiled and placed the Polaroid on the bed beside her. She got that I was spellbound by everything happening lately, and as always, she put me first, knowing I needed to see that picture. It was the security that my life was now infinitely better.

"You can get dressed now, Molly, and we'll see you again in about two months unless you experience any of the problems we discussed. If so, you need to come straight back." *High blood pressure, dizziness, extreme swelling, severe headaches, abdominal pain, blurred vision…* Fuck me, the list seemed endless. I knew I'd become an overbearing dick, but shit, there was no way I was losing the two most precious things in my life. I'd never forgive myself if I did.

"Can we find out the sex, then?" Molly asked quietly.

"Hopefully," the doctor replied and slapped my back, forcing me to look up from the tiny image of our baby. "Congratulations, son, I'll see you at the championship in Georgia and *Roll Tide*!"

"Roll Tide," I croaked out.

Dr. Adams left, and Molly put the picture in my hand before shuffling to get off the bed.

As I watched her contented face, a small, happy smile still there on her lips, I just needed to hold her. Picking her up in my arms, I crushed her to my chest, just breathing in her vanilla scent.

"Romeo what—" she asked.

"Thank you, Mol. Just… thank you…" I said and, wrapping her hands around my neck in response, she whispered, "Thank you, too."

An hour later, we were back in Molly's room and I ran her a bath. I took advantage of the time alone and went back out to my truck, retrieving the gift, and laid the white box on the bed.

A short while later, the bathroom door creaked open and Molly came out in my favorite purple nightdress. She looked beautiful with her long, wet hair hanging low and her glasses firmly on her nose. She frowned when she caught sight of the box.

"What's that?"

"A present," I answered proudly. Molly eyed me skeptically and moved to the bed, sitting down beside me.

"What is it?" she asked, running her finger over the lid.

"Open it."

Shaking her head and giggling, she opened the box slowly, so delicately that I felt like ripping it open for her. My heart sank when I realized she probably hadn't been given gifts too often, and I made a mental note to rectify that fact.

Peeling back the white tissue paper, her hand went to her mouth. "Rome…"

"What do you think?" I asked, seeing the tears in her eyes.

She loved it.

Lifting the tiny Tide jersey from the box, she studied the front, then turned it around, whispering, "Prince, number seven."

"I know it's apparently bad luck before the end of the first trimester to buy things, you know, because things are still fragile, but I thought one small gift wouldn't hurt."

Pressing the tiny crimson jersey to her chest, she looked up at me and crawled forward, leaning down and kissing me softly on my lips.

Breaking away and studying the jersey once more, she looked me dead in the eyes and whispered, "We're going to be parents, Rome…"

Smiling, I tackled her gently to the bed, tapping her nose. "Damn good ones too… and I can't fuckin' wait."

Losing her smile, she stared down at the bed and asked, "Seattle?"

My heart faltered. "Maybe." Lifting her chin with my finger, I said, "Hey, look at me." She did as I asked and I said, "You're used to rain, right, you know, being from England?"

Cracking a smile, she blushed, saying, "Romeo Prince, are you asking me to come to Seattle with you?"

"I'm asking you to come with me wherever I get drafted. It's you and me, baby."

Tilting her head, she corrected, "No, it's you, me, *and* our angel."

Raising my eyebrow, I joked, "The Shakespeare/Prince Trifecta?"

Laughing loudly, she agreed, "The Shakespeare/Prince Trifecta."

Shuffling to Molly's stomach, I whispered, "You hear that, angel? You've officially made the coolest gang in all 'a Bama!"

Molly giggled as I moved back to share her pillow. Her eyes closed for a moment and she ran her fingertips up and down my bare bicep.

"What you thinking, baby?"

Snapping her attention to me, she sighed happily. "I just can't wait to see our tiny bundle in your arms."

My heart felt like it jumped to my throat in excitement and, without saying a single word in response, I crushed my girl into my chest.

I couldn't wait for that either.

26

"One more, Rome, one more!"

My arms shook with the strain as I bench-pressed the three-hundred-pound weight, sweat dripping into my eyes, and with one final push, I let out a grunt as I locked my elbows straight and Austin took the barbell from my hands, placing it back on the rack.

"Rome!" he shouted in reaction to my new PB, shaking my shoulders.

I stood up. Austin threw me my towel and said, "You pumped or what? I thought you were gonna give yourself a friggin' coronary!"

Reaching down for my water, I glanced over to Chris Porter, who'd been staring at me on and off all session with a shit-eating grin on his damn ugly face.

Jimmy-Don walked over from Porter's little posse, shaking his head, prompting me to ask, "What the fuck's up with him?"

"He's with Shelly Blair and won't shut the hell up over it."

That stilled me. "*He's* with Shel?"

"Apparently," Jimmy-Don said in disbelief.

"Then why the fuck is he glaring at me all the time? I was starting to think he was into me."

"Just let it go, Rome," Austin said, slapping my back. "He's a douche, no more explanation needed."

"Let what go?" I asked, suspicion creeping into my veins.

I watched Austin glance at Jimmy-Don and shake his head—way to be inconspicuous.

Turning to them both, I snapped, "You tell me or I'll go over there myself and find out."

Jimmy-Don paled and went to say something, when Coach entered the room. "Prince, office, now," he shouted.

Frowning, I turned around, watching him head into the back rooms out of sight.

"What the fuck you done now?" Austin asked, concerned.

"Fuck knows." I began walking away, but not before catching Porter laughing again with his friends. Turning back to Austin and Jimmy-Don, I said, "You're going to tell me what the hell is going on when I get back."

As I approached Coach's door, I felt a wave of unease. I had no idea why the hell he needed to speak to me so urgently, but whatever it was, it didn't feel good.

"Come in, Rome!" he yelled when I rapped on the closed door, and I entered the office and he gestured for me to sit down.

He looked stressed, out of sorts, and my stomach fell. "What is it?"

Running his hand over his forehead, he said, "We've been given the details on the venue for the SEC Championship homecoming dinner."

"Okay…" I couldn't figure out why the hell it would matter to me.

"Rome, your momma and daddy are hosting it. Prince Oil is funding the whole party and the dinner is at your folks' place… the Prince Plantation."

I just stared. I have no idea for how long, but it was long enough to encourage Coach to ask, "Son, you okay?"

"She's pregnant," I whispered.

Coach leaned forward, asking, "What?"

"Mol, my girl… she's pregnant."

My eyes fixed on Coach as he sat back and blew out a long breath. "Hell, son! You sure know how to do things the hard way. Ain't you a bit young to be a daddy?"

"It wasn't planned." I ran my hands through my hair. "But we're keeping it. It's *our* child. We're going to make it work."

Coach seemed to accept that. "I take it your folks don't know?"

"I haven't spoken to them in months. The last time I saw them, they attacked me and Mol. It was a fuckin' nightmare." Panic swelled in my stomach, that sinking, empty feeling that almost makes you puke. My hands began to shake and I blurted, "We need to change it, Coach, the venue. We need to have it somewhere else where they can't run the show."

"I tried, Rome, I really did, but the director of sport already approved it. The damn governor's going to be there for goodness sake. Apparently your momma and daddy were real insistent, and hell, but folks don't argue with them 'round here. You know this."

Unable to sit still any longer, I jumped to my feet and began to pace. "It's a setup! You and I both know they've never given a shit about football. They've never even seen me play for the Tide once. Hell, they even tried to bribe you into revoking my scholarship four years ago!"

"I know, but I don't know what else to do."

"Fine." I met Coach's worried face and announced, "I just won't go."

"Rome!" Coach said tiredly and moved to stand before me. "You have to be there. We have the sponsors coming, the TV stations, journalists—they expect you to be there. *I* expect you to be there! You're the QB for the Tide. You *are* football in Bama!"

"I won't go and risk my girl getting hurt!"

"Then maybe leave her at home, son. Think of a plan B. Turn up, wear a smile, do your duty, and leave."

Do your duty. Where had I heard that before?

"Change it," I said through clenched teeth. "Change it… I'm begging you."

Coach reached out to lay a hand on my shoulder, but I jumped at the action and his face fell as he held up his palms. "Rome, I'm so sorry. I don't know the history with you and your parents, but I know it's bad. I hate to ask this of you, but you need to be there, and the venue choice is way out of my hands."

Coach checked his watch and cussed. "The coaching staff have a meeting now with the director about the travel plans to Georgia, and I can't get out of it. I've got to go." Stepping forward, he said, "Finish up your weights. Hell, go pass some balls, get out your anger, then go home and try to relax. Speak to Miss Shakespeare. And if needs be, we'll work out a way to protect you both." Laying a hand on my shoulder, he assured, "You're our priority, son. We're a team. We look out for each other."

I couldn't speak so I stood there silently as he left the room without another word.

I tried to keep calm, but I was too far gone, too enraged.

When I reentered the gym, Austin and Jimmy-Don signaled for me to go over to them, but I was rooted to the spot, lost, not knowing what to do. I couldn't let my folks get to me this way, but I needed football to leave their clutches once and for all. I was in total catch twenty-two. I needed a plan, but Christ, I couldn't think straight.

"Rome!" Austin shouted and, frowning at my weird mood, waved me over.

Breathing deep, I headed in his direction, when I heard Porter say, "Yeah, apparently she's a real slut. Shelly said she lets him do anything to her, and I mean anything. I see the attraction now. I could get past all that ugly if she'd let me fuck her up the ass too."

I could feel the wave of the blood rushing to my face and my teeth were clenched together so hard I was sure I felt them crack. I saw Austin glaring at Porter in disgust and tried my damnedest to gain my composure, but when the fucker added, "I mean, just hearing that English accent scream my name would almost have me shooting my load… and from what I hear, she swallows that down like a good little whore!"

I completely lost it.

Using the years and years of sprint training to my advantage, I flew at Porter, tackled his ass to the floor, and instantly began to wale on him. He didn't even get a chance to react properly, only getting in a few shit jabs before a right hook to his jaw knocked him the fuck out. His body went limp below me, but I couldn't stop. I needed to get out all the anger. It was tearing me the hell up—and the fucker deserved to pay for the shit he was spitting about Mol.

Two arms grabbed me from behind, yanking me off Porter, and scrambling to my feet, I saw Austin and Jimmy-Don were before me. On instinct, I swung out my fist, Austin ducking, showing he too wasn't unused to violence.

"Get him the hell out of here and cleaned up… All y'all move… Now!" Jimmy-Don screamed over my shoulder, and swerving, I watched what was left of the team, dragging a now semi-conscious Porter from the gym.

"What the fuck's up with you?" Austin barked out, clearly trying to keep hold of his own temper.

"Y'all need to leave me the hell alone," I said roughly.

"Rome, buddy—"

"I said leave!" I snapped at Jimmy-Don, who, disappointed, pulled on Austin's shirt to get him out of the gym, leaving me to deal with all this crap by myself.

I was so out of my depth with all this shit. I was twenty-one and was through with all the pressure. Through with having to fight every damn day to just to have a normal life, for me and my girl to just be together, away from anyone's business, and have our child in friggin' peace.

Temporarily losing my damn mind, I began tearing apart the gym as every fucked-up scenario of what my folks could be up to played through my mind. Throwing mats, overturning equipment, I panted harder and harder until I was completely breathless. My shirt was soaked with sweat and blood, so I ripped it off, throwing it across the room, and slumped down to the bench, fighting back the tears.

I'd never felt so damn helpless in my life.

After several minutes of just staring at the ceiling, I heard the gym door creak open, and I stilled. When I dropped my head, I saw Molly stepping through, mouth gaping open at the state of the gym and then turning her attention on me, her face paling and her eyes huge.

She walked forward and I hissed, "Guess who's hosting the fucking SEC Division Championship dinner two days after we get back from the game in Georgia?"

"Oh no, baby—" she whispered and her hands immediately went to protect her stomach. I don't think she even realized what she'd done, but that action alone had me dying inside—she feared what my folks were going to do to our child.

"It's a fuckin' joke! They've never given a shit about football my whole life and now they suddenly volunteer to host the biggest dinner of the year… at the plantation? It's a fuckin' trap to get us there, Mol!"

She tried to comfort me, to get closer, but I couldn't let her. I was so damn livid. Couldn't have her trying to soothe me.

"Romeo, you need to calm down! Half the college is out front. You've beat a teammate to a pulp—"

At the mention of that fucker, my skin pricked. "He fuckin' deserved it. He started spouting shit about you… to me! He had a fuckin' death wish the minute he opened his stupid mouth!"

"I don't care what the hell he said about me. Look at the state of you! You're acting insane!"

Was she kidding? Didn't she realize why things were so bad, why I was so riled up? "My parents have staged this whole thing. Remember last time, the way they attacked us? This is just a more elaborate trap. They knew I'd never go back voluntarily. Coach has agreed to it. They've already invited the governor, mayor, and a million other boosters who've all eagerly accepted. They made sure the college couldn't refuse! Fuck!"

Molly moved to the bench out of the way of my warpath, and facing her, I stated, "We're not going. There's no fuckin' way you're going to them in your condition."

I couldn't take my eyes off my girl as a hand rubbed across her tired head. She went on and tried to convince me to go, even going so far as to offer to stay at home. But there wasn't a chance. Didn't she know how much I needed her?

Moving before her, I said, "No! No fuckin' way! Why shouldn't you be there with me? The college needs to change the venue. Fuck my parents. I know them, Mol. Something is going on, I just know it, and I won't have them destroying my family—I'm over their mind games."

Loving sympathy flooded her features and I breathed deep, using Mol's presence to calm me—she always calmed me—and I could tell I was upsetting her being so charged up. I walked slowly to where she sat and, dropping to my knees, laid my head on her lap, pressing kisses to her stomach. "If they find out about our little angel in there, fuck knows what they'll do. I can't lose you both."

Soft hands ran through my hair and I used the touch to lose the rest of my rage.

"Romeo, I understand why you're like this, but it's one party, with hundreds of people around. They won't do anything so publicly. They wouldn't want the embarrassment. I'll stay by your side the whole night. They won't have a chance to get to me. You'll protect me. I know you will."

I would, with my life if needs be.

Molly set to cleaning me up, caring for me like she always did. "I wouldn't be able to live with myself if they hurt you or our little angel, baby," I said.

She took my face in her hands and insisted, "Nothing will happen."

I felt like I was six again, trapped under my parents' hold. For the last few months I'd been happy, and in one fell swoop, they managed to drop me back to being the abused kid they'd ripped on for years.

I could feel the tears, but I couldn't stop. "Why do they always have to interfere? We're doing so good. You're healthy, our baby's going strong, and the Tide's the clear winner of the SEC Western Division and heading to the National Championship. Then they come in with their plotting and scheming, ruining my life again. I'm telling you, it's all rigged. They're planning something. Something big."

I knew it, could just feel it within me.

"They're powerful people, Romeo. The party won't be moved. We need to go and put on a united front. You need to be a leader for your team."

I held her tightly. Then, inching back, she said softly, "You really lost it."

I knew I'd fucked up again, so I told her about the conversation I had with Coach, what he'd tried to do for me.

As she continued to clean me up, she shook her head and said curtly, "I don't like it when you lose control. You need to be better than this, Romeo. I don't want to have to worry about your temper, especially when the little one arrives."

I fucking loved this girl. Here we were, in a wrecked gym, my body covered in blood, and she was still trying to make me a better man, still admonishing me for my bad behavior.

I couldn't help but smile wryly.

"What?" she asked, confusion contorting her beautiful face.

"I love you," I announced, placing a kiss on her throat, and I could see the need for me building in her eyes. Pregnancy had us fucking like rabbits... something I wasn't complaining about.

Pushing on my chest, Molly chastised, "That won't get you out of my bad books! Look at the state of this place, of you!" But when her nostrils flared and her hand ran down my sweaty stomach, I knew she was two seconds away from letting me sink into her warmth.

My cock throbbed in my shorts, and pressing right up against my girl, I said, "I want to fuck you right now, so bad."

"Not here. And not until you promise me that you'll never act like this again."

Was she fucking kidding me? I could see she was on the edge too and the damn door was shut; we were good. "I'm all riled up and need a release, the kind that only you can give me."

Pushing on my chest again, she said, with conviction this time, "I mean it. Don't ignore me. My child won't grow up with a daddy who can't control himself when things go wrong."

That sentence was like a hammer to my heart. I would never hurt our angel.

"You get that, don't you?" she asked, using my own words against me.

"I get it. It stops now. I won't be anything like my daddy with our angel. I promise you that."

Needing to get away from this place, and *really* needing to fuck her, I said, "We're going to the cabin. I'm going to strip you down and you're going to do everything I say, until neither of us can stand. You get me?"

"Ugh! Fine! I get you!"

Tilting my head, I assured, "I'm going to make sure you're protected at the party, baby."

"I know you will."

Moving to the bench, I pulled her onto my lap, feeling a million times better. "It's déjà vu," she said, "you, cut up and bleeding and me, cleaning you up. But let's not make this our 'thing,' okay?"

"Last time, I promise. I'm going to change. No more cleaning up my messes. Scout's honour." I held up my hands, joining the appropriate fingers together.

"You were never a scout, Romeo," Molly chuckled.

"I joined…" I informed.

Fixing her eyes on mine, she asked, "Really, you did?"

"Mm-hmm… but I was kicked out for fighting." Sad but true… The fucker probably deserved it back then too.

"Why am I not surprised?" she said, curling farther into my chest, her breath warm on my skin.

Our friends let themselves in a short while later, where I explained about my folks and the party, much to their dismay, and then I told Austin and Jimmy-Don about the baby. They were, unsurprisingly, shocked, but meeting eyes with Austin, I knew he was going to help me protect Molly and our angel.

27

The Prince Plantation
SEC Championship Homecoming Dinner

"My husband and I couldn't be more proud of our son, Rome. He was always so talented growing up, and y'all love and respect him too—that only increases our admiration."

A soothing vanilla scent drifted on the breeze as Molly leaned in, rubbing my arm, and took my tightly gripped fist off the edge of the table, placing it on her slightly rounded stomach. Squeezing my eyes, I calmed some but tensed once more when my momma continued talking from the top table, addressing the heavy crowd.

"My husband and I couldn't make it to the game in Georgia, unfortunately, as we had prior engagements with our company here in Alabama, but we watched the SEC

324

Division Championship on TV, seeing y'all win over the Gators and lift that trophy for everyone here back home."

Screams and cheers went up from around the room, except for our table. Coach looked over to me, shaking his head at my momma in disgust.

"We couldn't be more proud of our son who threw like a true professional in all four quarters, or all of the Tide for that matter. Your state and school adore y'all."

I actually felt nauseous as she lied her way through the speech. Proud? Talented? They'd never been proud of me, but here they were, fucking showboating to the crowd, the cream of Tuscaloosa society smiling at me, congratulating me on my amazingly supportive parents.

They had no friggin' idea.

"I love you, baby," Molly whispered into my ear, and I turned toward her face, slackening my tense jaw and pressing my lips against hers, breaking only momentarily to say, "I love you too."

My folks didn't even acknowledge me much after that, too busy networking and putting on their show.

We had nothing left to say to one another anyhow.

The dinner moved on to the party side of things, and I relaxed when I managed to convince Molly to dance—keeping her close, keeping her protected.

"Rome?" The band finished playing "Sweet Home Alabama" to rapturous applause from the team and fellow guests, and, turning at the sound of my name, I saw Coach behind me.

"Oh, hey, Coach."

Facing Molly, he said, "Miss Shakespeare, can I borrow Rome for a while?"

I stiffened, not wanting to leave my girl, but, giving Coach a big smile back, she nodded. "Sure, my feet are killing me anyway. I need to sit down. My damn ankles are like balloons!"

Taking Molly back to the table and sitting her down with her friends, I said, "I'll be back as soon as I can. Stay with someone, okay?"

Pressing a kiss on my cheek, she answered, "I promise."

Turning back toward Coach, I managed to signal to Austin and Jimmy-Don to watch out for Molly, and they both gave me a thumbs-up.

Over an hour passed, and I was still talking over game tactics for the BCS against Notre Dame—the most effective plays and the weaker parts of the Dame defense. I felt as though my eyes were crossing with boredom, and when my daddy joined the mass of business men and boosters, also throwing in his two cents, I had to hold back from launching across the group and throttling the bastard, especially when he looked at me and smiled—no, not smiled, *gloated*—my heart sank.

Something was up.

I began backing away from my daddy's smug face, Coach frowning worriedly at my behavior, and I ran around the house, bursting into the backyard, and searched furiously for Mol. I beelined for the table we'd been sitting at and did a quick count: Cass, Austin, Lexi, Ally, and Jimmy-Don.

No Mol.

Jimmy-Don stood and looked behind me, beaming. "Where is she, man? You made her damn night with that note, you cheesy bastard!"

My hands began to shake, my breath choppy. "Where's Molly? What're you talking about?" I gripped onto his arms, my move silencing the table. Jimmy-Don's mouth worked, but nothing came out.

"Where is she?" My hold on his arm tightened, hurting him, until a sharp push from Ally stopped me. Jimmy-Don stumbled back into Cass's arms, completely white.

I looked down at my cousin and whispered, "Mol?"

And then I heard it…

"Rome! *ROME!!!*"

Whipping my head to the entrance of the house, I saw Shelly practically sprinting down the stairs in my direction.

All the blood in my body seemed to drain away as she approached me, panicked and hysterical, her face laced with tears.

I began to run and, grabbing her, asked, "Where's Mol?"

"She's… we didn't know… the library… She's… Oh my God, Rome…" was all she could get out.

Throwing her to the side, I ran into the hallway, tens of my teammates staring at me with a mix of sadness or shock. I had no idea why, but it only served to scare me further.

I could vaguely make out our friends following behind me, and seeing the heavy crowd blocking the entrance to the library, I shouted, "Move the fuck out of my way! MOVE!!!"

Scattering at my command, the doorway cleared and I almost collapsed at the sight of what I found, my legs buckling with instant terror: Molly curled on the floor, covered in blood, screaming and writhing in pain.

No…

In seconds, I was by her side. "Mol! Fuck! Baby, I'm here! I'm here!" I didn't know where to hold her, how to stop her pain.

Golden eyes, dulled with pain and sadness, looked my way, and she whispered, "Romeo, our baby, our baby… I-I think I'm losing it. Help me… Please…" and she wailed in pain again, clenching her legs together and hugging her stomach before crying so hard into the carpet she could barely breathe.

Lifting my head, I saw our friends staring at us in horror, and I shouted, "Somebody call 9-1-1. She's losing our baby!"

Fuck. She was losing our baby… Questions of how and why were circling my mind, but I couldn't tear my attention from Mol, who looked like she was dying—fuck! *Was* she dying?

I flinched as someone touched my shoulder—Jimmy-Don telling me the ambulance was on the way.

Desperately needing to hold my girl, I picked her up, having no idea whether it was a good thing or not, and brought her to my lap. Rocking back and forth, I tried to soothe her, but her jerks of agony were tearing me apart. "Shh, baby, I'm so sorry. I'm so, so sorry," I cried out, my tears like never-ending torrents.

Her skin slowly paled to a deathly white, and she touched my cheek, her weak hand like a feather against my skin. "I think our baby's gone. It hurts so much. I think our baby's gone..." She tried to finish, but her eyes widened, body stiffened, and she screamed, the most haunting fucking scream I'd ever heard, as I felt a sudden wetness on my legs and, looking down, saw blood trickling down her thighs onto our intertwined bodies.

I didn't know what to do. Hell... *I didn't know what to do!*

Molly's eyes began to flutter closed, her clutch on my shirt slackening, and a fresh bolt of panic felt like open blades shredding my chest. "Where's the fucking ambulance? She's pregnant, goddamn it... She's pregnant... Our little angel..." I trailed off, helpless to do anything.

Searching Molly's body, wading through the mass of white fabric of her dress now coated in blood, I tried to find something I could do. I couldn't. I wasn't a damn doctor. I wasn't prepared for this shit.

Her breath shallowed, and, whipping my attention back to her face, I spotted a gash on her lip. Using my thumb to take a closer look, I frowned. "Baby? Why's your lip bleeding? What the hell happened to you?"

I was losing her. Her eyes were glazing and her body was no longer reacting to the pain. I sent prayer after prayer to God, begging him to save my girl. I couldn't lose her. She was my everything.

"Mol?" I asked, and my body stilled as her eyes began to close. "Mol! Stay with me, Mol!" I screamed, holding her closer in my arms.

"Y-your mother hit her and she fell against the table. W-we… I d-didn't know she was pregnant… We were just trying to scare her off. Things got out of control…"

Shelly. Shelly stood shaking beside me.

Rage like never before surged through my body like pure octane at Shelly's confession. She went on to inform me that my momma had snuck away, and, acting on pure instinct, I made to move, to go after her. I wanted to end all this shit once and for all, but when Molly's trembling hand laid on mine and she begged me to stay with her, I could do nothing else but break down in sadness, whispering, "Baby, I'm so sorry… Our angel… Our angel…"

But she'd gone. Molly had gone still in my arms, her breath almost nonexistent as her blood continued to pour out.

"Rome," Ally's broken voice sounded beside me. "The EMTs are here. They need to take Molly to the hospital now. Come on, darlin', let them do their job."

Looking up, two men were moving frantically into the room and took Molly immediately from my arms. Standing, completely numb, I registered the mass of eyes watching the scene, and gripping Molly's limp hand on the gurney, I followed her out to the ambulance, ignoring the flash of cameras and whispers from the horrified guests.

The EMTs pushed the gurney into the ambulance and began firing questions at me.

"How far along is she?"

"Nearly three months."

"What happened?"

"Apparently she was hit and fell against a table edge… I wasn't there… I couldn't help her…"

The paramedic worked nonstop on my girl, attaching IVs and Christ knows what else. The ambulance flew through the city, but I never let go of my girl's hand. She'd asked me not to leave her; it was one promise I wouldn't break.

* * *

"Your girlfriend has suffered a severe blow to the stomach and that caused irreparable damage to the placenta, and I'm sorry to have to tell you, but she lost the baby. We have also found evidence of internal bleeding and are prepping for surgery as we speak."

I didn't know how to deal. I'd lost all feeling.

"Will she survive?" I rasped out, my voice rough from crying.

"We're going to try our best, son. Someone will be out to keep you informed of her progress." And with that, the doctor left me alone in an empty family room while he raced off to patch my girl back together. He might be able to repair her body, but fuck knows what her mind would be like when she woke.

A light knocking on the door sounded, but I couldn't look up, too entranced by the speckled pattern in the linoleum flooring.

"Rome!" a female voice cried, and I recognized it as belonging to Ally.

She wrapped her arms around my shoulders and sobbed uncontrollably. It went that way for a while—all of my friends crying, hugging me close. Even Austin, the strongest person I'd ever known, broke down, hugging Lexi afterward. Then when there were no more tears to be shed, we each took a seat in the room and sat in silence.

"Bullet, I can't tell you how sorry I am, man. Molly and I were given a note when I took her to the bathroom. We thought it was from you. I can't stop blaming myself." Cass rubbed at his back as tears streamed down her face.

"What did it say?" I asked tiredly.

Ally shifted forward, her eyes darting to the floor nervously. "I managed to speak to Shelly before we left. Your momma set it up, darlin'. Apparently she wanted to scare Molly away for good. Shelly admitted she'd told your momma about the notes you give Molly before a game, and while your daddy stalled you with football talk, she used it to get her alone."

I caught Jimmy-Don throwing his head in his hands at that bit of information, explaining, "The note said to meet you in the library, that you needed a break from the party, and for Molly to meet you there. I never doubted it was from you, not even for a second."

Ally's sympathetic gaze landed on Jimmy-Don, who'd broken into tears, but she managed to continue. "Apparently your momma starting telling Molly to leave you, had some private detective find out some real nasty things about Molly's past and started using it against her.

It didn't work. Molly was unmoved, but when Aunt Kathryn began talking crap about you, Molly fought back, apparently in your defense and that's when your momma lashed out. She was drunk off her ass again. Molls fell against the table and, well, we know the rest. Your momma and daddy were nowhere to be found afterward. The police want to speak to your momma, but she's completely disappeared."

If I wasn't so numb, I'd have torn this room apart, but even my anger, this time, wasn't enough to make my body move. My momma investigated shit about her? Most likely about her daddy and grandma dying. I vowed at that moment that if I ever saw her again, I'd make her pay. Christ, all this happened because my girl defended me. Like that didn't make me feel even worse. She'd lost our angel because of me…

"I hate them. I hate them so damn much," I whispered, almost breaking the sides of the plastic chair with my grip. "They're dead to me. Fuckin' six feet under, dead."

My friends' silence told me they completely agreed.

28

After several hours and a stupid amount of coffee, a nurse wearing pink scrubs entered the room and I froze and held my breath as my heart tried to cope with the fear suffocating my body.

"Rome?" the nurse asked as she searched the room. I stood and she moved before me. "Miss Shakespeare has made it out of surgery and she's stable in ICU. We were able to repair the stomach rupture she suffered and transfused her with blood to replace the heavy blood loss from the miscarriage."

"Can I see her?" I asked desperately. I needed to be there when she woke up.

"Soon. I'll send someone to fetch you."

After the nurse left, I slumped back on my chair and heard the sighs of relief from my friends.

"She's going to be fine, Rome," Ally said emphatically, trying her damnedest to be positive.

Nodding slowly, I replied, "Her body may heal, sure. But I still have to tell her we lost our baby, and I can tell you now, she's going to be anything but fine."

Silence resumed once again.

As I entered the small private hospital room, I had to grip onto the doorframe to stop myself from falling to my knees. Tubes and wires were coming from her pale skin, deep, dark shadows hung under her eyes, and she looked so small and broken, swamped under a mass of white cotton.

I focused on the constant beat from the heart monitor to control my breathing and slowly moved to the bed, kissing Molly's cold cheek and pulling a chair beside her, holding her hand in mine, and began the wait for her to wake up.

I must have drifted off, and a hand running through my hair woke me from my sleep. Convinced I was dreaming, I startled when confused golden eyes focused on me, Molly's hand weakly dropping to her stomach.

"Romeo? Did... did...?"

I knew what she was asking, but my voice was taken by grief, so I simply nodded, watching the complete fucking agony set on her pale, beautiful face and tears begin streaming from her eyes.

After days of missing my girl, needing her to share in my grief, I leaned over, holding her waif body in my arms, and whispered, "I'm so sorry... It's all my fault."

But Molly being Molly wouldn't hear of it, and pulling me on the mattress beside her, assured me there was nothing I could have done when I told her I'd let her down. I explained to her what happened—the note, Shelly, my momma, everything—and with every sentence, she grew more and more distant.

Over the next couple of days, Molly gradually turned in on herself. She wouldn't eat, barely spoke, and when she wasn't sleeping, she stared unseeing at the ceiling, ignoring me, ignoring our friends.

The guys came to see her and tried their best to cheer her up, but the worried glances coming my way showed me they knew Molly was fucking depressed. I didn't know what the hell to do to pull her out of it.

I couldn't bear it, day in and day out being in that fucking hospital, watching Mol drown in misery, watching the hours turn into days, and my girl letting the grief tear her apart from the inside out. So when the doctor came in and told us Molly was being released, I was so damn happy, thinking that once out of the prison cell of a hospital room, she would start to heal, start to help me heal too.

I was busy packing her bag when a text came through on my cell.

Coach: Rome, I hate to ask this of you now, but I really need you at this function tonight. You don't have to come for long, but you need to be here for the team, for the press.

Sighing and pinching my nose, I cursed inwardly. Coach had been great lately, but the fact of the matter was that football stops for no one, and our baby's loss was not going to change the fact that the championship was right around the corner.

"What is it?" Mol asked from the bed.

I turned to see her looking at me with her usual indifference, and answered, "It's Coach. He needs me to attend a charity function at the stadium tonight. I've missed a lot of game prep, and he needs the QB to be there to show I'm with the team all the way to the championship."

"Then go."

I stilled and dropped the packed bag to the floor. "I can't leave you like this."

"Yes, you can. I'm tired anyway. I need to sleep."

Anger seeped into my muscles. I was through with this fucking imposter lying on the bed, pretending to be my girl. I hardly recognized her. I wanted the old Molly back. The one who would laugh with me, the one who would make everything better... the one who friggin' loved me. I'd coped on my own for the last several days, supressing my grief to get her through hers, but I couldn't fucking do it anymore, and losing my grip on my anger, I swung a fist into the wall.

"For Christ's sake, Mol! How can you be tired? You've slept for days, done nothing for days! I understand you've had surgery, but the doctors said you should be feeling a lot better by now. You're wallowing, Shakespeare. You need to snap the hell out of it! I've tried, been trying to be patient, but enough is enough! I've lost a baby too, not just you, but you shut me out and act like I'm a damn stranger to you. I was the daddy, for fuck's sake! I can't do it alone. I have too much to think about—you being like this, leading the team to the championship, the hopes of an entire state on my head. I need you to help me, Mol, not to drown in your own fuckin' misery. Who's supporting me? I'm grieving too!"

Her lifeless eyes regarded me, unseeing, and pure desperation took hold as I pounded to the bed, all gentleness gone. I pressed my lips to hers, aggressive, rough, and how we usually liked it. But her lips didn't move. It was like kissing a fucking corpse.

I was scared.

When I saw her on the floor, covered in blood at my folks' place, I'd been scared. When I knew I had to tell her our baby had died, I was scared, but the fear of the girl I loved, the girl who *saved* me, being lost for good had me almost insane with panic.

"For fuck's sake! Please. Please. You're scaring the shit outta me! You need to start dealing with it, dealing with everything that's happened." I pleaded. But she turned away, not wanting to listen… and it felt like I was dying a slow and painful death.

"You can't even bear to look at me, can you?"

Her back stiffened, she whipped to face me, pure anger distorting her features, and she screamed, "*There!* I'm looking at you! Tell me, Rome, what would like me to deal with exactly? The fact that your mother killed my fucking baby?"

And there it was... *My* baby. She no longer saw us together... We were no longer in this together.

"Our baby, and don't you ever forget that. I was with you all the way until the end... still am! I'm still fucking here, trying to pull you out of hell!"

But there was nothing, not even a flicker of understanding in her eyes. She'd given up on us, and in that moment, I didn't care either. I was over this whole friggin' year.

"You know what? Fuck this! I'm out!"

I attended the dinner as requested and hours later found myself tearing through the hospital, my girl gone and nowhere to be found. Sitting in her empty room, one thing was abundantly clear: Molly had given up.

She'd left me. She'd run.

29

Present Day…

"My God, Rome," Ally whispered, wiping at her eyes. "I never knew… never realized you both went through so much. How much you meant to each other. Saved each other."

"Yeah," I croaked out. "Now you do." I turned to Ally, who was looking around the room, biting her lip in worry. "We need to find her, Al. What if she does something stupid? She's not thinking straight. Hasn't been for days."

Her hand suddenly slapped on my arm and she pointed to the wall. "Rome, look at the date on Molly's calendar."

"Flight to Heathrow. Oxford presentation," I read out loud.

Shit. She'd gone back to England for the presentation she'd been working on. Of course. Professor Ross would have been the person in the car at the hospital. But the flight was long gone. *She* was long gone.

I immediately jumped from the bed, planning my next step.

"Where are you going?" Ally asked frantically.

"To Oxford. I need to get her back."

Ally's hand gripped my arm. "You can't, Rome! What about the National Championship? You'd jeopardize the draft! You can't just leave. It's your whole future we're talking about here!"

I let out a guttural scream and swiped the top of Mol's drawers with my arm, watching all her shit fall to the floor, then turned to face Ally once more. "No, that's where you're wrong! Molly's my fuckin' life, my fuckin' future! And right now she's on a 747 to Heathrow Airport, friggin' dying inside because of me, because of my psycho mother! Fuck the championship!"

For the first time in our lives, I could see I'd scared Ally. I could see it in her ashen face, her usual olive skin bleached white with shock.

Raking my hands through my hair, I dropped my ass to the edge of the nightstand. "Shit, Al. Sorry. I'm so sorry… I'm just going outta my mind. I don't know what the hell to do." It was no good; the tears I was fighting began pouring out of me. My shoulders shook and I buried my face in my hands.

Ally's arms embraced me while I let it all out. "Here's what I think, Rome." She paused, waiting for me to speak, but I couldn't. "I say we get outta here now and go to my folks' in Birmingham. We were scheduled to leave in a couple of days for Christmas anyway." I stiffened and went to argue, but she continued. "Give Molls some time. She'll come around. I know she will. I've never seen a couple like you two. You're perfect together. Just let her digest everything. She's sensitive, needs time to heal. Ring Coach. Tell him you're going to have to take a few days away, then return for training and win the National Championship. If she still hasn't returned, then do something. Hell, I'll fly to England with you if needs be."

I knew she was right, but even spending a day apart from my girl, without hearing her voice, was going to kill me.

Fuck. How did it all go so wrong?

I couldn't help but think of my folks and what they'd done. Year and years of their abuse flashed before my eyes and I hated myself for never fighting back. I wanted to hurt them, just like they'd hurt me, hurt Mol... our fucking baby! My palms felt like they were on fire and my hands curled into fists.

"Rome?" Ally said nervously.

"I can't go!" I shouted, Ally cautiously stepping back across the room. "I need to find my folks. They need to be held accountable for what they've done!"

"And where you gonna look?"

"I don't know. Everywhere. I can't just do nothing. They've taken everything from me... *Everything!*"

Ally moved right in front of me, panic all over her features. "Rome, I understand the need for justice, I really do, but be logical. Let the police do their job. They'll be found and dealt with in the right way."

"Al…" I whispered, unable to find my voice.

"Promise me. Don't let them ruin your life anymore. You go after them, and you'll end up in trouble. I know you Rome, you'll lose it."

"Goddamn it, Al!" I complained, but slumping my shoulders, I reluctantly nodded my head. "Okay, we'll go to Birmingham but… let's go now, before I change my mind."

Ally tentatively placed her hand on my shoulder. "We'll get our bags packed and get straight on the road. I'll drive."

I stood numbly and reluctantly left Mol's bedroom, following Ally to her room while she got her stuff together. Everywhere I stood felt suffocating, so I stepped out on the balcony to think. It was the wrong choice; it was out here where Mol and I had really hit it off. It was the beginning of us.

After about ten minutes, there was a panicked knock on the door, and Lexi and Cass ran in, their faces dropping when they saw me standing outside, looking at them blankly.

"Hey, Rome. We're sorry. We didn't know you'd be in here," Lexi said. I didn't reply, just turned away again to stare out at the trees once more.

"Where's Molls?" Cass whispered, trying to be discreet, but her thick Texan accent sounded like a foghorn in the quiet room.

"Gone," Ally whispered back, causing all my muscles to tense.

"Jesus! Gone where?" Cass asked, her own anger seeping through her words. "Wherever it is, we need to go and get her! Now!"

"Too late, Cass. Looks like she's gone back to Oxford, caught a flight outta here earlier tonight, hitched a ride from the hospital with the professor," Ally informed her, and for the first time that night, I heard her own tired sadness leak through.

Someone sniffed, and then Lexi's soft, broken voice cut in. "Poor Molly, what must she be feeling? I want her back where she has friends. I want to hold her, comfort her, and tell her everything will be okay. No wonder she left. How's she expected to cope with everything that happened?"

"With me!" I screamed, almost involuntarily, and whipped to face our shell-shocked friends. Lexi's heavy black makeup was smudged down her face, her bottom lip trembling as she stared at me, eyes wide.

"I'm sorry, Rome, I—"

"She had me!" I shouted again, approaching them furiously. Ally moved before me, trying to stop me with her hands flat on my chest. I cast her aside, yelling over her shoulder. "We were meant to get through all of this shit together! She promised me, over and over! I'm so fuckin' mad at her! You all stand here crying, but she ran out on you too. She left all of us! She's almost twenty-one and she still runs when shit gets tough! She should have fuckin' stayed, stayed and got through our baby's death with me!"

Lexi and Cass stood rooted to the spot, tears streaming down their faces. I actually felt some semblance of guilt seeing Cass reduced to a weeping mess. But I was pent up with rage, stuck in fucking limbo, unable to see past my own grief.

The door burst open, and Jimmy-Don and Austin stepped in. Austin glared at me as Jimmy-Don wrapped Cass in his arms, eyebrows furrowed in confusion as he registered the scene. Austin pulled Lexi beside him, cupping her face, then turned to look at me, mouth tight. He was pissed at me too?

Perfect.

"Rome, you need to calm the hell down and stop ripping on the girls," Austin said calmly, but I could hear the heavy threat in his voice.

"Fuck off, Austin. You have no idea what I'm going through," I snapped, moving to walk away.

His already dark eyes seemed to blacken even more, and he grabbed my arm. I looked down at his hand wrapped around my bicep and clenched my jaw.

Austin watched me, lurching back slightly, but hissed, "You're right, I don't, none of us do, but don't give Lexi shit because Molls left you, okay?" That caused me to pause, and Lexi lowered her head in embarrassment, avoiding my gaze.

Whatever. I couldn't give a rat's ass as to what was going on between those two right now.

Ripping my arm free, I looked to Ally and asked, "You ready?"

She nodded, exhausted, and addressed the rest of our friends. "We're going to my momma and daddy's early. Have a nice Christmas, y'all, and we'll catch you when we get back." She hugged each person tightly, but I just pushed past them to the door—I wasn't exactly full of Christmas cheer.

A firm hand landed on my shoulder.

Austin.

"You okay, man?" he asked, no longer pissed, just worried.

Shit. This was Austin, my best damn friend. I sagged and shook my head no. "She'll come back," he assured me.

I met his eyes, then Cass's and Lexi's. "Look, about before—"

Austin grasped my face in both of his hands, interrupting me mid-sentence. "Don't apologize. Just get the hell out of here and get your shit together. We got a championship to bring back, and you need to be in top form." He planted a typical Sicilian kiss to my forehead.

Stepping back, I ran down the stairs, past all of Mol's sorority sisters watching me in pity, and out into the crisp winter air, making my way straight over to the Mustang.

Ally joined me seconds later and in silence, we drove to my frat house, I gathered some clothes, rang my coach, and we hit the road.

Destination: Birmingham.

30

"Rome, we're here," I heard Ally say from beside me as the roaring engine of the Mustang grew to a stop. At first I was disorientated, but then I remembered... everything... and that excruciating pain that had subsided, if only for a short time during sleep, stabbed back into my chest with vengeance.

Taking a deep breath and opening the passenger door, I smiled at Aunt Alita, who was running from the small country cottage, arms spread, tears running down her face, shouting, "Rome, mia Rome! Viene aqui, viene aqui!"

Smashing against my chest and squeezing her arms around my waist, my tiny Spanish aunt cried into my shirt. The lump in my throat expanded with her over-the-top affection. It was how a mother should be—nurturing, protective, loving—and that thought sliced my heart more.

Even though unborn, Molly had been all those things to our child.

Pulling back, Aunt Alita asked, "My darling, are you okay?" in her heavily accented tongue. "Ay dios mio! Such a tragedy. May the Lord strike down your parents for such cruelty!"

My uncle stepped onto the small porch, pulling my attention, a sympathetic frown on his face—his face that looked too similar to my father's to bring any comfort.

"Mama! Leave him be," Ally said, rolling her eyes in my direction, ushering her mother away and into the house.

With a deep breath, I walked to my uncle, stiffening as he laid his hands on my shoulders. He immediately lifted his palms into the air. "Sorry, son. I forget how much your daddy and I look alike."

"No, it's fine. I'm just not used to people touching me, that's all. And yeah, you do look so much like him at times it's uncanny."

Uncle Gabe smiled sadly. "Though nothing alike, I hope?" Placing his hand on the back of my head, he pulled me close. "That man is evil, Rome. I knew he wasn't a good man. Hell, even growing up, he was an ass, but for both your momma and daddy to do what they have lately... Well, I could never have believed them capable of such behavior."

Letting out a humorless laugh, I said, "Yeah, well, I'm sure Charles Manson's family thought the same about him too. Some folks are just born to be bad and no one can stop them."

Uncle Gabe's brown eyes glistened, a tortured expression on his face. "I should've done more for you, took you away from it all… fought for you harder. I've let you down." There was a pause in his breathing before he whispered, "I failed you so bad, son."

Shifting out of his embrace, I replied, "No, you didn't. My bastard parents keep getting away with this shit, everyone blaming themselves for their actions. But no one's to blame but them. For reasons only they will ever know, they take enjoyment in destroying people, people they should've loved."

Uncle Gabe's eyes dipped, and putting his arm around my shoulder, he guided me into the small house, revealing, "Well, it seems karma may have caught up with them at long last."

Stopping dead, I asked quickly, "What are you talking about?"

Walking ahead into the front room, my uncle pointed to the TV. "It's all over the news. Hell, it's everywhere…"

Heart pounding, I raced into the room where Ally and Aunt Alita where already sitting on the couch, eyes glued to the screen.

Ally went to say something, but the images on the news almost brought me to my knees, and she stayed silent.

Breaking News: Tide Star QB's Girlfriend Miscarries Amidst Prince Oil Money Laundering Scandal

My exhausted mind raced to take in all the images. They showed Molly on a gurney being ushered into the back of an ambulance, with me holding tightly onto her hand, her dress and my white suit covered in blood.

The reporter spoke in depth about the incident and the breaking story of how my momma assaulted Molly at the hospital and how she'd been arrested for assault. Next, a preview of tomorrow's paper covered the screen, with that same fucking image, and the anchors went on to talk about the night of the dinner and how Molly had miscarried later on. It infuriated me that they didn't even know to mention how she'd changed my fucking life, how she'd been brutally robbed of being the best fucking mother on Earth, and how she was the most important person in the world to me.

The next image was of my father in handcuffs, being taken from his home. The usual arrogant sneer was on his face, unchanged, as the police pushed him into the squad car. The camera switched back to the anchors, who went on to discuss the massive amount of money my father had been laundering from his own company's profits to cover what looked like some corrupt off-shore investments. They were suspecting that my father owed a set of dubious people a lot of money and that he'd drained his share of Prince Oil's profits over the last year—the only share left in the black belonging to Martin Blair, who had yet to make a statement.

And then it hit me. The marriage. My arranged marriage to Shelly would've given him access to Martin Blair's money as per the agreement the two of them had made. *The bastard!* The Princes of Alabama would've been penniless without it… ruined.

Money. It was always about fucking money!

Launching to my feet, I made a move for the door, but a hand on my shoulder held me back. I struggled to get away.

"Woah! Rome, calm down, son!" Uncle Gabe protested, backing away. Ally and Aunt Alita, all wide-eyed and nervous as they watched me fall apart.

Gripping my hair in anger, I let out a loud scream and left the room, apologizing over and over. "I'm sorry, I'm sorry... I just... I need to get out of here... I need air..."

Bursting out into the cold night, I kicked over anything in my path: the grill, chairs, Christ, every neatly potted plant I could see, and rammed my left fist against the large stone wall surrounding the yard, numb to the skin ripping apart at the impact.

All the shit I'd been put through this year was because my daddy was in debt up to his fucking eyeballs? My girl and my unborn angel destroyed because of my parents' fucking greed! I couldn't take it anymore. I couldn't take any more pain or disappointment. I was drowning, fucking drowning in misery.

Throwing myself down on a lawn chair, I pulled out my cell. Molly would still be in the air as she flew the hell away from me and the fall of the Prince Empire, but I had to call. I needed to hear her voice; it was the only thing, bar her touch, that calmed me.

Dialing her number, my heart flipped when her voicemail message immediately played:

Hi! You've reached Molly. Sorry I can't answer the phone right now, but if you leave your name and number after the tone, I'll get back to you when I can.

Ending the call, I dialed the number again... and again... head lowering and heart cracking with every English-accented, "Hi!"

After the fifth time of letting the message play out, I finally spoke:

"Mol. There's a story in the paper. It's about us... about losing our angel. Christ, Mol, there's a picture of you. It's breaking my heart and you're not here. My momma has been arrested for assault; my daddy has been arrested for money laundering. Please, call me. Tell me where you're at. It's all fucked up. I'm going crazy without you. I love you. Come back to me."

I hung on the line until it went dead, then succumbed to all the pain ripping me apart and, no longer able to stave them off, let out the wracking sobs. I couldn't breathe, couldn't stop the shaking of my body. I was completely falling apart.

Seconds later, I felt an arm wrap around my shoulder and I automatically flinched and moved to get up. Strong arms pushed me to stay seated, and as I looked up through my fallen hair and blurry eyes, Uncle Gabe pulled me to his chest, patting my head soothingly. "It's okay, son, let it all out. Don't fight it."

Giving in and taking comfort in his support, I gripped to his shirt, confiding, "I can't do it anymore. I can't be without her. What am I going to do? What if she never comes back for me?"

My uncle's strained and hoarse voice replied, "Shh, son. It'll be okay. None of this was your fault. Losing your baby should not be on your conscience."

Anger fused in my veins and I snapped, "It was, though. It was all my fault!" My face was wet with too many tears and, giving up the last of my resistance, I sagged and said brokenly, "Everybody leaves me. Nobody ever has faith in me. I'm never enough… I'm never fuckin' enough… What is it that makes everybody leave me…? What is it that makes them not love me enough to save me too?"

My uncle tightened me in his hold and then moved before me to grip my cheeks. "You are enough! It's not your fault, you hear me?"

My head shook in disagreement and my eyes closed, but the fucking stream of tears just wouldn't stop… anger and grief now the only emotions I had left.

31

I woke with a start, sitting up in bed, sweating, panting, and my cock so damn hard in my boxers. My hand felt beside me, searching for Mol, but the spot to my left was empty. Oh, yeah. She'd gone, and it was my third night at my uncle's place… alone.

I looked around the unfamiliar room, my eyes catching sight of the clock beside me—three in the morning. Shit. My thoughts were immediately on my girl, knowing she'd already be awake and going about her day in Oxford.

Was she missing me? Wanting to come back home?

Falling back onto the mattress, I groaned and squeezed my eyes shut, but the replay of images from my dream was a slow torture, a temptation—I'd broken from my sleep way too soon. I wanted the memory of making love to my girl to seem real, wanted to feel once again what it was like to be inside her, chest to chest, rocking together, hands intertwined... lost in her... saved by her.

Closing my eyes, my memories slammed into me like a fucking truck, but I embraced them. I wanted to remember...

"Romeo, what are you doing? The party... you've just won the SEC Championship, you should be with the team..." Molly panted into my hair as I held her against the wall of my room. As soon as the door slammed to a close, I began pushing down her panties.

Lifting the skirt of her dress, I wrapped her legs round my waist. "They've had me all day in that fuckin' parade, showboating me through town. The press has heard everything I gotta say. Now it's all about you, and me, and sinking my cock into this sweet little pussy," I said slowly, taking my hand and flicking my finger along her clit.

"Rome!"

Slipping back to reality and groaning with need, I reached down, stroking along my cock, trying to remember everything: how it felt being that close to my girl, how her face looked in the moonlight as I thrust into her against that wall. I was fucking desperate, searching for some connection to a time when things weren't so messed up...

I freed my dick from my jeans and guided it toward Mol's hot center. "You ready, baby? You ready for me?"

"Yes!"

I ran the tip around her warm hole, teasing, feeling her push down in frustration. "Mmm... I might just wait until you need it a bit more."

"Rome! No! Please..."

Smiling as she tilted her hips just right, I breeched her entrance, and with one fast slam, pushed right in to the hilt.

Christ, it felt so good.

Molly gripped the nape of my neck as I pressed kisses along the sides of her neck and the swells of her tits. "Shit, baby, you're so tight."

"Harder, Rome, harder..." she begged.

I gave her what she needed and pounded her against the wall, the rhythmic thuds of her back against the drywall sounding with each thrust.

"Ugh... Rome... I'm... I'm—" Her sentence cut off as she screamed against my neck, her tight channel milking my cock.

"Mol... Mol!" I croaked as I came, gripping my girl's legs and holding her off the floor with my torso.

Pulling back, Molly beamed her smile at me. "We should get back to the party now. People will be wondering where we are."

Grinning back, I said, "Fine," and leaned in to whisper in her ear, "but keep the panties off. There are more walls I'm wanting to try out..."

Staring at the ceiling, breathing fast with cum on my stomach, I felt a friggin' tear slip out of the corner of my eye. I couldn't get that feeling of contentment back, jerking off like a desperate fool in the middle of the night just to get a feeling even close to what we shared.

What Mol and I shared was never just a fuck; it was never just making love. It was fucking life-changing, life-affirming, and fear seized my chest at the thought of never having that back.

Yeah, the way we fucked was rough, intense, but it didn't make the connection any less real. In fact, it made it the total opposite. In those moments we were exactly who we were meant to be, and we'd been unashamed to expose that side of ourselves to one another. We fit like a friggin' puzzle.

Feeling like I'd taken a blow to the chest instead of reliving a happy memory, I sat up straight, swinging my legs off the bed, my head falling to my hands. My promise to my girl tormented my mind. *I'll make sure we get our happily ever after...* Like hell I did. She got a fucking nightmare, and she—no, *we* were still stuck in that damn hell.

Walking to the bathroom, I turned on the shower, letting the hot water pound on my head. Grabbing the soap, I ran it over my skin, staring at the tattoo on my hip. "*One Day*." I thought back to the day I got it—the day I told my daddy I'd gotten the UA football scholarship and was leaving home at the end of the school year. I was going to play for the Tide. It was the happiest day of my life, or had been until I met Mol. That tattoo was a symbol of my freedom, of my intention to get the hell away.

Switching off the shower, I toweled off and sat on the bed. The clock now read four a.m. Only a bastard hour had passed.

Reaching for my cell, I found the only number worth knowing.

Lying back on the bed, I listened to the voicemail greeting that kept me company most nights, then spoke:

"Hey, baby, just thought I'd call. It's four in the morning and I can't sleep… again. I dreamt about you tonight… God, I miss you. Being away from you is killing me. Come back, Shakespeare. I need you. I feel like I'm going insane. It's Christmas tomorrow, for fuck's sake. You should be here like we'd planned, just being with me, not in friggin' England on your own. If you can't talk yet, fine, but just let me know you're okay, text, email, just something—"

The long tone cut me off, telling me I'd run out of time, and, throwing my cell to the floor, I lay back, closed my eyes, and let more memories rip me into shreds.

32

I was right to come back to Tuscaloosa. It may've only been the day after Christmas but I'd pretty much spoiled most of the holidays for my aunt, uncle, and Ally. Getting the news on Christmas day that my momma was being released without charge for her assault on Molly at the hospital—a restraining order and a court issued rehab program, her only punishment—was a complete head fuck. The news got me so damn mad that I couldn't sit at the dinner table, celebrating the joys of Christmas, when my momma had gotten away with her crimes, and just to top it all off, I still hadn't heard from my girl.

Uncle Gabe had tried to help, asking the police about the fact that my momma was the cause of Molly's miscarriage and why wasn't she being held accountable? But the fact was my mother never knew Molly was even pregnant when they'd had their argument, and the placental abruption occurred when Molly fell against the edge of the table after my mother's slap. Molly hadn't pressed charges for that assault, too busy grieving to even care.

So here I was, pounding down the highway back to Tuscaloosa, reeling from my mother's lack of comeuppance and dreading the Tide's training for the BCS Championship that started tomorrow and the fact that I'd have to face all my teammates.

After an hour, I pulled into a familiar parking lot, and Luke was already waiting just inside the main door—inked from his completely shaven head to his toes.

Standing as I entered his shop, he shook my hand, stating, "Rome, I'm so sorry, man… I saw it on the news. I don't know what the hell to say."

Slapping him on the back and swallowing hard, I replied, "I know, man. Thanks."

I pointed at the black-padded table, all set up, and asked, "We good to go?"

Gesturing to the chair with one hand and giving me a thumbs-up with the other, Luke busied himself preparing the gun and ink as I peeled my shirt over my head and sat down, my jaw clenching.

Sitting down beside me, Luke asked, "So what are we going for?"

"Angel wings, white ones, big enough to cover most of my chest and torso."

Luke paused, then nodded sympathetically and went to begin marking them on my skin, when I stopped his hand, gripping his wrist, looking him dead in the eye. "You make this the best fuckin' work you've ever done. My previous ink is nothing compared to this. Any work you've ever done is nothing compared to *this,* you get me?"

"I get you. I promise, Rome, they'll be just right."

Sensing his sincerity, I freed his hand and an hour later, the outline was drawn.

"Go ahead, man, check it out."

When I stood before the mirror, I couldn't speak. The wings were just right, the perfect tribute to our child—two large wings starting on my chest and each tip ending low on my abs. Giving Luke an approving nod, I sat back on the chair, the buzzing of the gun blaring in the silent room.

"It'll take about eight hours all in all. We'll do half today, then finish up tomorrow if you'd like," Luke said, hovering the gun just above my stomach, waiting for my answer.

"No," I said harshly. "We start and finish today."

Luke frowned. "Hell, man, that's too much. Your body could go into shock. We're gonna be covering some damn painful areas."

"I don't give a fuck. We do this today," I growled, my voice coming out too strong. Luke was a friend and didn't deserve my shitty attitude, but I needed this, needed to get it done.

"Bullet, man, the pain—"

"Is what I want! Now are you going to do it or do I need to find someone else who will? I'm paying you a hell of a lot of money to get this done as soon as possible, but believe me, that can change."

Sighing, Luke answered, "Have it your way, man. But don't say I didn't warn you. Let me know if you want to stop at any point."

"I won't."

The minute the gun touched my skin, I closed my eyes. The pain would be worth it. Molly endured so much fucking pain; it was only right I did too, and our angel… our angel deserved this. Deserved to be remembered.

"Rome, man! Have you blacked out on me or what?"

Snapping back to reality, I flinched at the tightness of my raw torso and, looking to Luke, asked, "What?"

"We're done. You okay?"

Rubbing a hand down my face, I said, "Yeah, fuck, I zoned out."

"I know! You want to have a look before I cover it?"

Taking a deep breath, I nodded and, slowly getting off the table, walked to the floor-length mirror, my legs weak as hell from all my body had been put through.

This time, when I saw my new ink, there were no sharp inhales of breath, no painful regurgitated memories or tears. The wings commemorating our lost angel were meant to be on my chest; our child was meant to be remembered. I'd gone through the pain; I'd begun atoning for my failing as a daddy.

"They good, man?" Luke asked from behind me.

Turning and shaking his hand, I replied, "They're fucking perfect… just… beyond."

* * *

Later that night, I stood at the doorway of the place I never wanted to see again in my life. Too many memories—old and new—assaulted me as I opened the front door, and the first thing I noticed was how bare and cold the place felt without the usual antiques and artwork proudly and ostentatiously on display.

Footsteps sounded in the hall. My daddy's lawyer was at the entrance to the office, gesturing for me to step inside.

When I walked into the study, my father sat behind his desk, unkempt and looking older than his years. He looked up when I entered and let out a small, bitter laugh—even hitting rock bottom didn't change the bastard.

"Let you out on bail, then?" I drawled, taking a seat.

Shrugging, he answered, "Paid for it with the last of the Prince Oil share of the money, but don't worry, son, I'll be going to prison soon enough… and all because you were too fucking stubborn to do what you were told."

Leaning forward, I hissed, "You deserve to fester in a cold cell. You killed my baby, you sadistic fuck. You're lucky I don't kill your evil ass. *You* laundered the money. It's all on *you!*"

"Wow, Romeo, I can just feel the father-son love," he answered dryly. I almost had to sit on my hands to stop from knocking the bastard out. I wasn't going to hit him though. I didn't want anything to get in the way of his conviction.

"What's happened to Prince Oil? The Blairs?"

"The company is in administration. The Blairs are probably gonna declare bankruptcy." He turned his cold, dead eyes to me. "Bet that makes you happy, eh?"

"And Momma? Where's she? Off ruining more lives?" I asked, ignoring his shitty tone.

He waved his hand dismissively. "She's left town. She won't be back."

"She should be rotting in jail too!"

The suit entered the study at that moment, putting an end to our conversation, and sat down before me, pushing a contract into my hands. "From this day on, you are to cut all ties from your parents. That includes any inheritance of their fortune—or what's left of it when it's liquidized by the government—their properties, and their possessions."

"Done," I answered quickly, causing the no-nonsense lawyer to glare at me over his glasses.

"You have no problems with this?"

Smiling, I said, "Let me put this to you straight. I hate them. They're fuckin' horrible examples of people. I have my own money—money they can't touch—and I'm getting drafted by the NFL. I want nothing of theirs. Anything they've touched would only be cursed anyway."

"So you'll sign?" The lawyer confirmed again and I nodded. My daddy turned away from me in his chair, staring out the window.

The fucker was broken. And it was the best thing I'd ever seen.

Refocusing on the lawyer, I replied, "Gladly."

He passed me a fancy-ass pen, and three signatures later, I was officially and legally free.

Standing, I walked over to my daddy one last time and declared, "We're done. Never speak to me again. Never contact me again. If you come anywhere near me, Molly, or my friends, I'll kill you and that's a damn promise." Crouching right down before his aging face, seeing his lip curl in anger, I smiled. "And have fun rotting away in a cell, being someone's bitch for the rest of your miserable life. And while I'm sure y'all will think of me every minute for the rest of your days, I'll make sure to never think of either of you Ever. *Ever*. Again."

As I stepped out of the front door, I took one look at the old empty house that had held me an emotional prisoner for so long, and realized, my folks no longer had any power over me, not like before, and never would ever again.

* * *

Walking back into that locker room was hell.

As soon as I entered the doors, my rowdy teammates froze and stared at me as I made my way to my locker, dropping my bag and squeezing my eyes closed at the strength it was taking to face them all again.

I heard Coach walk into the room and clear his throat. "Rome?" he said, and turning, I looked to him, knowing my face was blank. "Damn glad to have you back, son." He walked over and shook my hand, pulling me into his embrace, and when he stepped back, each of my teammates did the same. My eyes blurred with the emotion of the moment.

Chris Porter was one of the last to approach me, and when he did, he shook his head. "Bullet, man, I'm so sorry." I could only squeeze his shoulder in response. The shit between him and me no longer mattered. Perspective—a wonderful thing.

"I finished with Shelly right away. Anyone who could be involved in something so sick isn't worth the damn air she breathes."

"How's Molly?" Jacob Thomsson, our linebacker, asked.

"She left me. I have no idea how she is."

The tension in the room intensified as I turned my back to the team and began to change into my training shorts, unable to bear the pity in their faces. They needed to know Molly wouldn't be around for the pregame kiss to which so many of my teammates and fans attributed my near perfect performance this season. I knew the majority of the guys would shit themselves at that information— going into the championship with a heartbroken QB wouldn't exactly fill them with confidence.

A tattooed arm hooked around my neck, and Austin whispered, "We'll get you through this, Rome. I swear to God we will."

I friggin' hoped so.

"She'll come back."

Smiling grimly, I said, "Ally, Jimmy-Don, Lexi, and Cass all tell me the same. But you guys don't know the half of it. You didn't see her face the night she left. She's gone, man. Gone for good."

"I wouldn't be so sure. What you fail to realize is that the rest of us saw how she looked at *you*, despite all the grief. She may be going through shit right now, but she loves you, Rome. She'll be back."

Cracking a smile and feeling a tiny bit of happiness for the first time in what felt like an age, I joked, "You going soft on me, Carillo?"

Barking out a laugh, he replied, "Nah, I just envy you, man. Who wouldn't want a girl sticking with you even when everything goes to shit? She may be gone now, but she won't be gone forever."

33

BCS National Championship
Rose Bowl Stadium, Pasadena, California

POD's "Here Comes The Boom" pumped out of the locker room's speakers as the team—the University of Alabama's famous Crimson Tide—prepped for the biggest game of the year. Some guys were shouting in excitement; some were quietly listening to earphones; some were puking in the john; most were simply waiting for the referee's whistle to start the game.

Ally and Cass were using my game tickets. They had flown out to California, along with thousands of Bama fans, to watch the showdown against the Fighting Irish of Notre Dame. As a senior, it was my very last game for the Tide. Fuck. It was my last game with a group of guys who were my family. I had to win the ballgame for them. I had to get in the zone and play the game of my life.

Coach entered the room and slowly surveyed the scene. We all fell silent. "Take a knee. Let's pray."

We did as he instructed and recited The Lord's Prayer. Each player then looked to Coach, who instructed, "Stand up. Listen good."

We all got to our feet and Coach took his place in the center of our player circle. Moving to look each of us in the eye, he stated, "Let's fight the Irish... all... over... the... field." Coach emphasized the last four words. My blood rushed in my ears and the energy building between the team was infectious.

"Defense, offense, special teams. Stay alert. Y'all know your assignments." Coach paused, pointing to his watch. "Sixty minutes, no more, no less. Don't take this win for me. Take it for each other. Let's leave it all on the field."

Bodies shook with adrenaline, players swayed where they stood, anxious to hit the field, and Coach turned cheerleader. "We're the reigning champions! Do y'all wanna *stay* champs? Well, do ya?!!!" he asked loudly.

"YEAH!" yelled back the locker room, the enthusiasm through the roof.

Shaking his head in disappointment, Coach yelled, "Not good enough, so I'll ask y'all again. Do ya wanna stay the champs?!!!"

"YEAH, YEAH, YEAHHHH!!!" chanted the team, the sound of shouting rumbling along the lockers, and players began pounding the doors and walls with their fists, the noise of the crowd outside building and the excitement of the players almost too much to take.

"Then grab your gear, hit the field, and... *ROLL TIDE!!!*"

Heading for the locker room door, in unison, the team, *my team*, chanted, "TIDE, TIDE, TIDE!"

As returning BCS champions, we had the honor of running out onto the field first. Rolling my shoulders and jumping on the spot, knees to chest, I gripped onto my helmet guard tightly, trying my damnedest to get psyched up.

I tried real hard not to let my mind drift to Molly. I'd been hoping she'd show after the voicemail I'd left her yesterday. But, as always, there was no reply. I'd made peace with myself that she wasn't coming back to the US. My plans were firmly in place—to win this fucking championship, then fly to Oxford and sort this shit out once and for all.

The announcement for the Tide came. Just like last year, it was a blur as the team ran onto the field. Austin and Jimmy-Don led the way, pumping up the crowd to a crazy volume.

Taking a sobering breath, I shot out of the tunnel, pyrotechnics going off all around me, keeping my head down as we swarmed onto the field. I robotically sang "The Star Spangled Banner" with all my heart and as *"...the home of the brave"* died away into the night air, it was time for the rival team captains to meet for the coin toss.

I enjoyed this calm before the storm.

The Fighting Irish captains called it correctly and elected to receive.

Toward the end of the coin toss, the Bama fans rose as one and began to chant, "Kiss, kiss, kiss…" so damn loud it was deafening. Now back on the sideline, I hung my head in embarrassment and squeezed my eyes tightly, trying to ignore the pain of Molly's absence. How could they know their good luck charm was across the fucking Atlantic? I cringed, knowing I couldn't deliver, as tens of thousands of Bama fans demanded the ritual they believed had carried the Tide through an undefeated season.

Even so, the ever-increasing volume took my breath away, the crescendo of noise from the fans almost intolerable.

I concentrated on my game plays, anything to block out the deafening roar. My teammates began walking forward, checking out a new commotion in the crowd, but like a pussy, I hung back—I wasn't interested. I couldn't wait for the damn referee's whistle to blow.

Someone suddenly jumped on me—Austin.

"Rome, look!" He pointed toward the Jumbotron. When I looked up, my heart exploded in my chest like a friggin' grenade.

Molly?

I whipped my head to the direction of the stands, scanning for a familiar face, and our gazes locked.

Fuck me. She looked stunning: brown hair long and loose, white dress… so goddamn beautiful.

Deep emotion surged through my body, but all I could think of as I walked as if on air toward her was she came— she actually friggin' came back for me.

The closer I got, the more my throat dried and my chest tightened. Her golden eyes widened with nerves.

I let go of my helmet, no longer needing it to stay centered… calm.

As I glided to a halt before my girl, I looked up and watched her take a deep breath, the stadium around us uncharacteristically still and quiet.

"Hey, Mol," I said in a rough voice.

"Hey, you," she whispered back. Then I closed my eyes for a moment, savoring that familiar accent once more.

"You going to give up that sweet kiss?"

"If that's what you want."

The heavy burden I'd been carrying around for weeks lifted, and I answered, "It most definitely fuckin' is."

Reaching forward, I lifted Mol over the barrier and wrapped her into my arms, crashing against her lips with my own, tasting the sweet vanilla taste that was so uniquely her.

My girl took everything I gave, her desperation matching mine as we let our crazed need for each other take over.

Needing a breath, I broke away and asked, "Are you really here?" running my hands over as much of her as I could.

Cupping my face, tears in her eyes, she cried, "Baby, I'm so sorry I left. I couldn't cope, but… I love you. I love you so, so much. Please forgive me. Please…"

She loved me. She fucking loved me, and the relief those words conjured had me literally dropping to the floor, still clutching Molly in my hold.

I was never letting her go again.

"Are you back for me? For good?"

Her warm breath breezed down my neck. "For the first time ever, baby, I ran back to something, to you... my Romeo."

I *was* hers; she had no idea how much.

"You won't ever run again. You get that now?" I said firmly, searching her eyes for any doubt. There was none.

"I get it."

"You left me alone for weeks, no word, no explanation. Do you know how mad I am at you for that?"

"I know." The sadness and regret in her soft voice almost cut me like a knife. But I had my answer. She *was* with me now for good.

Pressing my forehead to hers, I stated, "I'm going to win this game. Then I'm going to fuckin' brand you, once and for all. It seems I've been too lenient with you, Shakespeare." I pushed. "Maybe you didn't quite get that you're mine and as such can never, ever leave me—even if your heart is broken. Because if you're hurting, baby, you can bet I'm fuckin' hurting too."

My muscles felt invigorated and I stood, hoisting Molly back to her seat, ordering, "You, back in those stands. Now. I've got a championship title to take back home. Then I'll deal with you. Quite frankly, I don't know which one I'm more excited for."

Flushing beet red and throwing me a huge smile, she said, "Give them hell, baby," then planted another lucky sweet kiss full on my lips, the Bama fans roaring in reaction.

We played out of our skins, but Notre Dame was never too far behind us, never too far in front.

The final down of the game, fifteen seconds on the clock, fourth quarter. I had led a drive into the red zone. We had to score a touchdown; a field goal was not enough to secure the victory. Notre Dame's defense hadn't missed a damn beat all night and I had one last chance to wrestle the win from their stubborn clutches.

Calling a, "*Crimson Two, Crimson Two*," in the huddle, we moved into position, ready to execute an option play called by Coach himself. "Down... set... *Hut, hut*," I calmly yelled, taking the shotgun from the center.

I immediately looked for Porter. *Shit!* He was covered. I checked down to Carillo. *Fuck!* Not an option. Stepping back, I scanned the wider field, Jimmy-Don giving me precious few seconds.

Now!

Seeing a running lane, I set off, my breath echoing in the casing of my helmet as I powered onward, the end zone clear in my sights. I visualized making the touchdown. I felt the elation of winning the game, willing it into reality.

I pushed my tired legs to their absolute limits, every muscle screaming, and I broke the plane—*touchdown!*—then spiked the ball.

The sensation of victory hit me hard, but I didn't freeze. We'd taken it. We'd fucking won.

Staring up to the sky, I pulled down my jersey, kissed my hand, placed it on my tattooed wings, and held it up high, praying, "This one's for you, my angel. This one's for you…"

Suddenly the whole team dove on me. TV reporters, Tide staff, and fans alike flooded the field. "Sweet Home Alabama" blasted around the stadium as hundreds of fireworks burst in the sky, celebrating our win.

After many congratulations and hugs, I stared over a sea of heads to see my girl sat in her seat, crying, Ally holding Molly in her arms. I glanced to the Jumbotron, still showing replays of my celebration.

The wings. She'd seen the wings—I just hoped she loved them too.

The Tide was swiftly caught up in the whirlwind of our win. After the trophy presentation and painful TV interview eulogizing my award as the championship's MVP, I jumped off the stage and ran to my girl, immediately lifting her up and exclaiming, "We won, baby!"

Throwing me a smile, she replied, "I'm sooo proud of you."

One hand holding her gorgeous ass, the other caressing the bare skin of her back, I confided, "I need to be alone with you. Now."

We took off, heading for the player's tunnel, ignoring shouts from the coaching staff calling me back. Fuck them all. I needed to be alone with my girl.

Molly giggled, nuzzling my neck, and asked, "Don't you have to be with the team?"

"You want to give them all an after show? Because right now all I can think of is being inside you, and no matter where we are in thirty minutes, it's happening."

Golden-brown eyes widened, and she sucked in a low breath. "We need to go... like now."

Relaxing for the first time in weeks, I exhaled in relief. "Glad we're finally on the same fuckin' page."

34

NFL Draft
Radio City Music Hall, New York
Four Months Later...

"*The first draft... for the next NFL season... for Seattle Seahawks... is... quarterback... Romeo Prince... from... the Alabama Crimson Tide!!!*"

A warm wave of relief washed over my body, and I closed my eyes.

I'd done it. And hell, I was the first pick draft. I was the best fucking player in the country... I *was* worth something after all.

An excited high-pitched scream sounded in my ear and my girl pulled me to my feet. Unable to resist getting caught up in the moment, I lifted her to my lips and kissed her over and over. I pulled back and she whispered, "Baby, you did it."

As I looked into Molly's eyes, I remembered a time when I wasn't sure she'd ever come back to me, never mind be right here beside me as my life changed and my dream came true, or at least half of my dream.

A steward tapped me on the shoulder. "Mr. Prince, we need to go to the stage now. Please follow me."

Nodding and squeezing Molly's hand one more time, I turned to the corridor, a huge friggin' camera following me the entire way. I took the Seahawks baseball cap handed to me and, placing it on my head, walked onto the stage.

The lights and the noise were blinding.

The commissioner pulled me in close as he shook my hand, saying, "Well done, son! You got to be feeling pretty damn happy right now!"

Slightly dazed by all of the attention, I just nodded numbly, and he handed me my Seahawks jersey, the feel of it in my hands and the **PRINCE 7** on the back too much to take in.

I had to do a shitload of press, answering question after question about how I felt going to Seattle. How do you verbalize a dream coming true? I was excited, beyond excited, and told a thousand journalists so—it was the fucking NFL after all—but something just wasn't sitting right in my stomach. A sinking feeling of doubt was tugging at my mind. I knew what it was... Mol. She hadn't decided on a damn school yet for her PhD. We'd been living together for months now. After our stint apart, we moved into our own apartment almost immediately, and I'd seen her apply to lots of colleges and hadn't dared bring up my anxiety about us having to live apart. At this point in my life, I knew I couldn't be without her. Hell, I didn't sleep anymore if she wasn't curled into my side.

Those thoughts kept playing on my mind as I shook a million hands, met Seahawks staff by the dozen, and by the time I got back to the green room—my friends and Molly still giddy as all hell from my achievement—I was ready to tear my fucking hair out with worry.

Flashing me a huge smile, my girl launched into my arms, pressing kisses all over my face, singing, "I love you, I love you, I love you…"

Trying to ease my anxiety, I pulled her into my chest, probably holding her too tight. I obviously had, because when I let her go, her eyebrows were drawn and she asked, "What? What's wrong?"

She could read me like a book.

I glanced over her shoulder and noticed our friends staring at us, smiling… Well, except for Ally. She was frowning too, sensing my weird turn in mood.

I held up my hand to our friends, excusing Molly and myself, and, needing to deal with this crap now, pulled her down a corridor, making sure we were alone. She smiled and playfully tugged on the peak of my cap, but I could see the strain around her eyes… She thought I wasn't happy.

Reaching for the cap and pulling it off, I said, "I am happy, baby." I didn't want her to misunderstand that. "But I can't do it without you. Seattle. I'm going to Seattle. You applied to Harvard, Yale, and Stanford that I know of. You've been so fuckin' secretive, and I'm going

379

insane. We could be on different sides of the country for all I know, and I need you with me. I don't think I can do this without you."

"Rome—" She tried to interrupt, but I had to get all of this out before it ate me alive.

"I feel like just demanding it because I know you would drop everything for me. But I also want your dreams to come true. I don't know how to have both you and football."

Her face was unmoved, relaxed even, and I couldn't understand how she wasn't freaking out like me. Was she *actually* okay with us being apart?

Holding my hand, she pressed a kiss on each of my fingers before confiding, "Romeo, I've run away from my problems all my life, never to return, but you're the first person I've ever run back to. That means so much to me. You pulled me out of the darkness." I swallowed hard when she took my hand she'd just kissed and pressed it against her flat stomach. We'd decided to wait to have more children, wait until we were older, more settled, but it still ripped me to shreds knowing we should've been preparing for our angel's arrival if things had gone down differently.

With a soft squeeze of my hand, she made me refocus. "And gave me hope. Hope that one day I will be a good mother… when the time is right, and that I do have a family… in you."

I couldn't speak, and when she leaned forward and pressed a kiss to the angel wing tattoo on my chest, my eyes closed and I had to take a deep breath. "You once told me that one day you wanted to get away, that one day you would be your own person, and that one day you would get everything you wanted." I had, all those months ago in her room, but what I wanted now landed solely in her hands.

Cupping her face, I told her, "But what I want is you. Everything I want is with you. You're my 'one day.'"

She handed me an envelope from her pocket, and a small smile set on her lips. "Your 'one day' is finally here."

I immediately ripped it open and read the short paragraph:

Miss Shakespeare,

We at the University of Washington, Seattle, are pleased to inform you that you have been accepted on the PhD program for Religious Philosophy. To confirm your place, please contact us using one of the methods below.

My heart pounded and my hands were actually shaking. Looking up at my girl, I couldn't digest it. She was coming with me? She'd done this for me?

But… how?

Her gaze was expectant, but all I could get out of my mouth was, "You… Does…? What?"

Giggling, she removed the letter from my frozen hands and said, "I also applied to Seattle. When Doctor Adams, all those months ago, mentioned there was a possibility of you going there, I researched into how the draft worked and took a calculated chance on Seattle. I didn't want to say, just in case it didn't work out. But it's just paid off.

I'm coming to Seattle with you, baby. You're looking at the newest PhD student of philosophy. I sent my email confirmation about twenty-five minutes ago."

Fuck. As she said those words, I realized we'd done it. Against all the odds, against every obstacle thrown our way—the loss and all the pain—we'd friggin' done it. We'd both gotten what we wanted and we were still together.

Unable to contain my happiness, I smashed my lips against hers and my mind drifted to the one last missing step. I wanted Molly forever, and in my heart I knew there was only one thing that would make everything perfect.

Breaking away from her lips, I stared my girl right in the eyes and said, "Marry me."

Her mouth dropped in shock and she stuttered, "W-what?"

Holding her face in my hands, I repeated, "Marry me. Marry me tomorrow, tonight, as quickly as we can. Just… fuckin' marry me, Shakespeare. Let me make you officially mine."

"But… But…"

I pressed her against the wall and reiterated, "I love you. I love you more than anything. I can't and won't be without you ever again. I want to give you everything possible. I want to give you happiness… I want to one day give you children… Marry me. Be with me. Have forever… with *me*."

Her breath came quick as I kept my gaze locked on hers. A wash of contentment settled over her face, and then she made my fucking life.

"Yes!" she cried.

"Say it again." I needed to hear that one small—but powerful—word once more… just to be sure.

"Yes. Of course I'll marry you!" She giggled and I kissed her with everything I had until she chuckled against my lips.

"What the hell are you laughing at now, Shakespeare?" I asked, her happiness becoming infectious.

"That the two ill-fated lovers—in our story—found a way to be together against all the odds, all of the obstacles, finally getting their happily ever after."

Fucking Romeo and Juliet…

Ah, whatever. My girl wanted a fairy tale? She could damn well have one. Holding her close, I whispered, "For never was a truer story of love conquering woe than this of *Molly* Juliet and her Romeo."

We both paused for a moment, gazes locked, before we burst out in laughter.

"And where, Romeo Prince, did you learn that?"

Shrugging, I answered, "Google. Where else!" Molly couldn't stop herself from giggling.

Bringing her left hand to my mouth, I kissed her bare ring finger. "You need a ring."

"It's okay. We'll sort it later. I don't need a ring yet. I'm happy with just having you."

"Fuck that!" I said a bit too loudly. "We're sorting it right now."

"But… but… the draft…"

"Is done. We're going to Seattle. No need to stay here any longer, and right now we're getting you a ring." I paused and looked down at my flustered fiancé—fuck! my *fiancé*—and a question came to mind. "Or should we just get married now?"

Swallowing, she whispered, "What? Where?"

I shrugged. "Vegas? We can be there in a couple of hours." The excitement that thought brought was almost too much to take. She could be my wife in a couple of hours.

"No," she said in a low voice, and the excitement within me faded.

"No?"

Clutching my hand, she said, "I want to marry you, as soon as possible, but not at some cheap chapel or by some dodgy fat Elvis!"

Pulling her to my chest and wrapping my fist in her hair, I asked, "Then where?"

Smiling sadly, she said, "My parents eloped to Gretna Green."

"Where the fuck is that?"

"Scotland."

Scotland? Fine, whatever. "Done. We'll get the next flight out."

Shaking her head but laughing this time, she said, "No. I'm joking. I don't want that. I want us to have our own story. I want us to make our own memories. I want this wedding to be done right."

I groaned in exasperation. "Mol, for fuck sake, I just want to make you mine. You own me in every way, shape, and form. Just give me this, soon. Let me have you too."

Brushing a hand down my cheek, she pressed a kiss on my lips and whispered, "Okay, baby. However you want. Wherever you want."

"Done, we'll get married as soon as we're back in Bama, but right now, we're getting you a ring."

Taking Molly's hand, loving the sound of her excited squeal behind me, we reentered the green room, walked to our friends, and I put my arm around Molly's shoulders. Our friends threw each other questioning glances, watching us closely.

"We're getting married," I announced proudly, "and right now we're getting Mol an engagement ring. If you want to come, let's go." All their mouths hung open in shock before Cass beamed a huge grin, bellowed out a deafening whoop, and then they all began diving on us in excitement.

* * *

"So what kind of dress are you thinking about?"

"Well... I—"

"*Because*, I have some ideas, you know, about silhouettes that would suit your frame," Ally went on, and I couldn't help but laugh as Molly sat, stuttering her way through the barrage of questions her friends were firing her way. We'd been engaged all of three hours and her friends had all but planned the whole damn wedding day.

"And I can do your hair so you can check that off the to-do list. Oh, and I can get my momma to make the bridesmaid dresses." Lexi paused and her eyes widened.

"That is, of course, if we *are* your bridesmaids…" She gestured to the girls in the booth.

Molly reached over the table and clasped Lexi's hand. "Of course you guys are my bridesmaids. You're my best friends." Cass and Lexi beamed with excitement, and Molly turned to Ally. "And I was wondering if you would be my maid of honor?"

Ally gasped and water filled her dark brown eyes before she launched into my girl's shocked embrace. "Oh my God, darlin', I'd be honored!"

Molly awkwardly patted her on the back, a happy smile on her face, and she caught my watching gaze, rolling her eyes, causing me to laugh.

She was so damn cute.

After accepting my proposal, we'd all hit the bustling streets of New York and began our search for her engagement ring. Ally had only one place in mind and dragged us to *Tiffany's*, quipping, "Rome's rich as all hell. It's not like he can't afford it!"

When Molly caught the prices of most of the rings, her eyes had almost popped out of her head. Squeezing my hand, she said, "Rome, I… I can't, some of these rings are as expensive as a car. It's too much."

Shrugging and pulling her close, I replied, "You're worth it, baby. Get whatever you want." But I could see she was resolved in her decision.

Despite Ally's insistence on a huge rock and my willingness to buy her anything she damn well pleased, thirty minutes later, we found ourselves in a small, vintage jeweler in Little Italy. My girl picked out a 1930s simple, half-carat diamond ring. As soon as the seller had told her the story behind it, Molly was in love.

Apparently it had belonged to a couple who'd spent their whole lives together, never once spending a day apart, after surviving religious persecution in Germany, and came to the States after World War II. They'd lived until an old age, had a huge family with lots of kids, and passed away within days of one another, the one left behind unable to survive on their own. In their will, they had asked that the ring be sold to a young woman who truly loved and deserved it.

Molly had listened to the old jeweler with tears glistening in her eyes, and I knew she'd found her ring of choice. She was all about the deeper significance of things, and thought that this ring, after everything we'd been through, was perfect.

And seeing that thin piece of gold on her finger was fucking perfection to me too.

Jimmy-Don's girly shriek shook me from the recent memory, and I watched him jump up and down in the booth of the bar and swerve to me, hands pressed to his chest. "Gee, Rome, please say I'm your groomsman. I have the perfect tux in mind! I have the whole day envisioned… It'll be just… just magical!"

Cass scowled at his mockery of the girls' excitement and laid a punch on his arm. Molly broke into fits of giggles at her friend.

I slapped Jimmy-Don on the back and said with all seriousness, "You know it, man. Reece too." That quickly stopped their jokes and I could see that the two of them were genuinely taken aback, speechless even.

"I'm getting us champagne to celebrate," I said, standing from the booth and tipping my chin at Austin. "Carillo, coming?"

He nodded his head and joined me walking to the bar. "How you feeling, man? Pretty fuckin' awesome, I imagine."

Taking a glance back at Mol and all our friends, happy and laughing, I said, "Too right, man. I can't believe a chick like her is actually going to marry me. I'm one lucky bastard."

Turning back to the bar, I ordered a bottle of Cristal and faced Austin. "So you gonna be my best man or what?"

Austin swallowed and a slow grin spread on his face. Slapping his hand in mine, he moved in to grip my shoulder. "Fuck, man, of course I will!"

"Only seems right after knowing you my whole damn life. Plus, you're the closest thing I have to a brother. We've both been put through the ringer and both still here to see another day." The poor bastard had had a rough six months, but thank fuck, he was now in a better place.

"I'm fuckin' honored, man, honored!" He flicked his gaze to Lexi sitting next to Molly, and a contented expression set on his face. "Only if you return the favor one day."

Smiling now myself, I said, "Done deal."

For the rest of the night we celebrated hard and I'd never felt so happy. Molly and I were going to Seattle, my little Shakespeare had agreed to be my wife, and on our return to Tuscaloosa, we had a wedding to plan.

35

"Are we all set?"

"We're good, son. Just need to get y'all changed into your tuxes and wait for the bride to show her face."

It had been a month since the draft, and on my and Molly's return to Bama, my aunt and uncle heard the news of our engagement and offered us the use of their house in Birmingham for our wedding. We'd decided to keep it small. In fact, only our friends knew of it. It wasn't a day for the press or for people to ooh and ahh at the real-life Romeo and Juliet of Alabama, the friggin' 'tragic lovers' the papers had made us out to be.

Since the Tide had won the championship, the hype surrounding Molly and me had been crazy, the draft only heightening the attention further, and we needed to get the hell away, get away from the media circus our marriage would no doubt become.

Our marriage was about us. No pomp, no ceremony.

"Is she okay?" I asked my uncle impatiently as he put the finishing touches to decorating the garden.

"She's great. Ally and the girls all slept in her room last night, giggling and staying up late. Your Aunt Alita is in her element, getting Molly all dolled up for today." He stopped and looked up from attaching the last fairy light to the white wooden altar. "Your girl looks absolutely breathtaking, son. Breathtaking… You've done good."

All I could do was scowl.

"What's that face for?" Uncle Gabe asked, smiling his fucking knowing smile at me, just as Austin, Reece, and Jimmy-Don entered the yard.

"That I wasn't with Mol last night! We haven't spent a damn night apart since I got her back, and I didn't sleep a wink in that hotel room, knowing she was here. I fuckin' hated it! You're lucky I didn't just screw tradition and turn up in her bed."

"Hey!" Jimmy-Don protested. "We were great company! Why wouldn't you want *this* over Molly?" He ran his hands down his body and licked his lips suggestively.

I ignored him, and my uncle patted me on my back. "You know your aunt wanted you guys to do it right. Believe me, son, it'll be worth it. Absence makes the heart grow fonder." My uncle gestured around the yard. "Well, what do you think?"

The garden area had been completely transformed. At the end of the lawn, masses of bright flowers and solar lamps made a footpath to a large, white wooden altar where the pastor would stand. Fairy lights were everywhere: in the trees, draped over the outside of the house, the fences... Mol was going to love it; it was the perfect romantic setting.

My uncle had been killing himself, getting the house ready for today. I knew it was because he still felt some guilt over what'd happened over the past year, hell, the past *twenty-two* years, but he shouldn't have. It was all under the bridge now that my daddy was in prison and my momma had apparently gone to live with her sister in Louisiana.

They were completely out of my life. For good.

"It's great, thank you," I replied, surprising him by slinging an arm around his shoulder and planting a kiss on his head. Yeah, yeah, I was all caught up in the moment too.

Suddenly, a loud slam of a door caused us all to look around.

Aunt Alita bolted out of the house, all flustered. "Gabe! Rome! The pastor is here." She gestured wildly with her hands at the five of us, still in our jeans and shirts, "Ay, ay! You're not even dressed! *Vamose!* You have thirty minutes!" Screaming like a Spanish banshee, she reentered the house almost as quickly as she came out.

Austin, Jimmy-Don, and Reece just stared at the now-empty doorway, and laughing, my uncle put two hands on my shoulders from behind. "The joys of married life… something for you to look forward to!"

Even though my fucker friends snickered at my uncle's comment, all I could think was that those thirty minutes couldn't pass quickly enough.

Standing at the altar was surreal, and the friggin' penguin suit I was trapped in almost choked me. Austin stood to my left as my best man, Jimmy-Don, Reece, and Uncle Gabe as my groomsmen.

Music started playing, some classical shit my aunt had picked out, and it immediately set off the nerves. I wanted to be married. I wanted to marry Molly so much that the reality of this moment was hard for me to digest.

It was actually happening.

Aunt Alita walked out of the house first and my uncle beamed with pride as he looked at his wife. Aunt Alita was Ally in twenty years: long brown hair, brown eyes, olive skin—very beautiful. Even after all these years of marriage, he was obviously still crazy about her. He had walked away from my grandparents and all his family for her, and it was comforting to see that true love could stand the test of time.

Cass and Lexi walked out next, wearing matching pink dresses and holding small bouquets of white flowers. Lexi was stripped of her usual heavy makeup, and Austin shifted beside me, a huge damn grin on his face as he watched her walk closer.

Ally was the last of the bridesmaids—Molly's maid of honor—and I knew that in just a few minutes, my girl would step out of that door. My heart beat furiously in anticipation.

As Ally took her place next to Cass and Lexi on the opposite side of the altar, I closed my eyes, taking a long, calming breath, and when I opened them again, that same breath was knocked right out of me.

Fuck. Me.

Molly had just stepped out of the house and was walking slowly toward me… and she was so beautiful. Her long, brown hair had been swept away from her face, held up by a white rose. Her dress was white lace, sleeveless, high-necked, and hugged every part of her stunning body. Finally, she held a bouquet of white roses in her hands—and she was gripping onto them as though her life depended on it.

I couldn't help but smile as she kept her eyes on the floor. She hated attention, even this small affair, but when she nervously darted those golden browns to meet mine, a relieved smile tugged on her lips, her shoulders relaxed, and she never looked away from me as she made it to my outstretched hand.

As soon as her hand met mine, I leaned in and whispered, "Hey, Mol."

Blushing, she replied, "Hey, you," and we both broke into laughter, the tension dissipating to excitement and happiness.

"You look beautiful," I said quietly, and the pastor cleared his throat. His face was humored, and narrowing my eyes at his subtle reprimand, I stepped back, signaling for him to begin the ceremony.

I couldn't exactly go apeshit at a man of God now, could I?

After listening to the pastor's advice and prayers, and bible readings from Uncle Gabe and Ally, it was time for the vows. We'd decided to write our own, and, gripping onto Mol's hands and clearing my throat, I began.

"Molly. Last year, you captured my heart, being exactly who you are—the kindest, most supportive person I've ever known. Not only did you make me fall madly in love with you, but you became my best friend and got me through both good and bad times. You're the reason I smile every morning and you are the person who gives me comfort when I'm down. You believed in me when no one else did, and you showed me how to love when I never thought I could. But most of all, you gave me your unconditional acceptance."

Reaching out, I wiped a tear from Mol's eye. "I'm not sure a lifetime is long enough to try to give you all that you have given me, but I promise I will spend all of my days striving to make you happy. I will laugh and cry with you, and if you run, I'll be right there running beside you. I promise to love you forever, and I promise, when the day comes, that I will be the best daddy a child could hope for."

Tears blurred my vision, but I needed to finish. "I have never been more certain of anything in my life as I am that we were always meant to be. We are better together than apart, and no matter what happens in our lives, I know that waking up and seeing you each morning will always be the best part of my day."

"Romeo... that was beautiful..." Molly whispered tearfully, and I had to fight to keep my emotions in check too. Sniffing and crying sounded all around us, but I only had eyes for my girl.

"Molly, your vows, please," the pastor instructed, even his voice sounding a little husky.

Pulling herself together and straightening her shoulders, Molly spoke. "Romeo. If someone had told me a year ago that I would be standing here, marrying my soul mate at age twenty-one, I would never have believed them. If someone would've told me all that we would go through as a couple, I would never have believed them." She shook her head in disbelief and pressed her soft hand against my chest, her golden eyes fixed on mine. "You saved me, Rome. You saved me from a life of loneliness. You showed me there was more to life than I'd been awarding myself, and you showed me how to depend on you and to let you into my heart. I will laugh and cry with you too, and I promise you I will never run from you again and will forever stand by your side. My father told me that one day I would understand what it would be like to give someone the gift of my soul, and I *do* understand—I gave it to you from the very first moment we met. You are my everything, Romeo Prince, and I can't wait to spend the rest of my life next to the best man I've ever known."

The minute she finished, I dived on her lips. Fuck waiting. Her vow to me was incredible and more than I could ever have hoped for.

Breaking away, I stroked her face and said, "I love you, baby. I love you so much."

"I love you, too," she said through happy tears.

A cough pulled our attention, and the pastor smiled, holding up an open Bible. "If we exchange the rings, I can pronounce y'all husband and wife, and you can get back to your kissing."

Looking at Molly and our friends, we all started to laugh, and Austin handed me the ring.

"Molly, I love you. With this ring, let it be known that I choose you above all others. Let it be known that with this ring, I promise to be with you for eternity, until death do us part." Slipping that platinum ring on Mol's finger did something to me. I felt reborn. Like the past, all the abuse and unhappiness, was finally buried, and only an exciting and perfect future with my girl awaited. I felt like, for the first time in years, I truly liked who I was, and it was all due to the girl before me, binding herself to me forever in every possible way.

Ally handed Molly the ring, and she took hold of my left hand. "Romeo, I love you. With this ring, let it be known that I choose you above all others. Let it be known that with this ring, I promise to be with you for eternity, until death do us part."

"And by the power vested in me, I now pronounce you husband and wife." The pastor faced me with an amused smile. "Romeo, you may now kiss your bride... *again*."

I didn't waste any time and took Molly's mouth with mine, softly, savoring every moment of this unbelievable feeling taking hold.

Molly was my wife.

36

Pulling my new wife closer in my arms, I whispered, "You ready to go?"

Her bite on her bottom lip and her hooded eyes told me she was. I stood and faced our guests, who were finishing up eating. "Guys, we're heading out."

Ally jumped to her feet in protest. "No, you haven't done the first dance yet!"

Shit. I looked down to Molly, who had surprise written all over her face.

"First dance? But there's hardly anyone here. We don't have to do a first dance." I smiled as she tried to get out of it, but I held out my hand, an expectant look on my face.

Sighing in defeat, she took my offered hand and I pulled her to the small patio, surrounded by thousands of white lights. Ally ran to the stereo and the opening bars of our wedding song played. Molly glanced up at me, eyes glistening.

"Romeo... how?"

Stroking a loose piece of hair from her face, I said, "A few months ago you told me about this song. I thought it could be our tribute to your folks by making it our song too."

I remembered that day so well...

"Mol? Where are you, baby?"

I found Molly stood in the kitchen of our new place, making breakfast, music playing beside her from her iPhone speakers. I saw her shoulders shaking and I panicked. I instantly moved in behind her, wrapping my arms around her waist.

"What's wrong, baby?"

Turning into my chest, she smiled a watery smile and set to wiping at her tears. "It's silly. I'm being silly."

I knew I was frowning. I was so lost as to what the hell was happening. "Mol, tell me what's wrong. Has something bad happened?"

Laughing through her sobs, she said, "No, I promise, Rome. It's just..."

"What?"

"This song." Her eyes met mine, and I knew I still looked just as confused.

"You're upset because of this song?"

"Not upset." I watched as she took a deep breath, and I lifted her to the counter, cupping her face so I could see her better as I placed myself between her legs.

"You're going to have to explain, baby. Why are you crying because of a song?"

"It was my mother's favorite song. My dad would play it on their wedding anniversary, a kind of tribute, I suppose. It's kind of a tradition... a good one. I loved it, looked forward to it every year. He did it so I would know my mum in some small way, and you know what? It did make me understand her a little. After Dad died, my grandma continued to do it for them both. And well, when she passed too, it was something I continued doing for myself. When I hear it, it feels like they are all somehow still with me."

I let myself exhale and pressed my forehead to hers. It was her parents' wedding anniversary? Fuck. I didn't know what the hell to say in response, so I simply said, *"I love you, baby."*

Brushing a kiss on my lips, she whispered, *"I love you too."*

Sting's "Fields of Gold" played as my wife and I swayed on the spot, happy tears falling from Molly's eyes. I knew I'd done right by this song. It was meaningful to her, and now it would forever remind her of this day. No words needed to be said, and I knew she would understand why I'd chosen it—I wanted her to feel like her family was here, in some small way.

Our family and friends stood and watched us take our first dance as man and wife and eventually joined us on the floor.

It was perfect.

As the last few bars played out, Molly lifted her head, her hand pressed to my cheek, and she whispered, "Let's go, Rome. I need to have you alone."

"Christ, how many damn buttons are on this dress!" I complained as I tried to get my girl naked, the long line of tiny pearl buttons at the back of the dress dangerously close to being ripped apart due to my increasing frustration.

"Hurry," Molly ordered, her voice rough with need. We were in a private luxury cabin. We picked somewhere off the beaten track, completely secluded, for our first night together as a married couple.

As I unfastened the last button, I pushed the tight dress apart and it fell to the floor.

Fuck. Me.

"Mol, you're friggin' killing me," I groaned as she stood before me in a white lace bustier, tiny white lace panties, white stockings and a friggin' garter wrapped around her thigh.

Smiling, she asked, "You like?"

"I fuckin' love!" I croaked, my cock nearly bursting through the zipper in my damn tight pants. I quickly rid myself of my jacket and shirt, snapping the fly to give my crushed dick some relief.

Molly stood before me, looking like a virginal goddess, and my hands twitched, needing to touch her. "Get on the bed, baby," I instructed, watching her tight ass as she climbed on the mattress and sat up on her knees, waiting for what came next.

"Lose the bustier."

With an excited smile, Molly began unhooking the tight contraption. She was pushing her luck, taking her sweet time, and by the playful glint in her eyes, she knew she almost had me at my breaking point.

"Don't fuck with me, Mol." I warned. "I'm barely holding it together here."

Reaching into my boxers, I stroked along my dick. Her wide eyes watched the movement, and with a final pull, the lingerie dropped to the cream-colored bed and her full breasts were completely on show.

"Touch them," I growled, pointing to her breasts. I roved my eyes down her insane body. The only thing left was the stockings, garter belt and the panties. The panties were a problem.

Flushing in excitement, Molly moved her hands over her chest, slowly palming the flesh, tugging on her nipples, and closing her eyes in pleasure.

I fucking broke.

Marching to the bed, I crawled over Molly, knocking away her hands. "Enough, they're mine now."

I cut off her surprised giggle with my lips. I plunged my tongue straight in her mouth and she pushed hers against mine, her fingernails scratching along my back. My hand wandered south and I stroked my fingers over her hip and into the waistband of her panties.

"I need these off," I said as I broke my lips from Molly's and shifted until my face was met with the tiny scrap of white lace.

"Romeo... please..." Mol moaned as she ran her fingers through my hair.

The panties took all of two seconds to remove, and I sat back, just drinking in the amazing picture that was my wife. *Christ!* My wife. I almost groaned out loud at how fucking happy that thought made me.

Smoothing my hands back up Mol's thighs, I lifted her right knee and placed it across my shoulder. Laying a kiss on her white-and-blue garter, I smiled up at her half-closed eyes and said, "This stays on," and hooking my finger under the top of the white stockings, said, "These too."

"Okay."

Focusing between her legs, I leaned in and licked along her center in one long swipe, her hips rocketing forward at the action. "Mmm, baby, so fuckin' sweet."

"Romeo, please, I need... need..." she murmured, fisting my hair.

"Say it, baby. I want to hear you say it," I demanded.

With a shuddering breath, she rasped out, "Lick me... please..."

Moving back in, my girl's pleas spurring me on, I sucked on her clit, sinking two fingers into her channel. I worked her good, each passing second bringing her closer to the edge and my need growing more and more desperate.

"Rome! I'm... I'm..." Molly's legs stiffened and with a loud scream, she broke, coming hard against my tongue.

I moved back, watching my girl catch her breath, her eyes closed, and I lost all restraint. In seconds, I yanked off my pants and boxers and, pulling Mol's leg toward me, ran the garter down her thigh, her calf, and off her foot.

Opening her eyes, she asked, "What...?"

"Move to the headboard, baby." Molly did as I asked. "Clasp your hands around one of the railings. I want to play." She lifted her hands slowly, intertwining her hands on one of the white metal railings, and, taking the garter, I moved above her, securing her hands so she couldn't move. Her brown eyes brightened with excitement and her foot ran up my thigh and rubbed up against my cock.

"You want it, Mrs. Prince?" I asked, shifting closer until I straddled her chest.

"Come here," Mol said and took me into her mouth, my head snapping back on a hiss.

"Fuck, baby, that feels so good."

She moaned and the vibrations almost drove me insane. It was too much. I needed to be in her, needed to take the final steps in making her my wife.

Pulling out of her mouth, I shifted between her legs and wrapped her ankles around my back. Molly tested the strength of the garter with a pull on her hands, but it held tight, and an eager flush crept up her tanned skin.

"You ready, baby?"

"God, yes. Make love to me, Rome." That was all the encouragement I needed, and in one quick thrust, I pushed in to the hilt, both of us groaning out in pleasure.

Reaching up, I ran my fingers through her hair, staring right in her eyes as I pushed in and out of her warmth. "I love you, Mol. I love you so much," I said, pressing kisses along her cheeks and lips.

"I love you too, babe."

Her hips rocked against mine, and as I stared into her eyes, I knew I needed to feel her hands on me, her wrapped arms around me as I came.

Reaching up with one hand, I snapped the material loose, and Molly immediately held me close, her nose tucking into the crook of my neck.

Her moans increased, her breath getting faster as my pace increased. "Romeo… I'm going to come," she whispered, clutching my arms.

I pounded into my girl even faster, the motion making her scream out her release, the feel of her tight core taking me with her too.

"Fuuccckkkkkk…" I groaned as I stilled and came, the muscles in my neck straining with the severity of my orgasm.

Molly relaxed below me, her fingers slowly combing through my hair. As I looked down at her sated, smiling face, she put her hand to my cheek, eyes glistening, and whispered, "My husband."

In that moment, I was convinced that no two other people had ever shared something so strong, so crushing her mouth with mine, I pulled back, stared at the most beautiful girl on Earth, and whispered, "My wife."

37

Seattle, Washington
Twenty years later…

"Hello?"

"Rome Prince! Long time no see, son!"

"Coach?"

There was a gruff laugh before he said, "Yeah, it's your old coach! Still going strong here at the Tide. Twenty-five years this year!"

Smiling at the familiar sound of the man who helped me get through so much in my college years, I said, "I know, Coach. All-time record breaker for winning the BCS Championship. Not too shabby! I've watched your games every year. You've become a damn legend."

"And I've watched you too, son. You'll be a hall of famer, no doubt about it. In a few years, you'll be getting inducted."

"Thanks, Coach. I certainly hope so." I poured a coffee from the machine and moved to the kitchen table, sitting down. "So to what do I owe this pleasure?"

"I'm in Seattle and wanted to invite you and your wife out to dinner tonight if you're free."

"Of course! Tell me where and when and we'll be there. It'll be good to see you again."

"You too, son. I have a meeting in five minutes, but give me a couple of hours and I'll text you the details."

"No problem. See you tonight."

"See you, son."

Ending the call, I sat back in my chair, taking a deep breath. Damn, hearing his voice brought back so many memories. Was it really twenty years since I'd played for the Tide?

Shit! I was getting old.

The front door slammed shut and I looked to the hallway. It was only one in the afternoon and Molly shouldn't be back yet.

"Rome? You here?" she shouted, and a smile pulled on my lips.

"Yeah, baby, I'm in the kitchen."

A few seconds later, she walked in, dressed in a tight black knee-length dress, her hair pulled back in a loose bun, and the most sexy-as-fuck glasses perched on her nose.

Standing, I took the heavy briefcase from her hands and pressed a kiss on her lips. "You're back early."

"Yeah, my meeting was canceled so I thought, bugger it, I'm going home." Molly leaned in and wrapped her arms around my waist, pressing her cheek against my chest. "Mmm, I missed you."

"Missed you too, gorgeous." Her arms squeezed my waist in response, and I said, "I've just had an interesting call."

"Really?"

"Yeah. It was Coach. I haven't heard from him for years, but he's in town and wants to grab dinner with us tonight."

"The Alabama coach?" she asked, her surprised eyes fixing on mine.

"Yeah." I laughed. "The Alabama coach."

Her eyebrows pulled together in thought. "I wonder what he wants."

"To have dinner," I replied, slightly confused at why she thought it was anything more.

Stepping back to the opposite marble counter, she tilted her head as she stared at me. "Rome, you're retiring this season, and suddenly the coach of the Tide just so happens to be in Seattle?"

Hmm… Maybe she was right. Her smug smile told me she knew it too. "Okay, Shakespeare, I'm listening. What do you think he wants?"

Moving before me, her fingers crept up my torso, and she gave me a quick kiss on the lips. "You."

A strange excitement set in my bones. I'd never really thought about going back to Tuscaloosa. I love it, it's my home, but we left a lot of shit behind all those years ago, and we had made a good life for ourselves in Seattle.

I glanced down to Molly again and asked, "You really think that's what it could be?"

"I'd bet my life on it. He'll want you to coach. Bloody hell, Rome, you're one of the most successful quarterbacks in NFL history. If you joined the Tide, can you imagine how much better they could be? The recruits they could acquire?"

"And how would you feel about going back?"

Her eyes dropped to the floor. "I—I don't know. I love it here. Our lives are here and Tuscaloosa… I don't know, holds a lot of conflicting memories for me… for *us*."

I stroked a finger down her cheek. "Then we won't go, *if* he offers me anything at all."

"Is coaching something *you* would want, though? Is it something you could see yourself doing with the rest of your life?"

"Probably. It's the Tide. I didn't know what I would do when football came to an end, but the thought of being involved again with Bama football… I've got to say it excites me. It's in my blood. I'm Tide 'til I die."

Nodding her head slowly, Molly looked up at me and said, "Let's hear him out. If he offers you something, we'll talk about it and decide what's right for us all."

She began biting on her lip and her hand ran down my body to snap the button on my jeans. I fucking loved that look in her eyes. "Now, I've come home early from work, we have a couple of hours before we need to pick up the kids from school, and you're looking pretty damn hot, Mr. Prince, hot enough to make me think up some pretty naughty ways to spend the afternoon."

I felt my cock harden under her light touch, and, instantly whipping her up off the floor, began running for the bedroom, Molly giggling over my shoulder, screaming, "*Romeo!*"

"Oh, don't you dare, Shakespeare," I said with a hard crack on her ass. "You started this shit and I'm going to make sure I fucking finish it… at least three times!"

* * *

Centurylink Field, Seattle
A few months later…

"Taylor, Isaac, Archie, Elias! Come here, we have to go on the field in a minute! You all need to calm down!"

The roar of the crowd boomed all around the stadium, shaking the rafters, as we waited at the back of the players' tunnel. Molly was busy running around after the kids, trying to get them straight. I couldn't help but smile at them all in their Seahawks PRINCE jerseys, Elias's jersey so tiny as he tottered around his momma's legs—hell, he'd just begun walking and was already running rings around us both. And then there was Molly, long hair loose, tight jeans, her favorite brown cowboy boots and she too wearing my number. I could tell she was nervous; years of sitting in the "wives' section" hadn't prepared her at all for the craziness of today.

I was retiring. After nearly twenty years playing for the Hawks, I was calling it a day, and because of that, the Hawks were sending me off in the only way they knew how... big and loud.

Someone tugged on my jeans, and when I looked down, Archie, my son, was looking up at me with a strange expression on his cute-as-hell face.

Crouching down to his height, I asked, "You okay, little man?"

He pointed to the direction of the screaming crowd, all wide brown eyes, red flushed cheeks, and whispered, "Are you a superhero, Daddy?"

Smiling, I replied, "No, son. Why d'you ask that?"

He stepped forward, placing his chubby five-year-old hand on my shoulder, and said, "Because all those people are here today for you. They keep saying you are the best, *ever*, and the only other people who get treated like that are superheroes."

Lifting him into my arms, I said, "I'm not a hero, little man. I just threw a football good for a lot of years and that's why we're here today, to say good-bye to all the supporters before we head to Alabama."

He nodded his head in understanding, but pursing his lips, he leaned in and whispered, "I have a secret."

I pulled back, dropping my mouth in playful exaggeration, and said, "You do?"

He nodded his head sagely.

"Am I allowed to know it too?"

Pausing for a moment and thinking hard, Archie finally sighed and nodded his head. His little mouth went to my ear and he whispered, "I think you're a secret superhero and you're saying you're not because superheroes are not allowed to tell no one, are they? Just look at Superman; no one knew about the real him."

"And what's my power?" I asked, playing along.

"That you can throw a football farther than anyone, *ever*, and…" He motioned for me to lean in closer to his mouth, whispering, "You're the bestest daddy in the world. The kids at school are always telling me how lucky I am. But they don't need to. I know it."

I stilled and closed my eyes, his words choking the fuck out of me, but two strong little hands pushed on my cheeks. "No telling the others, though, okay? It's our secret."

"Okay," I agreed with a graveled voice, placing him back to the floor, letting him rejoin his brothers and sister playing across the way with a pigskin—they were football to the core.

A soothing hand rubbed at my back and Molly flashed me a wide, knowing grin. "You okay, baby?" A proud glint was shining in her golden eyes, and it was clear she'd heard what our son had just said.

Inching forward, I pressed a kiss to her lips. "Mm-hmm, more than okay."

She placed her mouth at my ear and whispered, "I believe you're the best daddy in the world too… and the best husband."

Clasping both hands on her face, I pressed my lips firmly against hers again, laughing at her surprised squeal.

A throat cleared beside us, and, glancing beside me, I saw the field manager, embarrassed. "Mr. Prince, we're almost ready."

Molly quickly fixed her hair and squeezed my hand in reassurance. She was always there for me, today being no different. She'd attended every game, Superbowl, charity function—you name it—for years and most of all, she'd given me four beautiful children. I loved my girl more now than ever and still thanked God every day that he brought her into my life.

"Okay, kids, come here," Molly shouted, and the four of them ran over, all smiles and hyper with excitement. Molly crouched down, meeting each of their eyes, and explained, "Now we're about to go out into the stadium. It's going to be super loud, so just prepare yourselves, okay?"

A chorus of, "Yeah, Momma," came out in reply, and Molly moved to Elias and wrestled with him, trying to secure his noise-cancelling headphones in place.

After giving up and leaving them hanging around his neck, she said, "Now, what do you all have to say to your daddy?"

I narrowed my eyes at Molly and caught the happy expression on her face.

Taylor, our daughter, our eldest child... our *teenager,* stepped forward, and I bent down as she hugged me. "We're all very proud of you, Daddy, and we wanted to let you know how much we love you." She presented me with a handmade card, a hand-drawn picture of us all in our yard on the front and a framed picture of the six of us at last year's Superbowl, all four of my children in my arms in the center of the field, huge, happy smiles on their faces and Mol kissing my cheek. "The boys made the card, but we all signed it for you. I chose the picture, well along with Momma—it's our favorite." I glanced to the picture again. It was my favorite too. A hand landed on my shoulder. "I really am so proud of you, Daddy."

Kissing her cheek, I rasped, "Thank you, princess."

Our three boys came to me next, and I could barely fucking speak through each hug and "I love you, Daddy." Molly stood beside me, clicking away on her camera and unashamedly crying as she watched the impromptu presentation.

My kids had clearly caught my battle with my emotions, if their wide-eyed looks were any indication. And I had to turn away for a moment, trying my best to pull myself together. The last thing I wanted was to walk out onto the field a friggin' emotional mess.

And after all, superheroes never cried.

As I looked at my beautiful kids, my chest swelled. I've never let myself forget how friggin' lucky I am that I got this life. Got my girl when I nearly lost her and got four perfect kids on Earth—and one in heaven—when I never thought I'd have any.

"Mr. Prince, we're ready. Please follow," the field manager announced, and I heard Molly instruct behind me, "Okay, two of you take my hands; two take Daddy's."

Two hands instantly encased mine; I knew who'd be with me and who'd be with Mol. Glancing down, I smirked to see I was right: Taylor, our girl, and Archie, who apparently believed I was a superhero.

I turned to Molly, who was holding hands with Isaac and Elias—now happily in his headphones—took a deep breath, and mouthed, "You ready?"

Rolling her eyes, she shook her head dramatically and mouthed back, "*No!*"

Music began playing, and the announcer hyped up the crowd as I laughed and winked at my wife's worried face. "*Seattle, please welcome to the field, for the final time, your quarterback, Romeo 'The Bullet' Prince!*"

With a squeeze of my hands, my family and I walked forward out of the tunnel. As we stepped on the field to fireworks and the roar of the crowd, I finally let myself exhale. This field, these supporters were my second home and I was going to miss them so damn much.

After a lap of the field, waving and thanking the fans, we were ushered to a stage on the fifty-yard line. Molly and the children stood beside me as I walked to the microphone to address the crowd.

"Good evening, Seattle!" The booming response from the crowd was deafening; the sea of flashing cameras and applauding fans, all of them on their feet, was a sight I would never forget. They were all here tonight for me, and my legs shook slightly from the enormity of the moment.

I waved to the crowd; they gradually quieted to silence.

"When I came to y'all twenty years ago, I had no idea what to expect." I laughed into the microphone and turned to Molly, who nodded in agreement. "I'd never left Alabama for any real period of time, had just got married to my girl." I reached out my hand, and Molly moved beside me, holding it right back. "And suddenly we were thrust into the crazy world of the NFL, and y'all welcomed us with open arms." The crowd stamped their feet in the stands and bullhorns sounded around the packed stadium.

I watched my children drop their mouths at the deafening reaction and gape in shock at the thousands of people all screaming for their daddy. Turning back to the mic, I waited until they quieted and continued. "The team and staff are my family, you guys who support us week after week are my family, and we're going to miss y'all so damn much. I never knew what I'd do after retiring from pro ball, but an opportunity has come up, and I am happy to announce that I have accepted the position of Quarterback Coach at the Alabama Crimson Tide. After many happy years in Seattle, my family and I are going back down south, back to my home, but I'll never forget Seattle and all the amazing years we've enjoyed here."

Squeezing Molly's hand for strength, I brought it to my lips and pressed a kiss to her wedding ring. Coach had offered me a position with the Tide coaching team the night we went to dinner, and Molly agreed I should take it. She thought a change would be good for us all.

"My wife has been a professor at the University of Washington for over ten years now, and my kids, well, all my kids are Seattle born and bred, something I'll never let them forget."

Roving a gaze around the huge stadium one last time, I lowered my eyes, holding back the threatening lump inching up my throat, and said, "Thanks to y'all for making my career here the best time of my life."

The crowd erupted once more, and with a drum roll from the band, a large banner dropped from the rafters: my name and jersey number, now officially retired in my honor.

Staring up at the banner, a sense of accomplishment filled me. I'd lived my dream to the best of my ability and loved every minute of playing for this team.

Suddenly several sets of hands wrapped around my waist and legs, as my children ran to me in support, and a familiar arm slipped around my waist: Shakespeare.

"You did it, baby," she whispered, still staring proudly at my banner, happy tears in her eyes. "You did it all."

Cupping her face, I pressed a kiss to her lips and said, "You ready to get back to Bama, Mrs. Prince?"

Moving in for another kiss, she giggled and replied, *"Roll Tide!"*

EPILOGUE

Tuscaloosa, Alabama
Six months later...

Shit. The Tide QB I was watching on the new game tapes Coach'd just sent me had rendered me speechless. His quick feet, the power of his passes and his running game were sick. He was a triple threat and, no doubt, the kid had some serious friggin' skills.

Hearing the quick stomping of feet coming up the stairs, I quickly switched off the TV, fumbling the remote and jumped to my feet just a Mol came through the door.

She met my eyes and frowned. "Romeo Prince! Are you watching game tapes when you are meant to be helping me sort everything out for this bloody housewarming get together you planned?"

Shit. There was no winning this one.

"I—"

"I don't want to hear it!" Molly held up her hand, silencing me. "I'm running around this house like a blue-arsed fly, sorting the food, sorting the kids, and *you* hide out up here in our room?" She walked forward and prodded me in the chest. "A week Romeo! We've been back a week and you plan a party... *Thanks!* We've barely unpacked!"

Molly stood before me, all in a fluster, dressed in a lilac summer dress—she looked fucking beautiful.

"Oh, no," she warned with a firm shake of her index finger.

Reaching out, I grabbed the material of her dress and pulled her close. "What?" I asked with a smirk.

Pushing on my chest, she shook her head. "Don't even think it."

"But, baby—"

"'But, baby', nothing." Molly removed my hand from her waist and stepped back. "Now get your arse in that backyard and fire up the grill."

Narrowing my eyes, I leaned in, whispering, "I'm so gonna fuck you tonight for that attitude, Shakespeare." Then walked out of the bedroom door and headed downstairs, laughing as I heard my wife's long, sexually frustrated sigh.

The sound of the kids playing in their game room filtered into the hall, and just as I was heading into the kitchen, the front door rang. Checking the clock on the wall, I groaned in exasperation. Our friends were an hour early. Molly was gonna kill me.

Swinging open the door, I immediately froze. A teenage kid—no, correction—a teenage boy; tall, big in build, with the cockiest smirk spread on his face.

"Bullet Prince! Big fan, man." He moved in for a fist bump, but I didn't even bother lifting my hand.

"Who the fuck are you?" I asked, and the kid paled a little as I crossed my arms over my chest. Yeah, I may have just retired but I still had a good set of guns.

"Err... I... I'm..."

"*Asher!*" My head swung around only to see my daughter walking my way, all smiles for the douche on my doorstep.

Oh. Hell. No.

Fully facing Taylor, and blocking the entire doorway, I asked, "Who's he and what the hell is he doing at my door?"

Taylor stopped in her tracks and her face beamed red. "Daddy! Stop it! You're embarrassing me!"

"Who is he? I won't ask again."

Rolling her eyes, she said, "He's my date."

I was pretty fucking sure smoke began blowing from my ears, because those three words just about made me combust.

"Come again?" I asked tersely, you know, just for clarification.

"He's. My. *Date*," she said slowly, each word exaggerated.

Fuck. Not only did she look exactly like me: blond hair and brown eyes, but she had the pissy, no-shit attitude to match. I could now see Molly's point on how damn annoying this moody shit could be to deal with.

"Bullet, come on. We can work this—"

I swung to face the kid on my doorstep as he spoke and without a single word in response, I slammed the door in his fucking face.

"Daddy!" Taylor screamed. "I was going on a date with him!"

"Like hell you were! Since when do you date, and why the hell haven't you asked permission? Because I'll tell you now, girl, that kid only has one thing on his mind, and like hell he's doing those things to my fourteen-year-old daughter! You get me?"

"*Momma!*"

"*Mol!*"

Molly came gunning down the stairs as I faced off against my daughter, her stance now mimicking mine, our gazes locked.

"What's going on? Why are you both shouting at each other?"

Turning to Mol, I asked, "Did you know she was planning on going on a date today?"

Molly's wide eyes snapped to our daughter. "Taylor, you know you're not old enough to date."

"But, Momma! I—" In true teenage fashion, she slammed her hands on her hips.

"But nothing. You're grounded for a week for being so sneaky and going against our rules. Now, get in there and watch your brothers. Our guests will be arriving soon and I don't have time for this."

Spinning on her heel with an angry shrill, Taylor stomped into the game room, screaming, "*Fascists!*"

When the door slammed, I exhaled slowly to calm the hell down and looked to Molly who was still on the stairs, blinking in shock. "Dating, Mol? I'm so not ready for this shit."

Molly cracked a smile and started giggling. "She's a teen, it was bound to start sooner or later. That's what you get when you have a girl, babe. Years and years of dating to look forward to."

"We've been back in Bama a week and suddenly she has hormonally-charged fuckers chasing her tail?" I leaned back against the wall and ran my hand down my face. "*I* was one of those fuckers, Mol. I know exactly what they want to do with her. *Christ!* I'll kill them! This shit's gonna make me go prematurely gray!"

Molly shook her head and passed by me, laughing. "She knows she can't date until she's sixteen, so relax, you have two years to prepare for the real thing." She continued strutting into the kitchen, glancing over her shoulder to add, "And two years to stock up on 'Just For Men', of course. You know, for all the premature gray hairs you'll get."

Flashing me a teasing smile, Molly quickly headed to the backyard—Oh, she'd done it now.

Running after my wife, I scooped her up in my arms, making her yelp out in surprise. I sat down on the secluded bench, way out of sight, laying her across my lap. Diving onto her soft lips, I fisted bunches of her long brown hair, and took what I wanted.

As always, she submitted to my demands.

We broke from the embrace several minutes later, both panting, and Molly squirmed against the hardness in my jeans.

"Mol…" I warned.

"Mm-hmm?" she answered innocently, a fucking horny-as-hell twinkle in her golden-browns.

My jaw clenched as I fought my need, and I hissed through gritted teeth, "Don't play with fire, Shakespeare. It's too much for pretty little English girls to cope with."

"What can I say…? I'm a risk taker." She shrugged and smiled widely.

Mol watched as my lip twitched, and within seconds, the two of us burst into laughter and I gripped her tight around her neck, tucking my head into her hair.

When we had both calmed down, I lifted my head and said, "I can't believe I said that to you back then. I was so fucked up and full of my own shit."

"Are you kidding me? You had me so pent up for you that I almost combusted on the spot! I could've stayed at that creek forever."

I leaned in close and whispered seductively, "If I'm not mistaken, you did combust around three of my fingers shortly after."

Slapping my chest playfully, Mol replied, "Yeah, and I tossed you off onto the grass!"

I froze at her comeback and practically dropped her to the floor, unable to contain my hysterical laughter. "Tossed me off?"

Molly pushed out her tongue and I slapped her tight ass. "How is it that even after living in the States for over twenty years, that accent of yours is still as thick as ever?"

"Says you! There's no shaking that southern drawl out of you, is there?"

Oh, she was just asking for trouble.

Gripping her thighs, I pulled her to straddle my waist, making her moan as I instantly ground my cock against her core, my hands locked on her cheeks, and I hushed out, "I should take you to the old cabin and fuck the living shit outta you for old time's sake. There's something in the Bama water that makes me want to own every fuckin' part of you, to fill every hole."

"Well, I think the new owners might have something to say about that," she muttered, trying to restrain herself from moaning out loud.

"I couldn't give a shit about the new owners!" I said curtly, and my eyes closed when she began rocking back and forth against my dick.

"I'll take you right here, Mol. Don't think I won't," I threatened, this time without humor, as I dragged my teeth along my bottom lip, my hands dropping from Mol's face to squeeze and nip at her breasts.

"It's good that you still want me after all these years. Four kids aren't exactly flattering on a woman's body."

I laid kisses along the side of her neck, licking and biting as I went. "Are you fuckin' kidding me? You're so damn hot it's unreal. *Christ*, I want you more now than ever."

"Yeah, again, four kids kind of shows that! You're insatiable, always have been."

My eyebrows danced. "Wanna try for number five?"

I was deadly serious.

"Not a bloody chance!"

My break of laughter relaxed her. I knew she loved having kids, adored being a momma, but she kept telling me that three boys under the age of seven and a pubescent teenage girl was quite enough to deal with alongside being a full-time professor.

"Just so you know, though, I'm ready when you are. I want as many children as we can produce," I said meaningfully. I loved having a huge family and would pop one out a year if I had my way. I loved being a daddy. It was the best damn thing in the world.

Those caramel eyes narrowed in jest. "You're trying for your own football team, aren't you?"

"Yep, and that's a hell of a lotta kids. We need a strong offense, defense, oh, and the special teams of course..." Mol giggled and shut me up by smashing her lips against mine.

"Eww! That's *gross!*" A high-pitched shriek stilled us both and we rolled our heads to the side, taking in the face of our disgusted, shocked daughter glaring at our compromising position.

If that Asher kid was back, I was gonna castrate the fucker.

Immediately straightening her hair, Molly went to move off my lap, but I held on tightly to her waist, whispering in her ear, "Do not move unless you want to scar our girl for life." I knew the moment she felt it, my hardness, and she couldn't help but blush as she kept still, hiding my... umm... awkward situation.

"What do you need, honey?" Molly asked, feigning normalcy.

Taylor shook her head in horror, her attitude still in place from before. "I've been calling for you both, but you never heard me. Now I can see why!" Molly glanced down at me and we had to force ourselves not to laugh at our daughters reprimand.

"*Whatever*. Look, you're the main feature on the nightly news, I thought you'd wanna know. It's about Daddy taking the QB coaching job at the Tide. And you too, Momma, 'bout you becoming a professor at UA, and that you've both taken positions at the same school. Said they're gonna tell the story of your life or something."

Molly turned to me and raised her eyebrows. "You know about this?"

I didn't have a clue and shook my head in bewilderment.

"We'll be there soon, princess. You go on back inside." Taylor turned and ran back inside without looking back.

Molly immediately jumped off my lap and ran her hand across her forehead. "I wonder what they'll be saying?"

Even after all this time, she hated being the center of attention.

I stood, fixing my jeans, and held out my hand for her to take. "Let's go see, eh?" Clasping her hand in mine, we followed the path to the house and straight into the family room. Our four kids were lined up on the huge black leather sectional, their eyes glued to the screen. And Mol froze on the spot, a loving smile ghosting her lips.

When I turned to the TV, a montage of us was playing to the music "Hall of Fame" by The Script. It was all there, a reel of our lives: the kisses before the Tide games when we were at college… the two of us holding hands as we walked around campus… the kisses at the SEC Championship… Mol's dramatic return at the National Championship… the Tide's homecoming parade where I'd refused to let go of her hand… the NFL draft where I'd been first pick and proposed to my girl… our graduation day, hugging and laughing in our gowns… the paparazzi picture from the airport as we left for Seattle, all of our friends in the background, waving us off… my first game for the Seahawks and Molly sitting in the stands, cheering me on… shots of Mol over the years, pregnant with each of our four children… the many Superbowl wins and finally, me, a few months ago at the Centurylink Stadium, as they retired my jersey, surrounded by my wife and our four children. The montage ended with a simple script, the text reading:

"Welcome home, Romeo and Molly Prince.
Forever Roll Tide!"

The presenters went on to discuss the game plan for the Tide's upcoming season and when I looked to our children—who were silently staring up at us—I realized Mol was crying. I was pretty choked up too.

"Momma, Daddy, you looked so young in those pictures," Isaac, our eldest boy, said quietly. With his curly brown hair and glasses, he was the only one of the four who was just like Mol, with an IQ to match… a cute little geek through and through.

"We were young, little man," I murmured, still staring at the commentators on the screen, but not listening to a word they had to say, my hand gripping almost painfully onto Mol's. "It seems like so long ago yet weirdly, just like yesterday."

"They called you Bama's own Romeo and Juliet," Taylor said softly, her mood forgotten. "At the beginning, they said your story was famous around here."

Laughing, Molly nodded her head. "That's what the press began to call us. Because of all the trouble we had in being together—publicly, unfortunately."

"With Daddy's parents?" she asked tentatively, and that old stab to the chest ripped through me in an instant.

"Yeah, honey," Mol replied as she slid her arm around my back, rubbing it up and down in soothing motions. I hated any reminder of my parents and the years of shit I suffered at their hands… especially the miscarriage. I never saw them again after the meeting in my daddy's study that day. And they were both long gone now. My Momma drank herself into an early grave only two years after she left Bama and my daddy suffered a heart attack ten years ago while incarcerated. We'd decided long ago to always be honest with our children—well, as honest as their ages would allow. Our troubles had been well documented and we didn't want them to hear any of our past from anyone but us.

"Go, Daddy!" Eli and Archie suddenly shouted from the sofa, completely ignoring our conversation, both jumping up and down excitedly, pulling our attention back to them. Our youngest boys ran to the front of the large TV, clapping and screaming as shot after shot of me playing football rolled: sprinting, passing, scoring touchdowns. We all burst out laughing when Eli, the youngest, ran full out at Archie, tackling him to the floor, screaming, *"Boom!"* and patting his chest, holding it to the sky, my—now famous—touchdown celebration.

Breaking from Mol's hand and running at Eli playfully, I lifted him above my head, tackling him to the ground. Squealing and laughing, Eli wriggled on the floor as I tickled him and Archie then jumped on my back, wrapping his tiny arms around my neck. As I glanced up at the other two on the couch, Isaac threw down his iPad, piling on too. Even Taylor, who at first rolled her eyes at us, finally succumbed to temptation and, with a squeal, ran and jumped on top.

"Let me up, you monsters!" I shouted dramatically as I tried to throw them of my back.

"Never!"

"We got you pinned, Daddy!"

"We brought down the Bullet!"

We were a mass of arms and legs, giggles and screams. And then I looked up at Mol watching, laughing at us all, and then it went quiet as five sets of eyes zeroed in on her, and she quickly lost her smile.

Backing away with her palms held up, Molly warned, "Oh, no. Don't you even think about it, I don't have time…"

My eyebrows danced as I said, "Kids, Momma is getting away. Defense, are you with me? One, two, three, break…"

Yells of agreement echoed around the large room as the five of us launched to a chase. With a scream, Mol turned and ran toward the kitchen, beelining for the huge backyard. She'd made it onto the first patch of grass when I hit her from behind, protecting her from being hurt with my body as we tumbled to the ground, our four crazy children piling on top.

"Do you give?" I shouted as we all tickled her into submission, her body jumping and jerking on the soft grass.

"I give, I give!" She choked on hysterical laughter, unable to stand the tickles to her ribs—it was her weak spot.

"Kids, go get a pigskin. Me and Momma need to get everything ready for the party," I ordered and, still hyper, all four of our beautiful kids ran to the game shed and out of our sight. Taylor glanced back at me and threw me a small, apologetic smile—we were good again.

Looking down at my hot and flustered wife, I pinned her arms above her head and straddled her hips. "Mmm… I'm kinda liking this position I got you in."

Molly bucked her hips, trying in vain to throw me off, pursing her soft lips.

Shaking my head disapprovingly, I whispered, "You want it rough, baby?"

"Romeo!" she screamed again, and I cut her off by slamming my lips against hers, my tongue immediately plunging into her hot mouth. Groaning against the assault, Mol let out a reluctant whimper, and I pulled back, teasingly licking the edge of her cupid's bow.

"Hey, Mol," I said with a smile.

Feeling her racing heart against my chest, she answered, "Hey, you."

"You gonna give up that lucky sweet kiss?"

Mol couldn't contain her giggle at the use of our old pre-game ritual. "If that's what you want."

My face broke out in the biggest fucking smile, and I replied, "Oh, it most definitely fuckin' is!" Releasing Molly's trapped arms, I cupped her cheek, moving in for the softest of kisses.

But all good things never last, or should I say they get cut short by a loud-mouthed, friggin' Texan. "Hot damn, guys! Get a fuckin' room!"

Sighing against Molly's lips, I withdrew my head a fraction. "Looks like our friends are here early," I announced with mock-disappointment. A pair of black cowboy boots landed next to our heads, and Cass looked down at the two of us, grinding her hips and biting her lip. "Still fuckin' like rabbits, I see! 'Yeah, Rome, yeahhhhh!!!'"

"Hey, Cass," Molly said, slumping back in frustration, ignoring Cass's usual inappropriate jokes. I began getting to my feet, smirking at Cass and hoisting Mol off the floor as I did so.

"Hey, Molls! I've missed you, honey!" Cass screamed, holding out her hands and pulling Molly to her huge chest, the impact robbing her of her breath.

A hand slapped on my back, and when I turned around, Jimmy-Don was holding out his arms. "Bullet, get the hell here, boy!"

I couldn't help but laugh as he jerked me in for a full-body hug, only withdrawing to say, "Everyone's here, guys. The adults are already inside drinking beer."

"Fuck, Yeah! We're gonna get wasted!" Cass hollered and, eying me with affection, proceeded to bear hug me too.

"Where are all the kids?" I heard Molly ask, waving to Lexi, Austin, Ally, and her husband inside the house. Ally's husband. Shit. I still struggled with who that was.

"Playing ball behind the trees. They're all having a blast, don't worry!" Cass said and, with a wink and a slap on my ass, walked ahead to take Jimmy-Don's proffered arm and set off toward the house.

I walked over to my wife, hooking an arm around her neck, and laid a soft kiss on her head, whispering, "God, I fuckin' love you, baby. We'll be finishing what we started later."

"I *fucking* love you too. And I can't bloody wait," Mol whispered back, squeezing both of her arms around my stomach, and I couldn't help but chuckle at that proper English accent cussing.

She was so fucking cute.

Laughter from all our best friends spilled out from inside of our house, echoes of our children's laughter carried on the summer breeze, and I held on tight to the most perfect gal in the world.

All was how it should be, how it was *meant* to be. We had happiness, we had a family, we always had each other, and as I tucked my amazing wife under the protection of my arm, I felt like the luckiest bastard in the world.

Molly Juliet Prince is, and always will be, my home.

THE END

BONUS CHAPTER

Molly
Aged Twenty-Six
Seattle, Washington

"Molly… Molly… Wake up for me, darling… Come on now…"

I was floating weightlessly in some transient dream, but a distant voice had me slamming back to my body with a jolt, and my eyes rolled open to fix on a blurry white ceiling.

"Welcome back, Mrs. Prince." A blond woman wearing peach scrubs was above me, coaxing me back to consciousness. I glanced around the room with heavy eyes and noted we were alone.

Where's Romeo?

"What…?" I tried to clear my dry throat. "W-where am I?"

"Shh… drink first." A blue beaker with a long straw met my lips. I took the offered drink and after a huge gulp of water, the liquid moistening my dry throat, I tried next to clear the thick fog from my mind.

No!

Stiffening, my hand flew to my stomach and I winced in pain. I felt like I'd been sawed wide open. Fear hit me in the chest. *Not again… This can* not *be happening again…*

The nurse's knowing blue eyes met mine, and rubbing a hand on my arm, she said, "We had to give you an emergency caesarean, due to your preeclampsia. The baby was in distress and your blood pressure was getting to a dangerous level."

Flashes of memory came back to me. Me on bed rest for the last three months, then hazy, scattered recounts of Romeo carrying me into the hospital in his arms, frantic, terrified, desperate even, and Ally… Ally drove us here to the hospital? That's right. Ally was staying with us here in Seattle. She'd secured a co-curating commission at the Burke Museum on The University of Washington's campus not too long ago and was in our spare room until she left again for her regular position at the Smithsonian in Washington D.C.

I forced my groggy mind to refocus… The baby… *Our baby!*

I opened my mouth, about to speak in guttering panic, when the nurse smiled down at me. "It was a successful delivery, Molly. Your baby is fine, absolutely beautiful." She lowered down farther to whisper, "And eager to meet Mommy."

A feeling of nervous excitement burst in my chest, but a hint of fear was evident too. My emotions were off the chart, and the nurse squeezed my hand in support.

My God... I was a mammy.

Reaching out, I gripped onto the nurse's wrist as she began to walk away. "I want to see my baby, please. *Wait!*" I jerked slightly forward. "What did we have?" My eyes scoured around every inch of the room. "And where's my husband? Where's my baby?"

"They're both just outside." Her kind face broke into a huge smile. "Your husband is one pushy man, Mrs. Prince. He's been relentless in his questions after your well-being while we brought you around from the procedure. We had no choice but to put you under general anesthesia. Things were getting too risky to give you an epidural. Your husband hasn't let go of your little one since, refusing to move from the family room next door until you were conscious again. He's causing quite a stir here in the hospital. The heartthrob Seahawks QB with a newborn cradled in his arms, pining for his wife... *Whew!* That man is reducing the nurses to teenagers out there, even in his blue scrubs!"

My heart melted. Knowing my Rome, he'd be scared to death. My miscarriage six years ago had almost killed him. I imagine holding our baby in his arms while he sat there all alone was scaring him shitless. He'd been so overprotective over the past few months, terrified of the risks of my condition.

It was too much like déjà vu.

"Please let him in. I need to see him… need to see them both," I instructed hurriedly, my voice hoarse with emotion. The nurse nodded, understanding my anxiousness, and left the room. My palms grew clammy and my breathing came fast.

I was a mommy. It had actually happened… *finally*. It had been one hell of a bad pregnancy, and as I sat here in this strange bed, I felt robbed of the full birthing experience. But we had a child. Words couldn't express the joy that came with that knowledge. I was more than lucky.

The door to the small room suddenly burst open and Romeo hurried in wearing blue scrubs, I assumed still left on from the OR, and I agreed with the nurses; he was a heartthrob, but then again, he was always beautiful to me.

My eyes immediately fixed on the tiny bundle in his arms, then back to my husband. His eyes were tired, his dirty-blond hair sticking out in clumps from where he'd been running his hand through, no doubt in stress, and his cheeks were red raw.

He'd been crying.

As soon as our eyes locked, relief flooded Rome's face and he released a long, pained breath. "*Molly!*" he groaned and, glancing quickly at our baby in his arms, carefully walked towards me and gripped my outstretched hand, kissing the palm, the back, and each finger before placing it on his cheek, pressing it against his skin.

"God, Mol, I thought I'd lost you… Fuck, baby, I've been freaking the hell out…" His words were strained and I stroked along his stubble to relax him.

"I'm fine, babe. We're all fine. It was just a C-section. We knew it was probable. They happen thousands of times a day. I was in safe hands."

He nodded once, then, looking slightly "fish out of water," glanced down at our baby wrapped in a yellow blanket, the colour no indication to their gender.

"Romeo…" I whispered in awe, seeing a tiny hand reaching north, my hand reaching out too in reaction, but my stomach tightened at the movement and I flinched and hissed at the sharp stab of pain.

Rome noticed, a worried expression set on his face, and he stood slowly, bending down to my level. "How about I bring our little princess to you?" And a huge proud smile lit up his face.

Princess… I exhaled slowly, closed my eyes, and smiled. We'd had a little girl. We had a daughter.

A happy whimper escaped my mouth and relieved hot tears began streaming down my cheeks. I'd managed to carry full term despite my health problems, and I was a mommy and my Rome was a daddy.

I immediately held out my arms and Romeo gently placed our daughter against my chest, taking any weight away from my injured stomach, the bare warmth of her skin against mine. The movement disturbed our sleeping little girl, and when she squirmed, her eyes opened and straight away met mine.

Sucking in a sharp breath, I stared down at my child. Dark brown eyes… just like her daddy, chubby little rosy cheeks, and pouting pink lips with a perfect cupid's bow.

I'd read her eyes could be blue, but just like her daddy, his brown-eyed genes were apparently beyond dominant.

Time suspended. It was as though the world had fallen away and just the two of us remained. We stayed staring at each other for what felt like days; it was like she already knew who I was. Her mammy.

Lifting my left hand, my right still clutching her close, I ran a fingertip down her soft, pink cheek and cooed, "Hey, my baby girl. I'm your mammy and I love you so, so much." I heard a contented sigh from beside me— Romeo—but I couldn't seem to look away from my daughter to pay him any attention.

With a long yawn, our baby girl's eyes fought the heavy pull of sleep but eventually dropped to a close, her breath evening out, and she fell asleep, the sound of her rhythmic breathing soothing me.

Water hazed my vision and two thumbs rubbed at my cheeks, wiping away the tears. As I glanced up, Romeo had sat next to us both, his arm protectively over my outstretched body, careful not to touch my C-section incision.

"She's beautiful," I said quietly, and Rome stroked a finger over her tiny forehead. My heart skipped a beat as I watched him show so much affection to our little girl, causing me to add, "Just like you."

"Baby… yeah," he said in return, his eyes briefly flitting to mine.

At his choked reaction, I looked up at him and gripped his hand. "Are you okay?"

Huffing out a controlled breath, he smiled wryly and rubbed at his eyes. "Yeah, I'm just so overwhelmed by everything. The idea of being a parent and the reality of it… I… I can't wrap my head around it." His bright-brown stare fixed on our sleeping daughter on my chest, clearly expressing utter shock and disbelief.

"You did good, baby, looking after her while I was unable to. She's so perfect," I gushed, and fresh tears fell from Rome's eyes, but there were no sobs, just free-falling happy droplets.

Rubbing a shaky hand over his face, he confided, "I thought I'd lost you both for a while there. I found you unconscious in bed. You were so still and pale and there was blood. I felt like everything was just falling apart again." He took a long breath. "Then when our princess—"

"*Princess?*"

Romeo smiled shyly. "We had no name decided, did we? You wanted to see her first, see what name felt right, and I refused to name her without you, and princess was the first thing I thought of. 'Baby Prince' just didn't seem right." Pressing a kiss to our daughter's head, he added, "She *is* my princess, and I'll forever treat her as one. You're both my everything."

Lifting his hand to my lips, I brushed a kiss to his palm and whispered, "Thank you."

He returned the kiss, and stroking back my messy hair, he continued. "When our princess was born and healthy, the nurses put her in my arms. It was all so surreal. I looked down at you in amazement, just wanting to share the moment with you, but you were out cold, tape over your eyes, a tube in your throat, and I couldn't see you from the waist down, some boxy contraption in the way. The OR got crazy with getting you fixed up. Machines were blaring, people were rushing around, you were just lying there still, but the two of us—me and our little girl—were just stood there watching it all happen. Helpless. For a moment, I panicked at the thought that it could just be me and her forever if something went wrong, no more you. I just couldn't help thinking of the worst. You know I can't live without you, baby. Not now... not ever."

"Hey now, I'm not going anywhere." I squeezed his hand again, catching his long, relieved exhale, and I inched in to cuddle in to my daughter. I couldn't help but smile as I inhaled.

"Crazy, ain't it?" My attention snapped to Rome, who seemed to be marginally happier from seconds before.

"What's crazy?"

"How good she smells. Like all newborn, different. Nice. You know?" He shook his head and blushed. "It's crazy. I've been tucking my nose into her neck the whole time you were in here. Her scent calmed me. Stopped me from losing it. The only other person who can do that for me... is you."

I sighed as he tried to put the impossible into words and held out our daughter for him to take. Rome took her willingly and brought her in for another kiss, his face completely bewildered and full of awe as he watched her every tiny move.

I never thought it was possible to love Romeo Prince more than I did, but seeing him with our child just brought things to a whole other level. The way he looked at her with complete adoration proved me right from all those years ago.

Rome had always worried he'd be a bad daddy like his father was, due to genetics. But seeing him now, how gently and protective he was with our daughter, showed me in an instant how good of a father he would be... *Already is.*

"I love you," I said quietly, completely in love with my soul mate and the living embodiment of that love sleeping softly in his arms. Something fundamental had changed within me.

Turning to smile down at me, Rome said, "I love you too, so much. You're amazing to me." The biggest smile set on his face and he edged in and kissed me softly, pulling back to say, "We're finally parents, baby. We've wanted this for so long."

Weeping in happiness, I tucked my head in the crook between Romeo's shoulder and neck as he joined me on the bed, our tiny gift from God soundly content in his arms.

The two of us sat in that hospital room for hours, just staring at our little girl and kissing one another in complete bliss. I was instantly in love. And I couldn't imagine anything changing this special feeling.

According to C. S. Lewis, The greatest form of love is *unconditional* love. It is argued that this love is the strongest one can express toward another person and it survives no matter any life change or circumstance. It is pure and untainted and will never be shaken or taken away.

Looking down at our baby girl in my husband's strong hold, I knew Lewis was right, at least to me. I'd carried our baby for nine months, nurturing and protecting her. She was conceived in absolute love, and as Rome and I watched her sleep in silence, I knew it was all true.

I had captured the greatest form of love, right here, right now, with my little perfect family, adoring them both so much it almost felt too much to contain—completely, whole-heartedly…

Unconditionally.

See More of Romeo and Molly's story in the upcoming Sweet Home Series novels:

Sweet Fall: The story of Lexi and Austin
Sweet Hope: Ally's story

Both coming 2014!

PLAYLIST

Imagine dragons — Demons

Zac Brown Band — Goodbye In Her Eyes

POD — Here Comes the Boom!

Sting — Fields of Gold

Blake Shelton — Kiss My Country Ass

Fall Out Boy — My Songs Know What You Did In The Dark

The Kooks — Got No Love

The Killers — Romeo & Juliet

Kings of Leon — Back Down South

Biffy Clyro — Mountains

The Fears — Heart of Trouble

John Mayer — Heart of Life

AWOLNATION — Sail

Coldplay — Fix You

Lynyrd Skynyrd — Sweet Home Alabama

Luke Bryan — Crash My party

The Script feat. Wil.i.Am — Hall Of Fame

To listen to this playlist, please follow the link: http://tilliecole.com/sweet-rome/

OTHER WORKS

Sweet Home

At age twenty, Molly Shakespeare knows a lot.

She knows Descartes and Kant.

She knows academia and Oxford.

She knows that the people who love you leave you.

She knows how to be alone.

But when Molly leaves England's grey skies behind to start a new life at the University of Alabama, she finds that she has a lot to learn — she didn't know a summer could be so hot, she didn't know students could be so intimidating, and she certainly didn't know just how much the folks of Alabama love their football.

When a chance encounter with notorious star quarterback, Romeo Prince, leaves her unable to think of anything but his chocolate-brown eyes, dirty-blond hair and perfect physique, Molly soon realises that her quiet, solitary life is about to dramatically change forever...

Mature New Adult novel — contains adult content, highly sexual situations and mature topics. Suited for ages 18 and up*

It Ain't Me, Babe

A fortuitous encounter.

A meeting that should never have happened.

Many years ago, two children from completely different worlds forged a connection, a fateful connection, an unbreakable bond that would change their lives forever…

Salome Blake knows only one way to live—under Messiah David's rule. In the commune she calls home, Salome knows nothing of life beyond her strict faith, nor of life beyond the Fence—the fence that cages her, keeps her trapped in an endless cycle of misery. A life she believes she is destined to always lead, until a horrific event sets her free.

Fleeing the absolute safety of all she has ever known, Salome is thrust into the world outside, a frightening world full of uncertainty and sin; into the protective arms of a person she believed she would never see again.

River 'Styx' Nash knows one thing for certain in life—he was born and bred to wear a cut. Raised in a turbulent world of sex, Harleys, and drugs, Styx, unexpectedly has the heavy burden of the Hades Hangmen gavel thrust upon him, and all at the ripe old age of twenty-six—much to his rivals' delight.

Haunted by a crushing speech impediment, Styx quickly learns to deal with his haters. Powerful fists, an iron jaw and the skillful use of his treasured German blade has earned him a fearsome reputation as a man not to be messed with in the shadowy world of outlaw MC's. A reputation that successfully keeps most people far, far away.

Styx has one rule in life—never let anyone get too close; not a chick, not even a fellow brother. It's a plan that he has stuck to for years, that is, until a young woman is found injured on his lot… a woman who looks uncannily familiar, a woman who clearly does not belong in his world, yet a woman he feels reluctant to let go…

New Adult Novel. Contains highly sexual situations, violence and mature topics. Recommended for age 18 years and up*

Released: April 2014

ACKNOWLEDGEMENTS

As always, I have lots of people to thank.

Mam, Dad, thank you so much for all your support. Dad, for your constant belief and positivity and Mam for reading every draft, oh, and for laughing at my mistakes— It's true, babies do smell of shit! (personal joke, please don't take offence!)

Stephen, my hubby. Even through the toughest year of your life, you stood by me and encouraged me all the way with my writing. I'm so happy I have you with me on this new adventure and I pray for wonderful things to come your way in the future.

Sam, what can I say? Thanks for popping out kid after kid and enlightening me on what it's like to be a parent! All those early morning stampedes have helped me create a wonderful family for Rome and Mol—nutter kids and all!

To my lovely Niece, Taylor, and my crazy, adorable nephews, Isaac, Archie and Elias. Thank you for making me the proudest, most doting Auntie ever, and, of course, for letting me use your names! You are forever immortalised in print!

Kia, as always you whipped this novel into shape and, I particularly enjoy your bluntness and comments that manage to scold, but are always so polite in doing so! You have been with me through every novel. I can't wait for the next one!

Rach, even though you were MIA for this novel, it doesn't mean I don't love you! As for the rest of the Teesside Massive, your life-long friendship always helps me shape my secondary characters. You've taught me what it is to have true friends and even though we are separated by an ocean, you're always close. Love ya's!

Cassie, my wonderful 'Bama' editor. Thank you for squeezing me in. You are wonderful to work with as always, and even though it pained me, I'm glad Auburn did so well for you this year! (

Kelly, thank you for the cover reveals and blog tours. You are an amazing blogger and friend. You have led me through the world of blogging with a steady hand and I appreciate everything you do for us authors!

Lysa! My absolutely favourite web designer ever! You have been unbelievable with your advice this year. When Sweet Home hit the best sellers lists, and I was completely lost, you pulled me from the unknown and guided me through—my personal Virgil! You are one of the funniest peeps ever and I can't wait to someday meet you face to face. I'm desperate to hear that Boston twang—*wicked!*

There are a few bloggers that I owe particular thanks. Jenny and Gitte at Totallybooked, you were the first blog to really give me a shot and I am forever grateful! Tessa, I think you're just bloody fabulous and I'm super excited for the next novel when you begin your role as 'Beta reader'— we're gonna kick biker ass! Smiten's book blog, again, one of my first supporters. Thank you so much for giving this small town gal a chance. Lesley-Lynn, although a new relationship, your love for Mol and Rome has been astounding. You rock, and I am pretty damn confident that your blog will hit the stratosphere!

And finally, to my readers. The success of Sweet Home will be something I'll never forget. I wrote the book as I just couldn't get the story from my head. Never in a million years did I think I would make the USA Today Bestsellers List, or top the Amazon and iBooks charts. It was all down to you. I hope you all enjoy Rome's story as much. Love you, guys!

ABOUT THE AUTHOR

Amazon and USA Today Bestselling Author, Tillie Cole, hails from a small town in the North-East of England. She grew up on a farm with her English mother, Scottish father and older sister and a multitude of rescue animals. As soon as she could, Tillie left her rural roots for the bright lights of the big city.

After graduating from Newcastle University, Tillie followed her Professional Rugby player husband around the world for a decade, becoming a teacher in between and thoroughly enjoyed teaching High School students Social Studies for seven years.

Tillie has now settled in Calgary, Canada, where she is finally able to sit down, write (without the threat of her husband being transferred), throwing herself into fantasy worlds and the fabulous minds of her characters.

Tillie writes both Romantic comedy and New Adult novels and happily shares her love of alpha-male leading men (mostly with muscles and tattoos) and strong female characters with her readers.

When she is not writing, Tillie enjoys nothing more than strutting her sparkly stuff on a dance floor (preferably to Lady Gaga), watching films (preferably anything with Tom Hardy or Will Ferrell—for very different reasons!), listening to music or spending time with friends and family.

FOLLOW TILLIE AT:

https://www.facebook.com/tilliecoleauthor

https://twitter.com/tillie_cole

Or drop me an email at: authortilliecole@gmail.com

Or check out my website:
www.tilliecole.com

7293326R00271

Printed in Great Britain
by Amazon.co.uk, Ltd.,
Marston Gate.